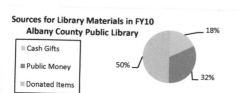

Sources for Library Materials in FY10
Albany County Public Library

- Cash Gifts
- Public Money
- Donated Items

18%

50%

32%

—THE—
WHITE
CITY

The Clockwork Dark
The Nine Pound Hammer
The Wolf Tree
The White City

—THE—
WHITE
CITY

JOHN
CLAUDE BEMIS

RANDOM HOUSE
NEW YORK

Text copyright © 2011 by John Claude Bemis
Jacket art copyright © 2011 by Alexander Jansson

Visit us on the Web! www.randomhouse.com/kids

Educators and librarians, for a variety of teaching tools, visit us at www.randomhouse.com/teachers

Library of Congress Cataloging-in-Publication Data
Bemis, John Claude.
The White City / John Claude Bemis. — 1st ed.
p. cm. — (Clockwork dark ; bk. 3)
Summary: Ray, Conker, and their Rambler friends face the Gog and his Machine in a final struggle at the 1893 Chicago Exposition.
ISBN 978-0-375-85568-9 (trade) — ISBN 978-0-375-95568-6 (lib. bdg.) — ISBN 978-0-375-89312-4 (ebook)
[1. Adventure and adventurers—Fiction.   2. World's Columbian Exposition (1893 : Chicago, Ill.)—Fiction.   3. Fantasy.]   I. Title.
PZ7.B4237Wh 2011
[Fic]—dc22
2010014252

Printed in the United States of America

10 9 8 7 6 5 4 3 2 1

First Edition

For my parents, Bill and Claudia

CONTENTS

—THE—
WHITE
CITY

BUCK RODE BEHIND THE KILLER STACKER LEE. BUCK'S HANDS were bound, his wrists tied with coarse rope to his belt. He sniffed, drawing in the smell of horsehair and sweat mixed with his own stench from days and days of riding. Stacker had little scent of his own except for the faint tang of steel emanating from his clockwork heart.

Although he was blind, Buck was keenly aware of his surroundings. Through his nose and the feel of wind on his skin, and with his ears, he had learned to be aware of the world in a way more powerful than those who simply viewed color, light, and form.

The two had crossed hundreds of miles since the badlands, where Stacker Lee had taken the Nine Pound Hammer from Conker. Eastward across the blazing prairie they had ridden, camping for a scant few hours each night and riding on again with the dampness of dawn still collected in Buck's knotted hair. Over and over, at night as he dreamed and by day as he jostled behind Stacker's saddle, Buck heard again the blast of gunfire and Si's screams. The cowboy could not rid his mind of the horrific memory.

Stacker and his men had captured Buck and Si and used them as hostages to get the Nine Pound Hammer from Conker. To ensure he would not be followed, Stacker had shot Si's tattooed hand and had kept Buck at gunpoint.

Buck gritted his teeth in fury at the memory. How could he not have helped Si? The gun had been right there, given to him by Stacker's man as a jest. And yet Buck had not taken it up, had not used the gun to murder the clockwork killer. Buck had thrown away his own guns back at the mountains around Shuckstack. A promise to himself that he would walk a new path, a path that would redeem him. A path that would make *her* proud, if ever he found her again.

Shame devoured Buck's heart. Whatever Stacker was going to do to him, whether torture or murder, Buck decided it was less than he deserved.

"Stay here," Stacker said.

Buck lifted his head slightly. The horse had stopped. Stacker slid down from the saddle.

Buck listened to Stacker's boot heels crunch on paving stones and then meet wooden planks of a sidewalk. Voices surrounded Buck, as well as the noise of carriages and wagons. They were in a town. No, not a town, he decided, for what prairie town had paving-stone streets? They had reached a city, or at least the outskirts of one. Tossing his head to one side to part the nest of hair covering his face, Buck let the breeze stroke his cheeks. He moved his head slowly back and forth, feeling, listening, smelling.

The street was lined with buildings. Shops, Buck guessed, from the large plates of glass he sensed at their fronts. After a few moments, Stacker's footsteps returned. He tied something to the side of the horse, below the Nine Pound Hammer, with the strips of rawhide that dangled from the saddle. Buck let his hair fall back over his face and leaned back as Stacker remounted.

Stacker turned in the saddle and put the mouth of a waterskin to Buck's lips. As Buck drank a few sips, with most of the water rushing into his thick beard, Stacker said, "We've reached Chicago."

Buck said nothing. He only swallowed the stale water.

Stacker gulped from the waterskin and hung it back on the saddle horn. "That man said we need only ride east and the crowds will lead us to the Expo grounds. We're nearly to the White City, as they call it."

Stacker led the horse back out into the busy street. "You make poor company, gunslinger. Fortunate for both of us I care nothing for conversation." He laughed dryly. "I suppose it makes little difference in me saying that when we meet with Mister Grevol, you'll let me tell him about . . . our accomplishments."

As they rode eastward, the noise and stench grew with each city block. There was the rumble of trains and the roar of factories, the whoosh and gasp of steel mills, and the lowing of thousands upon thousands of cows from stockyards. Among it all, taverns and broker's offices, hotels and saloons seemed oblivious to the haze of coal smoke and the reek of death.

Buck choked on the fumes, and Stacker laughed. "They say they butcher millions of animals a year in these pens. Rivers of blood run into the lake. Does it bother you? Have you become so sensitive to slaughter, Buckthorn, now that you've given up your guns?"

Buck spit to rid his mouth of the sickening taste the foul air left on his tongue. A string of spittle caught in his beard. Cinders fell like snowflakes onto his shoulders. He struggled to breathe as they rode for more blocks than Buck imagined any city could contain.

Finally they came into a neighborhood of small houses and streets lined with shady trees. A wind blew up from the east, moist and clean. They were nearing a lake. Buck adjusted his seat behind the saddle, his muscles knotted from so many miles of travel.

As the man had assured Stacker, the crowds herding into the World's Columbian Exposition couldn't be missed. Buck caught the lilt of excitement in the voices around him: children and couples and groups of men and women from rough and dirty tenements and wealthy Eastern manors, foreign tourists speaking any number of languages.

Stacker called out to a man, "Stables. Where can I bunk my horse?"

Buck sensed the stranger's hesitancy, the lingering of his gaze on the handsome man wearing the expensive Stetson and the grim man riding behind him, tousled and slumped like something half dead.

"Just around the block," he replied. "Past the pharmacy. The inn there keeps horses for an honest fee."

"Good day," Stacker called and shook the reins.

They reached the inn, and Stacker shuffled down from the horse. "Get off if you can," he said. Buck slid his leg over the saddle. His knees gave out as he landed, and he fell, his face scraping the sidewalk.

Stacker did nothing to help him stand again. "Wait here till I get back."

He led the horse away, and Buck heard the indistinct conversation between Stacker and the stable attendant through the hubbub of street sounds. Buck rose stiffly and settled back against a lamppost as passersby veered widely around him. His fingers felt numb from the ropes cinching his wrists to his belt. After a time, Stacker returned. "Let's go."

He led Buck by the elbow as they joined the crush of people entering the Expo. Stacker paid the admission with a few coins from his pocket, and they passed through the gate. Buck sensed enormous buildings rising up from the wide walkways. The air carried the smell of coffee, perfume, roasting meats, and the breeze of Lake Michigan. Such a mass of humanity buzzed around Buck as he had never felt. Soon Stacker was leading him up low steps away from the noise of the fairgoers. Stacker rapped on the wood frame of a door.

The door opened, letting cool air from inside leak out. "We're here to see Grevol," Stacker said.

Buck could not tell what the man looked like, of course, but he smelled the oil of his gun beneath his coat and the wool and sweat of a hat on his head.

"Is Mister Grevol expecting you?" the man asked.

"I'm Stacker Lee," he replied.

Buck caught the faint drawing in of the man's breath, the subtle retraction of his stance. "Wait here just a moment," the man said, and closed the door.

He opened it again after what seemed not more than a few seconds. "Come inside."

Stacker shoved Buck forward and they entered a narrow hallway. Other men were waiting down at the far end, other men Buck was certain were concealing guns. "Mister Tinley there will take you to see Mister Grevol," the agent who opened the door said.

Stacker and Buck went down the hall, where one of the men slid open the metal grate of a door. "Follow me," Tinley said.

The three stepped into a small chamber. As the man closed the thin metal door, Buck wondered why they were in this small room. Then his stomach lurched as the floor suddenly rose. He heard the *clank-clank-clank* of chains beyond the walls. They reached quite a height before the chamber stopped, and Tinley opened the metal door again.

"After you," he said.

Tinley led them down a winding hallway, through several offices where voices and the patter of machines silenced as they passed, and finally into a large room with thick carpet underfoot.

The agent continued across the room to a group of men seated together in leather chairs, smoking cigars and sipping cognacs. The conversation fell as Tinley whispered something. Then a man rose from one of the chairs. "Gentlemen . . ." Buck recognized the voice as Grevol's and could not stifle the cold constriction that drew at his throat like a noose. "We'll have to continue our discussion at a later time."

As the others stood one after the other, Mister Grevol added amicably, "Mister Burnham, you'll send word with your man on the attendance numbers . . . Mayor Harrison, get someone at the *Tribune* to write another piece. Publicity is still critical to our continued success. Have him send the story to papers back East. . . ."

The men exchanged promises and parting words, and as the group extinguished cigars and set down their glasses, Tinley returned to Stacker and Buck. "He'll see you in his office. This way."

He brought them to a room and closed the door behind him as he left Stacker and Buck to wait.

Stacker leaned close to Buck, his mouth near Buck's ear. "I don't know what he'll want to do with you." He snapped something open with a flick of his hand. Buck knew right away it was the long-handled razor that Stacker carried. "Kill you, most likely." Stacker pulled up Buck's sleeves and cut the rope binding his wrists. He closed the razor and put it back in his pocket. "Or maybe something worse."

The door opened, and Mister Grevol entered.

As he strode across the room toward his desk, he said, "Your man reeks. Have him stand at the door."

Mister Grevol rounded the desk and sat down. Stacker came forward, and Buck heard the clunk of something heavy being placed on Grevol's desk. "I was met with success, sir," Stacker said.

Mister Grevol was silent, and Buck made out the faint strokes of Grevol's fingers caressing worn wood and tapping at the iron head. "You're certain this is the Nine Pound Hammer?" he murmured.

"Of course," Stacker said.

Mister Grevol stood and drew something from his desk. Buck focused his attention, trying to discern what Grevol had picked up: the creak of leather gloves grasping a handle, the swish of air as Grevol moved what seemed to Buck a short staff toward the hammer. Grevol's cane. Buck remembered it from the battle on the trains. The walking stick that Grevol, otherwise known as the Gog, had used to battle Conker.

A hum rose from the end of the walking stick, a whirl of intricate gears and tiny machine parts alight with activity. Mister Grevol passed it over the hammer. "Yes," he said. "You have brought me the weapon."

The humming grew louder as Mister Grevol brought the walking stick up to Stacker's chest. Then abruptly the noise stopped. "Did you find it in the river?"

"No," Stacker replied. "John Henry's son, Conker. He had the hammer."

Mister Grevol gasped. "He survived the destruction of my train? How can this be?"

"I don't know. He travels with a siren. They have healing wells, or so I have been told."

The Gog came around the desk with a rapid flap of his coattails. "Why did you not kill him?"

"I was not able to."

"You?" Mister Grevol chuckled. "*You* were not able?"

"I had the Nine Pound Hammer. My job was to bring it back to you. If I could have . . . Conker took down both my men. I felt it best to leave before—"

"Both your men? Then who is this?" The humming of the walking stick returned, and the Gog turned sharply toward Buck. "Ah, yes . . . Why, it's the medicine show's sharpshooter. I remember."

Mister Grevol approached Buck, but Buck did not move. "You were there that night. You shot that boy. What is your name?"

Buck was silent.

Stacker said, "His name is Eustace Buckthorn."

"Has he gone mute as well as blind?" Mister Grevol asked.

"No," Stacker said. "He can speak when he wishes. He has been broken."

The Gog brought his walking stick up next to Buck's temple. Buck could hear it better now. The tiny, buzzing clockwork reverberated inside the sphere of glass that capped the end of the stick.

"Yes, I see," Mister Grevol said. "He feels shame and grief. . . ." The dizzying noise of the walking stick passed closer to Buck's ear. His knees began to buckle, and Mister Grevol grasped his arm, holding him up with an unnatural strength. This brought Buck back to his senses. The Gog was so close to him now that Buck could smell the faint hint of charred flesh, a network of scars covering Mister Grevol's skin.

Mister Grevol dropped Buck with a hiss. "Remorse over killings and for abandoning your child. Your self-pity sickens me."

"What of our agreement?" Stacker asked.

Mister Grevol said, "What of it?"

Stacker hesitated before saying, "The clockwork in me . . . I want it taken out. I brought you the Nine Pound Hammer. My service is complete."

"Don't be so hasty, dear Stacker. I have much greater opportunities for you."

Buck sensed something in Stacker's reaction. He drew in the smell slowly through his nostrils. Not fear. This clockwork killer was incapable of being afraid. But there was something in his reaction akin to fear, although Buck could find no name for it.

"Mister Grevol," Stacker said, "I wish to have my heart returned to me. I understood our last conversation to be a bargain between us. John Henry's hammer in exchange for . . . for my humanity."

"Yes, of course," Mister Grevol said. "I can return you to a lowly man again, but how sad that would be. I have given you something very special. Something very important to me and to my Machine. A gift that proves my faith in you. Don't you see? You, your clockwork heart, it is my finest creation so far. You are my guiding light in the coming war. A silent and swift war that will hoist this nation to heights its founders could never have imagined."

Mister Grevol struck the base of his walking stick to the floor. He spoke low. "Our country is young and bold and bloodthirsty. Just like you, Stacker. You are my ideal. You are my new America. You could be the general of my army. You, who have been perfected by my ingenuity. By my vision. By my

Machine. Once the Darkness rises over this city, a new society will be born. Fear will be our seed, for fear makes the weak docile and the strong angry and ready for change. We will have a perfect working class. A servile citizenry solely intent on making this world better. And a new race of men will lead—strong and pitiless men. Men who will bring freedom through the destruction of the old. We will build cities of industry, tall and sleek. We will shape this world, Stacker. Can you see it? Do you share my vision?"

Stacker Lee stood silently. Buck could sense the dark feeling that he could not name clouding Stacker.

Mister Grevol had stopped. "Wait awhile. Consider what I have said. See what our new society will be like and imagine your place in it. I need you now to amend for your cowardice."

"Cowardice?" Stacker hissed.

"You let John Henry's son live."

"What will you have me do?" Stacker asked, his voice dry and hoarse. "Destroy the hammer?"

Grevol chuckled. "No, we have nothing to fear from this relic. We will make a trophy of it. It will be displayed in the hall below us. Something that the rabble who flood to this exposition will relish."

"He will come for the hammer."

"Yes. And you will keep watch over it. Wait for Conker to arrive and try to take it back. This time, you will kill him."

"What of Buckthorn?"

"I assume you have not slit his throat already for a reason."

"A hostage," Stacker said.

"A pawn that will draw Conker and his friends into a fatal position. You, my knight, will strike. And when our opponents are defeated, you may do with him as you wish."

Stacker said, "There is the Rambler boy I have heard so much about."

"Rambler," Mister Grevol scoffed. "My men are hunting him as we speak. He flees across the prairie, running for his life like a hare before my hound. We'll capture him and his rabbit's foot. It undoubtedly is the source of the boy's power. With them both destroyed, there will be no threat of any *Ramblers* reaching my Machine in the Gloaming."

Buck's jaw tightened. He knew the Gog underestimated Ray and Conker but was not sure it made any difference. What hope was there left in stopping this enemy?

Mister Grevol strode around his desk, settling back into the large leather chair. "I have all the pieces in place to assure my success. My Machine has been completed in Omphalosa. It has been brought to Chicago. It is being hidden in the Gloaming beneath this very building as we speak. The sirens have been lured here. They are captive in the depths of my hall. I have filled them with my clockwork. They serve me now. And the last of the old Ramblers, Joe Nelson, that fool Peg Leg Nel, we know where he hides in his mountains. Yes, success is assured. It is within my grasp. I only need you, Stacker, to stop John Henry's son. Will you do this for me?"

"Yes," Stacker replied.

"Good," Mister Grevol said. "Then soon we will reconsider our bargain. But I expect by that time you will understand the folly of your desires. If you don't, then I can return you to your former state. Be assured. I am a man of my word."

As Stacker turned to walk toward Buck and the door, Buck understood the emotion he had been sensing in Stacker Lee. Remorse. Stacker regretted his bargain with the Gog.

Stacker opened the door, and Buck followed him out where Mister Tinley was waiting in the hallway.

Hope grew in Buck's chest. Hope in the form of a clock-work killer.

THE HORSE GALLOPED ACROSS THE SUN-BLEACHED PLAINS.
Ray leaned forward in the saddle, and Jolie, sitting behind him,
tightened her grip around his waist. A wake of dust rose behind
them as they crossed the wastelands of sagebrush and bone-
colored earth. Tumbleweeds broke loose and bounced across
their path before tangling again on gnarled shrubs.

"I do not see the steamcoach," Jolie called over the thundering hooves. "Where are they?"

"Don't worry," Ray assured her. "B'hoy sees them."

Ray squinted up from the shelter of his hat to spy the black
silhouette of the crow against the blue sky. He did not need to
link with the crow to see through the bird's eyes. He knew they
were not following the steamcoach any longer. How much
longer could he hide that fact from Jolie?

"Are they getting farther ahead?" Jolie asked.

"We'll catch up."

Saddle-sore and thirsty, Ray shook the reins and hoped they would reach the river by nightfall. They had set out three days earlier in pursuit of the steamcoach. The horse, who had belonged to one of the Gog's agents, had kept up the grueling pace better than Ray had hoped. There had been clumps of tough grass for her to eat. And they had found shallow trickles of streams for water. But she had two riders to carry, and the steamcoach rolled relentlessly westward. Somewhere beyond, farther than B'hoy had been able to see, Sally and the rougarou Quorl were moving even faster.

"We can't keep going like this," Ray said. "This horse will collapse if she doesn't rest soon. How are you holding up?"

Jolie said nothing, and after a moment he cocked his head to see if she was awake. She looked up at him, her thoughts clearly elsewhere. "Fine," she said.

The horse rode on and on as the land dipped and swelled like a stormy sea. At last, they climbed a low butte and stopped. The sun was veering down before them, casting its harsh glare into their eyes. Ray wiped the dust and sweat from his face.

"Mountains," Jolie murmured.

Far to the north, a snowcapped range jutted up from the plains. Ray whistled. "They're bigger than anything I've ever seen."

"How far away do you think they are?" Jolie asked.

"I can't tell," Ray said. "I'm not use to all this . . . openness. I'm used to the forests back home."

He turned in the saddle to check how Jolie was doing. Her dark, tangled hair was powdered with dust. Despite the days of riding in the blistering sun, her skin held its strange, unnatural pallor, glowing white like a piece of quartz. But her eyes showed she was weakening, and this worried him.

When he'd found her three days ago during the battle between the Gog's agents and the rougarou, he had hardly recognized her. The year spent watching over Conker as he healed in the siren well had changed her. She was stronger, more robust somehow. He wondered how he appeared to her. They had both grown up in so many ways. They were no longer the children sheltered aboard the medicine show's train.

"Look." Ray pointed to the left of the distant mountains. Much closer, maybe only a few miles away, the green tips of cottonwood trees peeked from a crack in the landscape. "A river's down there. We'll camp there tonight."

Jolie nodded wearily but then cocked her head toward the south. Over a series of patchy hills, a black ribbon of smoke rose in the air. "The steamcoach. I am certain it is farther away. We have ridden hard all day, so why are we losing ground?"

Ray shifted uncomfortably in the saddle. "You need water. There aren't any rivers in the direction they are traveling."

"You . . ." Jolie gripped Ray's elbow hard. "You are leading us farther from the agents because of me?"

"We'll catch back up. Don't worry about it." Ray kicked his heels against the horse's side and led them down the other side of the butte.

As night fell, Ray built a cookfire under the cottonwoods by the riverbank. The river was wide and swift-flowing, and when they had arrived, Jolie had done little more than slip down from the horse's back and walk quietly over to disappear beneath the currents.

Eating his supper, Ray cast a glance back toward the gurgling waters. Jolie would surely not emerge until morning. He put aside his bowl and closed his eyes. After a moment, his thoughts linked with B'hoy's.

He was high above the earth. Although the sagebrush country had grown dark gray, an orange and purple light still illuminated the cumulus cloudscape. From B'hoy's vantage, Ray watched as the ground grew closer and soon he saw the steamcoach, stopped for the night in a dry ravine. There was Muggeridge, the gray-bearded leader, sitting before the fire and eating. Beside him was Pike, his second-in-command, and keeping watch were Murphy and another agent. De Courcy had his arm bandaged and limped stiffly over to pick up his meal. Eight survived of the fourteen that had set out from Omphalosa, the others fallen in the battle against the rougarou.

Ray had not seen the Hoarhound since the battle, but he knew it was inside the large car at the back of the steamcoach. It was guiding the agents toward the rabbit's foot, guiding them unknowingly to Sally and not to Ray. B'hoy circled their camp, hesitating to go low enough to hear their conversations. After he and Marisol and Redfeather had been ambushed in the badlands before the battle, Ray worried that the agents had figured out that the lone, spying crow belonged to him.

As B'hoy began to return, Ray opened his eyes and got out his blanket. Unrolling it on the pebble-strewn earth, he thought of Sally. She had promised to keep the rabbit's foot at Shuckstack. Even if she believed the golden foot was leading her to their father, why would she have left Shuckstack alone? Surely one of the others could have gone with her, Buck or Si at least.

Did they even know where Sally had gone? Had they followed her, or were Buck and Si still back at Shuckstack?

As Ray lay down, he felt his jaw tighten with worry. Sally. How could she be so foolish? She desperately wanted to believe their father was still alive. But to risk the rabbit's foot, risk her own life, to cross the country on her hopeless quest . . .

B'hoy squawked as he landed on the branch of a cottonwood.

"I left you some," Ray said.

The crow descended with a flap to the bowl and pecked at the cold mashed tubers and pemmican.

"You're welcome," Ray added as he cocked his hands behind his head and closed his eyes.

Ray woke to B'hoy's croak. As he opened his eyes, he saw it was still dark. "Go back to sleep," he mumbled, but before he laid his head back down, he heard the crunch of feet on stones. He drew his knife swiftly from the sheath at his side and rolled over.

Silhouetted against the deep blue dawn, Jolie walked up from the riverbank, wringing the water from her tangled hair. "I did not expect you to be awake already."

Ray snorted and put the knife back. "Yeah, call me an early bird." He stood and stretched, feeling stiff from the saddle and hard ground. "How do you feel?"

Jolie came closer and poked a stick into the coals. "Better."

As a flame grew, it illuminated her face. "You look like it," Ray said.

He squatted and took a piece of pemmican from his rucksack, tearing it in half and handing part to Jolie. "I think there are more river crossings ahead, flowing out of those mountains. We should be fine."

Jolie ate with her eyes cast down and after a few moments murmured, "I wish I had brought the waters . . ."

"What waters?" Ray asked.

"From Élodie's Spring," she replied. "From the well where Conker healed. I took waters from there. Healing waters. But when your sister snuck away from the Wolf Tree and I followed her, I left them with Conker. If I had only thought to take them, I would not need to sleep in these rivers and we could reach Sally faster."

"You didn't know when you left." He shrugged. Then, wrinkling his brow, he said, "I keep trying to figure out why Sally didn't tell you who she was. She's never met you or Conker, but she must have known who you were."

"She knew us," Jolie said. "But when we met, she introduced herself as 'Coyote.' She kept her true name from us."

"But that's what I don't understand. Why would she do that?"

"Do you not see, Ray?" Jolie said. "She must have worried we would try to stop her. She has the rabbit's foot. She believes it is leading her to Little Bill, to your father."

"Is it?" Ray asked, uncertain himself whether he could believe after all this time his father was actually alive and trapped in the Gloaming.

Jolie shook her head. "I do not know. I loved Little Bill. I would like to believe he is alive, but I feel uncertain. Still, I hold a hope. You should too."

Ray frowned. "If he is alive, then she's leading those agents right to him."

"She may not know the Hoarhound follows her," Jolie replied. "Or the steamcoach. Which is why we have to move faster. We cannot let those agents catch her. We are losing too much ground, Ray." Her gaze hardened. "Next time, do not delay us without at least telling me first."

Ray held up his hands defensively. "I knew you wouldn't let me leave our course."

Jolie's eyes flashed with anger.

"You can't survive without the rivers," Ray added. "What else was I supposed to do?"

"Come on," Jolie said, walking over to the horse.

Ray stepped up into the saddle before helping Jolie on behind him. "We'll ride swiftly now that we're rested," he said. "We'll get ahead of them. Don't worry."

They rode hard throughout the morning, keeping the distant smoke of the steamcoach in their sight. At midday, they stopped to let the horse drink from the puddles in a nearly dry stream. Jolie got down to stretch her legs. As she went over to smooth the horse's mane, she said, "This horse is strong."

"Yeah, she's a tough one," Ray said, still sitting in the saddle. He took off his hat to wipe his hand through his damp hair and then brought the hat down lower over his brow to shield his eyes from the sun's hard glare.

"She should have a name," Jolie said.

Ray chuckled. "I'm guessing you already have one in mind."

Jolie nodded. "Élodie."

He held out a hand to help her back up. "That the well? Conker's well?"

"Yes." Jolie climbed on behind him. "The waters that

healed him were made because Élodie died. When a siren dies for love, her heart brings forth healing waters."

"Did you know Élodie?" Ray asked.

"She was my mother."

Ray turned to look back over his shoulder at Jolie. "Your mother? You've never told me anything about your mother."

Jolie frowned and lowered her gaze. When she said no more, Ray shook the reins, and they set off across the scrub brush and dust, picking up speed.

After a time, Jolie leaned closer so Ray could hear her. "My mother died when I was very young. I do not even remember her."

"How did she die?" Ray asked.

"My sisters say her heart was poisoned," Jolie said. "By my father. He was an outlaw who took refuge in the Terrebonne. My mother loved him. This was wrong."

"Didn't he love her?"

"My sisters never told me. They would not have acknowledged it if he had." Jolie paused as if thinking and then said, "I think he must have, if my mother felt so deeply for him. He had to have loved her."

Ray still didn't understand. "Then what was wrong with her loving him?" he asked.

"It is not our way," Jolie replied. "Sirens love only their sisters. Sirens care for no others. Our songs to father children enchant men, but they are not loved. My mother violated this law when she fell in love with my father."

Ray twisted in the saddle to peer back at Jolie. "You sound as if you think she was wrong for loving your father."

Jolie had a hardness to her expression. "She should never

have left her sisters to search for that bandit. She should have stayed with them."

Ray said bitterly, "Like your sisters should have stayed with you."

Jolie was silent. The horse Élodie galloped through the sagebrush. Finally Jolie said, "My sisters have returned."

"What?" Ray gasped. "How do you know?"

"When I was watching over Conker, one of my sisters, Cleoma, came to the well." Jolie took a deep breath before continuing. "She told me they are once more in the Terrebonne. I have forgiven them."

Ray bit at his lip, not sure what to say. He resented Jolie's sisters for abandoning her. He knew how much they had hurt her. Jolie might have found some way to put aside her resentment, but he couldn't.

"Cleoma, my sister," Jolie said, "she told me that they heard a strange voice coming from the waters of the Mississippi. I heard this voice too when Conker and I recovered the Nine Pound Hammer. Even last night, in this river. I cannot say who or what is calling out to the sirens, but I do not think it is in menace.

"Some sisters followed the voice up and into other rivers flowing out from the prairies. Cleoma said that the sisters turned back when they reached an unnatural night covering the prairie. They came back not knowing what this voice was or why it was calling them, but when they had returned, the ones that had gone out grew sick."

"Sick?" Ray asked. "How? Were they coughing? Did they go blind?"

"I do not know. Yes, I think Cleoma said they lost their sight. Why?"

"It's the Darkness. Your sisters went into the Darkness."

"The one you said covered the town—"

"Yes, Omphalosa. It must be." Then he hesitated before continuing, "Jolie, I'm not sure there's a cure for this sickness. Nel gave me and Redfeather and Marisol charms to protect us from it, but he didn't know how to cure it. A man came to Shuckstack who escaped from the Darkness. Nel couldn't find any way to save him. He died. I hope your sisters . . . I'm sorry . . ."

"Do not be," she said. "Cleoma carried waters back from Élodie's Spring. I am certain they have healed my sisters."

"You're sure?" Ray asked.

"There is nothing the siren springs cannot heal. Conker's body was broken by the train's explosion. And now he is whole. More than that. He is stronger yet. Who knows what he can endure having slept a year in Élodic's waters!"

"I wish I could have seen him," Ray said. "I've missed him." He added after a moment, "I've missed you too."

Jolie said nothing, but after a moment she tightened her grip around his waist.

Ray drove the horse, Élodie, farther across the plains, growing ever closer to the steamcoach. By nightfall, they spied a ribbon of thin, skeletal trees. Ray stopped the horse when they reached them and looked down on cracked brown mud-flats.

"I thought there would be a river here," Ray said. "It looked like it from a distance."

"It is okay," Jolie said, getting down from Élodie. "I am still all right. I do not need to sleep beneath the waters yet."

As they made camp and ate their meager supper, Ray sent B'hoy out into the gathering night. He found the steamcoach not more than twenty miles to the west. They would catch up with it soon.

But beyond, the crow saw only a worsening land—barren and without even sagebrush for vegetation. There was little water, and there were no more rivers.

BEFORE THEY RODE OUT THE FOLLOWING MORNING, RAY knelt to cut stems from the silvery sagebrush. Jolie, who was already seated on Élodie, called down to him, "Why are you taking that shrub? It grows all over these plains."

"Not ahead, I'm afraid," Ray replied as he sheathed the knife and tied the bunches to the saddle horn.

Jolie extended a hand to help him into the saddle before her. "Will we eat it?"

"No," Ray chuckled. "I hope it won't get that bad. We'll burn it. I've heard about this western sage. It's not like the sage back home. It has different properties, different hoodoo. There's a resin in the leaves and bark that makes a thin smoke. It'll help shield us from view, at least from a distance."

"From the steamcoach." Jolie nodded with understanding. "So we will not be seen?"

"Hopefully." He shook Élodie's reins. She kicked up clumps of rocky soil as she set off to the west.

The land rose gradually as they continued throughout the day, and the sagebrush and other tough grasses grew sparser and sparser. They came upon stagnant puddles where Élodie could water, but the creek beds were little more than baked networks of flat bricks. Ray did not mention to Jolie that B'hoy had seen no water ahead, but he didn't have to. Her somber expression and the way she cast her eyes around to the horizon told him she understood their dilemma.

Cresting a hill, they looked down on a large number of pronghorns with heads reared, standing statue-still. As Élodie galloped toward them, the deer all turned, flashing their white rumps and darting nervously, bunching together and then thundering away in a great herd. They reminded Ray that the last of Redfeather's pemmican was nearly gone. But there was no time now to hunt. He would have to hope the wasteland ahead could provide something to eat, even if only lizards.

As the herd disappeared, Ray noticed the toby was trembling ever so slightly against his chest. He took a hand from the reins to clutch it. There was a tickle in his fingers. He lifted his hand. A strange and soft pull began, as if tiny bits of string had been laced through the skin at his fingertips. He extended his arm and moved his hand slowly back and forth.

"What are you doing?" Jolie asked.

Ray pulled back his hand. "If I concentrate, I feel a tug." He held out his hand again, flexing the fingers wide. "It's like the lodestone. Do you remember? But also a warmth, like when it became the rabbit's foot."

"Is it your father you feel?"

"No," Ray said. "It's like there's something out there that shouldn't be. Something unwelcome in this wilderness."

"The Hoarhound," Jolie said.

Ray's heart gave a jolt and he drew his hand into a fist. He knew she was right. He had felt it before, back at the battle in those eerie badlands. He could feel the Hound. But how? he wondered. Where was this power coming from?

They did not make camp until well after dark. Even in the moonlight, Ray could see that Jolie looked weakened. Her skin had grown ashen, and dark circles rimmed her eyes.

"How much longer do you think you can go without sleeping in water?" Ray asked as he lay out his blanket for her.

Jolie slumped to the ground and curled up onto the soft padding. "I am not sure. A few more days, I hope. How far ahead is the steamcoach?"

"Close now. We might be able to pass them tomorrow. I've sent B'hoy to watch them." And to look ahead for water, but he knew better than to tell her this.

As Jolie fell into a fitful sleep, Ray closed his eyes to link with B'hoy. He found him perched beside a boulder several yards from the agents' camp. No guard was posted, and the Gog's agents huddled together around a cookfire, grumbling to one another.

". . . we're nearly out of water . . ."

". . . the most forsaken hellhole I've ever been in. Hot as blazes and not a patch of soft earth anywhere . . ."

". . . you sure the Hound is still leading us to the boy?"

De Courcy was asking this, and as he did, the other agents

grew quiet and shifted their narrowed eyes to Muggeridge. Muggeridge seemed at first to ignore them as he chewed and spooned more beans from his tin. He took another bite and frowned up at De Courcy.

"The Hound still has the scent," he said, smacking his food as he spoke. "The boy is heading west into the mountains."

"We haven't seen that crow of his," one of the agents said.

"Yeah!" another added. "And how could he cover ground faster than us, anyway?"

"Mister Muggeridge, you sure the Hound ain't broke somehow?" Murphy asked. "Possible one of them wolves damaged his sense of smell or whatnot."

"I'm the commanding officer," Muggeridge said coolly. "We have our orders, and we'll continue our pursuit even if it takes us to the Pacific Ocean. I've endured worse than this desert. The Rebs locked me up for a year in Anderson. So I know hardship. This ain't hardship! I want no more of this bellyaching or I'll have Pike here start drawing up terms for mutiny. We clear?"

The men turned their eyes down and grumbled. Pike shifted uncomfortably a moment before rising. "Get your rest, men. We've another hard day ahead. I'll take watch for the night."

Muggeridge nodded and cast his empty tin out into the shadows, scattering pebbles at B'hoy's breast. The crow rose in the dark, took flight on midnight wings, and soared on to the west.

The parched landscape seemed to stretch on endlessly. Barren hills rose one after the other like half-buried skulls. Tiny cyclones of dust and sand twirled up in the heat. They had seen no signs of humanity—no herds of cattle, no cowboys, no ranches, no long-distance wagons or stagecoaches carrying prospectors and westbound travelers. As Élodie rounded a butte, Ray spied the black sail of smoke and then the trudging locomotive.

"There they are!" Ray said, pointing. Jolie only gave a feeble nod.

Ray got down from Élodie and untied a branch of the sagebrush. He took a dash of saltpeter from the tin in his toby and blew it to make a flame as Redfeather had taught him. He lit the leaves, which began to burn slowly. A thin, fragrant smoke formed. He took a glass jar from his rucksack and dropped the burning sage inside. The smoke escaped from the jar's mouth. Climbing back into the saddle, he handed the jar to Jolie. "Can you hold it?"

She nodded.

"If it burns down, let me know and I'll get another branch."

She gave no reply but rested the smoking jar on her thigh. Ray kicked his heels to Élodie's side and shook the reins. The little quarter horse galloped across the land with the sweet-smelling smoke trailing behind her.

They grew ever closer to the steamcoach, keeping whenever possible to the north side of the hills out of the agents' sight. When they were only a mile apart, Ray could make out the men with their bowler hats tilted low over their brows. No head turned. No reaction showed that they had spied the horse and its two riders passing around them.

"It's working," Ray said. Jolie didn't reply.

Late in the day, Ray stopped Élodie in a dry riverbed. Kicking the mud with his boot heel, he opened up a small hole for the horse to drink from. Ray kicked open another and sifted the silty water through his bandana into the mouth of the waterskin. He looked up anxiously at Jolie. She sat on Élodie's back, her eyes half closed. Ray handed her the waterskin. "Drink," he said. She took the skin with a nod.

Ray walked out a ways while the horse continued watering. He reached a spire of earth and climbed it. Gazing around in the fierce late-day sun, he saw the enormous range of mountains to the west, rising like a wall beyond the flat waste. Turning around, he spied the steamcoach's smoke several miles behind.

"We're ahead of them!" Ray said excitedly. "And those huge mountains are up ahead. They have to be the Rockies. We'll hopefully catch up with Sally before—"

He looked back just as Jolie dropped the jar of smoking sagebrush and slumped forward across the saddle, her hands barely holding onto the horn.

"Jolie!" He scrambled down the spire, leaping the last eight feet. Élodie was stamping nervously, and Ray had to tug at her bridle and whisper in her ears to calm her. He put his hands to Jolie's shoulders to brace her as he asked, "Jolie? Can you hear me? Jolie!"

She lifted her head. "Keep going . . . ," she muttered. "Do not . . . lose . . . the steamcoach. . . ."

"Shut it," Ray said, climbing up behind Jolie to help hold her in the saddle. He forced the waterskin to her lips. "Drink some more."

But she didn't take the waterskin, and Ray felt her growing limp. He drew one arm tightly around her waist and with the other shook Élodie's reins. "Ride!" he called out.

Racing westward, Ray searched for B'hoy with his thoughts. He could not find him. B'hoy was still out scouting somewhere ahead. Ray raced Élodie, scattering dust and loose stones. Heat made the horizon wavy, and the blistering sun scorched through his coat. Ray squeezed his eyes shut against the glare and sand and the terror growing in his chest.

As the sun finally set behind the distant mountains, Ray spotted the black form of the crow ahead in the falling light. Ray quickly linked to him with his thoughts. B'hoy began a long stream of rasps and caws, but Ray had no energy to focus on the bird's speech. "Not now! We've got to find a river."

B'hoy swooped down across their path and began to lead the way. The horse raced through the night. The moon rose at their backs and the stars swung overhead. And when dawn eventually broke, Ray spied tufts of grass at Élodie's feet, and the hills ahead had low, gnarled trees. They had made it out of the wasteland.

"Are we getting near?" Ray called out to B'hoy, fear shaking in his voice. "She hasn't much time!"

Even as he said it, he saw the green tips of cottonwoods peeking from a depression in the ridge of hills. He kicked Élodie's flanks, and she raced down, foam flecking her jaws and blood speckling her distended nostrils. She wove back and forth to descend until they came to a rippling creek.

Ray leaped from the saddle and pulled Jolie off into his

arms. "You'll be all right. You'll be fine. We're here," he soothed over and over. Ray stumbled on the rocks at the shore but continued walking out into the slow-moving waters.

He lowered her down until her hair spilled out over the water's surface. Still holding her securely, Ray let her sink beneath the water. After a moment, she came up on her own, her bleary eyes searching for him.

"Ray . . . ," she said weakly.

He gave a heavy exhale of relief. "You . . . you were nearly . . ."

Holding onto his shoulders while she floated, Jolie dipped her cheek so that only part of her face was above the water. "His voice," she murmured. "I hear him . . . He is calling . . ."

"Who?" Ray asked.

Jolie seemed only half aware of what she was saying, her eyes dim and her voice thin. "He calls my sisters. . . ."

Ray held her for a while longer as she seemed to sleep, watching her anxiously.

With the sun glowing through the trees overhanging the creek, Jolie at last opened her eyes. Ray saw clarity in her gaze and knew she was finally alert, even if she wasn't quite recovered. He gave deep shudder.

"What is it?" Jolie asked.

"I thought . . . I was going to lose you."

"I am still here."

Ray gave a pained smile. "When we lost each other, after the train, the explosion . . ." He was not sure what he was trying to say, but he felt the words bubble up heedlessly. "All those times, once I started my new life at Shuckstack, I would go out into the wild. To be alone. I was learning to be a Rambler. I thought I did not mind being alone. But I did, Jolie. I kept thinking that I wished you could be there with me. And . . . I guess I thought I'd never see you again." He knew he wasn't making any sense.

Jolie simply stared at him, her fingers laced behind his neck.

Ray sighed. "I'm just glad you're here. Once we get through all this, we can go back to Shuckstack. You can see the mountains there. You'll love it—"

Jolie abruptly slid her fingers from his shoulders. "I should sleep. You need to also."

Ray was not sure if he had said something wrong, and his cheeks felt a little hot with embarrassment. But Jolie was right—the heavy weight of exhaustion was coming over him. "Right. I'll just be up on the bank."

Jolie nodded and gave a grateful smile before she slipped beneath the water.

Ray woke in the night, hungry and momentarily uncertain where he was. He looked around. Patches of shadow and moonlight crisscrossed the forest. He heard a whinny and found Élodie walking along the bank, her head bent down to the soft grass growing at the edge. Ray walked over and took her nose in his hands. "You're a good girl. You saved her."

The horse beat her head side to side and turned again to eating. No longer sleepy, Ray walked among the trees, prodding his knife here and there to dig up roots and collect mushrooms growing in the damp. He built up a cookfire and made a meal. Lifting his hand at one point, he again felt the pull and knew the Hoarhound was out there. Behind them and distant, yet still following.

When he had finished eating, Ray found B'hoy resting in the branches of a cottonwood.

The bird was awake and peering down at Ray with inky eyes. Ray could sense his exhaustion and his suppressed annoyance. "You tried to tell me something," Ray said. "When we were riding. I'm sorry I was short with you, but—"

The crow spoke in low, raspy croaks. Ray's eyes widened as he listened.

As B'hoy had been searching ahead for water, he had found a girl and a wolf. They were at the start of a pass going up into the mountains.

"How far away are they?" Ray asked.

B'hoy croaked: less than a day ahead.

Ray ran down to the riverbank and splashed into the water. He called Jolie's name, but she did not rise. She was beyond being roused, he realized. She would need to rest longer to recover.

But Sally was so close! He could almost reach her tonight if only . . .

He came up from the river and gazed at B'hoy. They might reach her by horse in less than a day, but a crow could fly faster.

Could I? Ray wondered.

He had mastered the crow's speech. He had learned to see from his eyes, to link with B'hoy's thoughts over a short distance. Was he ready?

B'hoy swooped down from the tree and landed in front of him momentarily before taking flight. Ray closed his eyes.

He took slow, deep breaths until he calmed his mind. He felt the moonlight on his skin. The damp forest and the vast wilderness surrounding him. He felt the weight of the earth beneath his knees. As B'hoy hovered above him, the bird's flapping wings became the only sound he could hear. His mind drew on all this and then went dark.

The crow beat its wings against the still night air. Ray looked down. In the dark of the forest floor, he saw himself tranquil and kneeling among the underbrush and fallen leaves. The crow beat its wings. The night was dark. Black feathers against black sky.

Ray looked down again. The forest floor was empty.

The horse let out a shuddering snort as Ray beat his wings and rose higher, flapping through the branches of the cottonwoods. He ascended above the treetops. A great field of stars shone overhead. He saw the crow silhouetted against them. B'hoy squawked and swooped forward, drifting ahead on the breeze that blew above the creek bed.

Ray stretched out his wings and followed.

With B'hoy leading, Ray flew up from the tree-filled bottomlands to the ridgeline above. The shadow of the mountains, rimmed in mist, stood ghostly against night. Ray flew farther and farther, the hills drifting past below.

Then he felt his fingers clutching at empty air. His arms were now heavy and long and no longer supporting him.

B'hoy circled around, cawing ferociously. Ray felt feathers

again where his fingers had been. He flapped but was descending, as if an anchor had been tied to his waist. Waves of pain shot through his body. He tumbled. The wings returned. He drifted closer to the ground and then he felt the helplessness of his arms and legs kicking. Back and forth, he struggled between forms, feathers and flesh, spinning and toppling until he struck the earth.

He gasped as he rolled over onto his stomach, with dust stinging his eyes. B'hoy was standing before him, blinking and cocking his head.

Ray groaned, "No . . . I almost . . ."

Sweat broke out over his body, and a cold chill shook him. His stomach knotted, and he struggled to rise to his elbows. He stood weakly, staggering a moment before recovering his balance.

"Lead me back," he whispered to B'hoy.

Ray opened his eyes. Jolie was kneeling over a cookfire, pulling bundles of blackened leaves from the coals with a stick. Ray grunted and Jolie turned.

"I thought I was exhausted," she said, "but you have not stirred all day."

Ray sat up, stiff but glad that the sickening effects had left him. "I did it, Jolie," he said. "I took crow form."

Jolie stared with astonishment as Ray recounted the events of the night. ". . . But I don't know what happened. I just lost the connection."

"You are lucky to be alive," Jolie said as she opened the bundles of burnt leaves to reveal steaming trout.

They ate together, and Ray told B'hoy to go out and search

for the steamcoach's position. When they finished the meal and were down at the river filling their waterskins, Jolie said, "Ray. There is something I need to tell you."

"What is it?" He felt suddenly anxious, but he wasn't sure why.

She took a deep breath and met his gaze. "Yesterday. In the river—"

"I'm sorry," he said quickly. "I shouldn't have gone on like that. I was just glad you were alive."

"I know." She gave a gentle smile. "But what you said. About coming with you back to Shuckstack. My sisters have returned. I belong with them, you must understand."

Ray felt his heart jump. "You'd leave?"

"I would go home," Jolie said.

"But Shuckstack . . . it could be your home. We're your friends. Your sisters . . . they left you! We care about you. Don't you see?"

"You do not understand," Jolie said, taking a deep breath before continuing. "I belong with my sisters."

"You belong with us!" Ray shouted. "You belong with those who love you."

Jolie's eyes flashed. "A siren loves only her sisters! I will not wind up like . . ."

"Like who?" Ray asked.

"Like my mother." She turned from the river and headed back to their camp.

"Jolie?" Ray called. "Jolie. Wait. I don't understand."

When he caught up with her, she was kicking dirt onto the dying coals of their cookfire. "You cannot understand," she said.

Ray waved his arms in frustration. "That's because you're not letting me. I thought you cared about us—"

"I do," Jolie said, snapping around to face him.

"Clearly you don't," Ray said. "You're just like your sisters. You only care about your own kind."

She grabbed his arm with a hard grip. "Would I be here if that were true?"

Ray looked away and pulled his arm from her grasp to walk past her. "Where's that horse? We need to go."

Jolie sighed. "I will find her."

When she left, Ray closed his eyes tightly and forced Jolie from his thoughts. He linked with B'hoy and saw the rough land on the other side of the ridge beyond the creek. B'hoy was soaring low, keeping from the sight of the steamcoach. Trudging along with its belching blasts of coal smoke and steam, the steamcoach roared across the hills. B'hoy circled so Ray could see their position coming up a ridge not far away.

Ray opened his eyes. "They've gotten ahead of us! We've got to hurry."

Jolie had Élodie by the reins. "She is exhausted. We have ridden her too hard. And look how she holds her back foot. I am not certain how fast she can go."

Ray knelt to inspect her hoof. "A stone bruise, maybe," he said, giving Élodie a gentle pat. "Sally's not far. Hopefully she can get us to her before those agents do."

Jolie frowned. She waited as Ray lit a branch of the sagebrush and dropped it into the jar before climbing into the saddle. She got on behind him and took the jar. Élodie ascended the hill up onto the ridgeline without faltering. When they reached the top, Ray spied the steamcoach's smoke over a series of hills to the west. He shook the reins, and Élodie began trotting.

She would not go into a gallop, but she rode up and down, over the rises, closer and closer to the steamcoach. With the mountains looming ever nearer, cottonwoods and other trees grew along the lower washes. B'hoy swooped back and forth across their path before sailing out ahead of them, keeping low to the earth. They were passing out of the barren sagebrush waste and into the eastern shadow of the Rockies.

Before long they crested a rise to see the steamcoach only a quarter mile to the south, atop a nearby ridge. Ray urged Élodie faster as Jolie kept watch on the agents.

"Ray!" she said sharply. "They have a—"

A rifle shot rang out. Élodie reared up with a whinny. Ray dropped low across the horse's neck and raced her down from the hilltop. Jolie was watching over her shoulder, and once they were out of sight of the steamcoach, she said, "They were not shooting at us."

Ray stopped Élodie and cocked his head to hear the shouting voices in the distance. "Are you sure?"

"The agent fired the rifle at something ahead of us," she said. "They were not even looking in our direction."

They got down from the saddle and crept to the hilltop. On the other ridge, the steamcoach had stopped. The agents were climbing out from the doors, pointing to something farther up the slope of the hill where Ray and Jolie hid, but not in their direction.

"What are they doing?" Jolie asked.

Then B'hoy flapped up behind them and landed at Ray's feet with a croak. "B'hoy!" Ray growled. "They must have spotted him."

Ray turned back to the agents. Muggeridge still sat on the driving bench, with the engine sputtering smoke, but other armed agents were spreading out slowly, searching the surrounding hilltops.

"We should go," Jolie said, pulling on Ray's elbow.

Ray did not move, his eyes narrowed with thought.

"Come," she said again.

"The Bowlers think the Hoarhound is leading them to me, right? They think I have the rabbit's foot. I'm who they're after."

"It does not matter—"

"It does!" Ray said. "Élodie is injured, and if we don't do something now, that steamcoach will catch Sally before we can reach her."

He turned back to Élodie and dug through the rucksack on the saddle to take out a piece of pemmican. Stuffing it in his pocket, he drank from the waterskin before handing it to Jolie.

"Do you think you can handle Élodie?" he asked.

"Yes. But why? What are you going to do?"

Voices grew louder.

Ray's expression hardened. "Let them capture me."

"What!" Jolie gasped.

He pointed toward the mountains. "I need you to go after Sally and Quorl. You know how to follow their tracks. You can find her."

"But this is madness!" Her eyes flashed fiercely. "You are hurt by what I said, and you are not thinking clearly—"

"I'm thinking fine," he grumbled.

"What will happen to you?"

"They won't kill me. They want to bring me to the Gog."

"And you will let them?"

Élodie was pulling nervously, and Ray took her reins to calm her. "Not if I can help it. We just need to hold those agents up long enough for you to reach Sally."

"But they will know . . . the Hoarhound can sense the rabbit's foot—"

"Get up," Ray said, motioning for Jolie to climb into the saddle. "I'll figure something out. I'll catch up with you if I can. Just go!"

Jolie opened her mouth as if to continue arguing but instead grabbed the saddle horn and swiftly pulled herself up. She took the reins from Ray and locked him in a furious gaze, but Ray saw her hand trembling.

They stared at each other until Jolie tossed her head, scattering her windblown hair from her face, and rode off toward the trees.

Wasting no time, Ray turned to B'hoy. "We need to get their attention. Move rapidly so they won't get a good shot and draw them back my way. I'll head down there." He pointed to the east, away from the direction Jolie rode, to the forest at the bottom of the hill.

B'hoy cawed and flew up to disappear over the hillcrest. Ray ran. As he reached the tree line, he heard gunfire resume. He looked back west, but Jolie had already vanished into the forest.

Shouting voices rose and the thudding and skittering of footsteps on loose earth came from beyond the ridge. B'hoy darted downward, arrow-like above the treetops. Ray watched a moment from the shadows as the first agent's bowler hat came over the ridgeline.

"There he is!" the man shouted.

Ray turned and ran into the forest. After a few dozen yards, he stopped and waited for the agents to arrive.

THE ROUGAROU FLICKED HIS HEAD UP AND AIMED HIS SILVER-
blue snout down at the sun-baked plains below.

"What is it, Quorl?" Sally asked, coming out from the comfortable shade of the trees and closer to the edge of the bluff.

"A gunshot." His human-like eyes, the only part of him
that still showed his true form, stared hard in the distance.
"There—another. And still more. Can you hear it, child?"

Sally cocked her head, holding back her blond curls from
her ear. "No. I don't hear anything."

"My hearing is very strong, little Coyote," Quorl said. "I
am not mistaken. They are guns."

"Maybe it's just hunters," Sally wondered.

"Of one sort or another," Quorl said.

Sally gave Quorl a worried look. "Do you mean that? Do
you think we're being followed?"

"Possibly . . . I have seen a strange black smoke at times in the distance behind us. It could be the locomotive that appeared at the Great Tree as we left."

As Quorl rose, Sally quickly said, "We don't have to go yet, do we? Why don't you rest longer? You've carried me so far, and I can tell you're weakening."

He took a few steps. "It is not the effort of our journey that weakens me."

"What is it, then?" Sally asked.

"As a steward of the Great Tree, I am not meant to be away from it. You know what happened to my pack when the Great Tree disappeared."

She remembered how the rougarou had lost their true forms, transforming first bodily into wolves and then in mind as well, eventually turning viciously on Quorl, the only one of the pack who had not forgotten he was a rougarou. They would have killed him had Sally not helped locate the Great Tree in time.

"We have gone too far away from it now," Quorl said in his grim, expressionless tone. "I feel its distance and will suffer for it. More so because the Great Tree is dying. That is why we must keep going. We must find your father if the Tree is to be healed."

Sally looked at the slope ahead and the rugged pass leading up into the mountains. The rabbit's foot had already led her nearly across the country. How much farther would she have to go?

She had left Shuckstack believing that only she could rescue her father. After all, she had given Nel back his leg and returned his Rambler powers. She could use the rabbit's foot—

her father's hand that had been severed by the Hoarhound—to help him as she had helped Nel. With his powers returned, her father could then escape from the Gloaming. He would surely be able to stop the Gog's Machine and save the Great Tree. If only she could reach him where he was trapped in the Gloaming . . .

But to return his hand to him would come at a terrible cost.

Sally had discovered through her father's book, *The Incunabula of Wandering,* that the rabbit's foot was needed to destroy the Gog's Machine. Mother Salagi had described it as "the light to pierce the Dark." If she saved her father, if she gave him back his hand and his powers, the weapon to stop the Gog would be lost.

But how could she not save her father? Although she had never met him, she believed, she had always hoped, that one day they would be together. Oh, what was she to do? Sally could hardly think on it all.

"Which way?" Quorl asked.

Sally gave a miserable sigh and took the rabbit's foot from her dress pocket to check the direction. "Quorl!"

He snapped his head around. "What is it?"

Sally held out the rabbit's foot, then moved it back and forth in front of her, watching the golden foot rotate in her palm until the tiny claws pointed west.

"Nothing . . . for a moment, I thought it was glowing." She put the rabbit's foot back in her pocket. "It must have just been the light reflecting off of it. Shall we go?" She pointed. "That way."

The two set out, slowly climbing farther up the pass into the mountain wilderness.

* * *

As evening fell, they made camp by a stream, where Quorl caught a few trout with his paws. Sally was used to eating the silky cold meat raw now, and with the bountiful wax currants and early season nuts Quorl had found for her, her stomach was full for the first time since she'd left the Great Tree.

"I don't know what I would do without you, dear Quorl," Sally said contentedly as she popped the last of the berries into her mouth. "I can figure out mysteries in the *Incunabula* but not how to start a fire or what's safe to eat. I'd never even be able to feed myself if you weren't here."

"You survived on the open prairie before you met me," he reminded her.

"Only because I had Hethy."

Quorl gave a soft chuckle. "Well, not to worry. I am with you. And the desert is behind us. We will eat much better now up in these mountains." Quorl stretched out on the mossy ground by the banks of the stream.

The first stars were coming out and the air was growing cool. Sally leaned closer to Quorl's warm side. "Quorl?" she began. "How will we reach my father?"

"What do you mean?" he asked. "The *Toninyan* is leading you, is it not?"

"What I mean is . . ." She paused to gather her thoughts. "Father is in the Gloaming. How are we going to cross over? Can you cross?"

"The rougarou's powers are not like those of the Ramblers," he said. "We cannot cross anywhere we wish. I can only cross using the Great Tree."

A sinking feeling came over Sally. "Then how will we ever reach Father?"

Quorl gave her an assuring look. "Your father is not in this world. He is in the Gloaming. And yet, the *Toninyan* pulls you toward something in this world. What do you think that is?"

"I have no idea,".Sally sighed.

"There are thresholds. Thin places in the fabric between the worlds where the Great Tree's branches come close to us. The rabbit's foot pulls you toward your father, so he must be just beyond one of these thresholds. I will be able to help you across."

Sally shifted anxiously. "Unless the branches of the Tree are too brittle."

"We will hope they are not," Quorl said. "We are a long way from the Gog's Machine here."

Sally felt better knowing that Quorl could help her across one of these thresholds, but her thoughts were awhirl with other worries. At last she asked, "What will happen if the Great Tree dies? Will . . . will *everyone* die? Would I die too?"

"No." His gruff voice was not especially reassuring. "You would not die. But if the Gog's Machine kills the Great Tree, it will bring something altogether worse than death for human-kind. You would be soulless. You would become something that felt no kinship or compassion for the rest of humanity or the world in which you live."

Sally shivered. "Would you know if the Tree died?"

"I would know, little Coyote," Quorl replied.

"How?" Sally asked.

"I would know," he repeated.

Sally wriggled back and forth, moving closer to Quorl. "Would you die with it?"

Quorl's voice was growing raspy. "Yes. I would pass from this world as well."

Sally wondered for a moment before asking, "Where did you come from, Quorl? Did the rougarou come from the top of the Great Tree—from that world beyond?"

"No, from beneath the earth, I think. I believe I recall that we ascended in our true forms from some lower world up to this one. Possibly up another Tree. Or maybe it was the same. I . . . I am having trouble . . . trouble r-r-r"—his voice broke into a low, guttural growl—"not . . . r-r-remember-r-ring now."

Sally lifted her head quickly from his fur. Quorl's tongue dangled from his long teeth. He was panting heavily all of a sudden. He rose to his feet and trod around in a circle.

"Quorl?" she asked anxiously.

He shook his head as if clearing away some thought. Then he spoke, his voice returning to its normal pitch. "I . . . I am sorry." He slumped back to the ground, panting. "I just need to rest. Let us sleep now." He laid his snout on his front paws and closed his eyes.

She had seen how Renamex and the other rougarou had lost themselves, their minds becoming those of wolves just as their bodies were. Quorl was too far from the Tree. He was changing.

She nestled against his side and hoped he was right. Maybe a good night's rest would help.

The following day as they continued to climb the pass, Sally watched Quorl closely and thankfully saw no noticeable return of the strange behavior from the night before. But Quorl seemed troubled and barely spoke as they traveled.

They crossed through lush forests of spruce and aspen, over meadows of wildflowers, and into still other forests of tall lodgepole pines. Ground squirrels and mule deer, marmots and coyotes scampered from them as they approached, and once Sally spied a golden eagle soaring above the mountainside.

"This is a marvelous place," Sally remarked. "So lovely, but it seems we travel so slow." She pointed to a snow-covered summit in the distance. "I've watched that mountain peak all day. Now it's late afternoon, and we seem no closer to it than when we started this morning."

With his head low, Quorl growled.

"What is it?" she asked.

He kept walking and did not answer.

Later that afternoon, they entered a broad valley with a meandering river, and the rabbit's foot led them toward a glacier squeezed between two sheer mountains. Quorl stopped as they reached the field of ice. A rumble reverberated from his chest, and he began trotting back the way they'd come.

"Where are you going?" Sally called, pointing to the glacier. "The rabbit's foot says that's the direction."

Quorl barked angrily, and Sally backed away a step.

The rougarou lowered his head and flipped his ears side to side. "That r-route." He paused, barked in frustration, and then tried once more. "Too steep. Go back." He threw his nose toward the range running up from the valley floor. "We go up on that r-r-ridge." He waited for her to follow.

With a shudder, Sally walked with Quorl back the way they had come. Soon he led them up a steep climb along a thickly timbered slope. When they reached the top of the ridge, Quorl began sniffing the ground.

"What is it?" she asked.

"Hor-r-rse," Quorl growled.

"A mustang, maybe," Sally said. "We saw some the other day." She watched as Quorl stood panting, his ribs sucking tightly against his silver body. "You're getting worse," she said. "Aren't you?"

"Ther-r-re is nothing we can do," he said quietly.

"What about those doorways, Quorl?" Sally said desperately. "You said there were places where you could cross over to the Great Tree. Find one of those and cross over! It will help you. It will make you better."

A whine sounded from his throat. He struggled to speak. "I would if I could. The Tr-r-ree is dying. And with it the door-r-rways are disappear-r-ring. We have to hope we r-r-reach your father befor-re that threshold is lost also."

Sally wrung her hands anxiously. "We should rest," she suggested, hoping it might help revive him. "I'm hungry. Could you find us some food?"

He nodded and lowered his nose to search.

"I'll go ahead and see if there's water," she called before continued along the ridgeline with the rabbit's foot in her hand. Was Quorl becoming irrational in this new state? He couldn't have smelled a horse. They had not seen another person since the dusty plains several days before, and that had only been a stagecoach traveling eastward in the distance.

The ridgeline eventually led her to a forest of aspens, where, after passing through the lonely groaning trees, she found herself in a cove with sheer rock rising up from a half-frozen lake.

She walked down to the lake to wait for Quorl. The snow crunched under her feet, and the wind whipping around the cove was chilly. She wondered, if the rabbit's foot was going to lead her much higher into the mountains, whether she had enough clothing. How much longer would they travel to find her father? Each morning brought hope, each day desperation, and each night disappointment.

Frowning with these glum thoughts, Sally looked out at the lake. Snow masked the shoreline, and a natural bridge of ice extended out over the cold black water. Sally put a tentative foot down on the bridge. The packed snow and ice seemed thick, but she knew the bridge was merely floating on the half-frozen lake. Looking around, she spied game trails beyond the lake, continuing from the cove to the west. That would be their route, she decided. She would wait for Quorl, and hopefully he would find something tasty for lunch.

Sally gazed up at the amphitheater of rock overhanging the lake. A heavy bank of snow hung over the top of the wall, dripping long icicles down the sides, and the wind blew powder down over the lake. Her attention caught on a little needle of snow and rock beyond the wall.

Was that the summit she had been watching all day? The illusive peak that she felt they could never quite reach?

With a few cautious steps, Sally ventured farther out onto the ice bridge. As she did, the summit came fully into the view. She gasped with joy. It was so close now! Just beyond the cove. She and Quorl would pass around the summit this very afternoon. She was not sure why, but this gave her a hopeful feeling, like there was some other presence in these lonesome mountains besides her and Quorl. Like her father might at last be close.

Behind her, footsteps crunched on the snow. With excitement swelling in her chest, Sally turned. "Quorl, look! We've—" Her voice fell short.

Standing barefoot in the snow at the start of the bridge, the siren Jolie watched her. Sally quickly scanned about. Quorl was nowhere around. A horse waited in the aspen trees, its reins dangling from its neck, and pushed its nose through the patches of snow for grass.

"Sally Cobb," Jolie said, her voice low but echoing off the sheer rock wall around them.

Sally's heart raced. Jolie had not called her Coyote. She had spoken her true name. How had the siren discovered that she was Ray's sister?

"What are you doing here?" Sally asked, and backed a few steps farther across the bridge. The path grew narrow as Sally neared the middle of the lake, the mineral-blue waters looming ominously on either side.

Jolie stepped out onto the bridge. The wind tangled her dark hair about her face. "Come back, Sally. Come so I may speak with you. It is dangerous out there."

"Why are you following us?" Sally cried, her voice reverberating around the cove and sending a few chunks of snow down from the high wall above them.

"Do not be afraid," Jolie said patiently. "I only need to speak to you. And if we talk too loudly, our voices might bring more of that snow down." Jolie walked slowly, her eyes darting with each footstep to the ice bridge beneath her feet.

Sally's foot broke through a slushy puddle that quickly filled with icy water.

Jolie held out a hand. "Please come back. Let me tell you what has happened to Hethy and to your—"

"Where is Hethy?" Sally asked, her gaze quickly scanning the shoreline. "Is she with you?"

"No," Jolie said. "Hethy was very sick when I left her at the Wolf Tree. From the Darkness."

Fear gripped Sally. She stepped back toward Jolie. "What will happen to her? Will she die?"

"I do not think so. I left healing waters with Conker. I am sure he has helped her. When I set off after you, Redfeather and Marisol were bringing Hethy to him—"

"Redfeather! Marisol. They were at the Great Tree too?"

"Yes," Jolie said. "They were with your brother. That is what I am trying to tell you. We have been following you. You have been in great danger. Agents of the Gog have been pursuing you."

"What?" Sally said in disbelief. "Why would they . . . but where is Ray? Where is he?"

"He gave himself up to the agents. To keep them from coming after you."

"No!" Sally cried. "Not Ray!"

Her voice fell as she saw Quorl burst from the aspens. He snarled ferociously and flashed a mouthful of fangs.

As he raced toward Jolie, Sally was too shocked to react. The Quorl she had known had a quality to him that was neither animal nor human, something altogether beyond this world. But this monster fixing his dark, rage-filled eyes on Jolie was nearly unrecognizable to her.

Jolie spun around and held out her hands. "Wait!"

The rougarou charged toward her, his roars echoing off the rock amphitheater. Sally felt the bridge trembling beneath her feet. There was a rumble from above. The snowbank broke apart, and enormous hunks of snow began to fall.

Sally ran across the ice bridge for the far bank as booms erupted behind her. She reached the far shore and kept running to the game trail leading from the cove. Only then did she look back.

The lake was gone.

Jolie was gone.

As the last of the avalanche settled into thin tendrils of snow, Sally dropped to her knees. An enormous mound of snow now filled the cove. Just as she was thinking Quorl was buried as well, the rougarou lurched up over the mound and stared down at her.

Sally scrambled to back away. She stifled a scream as he leaped from the mound of snow. But as he landed, Quorl simply collapsed. She trembled as she watched him, waiting to see what he would do. He lifted his head slowly and said, "I . . . did not mean . . . to bring down the snow. I thought she . . . What have I done?" The dark receded from his eyes, and clarity returned as the irises became blue once again.

"I don't know," Sally said. "Is—is Jolie dead?"

Quorl listened a moment longer. "I hear . . . nothing. Why . . . why was she following us?"

She did not know whether to tell him the truth, that he had

attacked Jolie and possibly brought about her death when she was simply trying to help them. "I can't say," she whispered.

Quorl turned his gaze back to her. "I am forgetting who I am."

"I know." Sally could fight back the tears no longer. Shaking with sobs, she wrapped her arms around his neck and buried her face in his fur. "Turn back, Quorl. Return to the Great Tree before it is too late."

"My little Coyote. I will not leave you," Quorl said. Sally could see how hard he was trying to speak, to keep from descending completely into a wolf. "I promise you . . . I will not harm you. Trust me. I may lose myself but I . . . never-r harm you. And no matter-r-r how much wor r-rse . . . I will lead you. I am-m-m bound-d-d . . . to you."

She stood and wiped her nose on her sleeve. "Let's go. Let's get away from here."

Sally cast one last look out at the avalanche, knowing there was nothing she could do for Jolie. She and Quorl set off, traveling side by side until they passed the summit the elusive summit she had watched with such hope—and continued on, following the rabbit's foot deeper into the mountains.

CONKER STRUCK A MATCH ON THE SIDE OF HIS BOOT AND LIT the lantern. As the wick lit, orange light illuminated the barn's interior. "It'll do," he grunted, brushing aside some cobwebs dangling from the rafters.

Si plopped onto a bale of straw, whipping her long braid of slick black hair over her shoulder. "Well? When are you going to check it?"

Conker hung the lantern back on the worn beam overhead and sat down across from her. "Whenever you're ready, I expect."

Si tucked her bandaged hand closer to her stomach. "Wait for Redfeather and Marisol to get back."

"Okay." The giant nodded. He took out the package of crackers and unwrapped the waxed paper before handing them to Si. The door to the barn opened, and Conker's hand reflexively grabbed Jolie's shell knife from his belt.

". . . but we can't build a fire in here," Redfeather was saying. "We should stay somewhere safe."

Marisol scowled at him as she closed the barn door behind her. "It doesn't matter. We've built a protective Five Spot every night since we left the rougarou and haven't had anyone even come near us. We'll be fine. Quit worrying."

Conker placed the knife on the straw bale beside him. He looked up at Si, who rolled her eyes at the arguing pair. Conker smirked.

"But what if Stacker Lee—" Redfeather began.

"I don't think Stacker's going to turn around to come back for us," Marisol said. "He's already in the city."

"Conker?" Redfeather waved an accusing hand at Marisol.

"I'm sure we'll be all right without a Five Spot tonight," Conker said in his low voice.

Redfeather opened his mouth and looked back at Marisol but then dropped his hand and sat down on the bale beside Conker, tucking his long hair behind his ears.

"What'd the farmer say?" Conker asked.

"We can stay here," Redfeather said. "There's a well behind the barn. Didn't offer us any supper, but he said he's going into the city in the morning to make a delivery. He'll give us a ride."

"You figured on how we'll find that boy?" Conker asked.

"Gigi." Marisol sat down next to Si and let her copperhead, Javidos, slither out from her shirtsleeve onto her lap. "No, but we'll ask around. Someone will know something about the workers from Omphalosa. If we can find where the machinery was brought, then we'll know where the Gog is."

"And once we find his building," Redfeather said, "we'll rescue Buck. We'll get back the Nine Pound Hammer."

"Good," Si said, a venomous snarl on her lips.

But Conker did not feel so hopeful.

Rubbing Javidos's chin, Marisol turned to Si. "Are you . . . going to take the bandage off?"

Si winced. Conker watched her impassively. He didn't want to rush her. After Stacker's man had shot her hand, Si had been unconscious. She had not seen the damage. Fortunately, Jolie had left the water from Élodie's Spring. Conker had poured the water over Si's hand before wrapping it. And as they had journeyed eastward across the prairie, he had given Si a sip from the waterskin each night. No blood had soaked into the bandages, nor had a fever taken her. And after only a few days, Si said that her hand no longer hurt.

Conker still worried what they would see when the bandage was taken off. But not nearly so much as Si, he imagined.

"All right, then," Si whispered, her eyes cast down to the dirt floor of the barn.

Redfeather and Marisol exchanged nervous glances. As Conker stood, Marisol got up and they switched seats.

When Conker settled beside her, Si didn't look at him but simply placed her hand in his lap.

Conker untied the knot of fabric at her wrist and slowly began unwinding the strips from her hand. "Reckon we could see things a little better?" he said.

Redfeather took down the lantern. He wiped at the sooty

glass, but it still gave off only a dim light. Opening the lantern, he dipped his hand inside and gathered a small flame to his fingertips. He kneeled before them. "How's that?"

Conker grunted and continued slowly pulling away the bandage. Redfeather's horse, Atsila, whinnied outside the barn. Conker stopped when he finally exposed the inky black skin of Si's palm. He looked up once at Redfeather and Marisol and then over at Si.

"Get on with it," she growled. Her chin twitched, and she turned her face away from Conker.

Gently Conker pulled the last of the bandage from her hand and let it fall to the dirt. As Redfeather held his flaming fingers closer, Marisol sucked in a sharp breath, causing Si to draw as tense as a knot.

Conker ran his fingers over Si's hand. The inky black skin. The black nails at the tips of her black fingers. He brought his hand over each knuckle, one, two, three, then stopped. The pinkie finger was gone, as was the knuckle and part of the side of her palm. But the skin was smooth, without even a scar, as if she had been born with only four fingers.

Conker folded his hands around Si's and gave it a gentle squeeze. "That hurt?"

Si shook her head.

"I suspect it's all healed," Conker said. "Do you want to look at it?"

Si turned her head slowly and stared down at her small hand lying in Conker's enormous one, gazing at it as if it were a thing not belonging to her but some awkward gift Conker was presenting.

"Move your fingers," Conker said.

The three fingers closed stiffly, her thumb covering them. She wiggled them a few times and then touched the missing part of her palm.

"Si," Redfeather said softly as he closed his fist to extinguish the flames. She stared at her hand, and Redfeather cleared his throat before continuing. "Do you . . . does . . . it still work?"

Si held up the hand toward the dark cobwebbed rafters at the top of the barn. She kept it outstretched for a long time, but no stars formed on the skin's surface, no celestial map, no firefly bits of illumination. Only the dark skin against the dark shadows.

Si lowered her hand. She stood up, walked over to the far side of the barn, and curled up on a bed of hay.

Conker looked back at Redfeather and Marisol, their faces awash in concern. "Let's all get some sleep," he murmured. "Got a big day ahead of us."

"Where'd you say you come from?" the farmer asked. He drove a pair of trudging mules along the road. Marisol and Si sat next to him on the wagon's bench, with Conker wedged in the back between the crates of corn and sacks of meal.

Riding Atsila beside the wagon, Redfeather said, "Started out in the Dakotas a few days ago."

"That's a fair distance, eh?" the farmer replied.

The sun was only just rising as the wagon rode through the western townships bordering the city. A shopkeeper paused from sweeping the sidewalk to watch curiously as the wagon passed.

"You all got jobs lined up on the Midway or something?" the farmer asked.

"The Midway?" Marisol asked uncertainly.

The farmer adjusted his cap as he glanced sideways at the girls. "Sure, the Midway. I haven't been, on account of all the work. The wife wants us to go once the harvest is all in. I hear the Midway is a sight more interesting than the rest of the fair. Aren't you folk performers?"

"We're just visiting the Expo," Redfeather said.

The farmer snapped his stick at the mules' hides. "You're Indian, eh?"

"Yes, sir."

"I hear there's a bunch on the Midway," the farmer explained. "Some Eskimos from way up in the Arctic. And Buffalo Bill's Indians at the Wild West show. Chinese folk too. Acrobats and the like. Tribes from who knows where, and a big volcano carried all the way from Hawaii. Bears that walk tightropes. You can kiss the Blarney Stone. Hear it's all quite a sight to see. Thought you all might be taking jobs there, is all."

"Nope," Conker said.

The farmer glanced back at Conker and laughed. "Don't think I've ever seen one as big as you." He laughed once more. "You could be John Henry's son."

"We just came to see the Expo," Redfeather said a little irritably.

The farmer's eyes traced over each of them, and he gave a sniff. "Well, lots of folks do." He snapped the stick again and drove the wagon until they reached the smoke and stench of Chicago.

* * *

Conker had never been to a city any bigger than Atlanta, and Chicago was nothing like Atlanta. The vastness surprised him, as well as the constant noise and overwhelming smell.

Finally, the farmer reached a distribution building, where other farmers had brought their wares to be sold to the city's groceries and restaurants. After helping the farmer unload the wagon, the four huddled together around Atsila, hardly knowing what to say amid all the chaos and confusion. The sidewalks were crowded with people and peddler carts, and the streets so busy with traffic that policemen in long blue ulster coats had to direct the intersections with shrieking whistles. The air was stale and filled with the noxiousness of black fumes and animal blood.

The farmer came back out from the warehouse, tucking the bills into his front pocket. "You all know where you're going?" he asked.

Redfeather shook his head.

The farmer pointed. "Head down until you come to State Street. Turn right. When you get to Fifty-Ninth Street, turn left. It'll take you all the way to the fair. You got money for lodging? Food? Entrance fee? Fair sure isn't cheap."

"I've got some coins," Marisol said.

The farmer reached into his pocket and took out a dollar. "That'll help, I hope," he said, handing it to Redfeather.

"Thank you, sir," Redfeather said. He slid the bill in his pocket.

"Nothing to it," the farmer said, climbing back into the wagon's bench and driving the mules out into the busy thoroughfare.

A cable car rattled noisily past them. Conker looked around at the others. "Well, let's go."

After about an hour of walking, they joined the crowd headed east on Fifty-Ninth Street. Signs everywhere announced rooms for rent and twenty-five-cent meals. Redfeather bartered with a stableman to get Atsila housed, and after casting a worrisome glance back at the stables, he came back to the others. Soon, with the noon sun beating down, they found themselves at the Midway's entrance.

"What are we looking for?" Conker asked as they waited in the long line to enter.

"The building will have to be huge," Redfeather said. "To house all that machinery they were building and all those workers."

"I just hope Gigi is all right," Marisol whispered.

"Fifty cents each," the attendant said. Marisol handed over the coins, and they passed through the gates to the Midway.

The long street leading down the Midway bustled with excited visitors. Jostled by laughing children and parasol-wielding ladies and neat-mustached gentlemen, the four walked with dumbfounded amazement.

Their medicine show had been nothing compared to the entertainment offered here. One moment they were walking through a picturesque Bavarian village with beer gardens, brass bands, and a grand town hall, the next they were in Cairo with towering mosques, belly dancers, and shouting vendors. A ruined Irish castle sat beside a long slide inexplicably made of snow. Masked Javanese hunters in grass huts were between a great tiled swimming pool full of raucous bathers and a colorful Japanese market.

Above the temples and coliseums and mock hamlets rose an enormous mechanical wheel, nearly three hundred feet tall. Conker kept his eyes cautiously on the monstrous wheel, fearing it would break off at any moment and roll down the Midway, crushing people in its wake.

"Look." Marisol pointed up. "There are people riding in that wheel!"

"How big are those cabins?" Redfeather gasped.

"Looks like railcars," Conker said.

A dapper young man in a white suit turned to them with amusement. "First time to the fair?" he asked.

Si glared at him suspiciously, but Marisol nodded with a smile.

"That's Mister Ferris's wheel," the young man explained. "Built it to rival Eiffel's tower in Paris. He's done it and more, hasn't he? A swell sight, don't you think?"

"It's remarkable," Marisol said. "Have you toured all the Expo?"

The man laughed. "I don't think anyone could see it all in a lifetime."

"There's more than this?" Redfeather asked.

"Sure there's more," he said. "This is just the Midway. Keep going and you'll be in the White City."

"The White City?" Marisol asked.

"That's what they call it, on account of nearly all the buildings being white. You'll think you're in Athens or Rome or somewhere. There's hundreds of buildings."

Conker felt his stomach sinking. Hundreds of buildings . . .

"We're looking for a friend of ours who works here," Marisol explained.

"Well, what exhibit does he work for?" the man asked, his eyes dancing over Marisol's and Redfeather's outfits and up to Conker and down to Si.

"We're not sure what it's called," Redfeather said. "But they built the display in a factory down in Kansas and loaded all this machinery for it on trains just a few weeks ago."

"Hmm . . ." The young man ran his finger thoughtfully along his sporting mustache. "I suppose it could be the Manufactures and Liberal Arts building. That's the largest. You can't miss it, all the way down on the lakefront. But there's also the Palace of Mechanic Arts and the Hall of Progress. Maybe the Transportation or the Electricity building? Boy, there's an awful lot it could be. Do you know what they display?"

"Not exactly," Marisol said, blinking at all the names. "Just a large machine of some sort."

"Well, sorry I can't help you, but go ask around in the buildings. Someone will know your friend."

They thanked the man and headed down the rest of the Midway, under the noisy raised railroad platform, and finally into the White City. The young man had not exaggerated. Great white buildings rose from the shorefront of Lake Michigan, looking more like temples from ancient Jerusalem than a modern fair. Among the buildings were ponds and fountains, some small and one so large it surrounded a tree-covered island with a Japanese temple and an elaborately manicured rose garden.

The four made their way from building to building, wandering through displays of various electric Edison lights and contraptions, huge sewing machines and conveyor belts, a grand telescope, bicycles of strange designs, the latest makes in warships and historical wagons and locomotives, as well as display after display of paintings, marble sculptures, beautiful glass and jewels, musical instruments, a replica of the Liberty Bell made of lemons and grapefruits, a stuffed mammoth, and an invention called an elevator that could carry people straight up to the tops of the buildings.

All the while, Marisol and Redfeather inquired with those working the exhibits about Gigi and the machine brought up from Kansas, but no one could tell them anything to help their search.

When it was late afternoon, they rested down at the waterfront. Marisol brought back stuffed cabbages and boiled dumplings from a Polish café, along with some sweets she said were called crackerjacks.

"We're never going to find Gigi," Redfeather complained as he gazed down at the water lapping at the breakwater.

"We have to," Marisol said.

Conker glanced over, anticipating the usual bickering between the two, but it seemed Redfeather was too exhausted or discouraged to argue. He turned to Si, to share a smirk as they often did, but her attention was on a group of men tying a dinghy up at the wharf.

"Think we should look for lodging somewhere?" Conker asked her.

Si continued watching the men.

"What is it?" Conker asked.

"You recognize them?"

Conker looked again, but the men had disappeared into the crowd strolling along the waterfront. "No. Were they Bowlers?"

"Not Bowlers," Si said, standing and craning her neck to look for them.

"Who, then?" Redfeather asked.

"I'm not sure, but two of them looked familiar." Si wrapped up the rest of her food and put it in her pocket.

"We wouldn't know anybody here—" Marisol began, but Si had already set off down the waterfront.

Conker scrambled to his feet, along with Redfeather and Marisol.

"Pardon me," Conker said as he tried to wade through the flood of people. "Si!" he called. "Slow down."

Si was already far ahead, crossing a bridge and disappearing behind an agricultural building. "Hurry," Redfeather urged, passing Conker to jog after Si. Cows were lowing from stock exhibits, and the crowds thinned on the back side of a pavilion. Conker spied Si again, and farther ahead the group of men, all dressed in cheap woolen suits and walking hurriedly down an alleyway that was clearly not where fairgoers ventured.

Donkey wagons filled with the fair's garbage waited in an alley, and Conker had to squeeze to get around the braying animals. "Si!" he called out, but she had already turned a corner in the alley. Redfeather pulled his rucksack off his shoulder and slid his tomahawk out, sheltering it against his leg as he rounded the corner.

"What's he doing now?" Marisol hissed from Conker's side.

But Conker was glad for Redfeather's caution, and he picked up his pace to turn the corner. They were now deep in a maze of dirty alleys that cut between warehouses at the edge of the Expo grounds. Si had stopped and was talking to Redfeather as Conker and Marisol caught up.

". . . I don't know which way they went," Si was saying. "But one of them saw me following them. I know them from somewhere. . . ."

The sun was setting, and dark shadows filled the alley. Conker said, "Come on. They're gone now."

"We should go," Marisol said.

A solitary man wearing a moth-eaten porkpie hat stepped out in front of them. He had bulging fish-like eyes and spoke through a mouth of silver-capped teeth. "You've been following me, girl," the man sneered, his hands cocked in his pockets. "That tattoo of yours leading you to more trouble?"

"Who are you?" Conker stepped between Si and the man. There was something familiar about him, but Conker could not place it.

"And you. Still looking for a fight you can't win, giant?" the fish-eyed man asked.

Conker's eyes flickered toward the man's hands as they dropped deeper into his pockets. "You asking for a fight with me?" Conker growled.

The man laughed. "Me, fight? No. But do you think you could still take him?" He nodded behind the four.

Conker spun around with the others. A group of six men blocked the alley, and at their front was an enormous man, massive gorilla arms hanging from swollen shoulders and a nonexistent neck. The huge man massaged his knuckles. "I don't know how you come back from the dead, but I had a good nap just a bit ago. Ghost or not, I think I could take you."

Redfeather brought up his tomahawk, and Marisol extended her arm so Javidos slid out from her sleeve, hissing angrily. But Conker only put a hand on Redfeather's shoulder, pushing past him.

"I almost didn't recognize you in those ugly suits." Conker laughed, rushing forward to clasp the huge man around the shoulders. The other men broke into merry jeers and slapped Conker's back.

"Si, my dearie." The fish-eyed man smiled, and Si rushed up to hug him.

Redfeather and Marisol looked at each other, perplexed by the reunion. "Who are these men?" Redfeather asked.

With an arm over the big man's shoulder, Conker said, "This here's Big Jimmie. And over there, that's Mister Lamprey. Here's Old Joshua and—"

"Wait a moment," Marisol said, her eyes wide. "I've seen them before too. After you destroyed the Gog's train . . ."

"They're pirates?" Redfeather balked.

"That's right," Mister Lamprey said with a roguish bow. "Greetings from the *Snapdragon*."

"What are you all doing here?" Si asked.

Mister Lamprey leaned close and in a low voice said, "The Pirate Queen is planning a robbery. You wouldn't believe all the riches they've got here. Various persons—wealthy folk, you see—have hired the Pirate Queen to pluck certain objects of great value from the Expo. Jewels that belonged to Queen Isabella of Spain. A coronet from India. Some Moorish diadem. You get the idea."

"Are you on your way now?" Redfeather asked.

Mister Lamprey chuckled and waved his hand dismissively. "No. No. Heists like these take lots of preparation. Lots to plan out. We're just gathering information, if you see. Doing reconnaissance."

"We're trash collectors," Big Jimmie added, running his thumbs under his suspenders.

"What?" Si asked.

"We've taken employ in the sanitation crew," Mister Lamprey said, winking. "That's why we're wearing these duds. Tonight, it's just work. Sweeping sidewalks. Emptying waste bins."

"But all the while," Big Jimmie said, "we're learning the layout. Watching the guards and their routines. Making notes."

"Aye," Mister Lamprey said. "But why are you here? And how come you're breathing and walking, Conker, after last we saw you blown to smithereens?"

One of the other pirates gave a cough, and they turned to see more sanitation workers coming down the alley. They stepped to the side to let them pass.

"Actually, your tale will have to wait," Lamprey said. "We'd best stay in good with our boss. Can't afford to get the boot, if you see. Where are you all staying?"

"We don't have anywhere," Si said.

Mister Lamprey smiled. "Then you'll be staying with us on the *Snapdragon*."

"It's here?" Redfeather gasped.

"Out in the lake." Mister Lamprey cocked a thumb back over his shoulder.

"We had to paint it pretty yellow," Big Jimmie added. "So it wouldn't look . . . what's the word?"

"Conspicuous," Lamprey said. "Meet us down at the big fountain. By the statue of Lady Liberty."

"Which one?" Si asked.

"The gold statue in the main fountain. She's called Big Mary. You can't miss her. Say, half past ten." Mister Lamprey tipped his porkpie hat to the four as the pirates headed for work. "Then we'll take you to the Pirate Queen."

WITH A SHOVE FROM THE AGENT, RAY FELL IN THE DIRT. HE sat up and ran the back of his hand across his bleeding lip. The agents surrounded him, their firearms drawn.

"Mister Muggeridge," Pike called out toward the steam-coach. "We've got the boy."

The door opened from the back of the steamcoach, and Muggeridge stepped down. He lifted his bowler hat to run his fingers through his mane of silver hair and, after replacing the black hat, brought his fingers to his beard, stroking the whiskers as he watched Ray.

"We got him, yes sir," the agent who had punched Ray said gleefully. He was one of the youngest of the remaining eight agents, a crop of red hair sprouting from the front of his bowler hat. "Caught him down in those trees, see."

"My vision hasn't failed me, Mister Sandusky," Muggeridge said. "You're certain he's the Rambler boy. Not just some kid off a ranch?"

Mister Pike answered, "The crow flew into the trees where the boy was hiding."

"Where's the crow now?" Muggeridge grumbled.

Sandusky exchanged a glance with Pike. "We didn't find the crow, sir," Mister Sandusky said.

"Mister Muggeridge," Pike said. "When we caught the boy, his actions were indicative of one who knows he's being followed."

Muggeridge frowned. "What kinds of actions would those be, Mister Pike?"

Pike didn't flinch, but the other agents anxiously watched the exchange between their commanding officer and his second-in-command. Pike said, "So he started running from us and put up a fight when he was caught. He hasn't spoken a word to explain who he'd be otherwise."

Muggeridge looked down at Ray. "You the Rambler boy?"

Ray locked eyes with Muggeridge but offered no reply.

"You hear me?" Muggeridge said, kicking a spray of gravel against Ray.

"Want me to get him to talk, sir?" Sandusky asked.

Muggeridge sneered but shook his head. "I've just been in the back with our Hound. He's still got the scent and it's still to the west. Doesn't sound like this would be our Rambler, does it?"

"But, sir—" Pike began, but his words were cut off.

"It's some Rambler trick, yeah!" De Courcy growled, nursing his injured arm against his side.

As an angry murmuring made its way around, Ray sensed

the Hoarhound's presence. He lifted a hand slightly and felt the tingling, the strange draw of the mechanical beast.

"The Hoarhound is following the Rambler's charm," Muggeridge barked. "Now, it could be that the boy there has hidden the rabbit's paw up in those mountains, but why would he do that? And why turn back toward us? Frankly I don't think we have the Rambler here."

"Damn if this ain't the Rambler!" Sandusky said. He holstered his pistol and charged forward at Ray, pulling him to his feet.

"What are you doing?" Muggeridge said.

"Look!" Sandusky began roughly feeling along Ray's pockets, down his legs, and then at his chest, where he stopped as his fingers clutched the toby sack. "What have we here, see?"

Ray twisted away from the agent, but Sandusky had him locked in his grip. With a tug, the agent popped open the top buttons of Ray's shirt. Ray fell back, and when he landed, the red flannel toby lay exposed.

Muggeridge's eyes widened. "Let me see that."

Mister Murphy ripped the toby from Ray's neck and handed it to him. Muggeridge opened the string and emptied the contents into his palm: roots, a dandelion petal, a twist of rue, dried herbs, and other charms. He continued shaking them out and letting them spill to the ground as he searched.

Mister Pike said, "The Ramblers were known to carry mojo pouches of these here hoodoo curios."

"But there's no rabbit's foot in it," Muggeridge said, throwing down the empty red flannel sack.

"The hell! He's got it hidden on him somewhere else!" Sandusky cried, and Pike tightened his grip on his arm.

"Strip him," Muggeridge ordered.

Ray tried to remain impassive as Murphy and another agent removed Ray's clothes until he stood in the baking sun in only his underclothes and socks. "Where is it?" Sandusky looked as if he were about to attack Ray again.

"Some sort of spell he's cast on it," one of the other agents suggested.

"To make it invisible," another agreed.

"I'm not looking for a discussion," Muggeridge barked. "I want some order here with you men!"

"We've been out here for weeks on these blasted plains!" Sandusky shouted. "How much farther we going to go? To the Pacific? To China? Yes sir, we're chasing a ghost!"

"Put Mister Sandusky in the coach," Muggeridge told Pike.

Sandusky furled his brow but allowed Pike to lead him away. Muggeridge said, "You men get to your posts. Ready the steamcoach." The men reluctantly backed away as ordered.

Muggeridge looked at Ray after they were alone. "Put your clothes back on, boy."

Ray began dressing. When Pike returned, he asked Muggeridge in a low voice, "Sir, are we going to continue pursuit?"

"We have orders to bring back the Rambler boy and his rabbit's paw," Muggeridge said. "And this kid isn't carrying it."

Pike's voice was tight. "The men are nearly mutinous, Mister Muggeridge. Supplies are low. Morale is worse. And I absolutely feel we have convincing evidence that this here boy is the Rambler we're after, even if we can't find the charm. Let's find out."

"What are you suggesting?"

"Bring out the Hound."

Ray had just fastened the last button of his shirt. He kept his gaze down, trying to mask the fear twitching at his jaw.

Muggeridge paused. "All right. You watch the boy."

He turned toward the back of the steamcoach. Pike thumbed the hammer back on his pistol and motioned toward Ray. "Sit on down there."

Ray sank to the dusty earth.

Muggeridge unlatched the door and entered the car. After a moment, he came back out, his hand clutching the Hoarhound at the throat. Ray had only ever seen the creature at night, images that had been blurred by darkness and the terror of the encounters. But now, as the frost-armored beast steamed in the hot air, Ray had time to see Grevol's creation more clearly. Bigger than a bull, the Hound had enormous jaws that hung slack, and its back was stitched up crudely from the battle with the rougarou.

Its head somewhat resembled a dog's, but with the features exaggerated and grotesque. The ears protruded back like splintered horns, and its muzzle hung with gruesome tendrils of skin. It moved with none of the grace of an animal but followed Muggeridge with a gait made stilted by rotating gears and pumping pistons.

Ray sucked in his breath as the Hound brought its steely eyes around to meet his. The monster snarled and lunged. Muggeridge tightened his grip and said, "Easy there. Slowly. Slowly. Over here."

As the Hoarhound approached, Ray sat back, leaning on his hands to stifle the trembling in his arms.

"Stay right there," Pike ordered him.

The other agents watched from the steamcoach. Muggeridge kept his eyes fixed on Ray.

The Hoarhound drew closer, closer. Ray could feel the cold seeping into the blistering earth, drawing small beads of moisture up through the parched dirt. The Hound panted, clouds of frost seeping from between its dagger-like teeth. Gears whined and machinery buzzed beneath the Hound's hide.

Ray cringed as the Hound brought its metallic nose within inches of his face and sniffed. A tingling grew in his limbs. His hands, which had been cold from the ground, grew warm and then hot. Ray felt something rising through the earth into his palms, up his arms, into his chest.

The spilled charms from his toby trembled in the dust. The twists of roots, the bundles of herbs, the stones, and objects were shaking as if a locomotive were passing. Even the empty flannel pouch was fluttering.

The Hoarhound growled.

Muggeridge gripped the Hound's frosty hide with both hands and pulled. "Back!" he ordered.

But the Hound snarled, its lips quivering around jagged fangs.

Ray should have been afraid, but somehow fear had been replaced by something else, something he seemed to have drawn from the earth. He raised his hand. It felt ripe with an intense pressure, an oppositional force. He brought his hand close to the Hound's jaws.

The Hoarhound's eyes widened. A terrible grinding of machinery whined from its innards. The Hound buckled and yipped.

Ray dropped his hand in surprise, and the Hound's metallic eyes flashed as it erupted in ferocious roars.

"Stay!" Muggeridge shouted at the Hound and drew a tin whistle from his pocket. Ray scrambled back from the snapping beast. When Muggeridge's whistle shrieked, the Hoarhound stopped and leaped back from Ray, knocking Muggeridge to the ground.

Agents rushed from the steamcoach, shouting, jabbing their rifles at Ray. "Down!" Pike yelled at Ray. "Get your hands down! Roll over!"

Ray flattened against the earth as the strange tingling drained from his arms. He was suddenly tired and, for a few moments, dazed. He glanced over at the contents of the toby, but they were no longer moving.

The agents kept shouting until Muggeridge hauled the Hoarhound back into the car and roared to restore order. "Back away, men! Firearms down. He's not going anywhere. We've got him."

Mister Pike approached Muggeridge and asked, "You all right there, sir?"

"I'm fine," Muggeridge said, brushing the dust from his black suit.

"You see those little curios from his mojo there moving?" Pike asked.

"I saw."

"So you agree he's the Rambler boy?" Pike asked.

"Of course he is, but where's that damn paw? That's what we've got to find out!"

Pike looked around at the men, their faces filled with anger and apprehension. In a whisper he said to Muggeridge, "I fear the men will kill the boy if we don't act quickly."

"They've got orders," Muggeridge snarled softly. "We've got orders. Return the boy and his rabbit's paw to Mister Grevol in Chicago. We've got to bring him that paw!"

"I figure Fort Hudson's near here," Pike said. "Just a frontier outpost. But the men can rest, see."

"And what about the paw?" Muggeridge asked.

"The boy knows where it is even if it's not on his person. He'll tell us with the proper motivation." Pike's nostrils flared. "Let's get him to the fort. Then . . . we'll interrogate him."

Muggeridge looked down at Ray. Ray still lay flat, his cheek in the gravel and dust. Muggeridge called to Murphy, "Gather the Rambler boy's mojo. We're taking him to Fort Hudson."

The interior of the steamcoach's carriage was little more than a stifling box with wooden benches. In the heat and half dark, the agents glared at Ray. Ray felt a grim comfort that Mister Pike was seated at his side. But even his presence did not keep the men from jeering and making cool threats.

"Maybe he's swallowed that golden paw, yeah. So want me to find out, Mister Pike?"

"Yes sir, some Rambler. Why don't you turn into a bullbat and fly away?"

Ray closed his eyes and leaned his head back against the plank wall, turning his thoughts to B'hoy. He searched for the crow but could not reach him. With luck, he was flying west, looking for Jolie and Sally.

What had happened with his toby back there? Had he drawn some strange power from the earth, or had it come from his toby? He had always used the objects individually or occasionally in pairs or small combinations. But this seemed like all of the objects were working together to give him some unexpected force. He had never known the toby to work that way nor heard of any Rambler using it like that.

Mile after jostling mile, hour after hour after hour, Ray rode with the agents of the Gog around him. He opened his eyes later to find darkness at the tiny windows. The steamcoach had stopped, and men were talking outside. One called out, "Open the gates!" The steamcoach continued a short distance and then stopped again. The men grumbled as they exited stiffly. Pike clutched Ray's arm and led him out.

Fort Hudson was a small collection of buildings and stables surrounded by a palisade of sharpened pine poles. Soldiers in blue uniforms peered curiously at the strange locomotive, while Muggeridge spoke with an officer. He gestured back toward Ray, and the officer nodded, pointing to a cabin. Muggeridge waved Pike over, and they led Ray to the cabin.

The officer opened the door. "Don't have any prisoners at the moment." The four walked inside the cobwebbed interior. The officer lit a lantern and placed it on the table. With a key, he unlocked a door to a back room. Pike shoved Ray inside as the officer spoke to Muggeridge. "There's two bunks for your men keeping guard. I'll show the rest of you to quarters. The cook will prepare a meal for your men and the prisoner."

"Thank you, Lieutenant Craig," Muggeridge said. "We appreciate your hospitality."

"What's the boy done that's brought Pinkerton agents this far west?"

"Horse thieving. A rancher over in Cheyenne hired us after the boy and his father stole nearly twenty horses. There was a gunfight. The boy killed the rancher. We'll bring him back to stand trial after he helps us locate his father hiding out in the mountains."

"Well, my men are at your disposal," the lieutenant said.

"We'll be fine, sir," Muggeridge said. "But don't be worried if you hear some noise. You know how it is trying to get information out of these types."

"I certainly do. We see the worst sort out here. . . ."

The men departed, leaving Ray alone in his cell. There was no bed or furnishings, just a chipped enamel pot. Ray slumped to the dirt floor.

He woke sometime in the night when Muggeridge unlocked the door. Ray blinked at the harsh lantern light. Muggeridge dropped a plate of beans and coarse bread to the floor. Most of the contents splashed out.

"Supper," Muggeridge said. "Enjoy it. After this, you'll have to earn your meals."

Ray sat up but didn't reach for the plate.

"That's how it is, huh?" Muggeridge said. The agent glared down at Ray a few moments before saying, "You know what we want. Tell us where the rabbit's paw is and you can go free."

Ray knew Muggeridge would never do that. And the Hound surely still sensed that the rabbit's foot was elsewhere. He might have stopped the agents temporarily from pursuing Sally, but he still had to hope they wouldn't send the Hound out.

"They'll come for me and you'll be sorry," Ray murmured coolly.

"What's that?" Muggeridge said with a surprised blink.

"You heard me," Ray said. "My friends have the rabbit's foot. They're Ramblers too. They'll come for me, and you'll wish you'd never captured me."

Muggeridge stroked his beard. "Will I, now? Your friends, these Ramblers. They have the rabbit's foot, huh?"

Ray simply glared up at the Bowler.

With a smug nod, Muggeridge turned, unlocked the door, and left. Ray heard him say, "Murphy, you and Anderson watch him tonight. We might have company soon. I'll get the men ready."

As Ray heard the door to the cabin shut, he picked up the plate and ate the beans and bread, wondering how he was possibly going to escape.

The following day Ray tried again to reach B'hoy, but the crow must have been too far away. He decided to try again to take crow form, hoping that if the men opened the door, he might fly out.

He closed his eyes as he sat on the dirt floor, thinking back. How had he done it? He had been sharply attuned to the forest, to the crow, to his surroundings, but as he tried now, all he could think of was the cell and his grumbling stomach and the miles of distance between him and Jolie and Sally.

"Rambler?" Sandusky called through the heavy wooden door. "I thought you said your friends were coming. Oh, hey.

Looks like they did come. And wouldn't you know, they ate your dinner, see. Sorry about that."

Ray could hear another agent snort before Sandusky left.

By the next morning, Ray's hunger was growing unbearable. The guards brought him water, but it was stale and offered no satisfaction to his stomach.

He woke in the afternoon with De Courcy standing over him. Ray had not heard him unlock the door, and this worried him because it meant he was becoming less aware without food.

De Courcy's bandages were gone, and he had his hands behind his back. Fearing that he might be carrying a club or some weapon, Ray scrambled to sit back against the wall.

"What's got you so jumpy already?" De Courcy asked. "I just came to tell you an interesting story, yeah." He took a step closer. "See, when I was a youngster, I used to make these slipknots. They're easy to make. You ever tried? No? Well, believe me, I got pretty good with them. If you set one of those slipknots up on a limb or fence, or in this case here tonight, the ground outside this brig, and you put something attractive in it—something like that little red pouch of yours, yeah—you can catch all kinds of things."

Ray felt his pulse quickening.

"I used to put bits of bread and food in them as a kid. Snag a dove or sometimes a squirrel. Yeah, positively lots of fun to be had with slipknots."

"No!" Ray lunged to his feet.

De Courcy swung a fist, catching him in the ear. Ray fell

back against the wall, toppling into the dirt. His vision swam, and as he tried to sit up, he saw De Courcy holding B'hoy by the neck and feet. The crow beat his wings against the agent's chest and squawked.

"Where are your pals, Rambler?"

Ray held up a hand. "Don't."

De Courcy tightened his grip. "Are you lying to us? Is anyone coming for you? Or is it just this stupid crow?"

"No," Ray pleaded.

De Courcy scowled down at him. Then, with a twist of his wrists, the wings stopped. De Courcy dropped B'hoy to the dirt and walked out, locking the door behind him.

"No. No." Ray crawled to him. Tears blurred his vision as he reached for the limp crow. He picked B'hoy up and held him to his chest. "No. Why did you come here? Oh, B'hoy . . ." He grew quiet as he heard the guards laughing in the other room.

Ray wiped his nose and sat with his back to the wall and B'hoy in his lap. He shook with silent sobs as he ran his fingers over B'hoy's black feathers.

Pike and Muggeridge did not come the following day. Ray no longer felt hunger, only weakness and a dull pain beneath his ribs as he thought of B'hoy. When De Courcy and Sandusky came on duty that night, De Courcy opened the door to put down a pail of water. Ray glared at the man angrily, B'hoy still in his lap.

Before De Courcy shut the door, Sandusky called, "Hey, why don't you let me go talk to our friend in there and find out if the Rambler cavalry is ever going to show."

De Courcy closed the door and locked it quickly. "Pike wanted me to make sure we didn't go in with the prisoner anymore."

"I only need a damn minute," Sandusky said. "Aren't you ready to get back home? There ain't no Ramblers coming for him. That paw is hid out there somewhere. Sooner we get him to tell us where, sooner we're back in Chicago."

"Come on, Sandy," De Courcy said. "We going to play cards already or what?"

Ray listened as the men settled down to the table and began shuffling the cards. "Look what I got us," Sandusky said. There was a tinkling of glass and the squeak of a cork being pulled out.

"That whiskey, yeah?"

"Kentucky bourbon!"

"Where'd you get that?" De Courcy laughed.

"Bought a few bottles off one of the soldiers."

"Well, pass it over, my friend."

The men began dealing cards and laughing more and more as they drank the bourbon. A plan formed in Ray's mind. It wasn't a particularly good plan, he admitted, but he was desperate. He got up to stand by the door, listening intently. After an hour, De Courcy stood, stumbling out of his chair as he rose. Sandusky laughed. "Where you going?"

"Relieve myself. Be right back."

After De Courcy left the cabin, Ray said through the door, "How about some food in here?"

Sandusky's chair clattered. "The hell? What you going on about?" His speech was slurred with the bourbon.

"I'm hungry."

"Yes sir, it gets to you, don't it?" Sandusky came over to the door. "You ready to tell us where that Rambler charm is?"

"I want some food first," Ray said.

Sandusky chuckled. "We ate it all, and believe me I ain't walking all the way to the blasted mess hall for more tricks from you."

"How about a drink of that liquor, then?" Ray asked.

"Kid, you're too young to drink."

"Do you want the rabbit's foot?"

"What are you going on about?"

"I've got it in here."

Sandusky snorted. "Got what?"

"The foot," Ray said

"You know something? If you're fooling around with me, I'm going to bust this damn bottle over your head."

"Unlock the door," Ray said. "It's right here."

With a jangling of keys, Sandusky opened the door. Ray backed into the shadows. Sandusky wasn't wearing his bowler hat, and with his mop of orange hair and disheveled shirt and drunken expression, he looked somewhat like an unruly child.

"So where is it already?" Sandusky said, an empty whiskey bottle dangling from his hand.

"Right over there," Ray said, pointing to the shadows on the other side of the cell.

Sandusky turned his bleary-eyed gaze to the floor. "Where—?"

Ray charged at Sandusky, catching him in the stomach. As he did, De Courcy staggered through the door. "What's going on?" he shouted.

Ray knocked Sandusky flat to the floor of the cell and made for the door. De Courcy drew his gun from his belt. "Back in that cell! Sandusky, get up."

Regaining his sense, Sandusky snapped around toward Ray. "Nope," De Courcy told him. "You fight him, we'll have Pike down here in a minute, yeah, and if he sees us drinking . . ."

Sandusky spat at Ray and grabbed the keys still in the lock. Before he pulled the door shut, Ray spied his red toby on a bench by the door of the cabin. The door closed, and darkness returned to the cell.

"What the blazes were you doing?" Ray heard De Courcy ask.

"He said he had that rabbit's foot with him."

"Yeah, and you believed him?"

"Shut up and deal another hand."

As Ray slumped to the floor, his eyes fell to something lying in the dirt. The empty whiskey bottle.

Ray may not have had his toby, but he had a charm now. He grabbed the bottle and looked at the floor. A sliver of light from under the door was enough to locate Sandusky's footprints in the loose dirt.

"Another pair of jacks?" De Coury scoffed. "Come on, Sandy. You've won the last four hands already."

Ray removed the cork and slowly sifted the dirt that formed Sandusky's footprint in through the narrow mouth of the bottle.

"Yes sir, going to win the next one too," Sandusky said.

Once the footprint was collected, Ray replaced the cork with a firm tap.

"We'll see about that," De Courcy laughed. "I'm dealing this hand."

Ray stood at the door and shook the dirt about the inside of the bottle. "I'm ready to come out," he called.

The two agents were silent, then a chair slid back. "You hear that, Sandy? The Rambler's ready to come out. Yeah, well, shut up in there so I can concentrate on my hand."

"Unlock the door," Ray ordered.

Keys jangled from the table. "What are you doing now?" De Courcy asked Sandusky. "Didn't I tell you we can't rough up the kid?"

Footsteps came to the door, and the bolt unlocked.

"Sandy?" De Courcy called out with a perplexed turn to his voice.

Ray put his hand to the door. "Mister Sandusky, knock Mister De Courcy out."

"That's it, Rambler!" De Courcy shouted. "Yeah, I'm coming in there to—"

There was a scuffle and then the sound of splintering wood before a body thumped to the floor.

Ray pushed open the door slowly. Sandusky stood there, looking dimly down at De Courcy's unconscious body with his bleary-eyed gaze.

Ray turned back to pick up B'hoy's body. He left the cell. "Put De Courcy in there," Ray said as he came out of the cell. Sandusky dropped the broken back of a chair and picked up De Courcy's feet, dragging him into the cell. Ray locked the door behind Sandusky and placed the whiskey bottle of dirt on the table. Grabbing his toby, Ray opened it. His charms were all stowed inside. He quickly tied a knot around his neck and tucked it beneath his shirt.

He pushed open the door and peered outside. A thin crescent moon was rising over the palisade. Dawn was not far off. Cautious to every sound, Ray made his way past the steam-coach and over to the stables. Crouching in the shadows, he heard the faint voices of guards standing watch at the entrance to the fort.

Ray went into the stables. In the first stall, a black mare turned her head. Ray whispered soothing words like he had often done with Élodie and saddled the horse. He led her out and tied her on the back side of the cabin. Then he went back in the stables and opened the gates for each of the horses, whispering all the while to the animals, explaining as best he could in their speech what he was planning.

Then, with the saltpeter, he lit a fire in the back of the stable and ran out to the black mare. Climbing onto her back, he whispered, "Be calm, girl. We're going for a ride."

Smoke rose from the stables, and soon one of the guards at the fort's entrance cried, "There's a fire!"

As the guards ran toward the stables, the horses stampeded out, whinnying and shrieking. The fort exploded with the thunder of horse hooves and men rousing from their barracks to help with the fire.

Kicking the black mare's haunches and weaving among the terrified horses, Ray rode to the fort's entrance. He leaped from the saddle and clutched the mare's reins, pulling the lever to open the gate.

"You there?" a soldier called. "Are you with those

Pinkertons?" He was only half dressed, without even boots or a sidearm on his belt.

Ray jumped into the saddle.

"What are you doing?" the soldier shouted.

Ray whistled loudly and shook the mare's reins. The horses turned at his call and scattered the soldiers as they clattered through the gate.

Ray heard the soldier crying behind him, "The prisoner! That horse thief, he's . . . stealing the horses. . . ."

He raced the black mare out into sagebrush prairie and toward the west, where the first rays of dawn were catching on the distant Rocky Mountains.

BUCK SAT ON THE STOOL WITH HIS BACK AGAINST THE wall, his hands folded in his lap, as he had done nearly every waking hour of every day for the past week. He sat, and he listened, and he learned.

The room where he was kept under the watchful eyes of Stacker Lee and the Gog's agents was high above the floor of Mister Grevol's Hall of Progress, as the agents called it. The Hall of Progress had an enormous open floor over a thousand feet long, containing hundreds of displays for what Mister Grevol and his staff considered "the future of America."

The hall was tall as well as vast, rising to a height of a hundred feet. Mounted to the girders and framework of the ceiling were a series of offices and rooms, accessible only by elevator, each with windows overlooking the exhibits below.

When he was first brought up to the room, Buck made sure to remember which way they had come from the elevators. He knew the number of steps from the elevators to the doors leading out from the hall. He knew how many tumblers clicked in the lock when the key turned the bolt. He knew the make of each gun carried by his guards, and that one of the agents had an old bullet wound in his hip by the sound his footsteps made.

Although Buck could not see the view from the windows in his room, Stacker Lee and the Bowlers could, and one of them was constantly on watch for John Henry's son or his three companions.

They expected Conker to come. The Nine Pound Hammer was mounted in a central display directly below their room. The legendary hammer apparently was drawing huge crowds.

"I'm going out," Stacker said.

Below, the voices of the last visitors to the hall had faded an hour earlier, and it was around this time, when Mister Grevol's agents left Stacker and Buck for the night, that Stacker would venture out. Buck rose from the stool and lay on his bed, the stiff mattress springs squeaking.

"I'm not partial to these cramped quarters, Buckthorn," Stacker said, as he did nearly every night. Stacker clamped the shackle that was bolted to the bed frame to Buck's ankle. "Need a little air to clear my head."

Buck said nothing. The swish of fabric and whisper of felt told him that Stacker was putting on his coat and donning his fine Stetson hat.

"Want me to leave the lantern on for you? Oh, of course

not." Stacker chuckled at his well-worn joke. The door closed with a thump, and the click of a key locked the bolt.

Buck woke later in the night. He lay thinking about the clockwork killer, unable to go back to sleep. After a while, he heard the lock click, Stacker's bootsteps as he came in, and the mattress groan and quiet once more. Eventually Buck slept.

In the morning, Stacker coughed and began getting dressed.

Buck sat up and asked in his low, gravelly voice, "Where do you go?"

"He speaks," Stacker said, his own voice raspy from sleep.

"What are you looking for?" Buck asked.

Stacker buckled his gun belt around his waist and poured a glass of water from a carafe. "The sirens."

Voices sounded in the hallway. The agents were arriving for their morning shift. Stacker unlocked the iron fetter from Buck's ankle. "Say nothing of my nighttime ventures if you still place a value on breathing."

The door opened and the agents came in, setting down a tray of sausages, toast, and overcooked eggs. Buck rose from his bed and went over to the stool. As he settled back against the wall, one of the agents shoved a warm plate of food onto his lap. Buck ate, all the while listening.

The days passed in tedious monotony. The roar of voices filling the Hall of Progress. The change of guards at noon and then at six. Dinner and supper ushered in with each arriving pair of agents. The voices below diminishing as evening turned to night. Then silence. The guards would leave and Buck was alone with Stacker.

Stacker rose, putting on his coat and hat.

"Going to look for the sirens?" Buck said.

"Get on the bed," Stacker ordered.

Buck stood and moved to his mattress, cocking his hands behind his head. Stacker knelt at his feet to lock the shackle.

"I know why you're looking for them," Buck said.

Stacker stood slowly and put the key in his pocket. "I liked you better when you knew when to be quiet."

"What I don't understand is why you want the clockwork removed," Buck said. "Why do you want your heart back?"

Stacker's razor clicked open. He took Buck's hair in a tight grip and jerked his head back against the hard mattress. Buck felt the cold edge of the razor pressed against his throat. "Your appearance is beginning to offend me, Buckthorn. When I shave a man, it's more than just his beard that might be lost."

"We share a goal, Stacker," Buck continued.

"We share nothing but this wretched room."

"You want to redeem yourself," Buck said. "The Gog is never going to remove the clockwork. You know this. But I can help you."

The blade crackled like a match across his bristly throat. Stacker pushed Buck's head to the side and stood. The door opened and then slammed, the sound reverberating. The lock clicked and Stacker's feet disappeared down the hallway.

Buck brought his hand to his throat. His fingers met a smooth patch of skin below his jawline and the warmth of blood. But the cut was not deep. Stacker had not meant it to be. It was only a warning after all.

* * *

As the evening shift of agents came in the following day, the one who handed Buck his supper said to the other, "Heard they spied the boy."

"Which boy?" another guard asked.

Buck froze.

"John Henry's son," the first said. "At least it was some big one. They think there was a couple of Reds with him. I don't know if they saw the China girl too."

Buck heard the shift in volume as the speaker turned his head toward Buck as he spoke. Buck scraped his fork across the plate, gathering up a mouthful of potatoes.

"What happened?" the other agent asked.

"They spotted them down at the waterfront, but you know how busy it gets down there. By the time McDevitt got there with his men, they were gone."

"They'll catch them."

"Soon enough."

After the afternoon guards left, the agent who had brought the news said, "You catch all that, scruffy?"

Buck continued eating, his expression placid.

"Think they'll come for him, Mister Lee?" the other agent asked.

"They'll come for the Nine Pound Hammer," Stacker Lee said, moving his fork across his plate. "If they're smart, they'll not waste a backward glance at this old gimp."

The agents laughed, and Buck took a bite of bread.

The guards went off duty, and Stacker left. Buck was still awake when Stacker returned. Rather than going to his bed,

Stacker came over to Buck and unlocked the shackle from his ankle.

"It's nearly morning," Buck said.

"Will be soon enough," Stacker replied. He removed his hat and dropped it to his bed, then took off his coat and gun belt. "You spent time with the sirens," he said.

Buck sat up, the mattress squeaking beneath him.

"I heard," Stacker continued, "you took up with a band of Ramblers that were guarding a siren down in Louisiana."

"That's right," Buck said. "Have you found the sirens the Gog has here?"

"They're locked below the hall. There are floors and floors in its depths. And deeper things still."

Buck sat without speaking.

"Have you ever seen one of their wells?" Stacker asked.

Buck nodded.

"Do the sirens conjure up the healing waters or do they simply stand guard over them?"

"They form when a siren dies," Buck answered.

"Is that right?"

Buck listened closely to Stacker's breathing, to his movements. Normally he could sense how a man felt in such a situation. Whether it was morbid curiosity or cold knowledge or compassion. But he could sense nothing in the clockwork man.

"We've killed plenty of men between us, Buckthorn. I know you've given up the gun, but killing for mercy . . . would you have the stomach for that?"

Buck frowned. "I don't know what you mean."

"Those sirens down there. If we killed them, it would be a piece of mercy, wouldn't it? No one should live with . . . this clockwork in them." Stacker poured a glass of water from the carafe and drank it in a long gulp. "And if they died and a spring rose, it would heal me. I believe it could."

"The water from a siren well might heal you. But a well only forms when a siren dies out of love. No spring would rise if you slaughtered those sirens down there."

"You sure about that?"

"I'm sure."

Stacker poured another glass of water but didn't drink. He put the glass down and gave a grim laugh.

"What?"

"I found a siren not long ago," Stacker said, "when I was searching for John Henry's son. I asked this siren if she knew where I could find a well of healing water."

Buck felt his pulse quicken. He tried to keep his face a mask.

"She said she didn't," Stacker continued. "But I knew she was lying. I have this power, you see. Not from the clockwork, but something I was born with. A way of knowing things about people. Just like I know secrets of yours, Buckthorn. Well, I knew this siren was protecting someone, and this was why she wouldn't reveal the well to me."

Buck could not help but tense. His neck muscles constricted and his hands clutched the sheets. "What happened to her?"

Stacker laughed. "That's the funny part. She was most likely protecting someone she loved. Why else would she not tell me of the well?"

Buck's voice came low through his gritted teeth. "What happened to her?"

"I killed her, of course. And all the while, if only I'd known that her death would have brought forth the very spring that could have—"

Buck lunged forward, bowling into Stacker and toppling him from his chair. The table overturned. The glass and carafe shattered on the floor. Buck twisted Stacker's collar so that it squeezed across his throat. Stacker gasped and spat, kicking his boot heels against the polished wood floor with awful squeaks.

"Who was she?" Buck roared. "Who was the siren?"

But Stacker could not speak, and his breath drew like a hissing valve from his open mouth. Buck heard Stacker's hand fumbling for something in his pocket. With one hand still squeezing the fabric of his collar, Buck reached down to clasp Stacker's wrist. The clockwork man was nearly unconscious. Buck beat Stacker's hand against the floor until the razor tumbled from his grasp. Stacker's body went limp as he passed out.

Buck pushed Stacker away and reached for the razor. As he felt for it on the floor, his fingers met a ring of keys that had fallen from Stacker's pocket.

Stacker began gulping deep breaths and coughing.

Buck had only a moment to decide. He had the keys. And Stacker's razor lay somewhere there on the floor. Had Stacker killed Jolie? Was she the siren he had murdered? Or was this all a bluff?

Buck picked up the razor and opened the blade. He knelt over Stacker and punched the razor into the floor, pinning Stacker's collar.

Then he rushed to the door and tried the keys hastily until he found the right one. How early was it? The morning guards had not arrived, but could they be on the way? He hurried down the hallway to the elevator, listening for any movement.

He opened the elevator door and stepped in. He felt around until he found the switch. The elevator groaned to life, jerking as it began its descent. As he came out on the main floor of the Hall of Progress, Buck heard the distant murmur of conversation and footsteps. No matter—they were not in the direction he needed to go.

Buck moved down the aisles of displays, his hip occasionally catching on a hard corner or brushing against the velvet ropes that kept visitors from the exhibits. He was nearly to the door when he remembered the Nine Pound Hammer.

When Conker had carried the Nine Pound Hammer, it had given off a powerful aura. Buck could always feel its presence, like something charged with electricity. He hesitated a moment before turning around. He had to get the hammer. Hurrying back through the displays, he tried to find that pulsating expression of the hammer's power.

Where was it? He couldn't feel it.

A faint clicking of gears and pulleys brought the elevator back to life. Buck turned and rushed toward the exit. He stumbled against exhibits.

The elevator door rattled open. "He's escaped!" Stacker's voice echoed through the great hall. "Buckthorn's escaped!"

A thundering of feet reverberated over the marble floors. Buck ran. His shoulder slammed into the door frame. Working key after key into the lock, he finally brought one around with a click. He pushed open the door and fell down several stone steps.

Morning birds twittered around the empty grounds. A cool wind blew up from the lake, and Buck turned to face it. He focused his senses. There was a fountain. And there a line of trees. And a building. On and on he went, keeping to the walkway, going as fast as he could.

He could hear the lapping of the water on the lake's shore. His feet reached the wooden boards of a pier. Buck ran, knocking into the railings as he went. The clatter of feet rose behind him. As he turned, Stacker pummeled into him. Buck fell backward, his skull cracking sharply on the wood. Stacker scrambled atop him, bringing his meaty fist against Buck's face again and again. At last Stacker hauled Buck up and dragged him toward the end of the pier.

Buck's legs gave out, but Stacker continued pulling him, the toes of Buck's boots thumping, thumping, thumping over the planks as they went. "The siren," Stacker hissed. "Her name was Cleoma. Does she mean something to you?"

Buck could not speak. His mouth was filled with blood.

Agents were shouting behind them.

Stacker snapped open the razor. "You were right, by the way," he said. "The Gog will never give me back my heart. But I will have my freedom. Fear not, Buckthorn." The agents' footsteps clattered on the boards of the pier. "Remember. Hope still lies at Liberty's feet."

Stacker brought the razor back and forth across Buck's chest in several sweeping slashes. Then with a shove, he knocked Buck into the lake.

RAY WATCHED THE TINY RIBBON OF BLACK SMOKE IN THE distance. Clutching the toby, he extended a hand. He closed his eyes and focused his attention over the vast distance. The toby trembled.

A tickle formed at his fingertips, like touching a wool coat charged with static. The sensation grew, tingling across his knuckles and into his palms. It pulled. Ray closed his hand and snapped open his eyes.

He kicked the mare's sides and rode her hard. To his left, the mountain range bore down like an enormous fortification, running north-south and stretching ahead and behind as far as Ray could see. The escape from the fort, and the days with nothing to fill his stomach but rank water, had left Ray weak in body and spirit. He was tempted to ride up into the high country, to catch game or forage for a meal, but travel in the mountains would be slow-going, and he couldn't risk the steamcoach catching up. So he rode northbound over the sagebrush hills, with only the faintest hope of happening upon something worth eating.

When twilight came, he camped by a stream. He drank thirstily and went up a rise to peer south. No billow of black smoke broke the flatlands. He had followed the steamcoach long enough now to know the agents had made camp for the night. So Ray also slept a few hours, until anxiety woke him.

The land was still dark, the hazy Milky Way casting the only light. Ray took B'hoy's body from his haversack and pried some rocks from the hard earth to stack them into a cairn. Tears beaded on his nose as Ray selected three feathers from each of B'hoy's wings and three from his tail. Putting the black feathers aside, Ray placed B'hoy atop the cairn. Feeling too weary to construct a prayer or poem to bless his companion, Ray simply said, "Return in peace, old boy."

He watched the night breeze rustle the feathers across B'hoy's back. He felt there was something right about leaving B'hoy exposed to the elements. Soon coyotes or vultures might eat him, or insects and grubs. This was the natural way of things: returning, providing nourishment for new life, continuing the cycle.

Ray took the toby from around his neck, opened it, and placed the nine feathers inside. He had no plans for the tokens but wanted something to remember the crow by. As Ray did this, his fingers brushed against the dandelion petal. He thought suddenly about Peter Hobnob.

Loneliness swelled in his chest, and Ray considered blowing on the flower, clapping his hands, and summoning his friend. But how long would it take the bumbling thief to arrive? And what purpose would it serve? Ray held the dandelion a moment longer, then with a sigh set the flower in his toby and hung the pouch back around his neck.

Under the noon sun, Ray rode near a mining camp. The wood of the shacks and the canvas of frayed tents were bleached a pale gray, like nearly everything else on the plains. He spied a man splitting wood to feed an open-air brick oven. Another man was cutting up food at a table in the shade of a tent. The faint whistling of "Silver Threads Among the Gold" wafted by. It was a tune Ray had not heard since his boyhood in the streets of lower Manhattan. How strange to hear the song again, out here in this rough country.

He could see no other inhabitants but caught the faint *tink* of hammers. He realized the other men were down in a mine somewhere, beating ore from the earth.

Ray wondered if he should ask the cooks if they could spare a meal. But what if they had a telegraph? Word might have come across the wires warning of a horse thief recently escaped from the fort. Ray saw no telegraph poles but feared news might have arrived by another route. He couldn't afford to risk capture again.

But he was so hungry, and this camp seemed the only opportunity for food. He would just have to be quick, he decided.

Ray led the mare down a slope and tied her reins to a trunk of sagebrush. She began eating the coarse leaves and tough grass immediately. Ray opened his shirt to take out the toby. He rustled through its contents until his fingers came upon a dried knob of poke root. A root worker in the Chesapeake lowlands had once shown him a driving-off spell. It would work, but only if Ray could find a candle in the mining camp and light it without drawing the men's attention. A risk, Ray had to admit, but one worth taking for some food.

Ray plucked a leaf off the sagebrush and tore it down the center. He snapped a corner of the poke root and crushed it with a rock into powder. Then, with the ingredients in his hand, Ray circled the mining camp until he reached the well for the miners' water.

He dropped one of the halves of the sagebrush leaf into the well, and then snuck up toward the camp. Through the tents and buildings, he spied the pair of cooks, whistling and chopping as they prepared the evening meal. His stomach whined painfully. Ray looked around until he decided they were the only two aboveground.

He went into the nearest tent and found a candle stub perched in a chipped teacup. He lit the candle and left the tent, cautious to the movement of the cooks. The first had finished chopping the wood and was talking to the other as he took loaves of bread from the oven.

". . . you say she lives down in Denver with her sister?"

"Yeah, I could have delivered the letters myself in less time than it took for the express rider to carry it. . . ."

Ray walked carefully with the lit candle until he was behind the cooks' tent. The side of canvas had been lowered to shade the men from the morning sun, and Ray knelt there to begin the spell. He snapped the candle from the wax in the cup and dropped the other half of the sagebrush leaf, along with the poke root powder, into the dried wax.

". . . this is the last of the beef. Have to hope the supply wagons get here soon."

"They're two days late as it is. . . ."

Ray tipped the candle and let the hot wax drip onto the leaf and powder. The wax cooled quickly, encasing the spell's ingredients until they were little more than faint brown and silver shadows in the yellow bubbles of the tallow. Ray licked his fingers and pinched out the candle's flame. He waited.

The men spoke idly about supplies and relatives and the irritations in their bowels, but after a few moments, Ray heard the one man's cleaver rattle on the chopping table and the other clapping his hands together to wipe off the flour. They walked together, speaking all the while, out from the tent. Ray slipped around the canvas wall and, crouching, watched them head toward the well.

Tricking them didn't bother him. They wouldn't know what possessed them with desire to go to the leaf's other half, floating in the well. They wouldn't give their actions a second thought. They would talk together and draw water from the well, maybe deciding that thirst had brought them there, until one of the two touched the other half of the sagebrush leaf and the spell would be broken.

Ray knew he wouldn't have much time, but he'd have enough. When the cooks had disappeared from sight, he scrambled out and collected loaves of bread into a large square of cloth. Into another he cut sections of roasting beefsteaks, still bloody from the spit, and stacked them with raw onions and cabbage. Among some hardware on the ground were several twines of rope. Ray tied the satchels of food to a coil of rope and put it over his shoulder. This was as much as he could carry and more than he felt right about stealing.

But he was hungry, and although suspicions and accusations might occur when the missing food was discovered, Ray would be far away. To settle his conscience, Ray selected a boneset leaf and a devil's shoestring root from his toby and tacked them to the underside of the cook's table.

The charms would protect the camp from illness, and although they would never know he had given them this compensation, Ray felt better about it. When he'd put a few miles behind him, he sat on the ground and ate until his stomach grew sore and happy.

The black ribbon of smoke followed him, edging ever closer as the steamcoach chased Ray across the rocky country. But at last, Ray reached the place where he saw the pass going up into the mountains. Sally and Quorl had gone that way with Jolie only a day behind them. Since the mare was not fretting, he pushed her on a little farther into the evening, ascending into the mountains' foothills and patchwork forests of the dry eastern slopes. He camped for the night, eating the last of the steaks, since they would spoil, and saving the rest to mix with whatever could be foraged in the high country ahead.

The following morning he spent some time searching out Élodie's hoofprints before climbing farther. Although it had been nearly a week since Jolie had passed this way, there had been no rain to wash out the tracks. Ray felt certain no other traveler had come this way and set off, following the prints up the slopes.

The course took him west, as he suspected it would, and the

high country was full of fine air and beautiful scenery. As he reached a point where he assumed he would lose the view of the dusty plains behind him, Ray looked back for the steam-coach. The black smoke showed it had nearly caught up to him.

He looked at the pass rising before him. The way was steep, a maze of loose rocks and boulders. With a sigh, Ray patted the mare's mane and said, "Good girl. They'll never be able to get that monstrosity up into these mountains."

He shook her reins and hoped he was right.

For a day, Ray rode into the high reaches of the mountains and saw no sign of the steamcoach. The following afternoon, he found himself in a wide valley carved out by a distant wall of glacier and a meandering river. In the grassy bottoms, he found a large wolf's tracks and scanned until he saw a girl's prints also.

Ray followed their tracks up the mountainside until he came onto the ridge and eventually reached a forest of aspens, white as ghostly spears staked to a battlefield. Coming out from the trees, Ray spied the heap of a recent avalanche and cast a nervous eye to the rock face above. Clouds of snow blew from the top, but it seemed the heaviest of the snowpack had already fallen and wouldn't fall again until the following spring thaw. As Ray urged the mare up into the snow, she sank to her belly, each step a struggle. He decided she'd have an easier time without him on her back, so he got down and led her by the reins.

When he was nearly halfway across, his eyes fell on a set of tracks—the enormous canine prints of the rougarou. Ray stopped and looked around. Where were Sally's tracks? Why wasn't she with the rougarou?

Then it struck Ray that Élodie's tracks did not cross the avalanche either. Jolie had not followed Quorl over the snow.

As he peered around in puzzlement, he heard a snort from the aspen grove. It was followed by the unmistakable flapping of a horse's mane. "Who's there?" Ray called, his hand going to his belt before he remembered that he no longer had his knife. He crouched in the snow behind the mare, peering back at the tree line.

A horse whinnied and clapped its hooves. Ray spotted the quarter horse's brown back and muttered, "Élodie."

Leaving the mare in the snow, Ray shuffled across the avalanche and, when he was back on hard earth, he ran to the horse. Élodie was still saddled, her reins hanging from her chin and tangled with leaves and bracken. "Jolie!" Ray shouted. "Are you here?"

Ray listened. There was a faint cry, but he could not detect where it was coming from or what was making it. "Élodie," Ray said, taking the horse's neck in his hands. "Where is Jolie? Where's she gone?"

He had learned to issue a few commands to the horse Unole that he and Marisol had ridden to Omphalosa. And he had used his limited speech to urge the horses at Fort Hudson to escape. But to understand Élodie now, Ray had to enter the horse's thoughts in a way he had never done before.

"What's happened to her?" Ray whispered.

Élodie flicked her ears and turned her big brown eyes to him. Ray closed his eyes.

The answer came not as speech, but as a flash of memory— the thunder of breaking ice and an enormous eruption of snow falling on a half-frozen lake.

Ray opened his eyes and turned back toward the avalanche of snow. "Jolie," he gasped.

What about Sally? Had she been with Jolie when the snow-pack broke?

Ray had no experience with snow of this magnitude. Was one crushed by the fall, or were they buried alive? And if the latter, could they survive for a while in a pocket of snow? It had been nearly a week, and frost or starvation would surely have set in.

Ray ran out onto the snow and began digging desperately with his hands. The snow was loose, and he managed to clear several holes before his fingers burned and throbbed with cold. He moved from spot to spot, calling out Jolie's and Sally's names as he plunged his hands into the powder and kicked the snow away like a fox building a den.

Sweating and half frozen at the same time, Ray knelt in the snow to catch his breath. "Sally!" he shouted. "Can you hear me? Jolie!"

He heard nothing. Élodie's memory formed again in his mind. Before the avalanche, this had been a lake. There was water beneath the mountain of snow.

Jolie might have survived in the water! But how was he to reach her? He had dug down deep in several spots and had reached nothing but harder snow. He couldn't reach the lake even if he had a shovel.

In desperation, fingers numb with cold, he pulled open the buttons of his shirt. He took out the toby and rummaged through the contents. What charm did he possess that could move this much snow? Nothing! But he didn't need to move the snow, he needed to find Jolie beneath it.

He had spent a month with a conjurer down in Georgia, a half Seminole who had used milk from an all-black cow to find buried treasure. He had said there was a better charm. What was it? A leafless plant. A little pale parasite that grew on the roots of some trees.

Gall of the Earth!

The conjurer had never used it because it was rare, growing only in cold places. Never in the marsh of southern Georgia.

Ray ran to the grove of aspens. He kicked away the hard earth from the roots of the first tree he came to. Clawing and throwing away the dirt in clumps, he searched for the pale plant. Nothing. He went from tree to tree. He was about to give up when he pried back a wedge of half-frozen earth and saw it. Growing among a thick fungus covering the damp roots was a ghostly stem with tiny droplet-shaped flowers. This was Gall of the Earth. He knew it as he plucked the plant from the roots.

As he hurried to Élodie, he tried to remember what the conjurer had taught him. To find buried treasure, he would need something that belonged to the person who hid the treasure. A button, a fingernail clipping, a . . . piece of hair! Ray searched the saddle until he found several strands of Jolie's long hair tangled around the saddle horn.

He took off Élodie's saddle and tore a corner from the saddle blanket. Wrapping the hair and the Gall of the Earth in the fabric, he had a sort of doll, a totem that represented Jolie. He hurried out until he was toward the middle of the avalanche, where he guessed the lake to be. He dropped the doll.

He watched the charm lying in the snow, the gray woolen sack stuffed with the Gall of Earth and Jolie's hair. For a few moments nothing happened, but then the doll twitched. The snow shifted beneath it, crunching ever so softly, until the doll turned, its lumpy head sliding over the loose surface of snow.

Ray followed the doll as it inched along. After a few yards, it stopped. Once more it twitched and nudged down into the crispy surface.

The snow around the doll began to melt, and a depression formed. The charm went deeper as the snow puddled and shrank. Ray's pant legs grew wet, and his boots filled with water. The snow melted inches at a time as he watched. Some areas upturned and collapsed more swiftly then others, and Ray backed away from the hole that was forming.

Soon, the snow shrank to reveal blue-black water. The doll splashed and disappeared into the depths. Ray crouched at the edge and peered down. He saw nothing but murky shadow. Then some distance down—he could not judge the depth in the freezing waters—he saw a shimmer of skin.

"Jolie!" he called. "Can you hear me?"

She did not move.

Ray ran back across the snow. From the saddle, he removed the coil of rope he'd taken from the mining camp. He tied one end to the mare's saddle horn and unwound the rest out toward the snow.

"Come on, old gal!" he shouted, pulling the horse reluctantly from her grazing. He stopped her at the edge of the snow and rushed out with the rope until he crouched again at the water's edge.

The limp form of Jolie's body floated down in the dark waters. Luminous pale arms extended. Strands of hair drifting out and mingling with the murk.

"Jolie!" he cried. He threw the bundle of rope into the water. "Grab it! Please take the rope."

The coil drifted down, knocking against her and disappearing into the black.

"Jolie! Take it. It's right there."

She did not move. It was clear she was unconscious. The lake couldn't have been more than a few degrees above freezing. How long could he survive in it?

Ray grabbed the rope and twirled it around the hole, trying to catch on Jolie. But the rope simply brushed against her shoulders.

He knew there was no choice left. He untied his laces and yanked off his boots. Throwing aside his hat, he took off his coat and shirt and pants. He dropped the toby on top of the pile.

Ray tried to prepare himself, to compose his courage as he stood shivering at the edge of the blue-black waters.

He plunged in. The cold was like nails driving into his skin. He kicked and fought to keep his mind from snapping shut. He dove deeper and opened his eyes to search for Jolie.

A little deeper, her pearly skin shone from the dark waters. He swam down until he grasped her about the waist and reached out for the rope. Kicking his way up, he followed the rope back to the hole of light. His face broke the surface and he gasped for air.

Holding tightly to Jolie's arm, he climbed out of the freezing water. Then he got down on his knees and pulled until he hoisted her up onto the snow.

Her eyes were shut, and her body fell limp and heavy against him. Ray lifted her into his arms and hurried off the frozen lake and back to the forest. "Jolie, can you h-hear me?" His teeth rattled. He shivered uncontrollably.

Ray knew he had to get dry quickly if he was to help her. He ran back for his clothes.

He could not imagine how Jolie had survived so long in the frozen lake. He had heard stories of trout frozen in Adirondack streams only to emerge in the spring, but he had always taken those for campfire tales.

When he returned, he wrapped the wool saddle blanket around his shoulders and tried to dry off as best he could. Stripping off his wet union suit, he put on his dry clothes and with stiff fingers tried to tie his bootlaces.

Jolie said nothing. Her eyes were open, but she seemed barely conscious as she lay on the ground. Her breathing came as shallow hisses. Her skin was an unnatural blue hue. Ray grabbed the saddle blanket and bundled it around her, thankful that her gown couldn't hold water.

"I'm going to build a fire," he said, before rushing to the aspens to break off dry branches. The effort of collecting wood helped warm him, but his skin burned from the cold. He moved hastily and soon had a fire roaring. He propped Jolie against Élodie's saddle before the blaze and hurriedly prepared teas from foraged herbs in his haversack.

As the concoctions warmed, Ray rubbed Jolie's arms and legs, trying to bring warmth and life back into them. The icy tinge was leaving her skin.

"Ray . . . ," she muttered weakly.

"Shh," Ray said. "Sip this. Slowly now."

"Where . . . what's happened?"

"Just drink," Ray said. As she drank the steaming liquid,

Jolie began shivering uncontrollably. Ray hoped this meant she was improving.

He poured himself a cup of the hot tea and drank it in a gulp. Warmth was returning to his frozen body.

With night falling, Ray nursed Jolie until her trembling subsided. He fed her bread and, later, a stew made from the onions and cabbage he'd taken from the miners. Jolie was too weak to speak but gazed at Ray with a gentle and grateful expression.

Later in the night, Ray said, "Jolie. I have to know. Was Sally . . . was she with you when the avalanche fell? Is she . . ."

"She escaped."

Ray exhaled with relief. "Did you speak to her?"

"She is in danger, Ray." Jolie managed to sit up slightly. "Quorl . . . there was something wrong with him. He has changed."

"What do you mean?"

"He was savage. Terrifying. Those eyes . . ."

"What about them?" Ray breathed.

The flickering firelight danced shadows across Jolie face. "They were the eyes of a monster."

SALLY WANDERED THROUGH THE TALL GRASS OF THE VALLEY. "Quorl! Where are you?"

She had only stopped to drink at the river and to clean up, and then moments later, when she looked around, he had gone. The valley was huge and sweeping—grasslands punctuated by occasional forests and, on the far side, blue mountains that sprang up from the valley floor into jagged peaks. It suddenly looked bigger and more desolate than she'd thought. Sally looked around for something to climb on, something to help her see where he might have gone.

"Quorl," she called out, her frustration edging toward panic.

She heard something ahead and tore her way into a thicket of bushes. Pushing the branches aside, the thicket ended abruptly, and Sally fell forward onto her hands and knees. She looked up and gave a startled gasp as she saw the rougarou. "Quorl! Why did you—"

She froze and then leaped to her feet.

Quorl was sitting atop a moose carcass. Blood stained the rougarou's snout as he bit into the moose's side and crunched into the sinew and bone. Sally backed away in horror. Quorl had hunted for her. She never would have been able to come this far if he hadn't. And she had seen him eat his catch, but this was different. From the flies buzzing about and the stench of rot, she knew this was a carcass he'd found, not something he had caught.

"Quorl!" she said sharply. "Get off that and come with me."

He kept eating, and if he understood her words, he gave no acknowledgment.

She dug into her rucksack and pulled out a handful of bistort bulbs. "You like these. Remember? Please come away from that thing, Quorl."

He eyed the bulbs but then returned to tearing at the moose's leg.

"Quorl, did you hear me?" she snapped. "Get up! We've got to find Father. Don't you remember what we have to do? I need you. I can't reach him without—" Her voice broke and she brushed angrily with her sleeve at the tears that sprang to her eyes.

He had promised he would lead her, that he would take care of her. But what if he had gone too far? What would happen when he was no longer a rougarou but became entirely a wolf? How would she find her father then?

Quorl had stopped eating, his dark eyes on her.

Sally took a deep breath and said firmly, "Get up now."

Quorl let go of the moose and rose to his feet.

Her voice trembled as she said, "You can't leave me again. Okay? Do you understand, Quorl? You promised, remember. You can't leave me."

Whether he understood her or not, Sally could no longer tell. But Quorl came toward her with his head lowered.

She took out the rabbit's foot and watched as it rotated in her palm until the little claws pointed to the sawtooth mountains rising from the far side of the valley floor. She took a few steps in that direction, peering back at Quorl. He looked back at the dead moose, his tongue dangling from his blood-speckled jaws, but then he trotted after her.

As they crossed the valley, Sally decided she no longer cared anymore whether she was able to return her father's Rambler powers to him. Mother Salagi had told her that only her father could make the spike that was needed to destroy the Machine, but she no longer cared whether he did that. All she wanted was to find him. Just to escape this wilderness and see him at long last.

If he could be her father, to watch over her and take care of her and be in her life, she wouldn't care what else happened.

By nightfall, she camped in a grove of aspens at the far side of the valley. When she woke the next morning, Quorl was still there. She was not sure whether to be relieved or not.

She found a pass leading up through the mountains. The climb was brutal, more like going up a ladder than walking.

They rose above the timberline into meadows of hard creeping plants and stunted shrubs. Sally looked at the looming mountains and steely sky ahead.

"How much higher can we go?" she wondered aloud.

She half expected Quorl to make one of his philosophical comments such as "There are paths that go higher," but Quorl said nothing.

They crossed the high mountains. Quorl stayed near as they traveled, but he no longer hunted for her or helped her gather roots and berries. Sally got by on the foraged food still in her rucksack, but by the time they reached a shadow-filled forest of spruce several days later, her supply was at its end.

After walking a short ways into the alpine grove, Quorl stopped and lifted his nose to sniff the air.

"What is it?" Sally asked anxiously. "Is something out there?"

Quorl trotted forward, his ears held high. Sally had to jog to keep up with him.

"Wait, Quorl," she panted. "Slow down."

The rougarou whined and began racing through the trees.

"Please, Quorl!" Sally called, running as fast as she could. "Slow down." She wound through the dark evergreens as Quorl got farther and farther ahead.

"Come back—" she began to yell, when her boot sank into a hole of loose dirt. Her foot twisted and Sally flipped sideways and fell. Pain shot up her leg. As she sat panting and trying to catch her breath, she eased her foot gently from the hole. Pulling up the hem of her dress and rolling down her sock, she saw her ankle had begun to swell.

"No, no . . . ," she gasped. She tried to stand, but as soon as her weight was on the foot, it gave way beneath her, erupting in fresh waves of pain. She looked around at the dim forest. She could no longer see Quorl, no longer hear his whines, no longer even remember which way he had gone.

A croak broke from the woods. She peered up to find a black congress of ravens watching her from the branches overhead. Sally tried once more to stand, this time careful not to put so much weight on her twisted ankle. She hopped a step and then shuffled another step, reaching out to hold on to a tree trunk for support.

"Quorl!" she called.

The ravens flapped their great black wings as they startled from the branches. Sally's voice echoed through the trees and vanished into the misty woods along with the ravens.

She began sobbing into her hands. What would she do? She had the rabbit's foot. It was still pulling her toward her father, but how would she cross into the Gloaming to reach him? She had to find Quorl. He would come back. He had to. She was limping along, calling out his name, when she emerged from the forest.

An enormous rock face rose up before her. A waterfall beginning hundreds of feet above cascaded down in a torrent of noise and misting spray. As Sally sank to the ground, she watched the last orange glow of the setting sun fade from the mountain wall.

WHEN THEY CAME DOWN INTO THE VALLEY, RAY CIRCLED THE mare and leaped from the saddle. He knelt in the tall grass and inspected the path of broken stems. Pushing back the blades revealed a footprint pressed into the soft earth. "She came through not more than two days ago," he said. "We're gaining on them."

Jolie looked down at the other trail parting the grasses. "Only because he is growing worse. When I tracked them up from the plains into the mountains, Quorl and Sally walked side by side. But now—"

"I see it," Ray said, and got back into the saddle. "He's not following a straight course like she is. He's drifting from side to side."

"Like an animal distracted by every scent and smell," Jolie said grimly.

Ray nodded. "Right, like an animal."

He surveyed the valley ahead and the distant mountains. "There's a lot of open country between here and that range."

Jolie rubbed Élodie's mane. "The horses are exhausted."

"Let's get them down to the river first, then they can rest."

With a crack of the reins, the horses set off through the belly-deep grasses. When they reached the river, Ray and Jolie dismounted and let the horses eat from the thistle growing along the banks. Ray dug up some of the starchy thistle roots to roast later. Under the tufts of grass, he found large, fleshy mushrooms and bright orange chanterelles. He cut up some to share with Jolie.

As they ate, Ray said, "Jolie, what happens after we find Sally?"

"What do you mean?"

"Your sisters," Ray said. "Are you . . . well, you said before that you belonged with them. Will you go back?"

"To the Terrebonne?" Jolie asked, her expression growing serious. "With the Machine still out there? Ray, the Gog must be stopped. I would not run from all there is to do, no matter how hopeless it might seem at times."

Ray nodded as he picked up another mushroom. "Good."

"But that still does not answer your question," Jolie said. "Where do we go after we catch up with your sister and Quorl? Chicago?"

"Where else would we go?" Ray asked.

She shrugged. "Do you not want to know what the rabbit's foot is pulling to?"

"It's not him," Ray said. "It can't be him. Even if he's

alive—and I have no reason to think he could be—my father's in the Gloaming. How could the lodestone possibly be pulling to something in the Gloaming? It doesn't make any sense that—"

The black mare whinnied and turned her head to the east. Ray and Jolie looked back. All they saw was the forest of cottonwoods from where they'd come. Élodie stamped her hooves anxiously.

"I thought you said the steamcoach could not follow us up into the mountains," Jolie said.

"It can't." Ray lifted his hand and held it out. He felt the jolt of current immediately.

Jolie's eyes were wide. "I do not see any smoke."

"Because there's no steamcoach out there. Get on Élodie!" he shouted as he leaped up into the saddle. "It's the Hound. They've sent the Hound after us."

The horses splashed across the river, and once they reached the far bank, Ray and Jolie drove them into a hard gallop. After they had covered a mile or more, Ray glanced back. On the other side of the river, a white form emerged from the cottonwoods.

Ray kicked his heels into the mare's haunches and leaned low across her neck, yelling, "Go! Go!"

The two horses raced side by side, hooves thundering. Ray searched for Sally and Quorl's passage, some sign of where they made their way out from the valley, but he had lost their trail. There was no time to stop and track them.

He looked up at the range ahead. "Do you see any sort of pass?" he shouted.

Jolie's eyes searched along the mountains. "I see gaps between the peaks, but to reach them would be impossible."

"Over there!" Ray steered the mare toward a grove of aspens slightly to the north. The mountains behind them came together in a narrow gap. "See that pass? It starts just on the other side of these trees."

"Can the horses climb that?" Jolie asked anxiously.

"Probably not." Ray pointed to the looming range. "But it's all too steep. We don't have time to search for a pass that the horses can manage!"

"So what should we do?"

"Get into the trees," Ray said. "Just keep riding."

Giving one last look back, he saw the pale form of the Hoarhound coming through the tall grass and knew they had only minutes before the Hound would reach the trees. Leading the horses into the dark grove, they ducked from low hanging branches and wound through the ferns and underbrush and around fallen branches and boulders.

"There it is," Jolie said as they came out the other side of the forest. A steep gully of broken rocks and debris jutted up into the mountains. "The horses cannot climb that."

"We'll go on foot," Ray said. "And we don't have time to argue about it. There's no other choice."

Jolie leaped from Élodie's back. "All right, but we cut the saddles and set the horses free."

Ray looked back as he dismounted. The trees were too thick for him to see how far away the Hound was, but he couldn't hear it yet.

"Okay," Ray said. "But hurry."

When they had gotten the saddles and harnesses stripped, the horses stamped their hooves anxiously, seeming uncertain of what to do. Jolie nuzzled Élodie's snout. "You are free. Go." She clapped her hands and the horses set off together, galloping swiftly away.

A roar broke, rumbling through the forest and echoing off the mountainside.

Ray shook his head and pointed to the pass. "We won't get beyond that first bend up there before the Hoarhound catches us."

"We cannot go back," Jolie said, clutching the handle of her knife.

Ray frowned at her knife. "And we can't fight it either! Our best hope is to hide. Up that tree," he said, running toward a tall leafy aspen.

"The Hound will have us cornered—"

"He already does," Ray said. "Climb!"

Jolie went first, grabbing the lowest branches of the aspen and hoisting herself up. "Higher," Ray said, climbing swiftly behind her.

Ray and Jolie scrambled to a cleft in the trunk nearly forty feet up. As Jolie scanned the forest below, she said, "If it sees us up here, it will topple this tree at the roots."

Ray was already taking out the saltpeter and a half-burned branch of sagebrush. "Then we've got to hope this keeps it from seeing us." He blew the saltpeter powder in his palm into a flame. After lighting the leaves, he dropped them into the jar.

Ray waved the sagebrush jar to scatter the smoke around them. The fragrant smoke drifted down through the limbs and leaves toward the earth. "Say nothing," Ray whispered, shifting his boots to find a secure perch. He and Jolie faced each other with the forked trunk at their backs. Jolie took a deep breath and looked down.

A snort sounded below. The Hoarhound's heavy footsteps approached until at last the beast came into view, winding its way slowly through the trees. Ray waved the jar once more, and Jolie had to put a hand to her mouth to stifle a cough.

From their high vantage, the clockwork monster looked more like a pacing bull. The ground crackled with frost under its heavy paws. The cold drifted up on the breeze. As the Hoarhound neared the trunk of their tree, it stopped and sniffed the ground.

Jolie squeezed the branch overhead anxiously, the skin across her knuckles tight and pale.

The Hound took a few more sniffs, then turned its enormous head side to side, searching the forest but not looking up. A guttural growl grew in the monster's throat. Ray tensed.

With a sharp exhale of frost, the Hoarhound bounded forward and trotted up toward the gully. When the monster had left the grove, Ray sighed with relief.

"I was certain it smelled us," Jolie whispered.

"The sage masks our scent," Ray said, holding out his hand to feel for the Hound. "Keep still and wait. It's not left yet."

"Ray," Jolie said with a note of alarm. "The jar."

The sagebrush in the jar was burning out. "Take out the branch," Ray said, tilting the jar her way as he got back out the saltpeter. She reached her slender hand in through the mouth to remove the sage, but it crumbled to ash.

"Is there any more?" Jolie asked.

"That was the last branch." Ray extended his hand toward the gully.

Jolie said, "Well, it will not matter if the Hound does not—"

Ray's eyes widened. "It's coming back!"

"What do we do?" Jolie asked, tensing again.

Juggling the jar and saltpeter tin, Ray opened the haversack. "Hurry! Look for even the tiniest piece. A few crushed leaves. Anything!"

As Jolie dug through the satchel, Ray watched for the Hound. He saw flashes of white, still at some distance, winding through the forest as the Hoarhound prowled.

"A leaf!" Jolie said.

"Give it here so I can light it." Ray tried to pass the jar and tin of saltpeter to Jolie while taking the sage leaf, but in the scramble, the leaf dropped.

"Catch it!" Ray hissed.

Jolie reached, but the sage flittered just past her fingertips. "I missed it!"

Ray heard the frost-crackled steps of the Hound coming nearer. He looked down at the leaf of sage, drifting to the ground. He knew the Hound would spot them without the charm. All it would take was one glance up. He had to get the leaf.

Ray shoved the haversack, the jar, and the tin into Jolie's arms.

"It is gone!" Jolie whispered urgently. "You cannot get down and back in time."

"Yes, I can."

He closed his eyes. He forced aside the thought of the Hound, the thought of the danger he and Jolie were in, the need to reach Sally. He leaned forward and dove through the branches.

He heard Jolie gasp, but he let the sound blend with the rushing of wind in his ears. He focused on the aspen, the forest, the mountains. He fell.

Ray sensed that he was about to hit a branch and opened his eyes. He waved his arms and felt the feathers catch the air and lift him up in time. Flapping his crow wings, Ray circled the trunk, spying the Hoarhound sniffing at the ground and edging closer to their tree.

He had only moments. He dove for the sage leaf and snapped it in his beak just before it touched the earth. Holding it tightly, Ray beat his wings to rise back up to Jolie. As he reached her perch in the cleft of the trunk, he transformed back.

He had to grab the trunk tightly as a swell of dizziness struck him. "Take the leaf," he gasped, holding it out to Jolie.

"I cannot light it," she said.

Like before when he had taken crow form, he felt nauseous and exhausted and could barely lift his head from where it rested against the rough bark. "Hand me the saltpeter," he murmured.

Leaning heavily against the tree, Ray shook a sprinkle of the saltpeter into his palm and blew on it to ignite the flame. Jolie shoved the leaf into the flame and, seeing fire brighten the edge of the sage, she dropped it into the jar. A moment later, smoke was drifting from the mouth of the jar, surrounding them and slowly settling along the aspen trunk toward the ground.

Ray held to the trunk, his eyelids threatening to close. The Hound was standing at the roots of their tree, sniffing. It backed away a few steps. Then slowly the Hound lifted its gaze until the mechanical eyes stopped at the cleft in the tree where Ray and Jolie sat.

Time seemed frozen. Ray realized it might be the after-effects of taking crow form, but there was something else to the moment. Jolie was at his back, one arm wrapped around him to keep him from falling from the tree, the other holding the jar, where thin wisps of smoke surrounded them. Below, the Hoarhound stared at them. Ray could read nothing from the mechanical monster's expression to know whether they were about to be attacked.

Then it sniffed, its eyes slowly moving from Ray and Jolie, scanning to the uppermost branches and then down, past the two of them and back to the ground.

The Hound circled around and then disappeared into the forest, jogging toward the gully.

"Is it gone?" Jolie asked.

"We'd better wait," Ray said.

Jolie smiled with amazement. "You did it, Ray! You flew. You were a crow!"

"It tires me," he said.

"You do not look as bad as last time," Jolie said. "Remember how long you slept?"

Ray realized he was feeling steadier already. He thought he might be able to climb down the tree in a few moments. He realized also how near Jolie was to him.

"You can . . . uh, let go of me now," he said.

"Oh," Jolie murmured, backing away from him and grabbing the trunk on the other side of the cleft. She looked around at the forest below. "Can you tell if the Hound is gone?"

Glad to turn his attention elsewhere, Ray lifted his hand. "I feel it less. It's leaving."

"Good," Jolie breathed.

"No," Ray said. "That's not good. The Hound is ahead of us now."

Jolie's eyes widened as she realized what this meant. "Sally," she said.

SALLY LIMPED THROUGH THE DARK FOREST BACK TO THE waterfall. She had called Quorl's name so many times her voice was hoarse. Kneeling down at the edge of the pool below the falls, she drank the cold, clear water until it filled her stomach enough to drive away the knots of hunger.

She sat on a boulder and took out the rabbit's foot. It pulled toward the fall, and her eyes traced the tower of mist and thundering water to the cliff high above. It was as if she had almost reached the top of the world. Staring at the cliff, she knew she would never be able to climb up there even if she hadn't injured herself. Besides, what good would it do? She had no way to reach her father now. Quorl was gone and all of her journey, all she had done and endured to get here, had come to nothing.

She jerked the laces from her boot and pulled the tattered

thing off. Her foot was swollen and splotched purple-black. A soft whimper escaped as she massaged the tender skin.

"I've got to reach Father," she mumbled. "I've just got to. There must be a way."

Opening her rucksack, she took out *The Incunabula of Wandering* and began leafing desperately through the pages. Somewhere there had to be a passage she had missed. Some spell to help her cross into the Gloaming. She simply had to look harder.

She turned page after page, seeing passages and poems along with the side notes in her father's hand, all that she had read dozens of times over. She knew the *Incunabula* forward and backward. She had not missed anything. The answer was not there.

With an angry shout, she heaved the book, pages fluttering, so that it landed on the stones near the pool. Grasping her rucksack by the straps, she flung it also, sending the bag tumbling over and over, spilling out some empty wrappers of waxed paper and pairs of dirty socks into the water.

"No!" she shouted. "No, no, no . . ."

Her vision was blurry with tears, but she thought she saw the rabbit's foot glowing as it lay in her lap. Sally wiped the corners of her eyes to rid the tears. As she looked down in her lap, she saw the rabbit's foot, golden yellow and gleaming in the sunlight.

But as she watched, the color began to lighten, the yellow becoming a bright, burning white until she had to squint against the glare. She grabbed the foot and found it surprisingly warm. She blinked hard. What was happening? She had thought it was glowing when she and Qurol were just coming up into the mountains days and days ago. But she had decided then that it was simply a bit of sunlight playing off the surface.

But the foot had also glowed before then. Back when she was leaving the Great Tree. Back when she heard gunfire and saw that strange locomotive coming over the dark plains.

And Ray had told her of other times. The rabbit's foot glowed when the Gog's mechanical Hound was near.

The rabbit's foot grew brighter. The warmth increased until it was nearly too hot to hold.

Sally turned to look back at the trees behind her. Heavy crunching steps were coming from the shadowy forest. Feeling a rush of panic, she looked around. She was wearing only one boot. The *Incunabula* and her belongings were strewn all over the ground.

She leaped up to rescue her father's book. Immediately her ankle gave way and she fell to her hands and knees, banging them hard on the stones. The rabbit's foot flew from her hand, bouncing toward the pool. She crawled forward, ignoring the pain. She was only halfway to the foot when she saw ice growing at the edge of the pool, encasing her floating belongings. A low growl began behind her.

She looked back over her shoulder. The monster stood at the tree line. Its white coat was mostly tufted into spikes of frost-hardened fur, but in places the hide had been torn, and oily machinery writhed beneath. The Hoarhound's gleaming eyes locked on Sally and then on the glowing rabbit's foot several yards away. The Hound growled once more and lowered its head. Tendrils of icy mist seeped from its jagged jaws.

Sally felt unable to move. But when the Hound began racing toward her with its steel claws tearing away hunks of earth, she found herself scrambling and kicking to escape. If she could reach the foot, she might have a chance of holding the Hound at bay. Ahead the cracking ice spread as the rest of the pool froze over into a solid sheet. She lunged for the foot, but even as she grabbed it, she knew she would never be able to use the rabbit's foot to stop the Hound, as Ray had. Fleeing onto the ice in desperation, she felt her hands slide out from under her, and she splayed out onto the slick surface.

Then something heavy landed with a crack on the ice behind her. It was little more than a blur at the corner of her vision, and then jaws locked onto her shoulder. The teeth did not pierce her skin. They held her firmly, without hurting her. She was flung out of the Hoarhound's path and sent sliding across the frozen pool, nearly into the spot where the waterfall's spray was freezing into a mound of splintered frost.

As she came to a stop, she rolled over to see Quorl stepping off the frozen pool and growling at the Hoarhound. The Hound locked his steely gaze on the rougarou. Slowly Quorl took a few steps to the side, drawing the Hound's attention away from Sally.

She knew her friend was far too small to be able to hold off the enormous Hound, and she nearly cried out to tell him to get away. Before she could find her voice, the Hound lunged for Quorl.

With a deft maneuver, Quorl flattened himself and rolled to one side. The Hound missed him, its front paws digging into the frozen pool. But as the Hound landed, the slick surface sent the creature sliding across the pool away from Sally and Quorl.

The Hoarhound slipped and scrambled and tried to rise while Quorl hurried to Sally. His blue eyes were wide and bright. "Get on my back!" he shouted.

Sally had no time to wonder at his transformation. She threw her arms around his neck, and he dashed toward the waterfall.

As he began to ascend a series of boulders to one side of the waterfall's frozen base, Sally cried out, "Where are we going?"

She looked back to see that the Hound was on its feet, digging its steel claws into the ice and racing after them.

"In here," Quorl said, and leaped from a rock into the spray of the waterfall.

For an instant, Sally lost her breath as the hammer of cold water struck her. But then they were through the waterfall and in a cave hidden behind. It was a tall but shallow space, little more than an alcove hollowed out by eons of tumbling water. Sally looked back at the sheet of water and said, "We're trapped! The Hound will be here in a moment."

Quorl faced the smooth rock at the back of the cave. "Yes, but we won't be."

A shadow grew in the bright sheet of water cascading down. Sally watched the waterfall begin to harden, its fall slowing as the water froze. A roar burst into the cave and she knew the Hound had nearly reached them.

"Hold on tightly to my neck," Quorl ordered.

"What—?" Sally began as he leaped at the cave wall. Bright blue light flashed and the rock disappeared, the cave disappeared, the roars of the Hound vanished. Quorl ran a few more paces and then stopped. Although it was nearly complete darkness, Sally could see the vague form of a bridge under Quorl's feet. Or was it a bridge? The ground was rounded, dropping off on either side into a swirling, howling darkness.

"Where are we?" Sally found herself shouting over the winds.

"On the Great Tree," Quorl said. "Little Coyote, I am so sorry. So sorry for all that you have had to endure, but mostly sorry that I abandoned you. I could not . . . help myself. I felt the presence of an opening to the Great Tree. I found the cave and crossed. But listen." He paused. "Can you hear it? The Great Tree is weak here. I must concentrate if I am to get us through."

Quorl walked slowly, with Sally clinging to his back. Under the screaming wind, Sally could hear the faint groans and whines of wood cracking. After a short distance, he said, "Here it is."

Quorl leaped forward, and there was another flash. Once again they were in a cave of rock, but not the one behind the waterfall. The wild wind was gone. Sally saw a dim light ahead and heard a faint, rhythmic *tink-tink-tink*.

"Just a little farther," Quorl said.

He brought her to the edge of a precipice, where they looked down at the floor of a vast cavern. Tangy smoke hung in the air. Drops of water falling from the shadows of the high ceiling caught the light and filled the space with a firefly shimmer. Stalagmites rose from the floor, and a dark lake crept out from the shadows at the far end of the cavern. Sally could not tell the source of the light, as it was coming from behind a large slab of rock, but it flickered like lantern light. There was a breathtaking quality to the place—the way the colors seemed richer, the way the edges of dark and light seemed to shimmer— that made her feel as if she'd entered a dream.

"Quorl," Sally whispered. Even her voice sounded strange and slightly melodic. "Where are we?"

"We're in the Gloaming," he answered.

Sally felt her heart jolt. She slid from Quorl's back. "Is he here?" she asked.

"Wait, Coyote! I need to explain first," Quorl said.

But Sally saw him. A man stepped out from behind the big rock slab. He had stringy gray-yellow hair, and his beard hung to his chest. His tattered clothes were bleached the same color as his hair. He walked over to what seemed to be an oven of red glowing coals set in a nook in the wall. With a pair of tongs, he drew out some glowing hot object from the oven and set it on a boulder to examine.

Sally leaped to a slope of rubble that led to the cavern's floor. "Father!" she shouted.

"Wait!" Quorl called from behind her.

As Sally raced down the slope of broken rocks, she realized her ankle no longer hurt. The hunger that had pained her stomach for the past few days was gone. But she had no time to wonder. She had to reach her father.

He picked up a small hammer and began striking the object on the anvil of rock, sending clanks of metal on metal echoing around the chamber.

"Father!" Sally cried again. Reaching the floor, she wound through the maze of stalagmites until she was only a few steps away from the man.

He looked wild and disheveled, like a castaway on a deserted island. His boots were split open to his bare toes beneath, and the left cuff of his britches had been torn away below the knee. There was an odd color, not only to his clothing but to his skin and hair as well. Unlike the otherworldly colors that shimmered around her in the cavern, her father's color had been bleached away. In his right hand, he held the hammer. The left hand was missing.

"Father," Sally breathed.

He did not respond to her or even take notice. Setting down the hammer, he picked up the tongs and lifted the little piece of metal he had been shaping. He went over to stick the object back into the mound of burning coal. Once the metal grew red, he took it out and returned it to the boulder.

As he brought the hammer up to strike, Sally called out, "Father!"

He hesitated for a moment but did not turn his gaze. He banged with the hammer, casting sparks and turning the hot metal with the tongs.

Quorl reached Sally's side. "Listen, Coyote. Let me explain."

"Isn't this my father, Quorl?" she asked.

"Yes it is, but—"

Sally rounded the makeshift anvil to place herself before Li'l Bill's line of sight. "Father?" She waved her hand at him. "Can't you see me?"

His eyes lifted just a moment to look at Sally and then over at Quorl. But then he resumed his work.

"What's the matter with him?" Sally asked. "Does he not know we're here? Are we separated from him somehow?"

"No," Quorl answered. "We are with him. In the

Gloaming. There is no reason he should not see us. That's what I wanted to tell you. There's something wrong."

"I don't understand," Sally said.

"Nor do I," Quorl answered. "When I came through before, I tried to speak with your father, but he won't acknowledge me. And his color . . . he has grown into a phantom, thin and fading. I do not know why, Coyote."

Sally looked up into her father's face. His mouth was working noiselessly, as if uttering some spell. "Can you hear me, Father? It's Sally. Sally Cobb. I'm your daughter."

Li'l Bill turned to place the tongs in the fire. Bringing them back out, his gaze flickered to her momentarily. "Father?" she said again, hoping to seize the opportunity. She ran to him and caught his arms before he resumed his work, but Li'l Bill gently pushed past her and picked up the hammer.

"Li'l Bill," Quorl said. "I am Quorl. We met once, long ago. I am one of the stewards of the Tree. The rougarou. Do you not remember?"

Li'l Bill brought the hammer down with a clank, and then another, hammering the metal until Sally thought her eardrums would burst. Stinging tears welled in her eyes.

"You came to the Great Tree," Quorl continued.

Li'l Bill's eyes blinked as the hammer reared up. His head cocked.

"You came seeking the counsel of the rougarou. You traveled with a companion, John Henry."

Li'l Bill lowered the hammer slowly, setting it beside the tongs. "John?"

"Yes, John," Quorl said.

"John," he repeated, his eyes half closing. "Where's John?"

"He's dead, Father," Sally said. "You were there. Remember?"

Li'l Bill turned at last to look at Sally. She was surprised to see that even the darkest portions of his pupils were grayed and ghostly. *"Father?"* he whispered. "Why are you calling me that?"

"Because I am your daughter. I'm Sally."

The chin beneath Li'l Bill's tangled beard trembled. "I don't recollect you, child. Why don't I know you?"

"You've never met me," Sally said. "You left before Mother knew she was having me."

"What is this trickery?" he murmured, as if to himself. He slowly reached out a hand and touched Sally's shoulder. "You're real."

"Of course I am," Sally said.

"You are my daughter?"

"Yes," Sally whispered.

Li'l Bill looked warily at Quorl and then back at Sally. "You . . . you aren't who I called for?" He picked his hammer back up and raised it above his head, but after a moment he lowered it slowly. He turned back to Sally, his faded spectral face glowering. "Why are you here? Why have you come?"

Sally felt dizzy with confusion. She looked down at her father's missing hand, the scarred stub of his wrist protruding from his tattered sleeve. "I came here to help you."

His expression softened, and he said sadly, "But you cannot help me." Then he turned and walked away to other side of his forge, where he began to rummage through a pile of stones and debris.

"What's wrong with him, Quorl?" Sally whispered. "Has he gone mad?"

"It's possible. He's been here alone for a long time."

Sally looked around at her father's corner of the cavern. There were no furnishings other than the lantern and the two tools he had been using to fashion the little piece of metal. "How has he survived? There's nothing to eat."

"This is the Gloaming," Quorl said. "The sustenance of our world is not needed here."

"How can that be?" Sally asked.

"This world is not the world of the material. It is a spirit world."

"Is he dead?" Sally cast a sharp glance at her father, who was squatting before the pile, inspecting a small object before tossing it aside irritably. "Is he a ghost?"

"No," Quorl replied. "He is not a ghost. He is flesh, but wholly different here." Then he called out, "How did you come to this place, Li'l Bill?"

Li'l Bill dropped the object back to the pile and stood. He looked back over his shoulder at them, his brow knit.

"Do you not remember?" Quorl said.

Li'l Bill paced a few steps, a finger pressed against his temple. "Yes, I know . . . so many tangled memories. I know. Somewhere in here."

After watching him ponder laboriously another moment, Sally said, "You fought a Hoarhound, Father. It took your hand."

Li'l Bill nodded. "Yes, one of his clockwork hunters. It had me . . . trapped for so long. And then I was freed."

"What happened then?" Quorl asked.

"Lost," Li'l Bill replied. "I was lost, I reckon. I wandered." He shook his head as if struggling to clear his thoughts. "I came to a place of darkness. There were roots. Yes, I reached its roots."

"The roots of the Great Tree?" Quorl said.

"Yes." Li'l Bill's eyes widened. "Such darkness. Such menace. The howl of his engines." He covered his ears as if being once again tormented by the noise. "I ran! I had to get away. I knew there was naught but death there and I couldn't save the Tree. Not then, anyway. Not yet. I wandered until I escaped the Darkness, until I found this place, a fierce distance from the Gog's clockwork. I've called to them. They will save it."

"Who will save the Tree?" Quorl asked.

Li'l Bill blinked hard and cast his hand back at the lake. "Them! The sirens. They're coming, don't you see?"

Quorl looked at the lake and narrowed his eyes.

Li'l Bill continued, "Yes. There is so much to be done. Look!" He hurried over to the pile and picked up a blackened object. "See! See, I've got a job of work to do yet. Oh, I do. Been making these." He placed it in Sally's hand and went back to the pile. The object was not a stone as she had thought, but a piece of iron that had been shaped by his hammer. It was heavier than Sally had imagined and looked like a pinecone before its bristles had opened.

Quorl looked skeptically at it and seemed about to say something to her when Li'l Bill came back with a handful of similarly fashioned objects. "I made them also." He dropped them with a clatter to the floor and went to collect others until dozens and dozens littered the area around Sally's feet. She looked closer now at the pile. There were hundreds, if not thousands, of the metal cones.

"What are they, Father?" she asked.

Li'l Bill came back with another scoop in his forearm. "To stop the Machine. Been practicing. Don't you see?" Irritation rose in his voice. He dropped the cones and rammed his fingers up into his knotted hair. "But they ain't right. I need it! I thought he would bring it to me."

"Who?" Sally asked, exasperated. "The sirens?"

He looked at her squarely, his manic energy suddenly gone. "Your brother, Sally."

"Ray?"

He smiled. "Why, of course. Where is he?"

Sally felt a wave of sickening fear come over her at the thought of her brother. He had been trying to find her, to help her, when the Gog's agents had captured him. And poor Jolie . . . she could not think about what had happened to her.

"He can't come, Father," she managed to say.

"But he . . . he has it." He began to pace back toward his forge. "I can't make it until he brings the rabbit's foot to me. He will bring it to me."

As Li'l Bill went back to sifting through his pile of iron cones, Quorl came closer to Sally. "Coyote? Why do you not tell your father that you have the *Toninyan*? You have what he wants."

"He's gone mad," Sally said, looking down at her feet.

"Not so mad as I first thought," Quorl replied.

She shifted anxiously. "It's too late," she said. "I can't save him."

"You won't know until you try," Quorl said, his voice growing deeper and more urgent. "I know it has been a shock to see him this way, but you must—"

She spun around. "Don't you think I want him the way he was? I want my father. I want him to be a Rambler again with all my heart. But I . . . I can't give him back his powers!"

Quorl's ears flattened and he turned his head questioningly. "Why not? There is nothing to lose by trying."

"Yes, there is." Tears welled up, and Sally tried to swallow the awful knot in her throat. "There is, Quorl. I can't give him back his power. If I do, the Machine will never be destroyed."

"I don't understand," Quorl said. "Your father was a powerful Rambler. To return his hand will return his powers, as it did with the Rambler Nel."

"But Mother Salagi told me that a weapon must be made, a 'light to pierce the Dark.' Only this weapon can destroy the Machine."

"What does this have to do with your father?" Quorl asked.

Sally took out the rabbit's foot. "This is the 'light to pierce the Dark.' This must be used to make the weapon."

Quorl stood frozen. He locked his blue eyes on her. "Then you are faced with a grave choice, Coyote," he said at last. His voice held no anger, no chastisement, no resentment, only a gentle grimness. "You might help your father, but what will be the cost in doing so?"

"It's not a choice, Quorl. We both know I can't give my father back his hand." She put her face in her hands, tears spilling into her palms. When she looked up, Li'l Bill had stopped his task. He squatted on his haunches and looked curiously over at her. As he rose slowly and approached Sally, Quorl turned and left them.

Li'l Bill sat on the floor next to her and gathered her against his side with an awkward arm. "Why are you crying, child?" he asked.

The simplicity of his question and the genuine concern in his voice overwhelmed Sally, and she buried her face against his shoulder and wept.

"I came here to save you," she said. "I wanted to give you back your powers. I wanted you to be a Rambler again, to be my father, to come away with me and be with me and Ray back at Shuckstack, but . . . but I can't save you."

He smoothed the curls of her hair with his hand. "It would not matter," he said. "I've been in the Gloaming too long. I cannot return to what I once was."

She looked up at him, blinking away the tears, surprised by how calm and lucid he seemed. "But you said you needed Ray to bring you the rabbit's foot."

"Not so that I could become a Rambler again."

"Then why?" Sally asked.

He sighed and stared up at the cavern's ceiling, his ghostly eyes distant for a moment. "John and I failed last time. We thought if I helped him cross into the Gloaming and he destroyed the Gog's engine with his hammer that the enemy would be defeated. We were wrong. The Gog's master, the Magog, inhabits the Machine. To destroy it, we needed a weapon of light to drive into the Machine's heart. A weapon John and I did not possess at the time. That is why I hoped Ray would come. I need him to help forge this weapon. He has it."

Sally looked over at the pile of cones her father had been making. He said he had been "practicing," and she thought it had been madness that had driven him to forge the innumerable iron cones. But now she understood.

"No, he doesn't," Sally said, and her father lifted an eyebrow.

He had been practicing making the spike, the weapon Mother Salagi had said was needed to destroy the Machine.

"Father," Sally said. "I have it." She placed the rabbit's foot in his hand.

"HOW FAR AHEAD IS IT?" JOLIE ASKED AS THEY CRESTED THE next ridge. Nothing but rocky sawtooth mountains surrounded them.

Ray held out his hand to feel for the Hoarhound. "I can't tell."

They raced on, ridge after ridge, higher and deeper into the mountain wilderness. They had rested only when Jolie needed to lie beneath the icy waters of a stream. Their food was nearly out. Ray wanted to try again to take crow form, to test the power once more, but he knew how much it weakened him. He needed all his strength for whatever was to come.

At last they entered a dark spruce forest. Ray stopped as he saw black forms swooping from the branches ahead. Jolie put a hand to her side as she tried to catch her breath. "What are they?" she asked.

"Ravens, I think." Ray called out to them in the speech of crows. A large, grizzled bird flew toward them, landing several yards away before hopping closer to Ray. The raven gave a few low croaks and cackles.

"What does it say?" Jolie asked.

Ray looked up with surprise. "They've seen them. A wolf, a girl, and a monstrous white devil. They passed through, but he's not sure where they went. They heard sounds of fighting, but then they disappeared. I can feel the Hound this way."

They raced through the forest until they reached a waterfall cascading down from an enormous bluff. As Ray came out from the shadows of the trees, he froze. A boot lay on the ground. And at the edge of the pool, he saw a rucksack, its contents drifting in the water. The water nearest to the waterfall was topped with ice, but as the pool became a swift-flowing stream, the ice broke apart and was carried away in chunks.

"What's happened to her?" Ray gasped. "Is she in the water? She . . . she hasn't drowned, has she?"

Jolie dove through the slushy ice and after a moment emerged in the middle of the pool. "I do not see anything. But I hear the echoes of voices."

"Like what you heard before in the river?" Ray asked.

"The voice is clearer, stronger here," Jolie said, coming out and wringing the water from her hair. "There are several voices now. But I cannot tell if it is—"

A loud thud sounded, stopping Jolie's words. She and Ray looked about. Another thud came, along with a crack.

Ray's eyes stopped at the base of the waterfall. The torrent of water seemed to be breaking over a large boulder at the bottom of the bluff. "It comes from that rock."

"That is not rock," Jolie said. "That is solid ice."

"Why would the waterfall freeze at the bottom like that?" But Ray's eyes widened as he realized. Another powerful blow cracked the ice at the foot of the waterfall. "The Hound is trapped."

"Not for long," Jolie said.

"Do you think it has Sally in there?" Ray gasped, feeling the toby trembling against his chest.

Jolie drew her knife, but before she could say anything, a final blow threw enormous frozen blocks out into the pool. The Hound burst from the waterfall and landed on the opposite side of the pool from them. Water and mist froze to its hide, plating the creature in a thick armor of frost. The ice on the surface of the pool crackled as it grew solid.

Jolie grabbed Ray's arm. "Quick! We must run."

"What about Sally?" he shouted.

"Being torn apart by that Hound will not help her!"

The Hound brought its mechanical eyes around until they locked on Ray. It stepped onto the frozen pool and began across.

Jolie pulled Ray so hard he staggered. "Go! Go!" she shouted.

They ran toward the trees, back into the shadows, leaping over fallen branches and racing through the undergrowth. Ray scanned the forest. Was there a place to hide? Was there a way to escape? They might be able to climb a tree, but the Hound would have no trouble knocking it down, and they had no more of the sagebrush.

The Hound roared. Its heavy steps thundered in pursuit. Cold saturated the forest. Saplings wilted around them. Leaves curled black. Ray and Jolie wound through the trees, not knowing where to go, only running.

Ray could hear the Hound breaking through trees and nearly upon them. He risked a glance over at Jolie.

"I can distract it," Ray panted. "You can get away."

"You know I will not let you do that," she said.

The whine of churning gears and the clank of steel teeth were a few yards behind them now. A bitter cold surrounded them.

"All right, then," Ray said. "You ready?"

Jolie flipped the knife around in her grasp, the blade down. She gritted her teeth and said, "Now."

Ray turned in one direction while Jolie split the other way. He swiveled behind the trunk of a tree and looked back. The Hound rushed toward him, jaws snapping. Ray rolled, barely managing to escape as the monster plowed into the tree, cracking the trunk and ripping up the roots on one side.

Ray scrambled to his feet as the Hound came around the tree. But before it leaped, Jolie landed atop the Hoarhound's shoulders. She punched her knife into its throat and ripped back the frosty hide, exposing churning black machinery. The Hound snapped its snout back but was unable to reach her.

As Ray searched for a way to help Jolie, he felt the toby blazing against his chest.

The Hoarhound bucked, trying to throw Jolie from its back. She stabbed at its head with the knife. Metallic clanks sounded with each blow, but she was unable to penetrate the monster's skull. The Hound flung its jaws side to side. Jolie plunged the knife, this time at the Hoarhound's steel eye. The blade sank, and the Hound unleashed a roar.

She brought the knife up to strike once more but paused. The blade was broken at the hilt.

The Hound rocked forward furiously, and Jolie lost her grip. She flew, tumbling end over end into the frost-brittle leaves.

"Jolie!" Ray shouted.

The Hoarhound swung its snout around to him. Steel gleamed from the Hound's exposed skull. The one eye was ruined, dangling from the socket by a jumble of cables.

Ray raised his hands protectively. The strange tingling he felt around the Hound was there. But it was stronger. There was something more, like an invisible resistance pushing back against his outturned palms.

The beast growled and then turned back to Jolie, where she lay dazed on the ground.

"No!" Ray cried. But the Hound was already lunging.

A welling of heat rose from the toby, flooding through his body and down his arm. A magnetic pressure grew in his hand and erupted from his outturned palm. The Hoarhound suddenly flipped to one side, missing Jolie and crashing to the forest floor on its back. He wasn't sure what was happening, but Ray held his hand out. The Hound flipped back to its paws and looked from Ray over to Jolie.

She scrambled to stand and ran toward Ray. The Hoarhound's claws dislodged clumps of dirt as it charged after her. Ray squeezed the toby with one hand. He extended his other hand toward the stampeding beast. Once again the repellent force burst from his palm. The Hound's front legs collapsed, and its clattering snout hit the ground hard.

"What did you just do?" Jolie gasped as she got behind Ray.

Ray didn't answer. He stared at the Hound. He focused on the heat welling from the toby. He focused on drawing out the repellent power, holding off the Hound for as long as he could.

The Hoarhound slowly rose to its feet.

A strange quiet seemed to have come over the forest. Ray could hear Jolie breathing behind him. He could hear the gears clicking within the Hound's neck as it lowered its head menacingly. Frost seeped from its jaws, causing the forest floor around it to crackle with rising splinters of ice.

The Hound crouched, ready to leap. The toby pulsated against Ray's skin over his heart.

"Get back," Ray said to Jolie through gritted teeth. He planted his feet wide and leaned forward with his arm outstretched.

The Hound sprang. Its jaws opened wide as it came down on Ray.

Jolie screamed.

Before the Hound reached him, it bashed into an invisible barrier and fell. Ray pushed the repellent force against the Hoarhound. The creature roared and snapped its icicle teeth, their tips catching on the invisible barrier. As Ray stepped closer, the Hound's mouth was wedged open. He could see twirling machinery in the depths of its throat.

The Hoarhound brought its head to one side, battering the invisible barrier. Ray braced his heels as he felt the blows strike again and again. The Hound turned to reposition its attack, and Ray reached out, locking its metal skull in the magnetic spell.

The Hound writhed, struggling to escape. Ray dug his heels into the dirt and held tight. How long could he hold off the beast? Maybe long enough for Jolie to get to safety. But he knew she would never do it.

Her hands gripped his shoulder. "Stay focused. Do not lose your concentration."

Ray pushed forward with the spell.

"You can destroy it," she said. "You can do that, Ray."

Ray held out his other hand, feeling the power grow. His muscles trembled against the might of the Hound struggling to escape.

"Destroy it!" Jolie urged.

Ray pushed harder, putting all of his strength into the enormous effort of crushing the Hound.

The ground shook and the dirt shifted around the Hoarhound's paws. A crack opened in the earth. Stones and loose soil slid into the fissure, and the Hoarhound began to fall in with them. A pair of spruces beyond the Hound tipped together, their roots breaking from the earth.

The Hoarhound thrashed and kicked to escape the sinkhole. Ray stepped forward, pressing with all his might. The Hound sank to its waist. The repellent pressure forced the Hound's head to one side. Ray took another step and crushed the Hound into the hole.

He felt the pull of the open void. Earth and stones and debris were sucked down. In a moment, he would be pulled in with the Hound.

Jolie clutched his waist. He kept his attention on the Hoarhound, only vaguely aware of her shouting as he dragged her with him. The earth collapsed beneath the Hound until only its head was still exposed, the jaws clapping desperately.

And then the dirt closed over it and the Hoarhound disappeared. Only a patch of upturned earth remained where the Hound had been consumed.

Ray dropped his hands and fell backward.

Jolie was still holding him around the waist, panting and trembling. Ray rolled over. He rose up weakly on his elbows and clutched the toby. It was still now. He listened to the sounds of the forest returning—wind in the treetops, birds calling.

Ray looked over at Jolie. She lay, winded, on her back. "What about Sally?" she murmured.

"The waterfall," Ray said. "She might be back behind it."

Stumbling with exhaustion, they made their way to the pool. Ray picked up the *Incunabula* and placed it along with the rest of Sally's belongings in her rucksack.

Jolie pointed. "Up those boulders. There seems to be a way behind the waterfall."

Ray followed her up the ice-slick rock. Although the spray dampened his clothes, he managed to avoid the powerful stream of falling water by staying close to the bluff and ducking beneath an overhang of ice still left by the Hoarhound's prison. Once he and Jolie were behind the fall, he looked around at the shallow cave.

"Where are they?" he asked.

"I thought they might have been trapped by the Hound's

ice," Jolie said. She knelt and touched her fingers to the ground. "It is all rock. There are no prints. No sign of whether they came this way."

Ray slipped Sally's bag from his shoulder. "But she left her belongings. At least part of them. And the *Incunabula* among them. She wouldn't have done that unless she was attacked suddenly. Maybe she and Quorl ran away somewhere."

"Then why would the Hound have come up here? It trapped itself accidentally behind the fall. It would not have come into this cave unless there was a reason."

"So why aren't they still in the cave?" Ray asked.

They looked at each other, and Jolie nodded. "The Gloaming."

"Yes," Ray said. "They crossed through this cave."

"How can we follow them?" Jolie asked.

"We can't! I don't know how."

"But you can, Ray." Jolie stepped closer to him, looking him fiercely in the eye. "You are a Rambler. You can cross."

"I can barely take crow form—"

"You have to believe you can." She pointed back toward the waterfall and the spruce forest on the other side of it. "Look at what you did to the Gog's Hound. How do you think you did that?"

"The toby," Ray said uncertainly. "Or maybe something from this wilderness."

"No," Jolie said sharply. "Do you not see? You did that. You! And you can cross. How did your father reach the Gloaming?"

"By taking animal form," Ray said.

"And Little Bill brought John Henry into the Gloaming to destroy the first Machine. You can carry me across too. Through this cave. I know you can."

Ray took the toby from around his neck and knelt to open it up. He took out B'hoy's feathers. Nine black feathers. A momentary ache filled his chest as he longed for his friend the crow. He couldn't bring himself to say so, but he did not think Jolie was right. It was the toby that gave him his powers. So maybe his old friend's feathers could guide him across.

He put the toby back over his neck and nodded to Jolie. "Okay."

Ray took a deep breath and gazed down at B'hoy's feathers. Then he closed his eyes and let the darkness surround him. He concentrated on the mountain above them, the roar of the waterfall behind them, the wilderness surrounding them.

He took a step forward and then another and let his body grow light. He flapped his arms and felt feathers catch the air and lift him. He opened his eyes and saw the waterfall before him. He rose up on beating wings and turned before he reached the wall of water. Soaring around in an arc, he saw Jolie watching him with awe. She laughed and turned to face the back of the cave. "I am ready," she called.

He whooshed down and caught her shoulder with his talons. Jolie disappeared.

He flew forward, feeling her within his grasp but with no weight to hold him down.

Light flashed as he soared into the rock. The cave was gone. The noise of the falls had disappeared. He saw faint branches and leaves and a vast distance below. A deafening groaning surrounded him, the sound of an enormous tree swaying. Ray flapped hard against the wild winds, struggling to follow the branch until lights flashed once more.

He flew out into a cavern. A great wolf—the rougarou Quorl, Ray realized, although he had not seen him before—looked up with alarm and leaped to his feet. Ray drifted over him and saw Sally run to Quorl. Away from the two, over by a dark lake, stood a man with a tangled beard, dressed in little more than rags. He watched Ray's flight with a bright smile. He looked older and stranger than the man from his childhood, but Ray knew this man. It was his father.

Ray descended between his father and Sally and Quorl. He opened his talons, and Jolie reappeared. As his feet met stone, he collapsed. Jolie tumbled and knelt, half dazed, at his side. Ray looked at his hands—for a fraction of a moment they were wings. Then they were fingers, the black receding into pink.

Sally ran to his side and took him around the neck. "Ray!" she cried. "I thought I would never see you!"

Dizzy with emotion and the effort of crossing, Ray squeezed Sally. "You found him, Sally. You did it. You found Father."

A FEVERISH SHAKING RACKED RAY. SALLY PUT HER HAND TO her brother's damp brow. "What's wrong, Ray? Are you sick?"

"No," he said. "It will pass. It's from crossing . . . from taking crow form. It happened before, but it was worse the last time. Is there something to drink?"

Sally said, "We've nothing to drink."

"Here, Ray," Jolie said. She tipped the waterskin to Ray's mouth.

Sally watched Jolie anxiously, her lips trembling to find words. After Jolie took the waterskin back, she glanced up at Sally.

Sally stammered, "Jolie . . . we . . . Quorl didn't mean to bring the avalanche down on you. It . . . it was all just a terrible accident!"

Jolie nodded to the rougarou. "I know. There are no ill feelings between us. All is forgiven. Think no more on it."

Ray felt his strength returning. He shifted, turning to look for Li'l Bill. "Father?" he called.

Li'l Bill was coming from the lake and stopped when he was still several yards away. "Ray? You are . . . so grown. I only remember the little boy. The one who took the lodestone, and now . . ." He looked from Ray over to Jolie and back. "And you, Jolie . . ." He gave a frail smile, a knot drawn between his brows.

Ray did not know what to do, but Jolie rushed up to him and hugged Li'l Bill. He awkwardly patted her back with his one hand, but a rush of emotion showed on his face. "Children, my mind has been clouded with darkness for so long. But now, with you all here, with the *Toninyan* returned, I feel it clearing."

"The *Toninyan*?" Ray asked, confused.

Li'l Bill nodded toward the lake. "The lodestone I gave you. The one that is now in my rabbit's paw. I can see that we have much to share. We ought to sit together and talk. Come."

As they gathered in the lantern light, Ray told about Omphalosa and the pursuit of the steamcoach, his discovery of the agents' aim and meeting up with Jolie. "I didn't know," Sally said. "If they had caught us . . ."

"They did not, thanks to your brother," Jolie said.

Sally looked stricken with guilt until Ray said, "It's okay, Sal. Tell us what happened to you." Sally recounted her journey before ever leaving Shuckstack, and Ray and Jolie were shocked to hear that she had returned Nel's leg and his Rambler powers. "Then you can save Father! You can take the rabbit's foot—"

"Hush now," Li'l Bill said kindly. "Let your sister finish. She's the one that ought to explain why she can't."

Ray's heart sank at those words, but he listened patiently. As Sally continued, he looked at his father, noticing how odd he looked, how ghostly he had become. At first he thought it was simply the Gloaming, since everything here had taken on a strange quality. But he realized, while Sally and Quorl and Jolie and even the rock of the cavern looked more richly colored, his father seemed as bleached as something from the wastelands he and Jolie had crossed.

Ray's attention was jerked back to Sally as she told about Mother Salagi's counsel and their discovery. "So this spike must be driven into the Machine?" Ray asked.

"Into its heart," Sally said. "That's what Mother Salagi and the seers said. Father's paw is the 'light to pierce the Dark,' and it has to be driven into the Machine's heart with the Nine Pound Hammer."

"Where is John's hammer now?" Li'l Bill asked.

"The handle was broken," Jolie said. "But Conker fixed it, with a branch from the Wolf Tree."

"Conker." Li'l Bill gave a sad smile. "John's son. I can hardly believe it. I remember when he was born. And now you dear ones have inherited our fight. It pains me that you all have to do so. If only John and I had known what was needed. If only we had destroyed the Magog the first time."

"All things happen for a reason," Quorl said. "You did not have the means to make the spike then. It is your powers placed into the golden foot that have made the weapon to destroy the Machine. It is through your sacrifice that this is possible, Bill."

He nodded grimly. "Yes. We are the wiser. But wisdom ain't going to assure success. The dangers have multiplied since John's death. And now Grevol is placing his new Machine at the very roots of the Great Tree. He's killing it. And with it the Gloaming."

Ray asked, "But if we destroy the Machine, the Tree will be healed, won't it?"

Sally looked anxiously from her father to Quorl.

Li'l Bill's gaze lingered on his hand and the scarred wrist where his other hand was missing. "No," he replied. "Terrible choices lie ahead, children. Impossible obstacles. Darkness. Darkness is covering everything. The enemies must be stopped. The only one to stop the Magog and its servant is the one who has mastery over his own Darkness. You see? It must be the one who can stand against his own black clockworks."

Ray suddenly remembered that Redfeather's teacher, Water Spider, had said something similar to Ray before they had set off to Omphalosa. But before he could remember exactly what, Li'l Bill continued, "Unfortunately even if these enemies are destroyed, the Great Tree will still die. It has been corrupted at its roots. I saw it, and I only barely escaped. The Great Tree will fall, and humanity will fall with it, as some other evil will rise to take possession over us all."

"But the Tree can be saved," Quorl said, rising up on his front paws. "You said before that you knew how to heal the Tree. You said the sirens could—"

"Sirens?" Jolie said.

Li'l Bill's face was pinched with pain, and he didn't look up.

"It is your voice I have been hearing, Little Bill?" Jolie said.

He nodded. "The waters have a powerful connection between our world and the world of the Gloaming. I used the lake over yonder to summon the sirens." He looked up at last at Jolie. Ray thought he saw fear welling in his father's gray eyes. "I never imagined it would be you, Jolie."

"My sisters heard your call too," Jolie said. "They followed it and journeyed up the rivers until they met a Darkness. They could pass no farther and returned. Now they are ill. The Darkness has sickened them, as it did the people of Omphalosa."

"No," Li'l Bill said. "I didn't mean . . . not for them . . ."

Jolie put a hand to his arm. "Fear not. My sister Cleoma brought waters from a siren well, with the hope that it would cure them."

"And cure them it must," Li'l Bill said. "For if they fall to the Darkness, they'll become servants to the Gog. They would be drawn to him, needing the Darkness for their survival. Your sisters would be under his charge. And with them, his means of controlling mankind will be unstoppable."

"What must be done?" Quorl asked. "How can the sirens heal the Great Tree?"

Li'l Bill looked at Jolie. "Only one of your sisters can save those that suffer at the Gog's dark mechanization. Just as the waters Cleoma is bringing to the Terrebonne can save your sisters from the Darkness, it is the waters of a siren well that are needed to heal the Great Tree."

"I know where Élodie's Spring lies!" Jolie said urgently. "It is a great distance, but we could go there to take waters—"

Li'l Bill shook his head slowly. "A spring must be formed that touches the Great Tree where it is being corrupted. The spring can be in our world as a siren well that draws its powers from the Gloaming. The waters will cross. But it must be made where the Gog has carried his Machine across to the Gloaming. Only such a spring will have the power to save us." Li'l Bill grew silent, his ghostly eyes lingering sadly on Jolie.

To anyone else her expression might have seemed impassive, but Ray could tell Jolie was deeply stricken by his father's words, and he wasn't sure why.

"What is it?" he asked. "I don't understand. What are you saying, Father?"

Li'l Bill turned to Ray. "There is only one way to bring forth this siren spring."

Jolie said, "My mother, Élodie, died out of her love for my father. Her place of death became the healing well that brought Conker back. To make a spring, a siren must give up her life for those she loves."

"But it does not have to be you!" Ray said. "Another siren. Another might choose to sacrifice her life to save the Great Tree, to save us all. It doesn't have to be you, Jolie!"

Jolie nodded, but whether she agreed with Ray or was quietly dismissing this possibility, he could not tell.

"The means of drawing forth this spring does not have to be decided now," Quorl said. "For it would be without purpose if the Machine is not also destroyed."

"Quorl is right," Li'l Bill said. "You all have a role, and it will take more than courage and a good heart to face all that is to come. There is little left that I can do to help you. But there has been one thing, thanks to Sally. Come and see."

They rose and followed Li'l Bill over to the lake, where a pair of tongs lay at the water's edge. The lake's surface was so smooth and black, it could have been polished stone. And it looked to Ray almost like a magic trick as his father dipped his hand in.

Li'l Bill reached around for something, saying, "Yes, it has cooled."

"What is it?" Ray asked.

As Li'l Bill brought it out, Ray and the others had to avert their eyes momentarily from the bright golden beam. "The light that pierces the Dark," Li'l Bill said.

Ray's eyes adjusted to the brilliance and he saw it was a shaft of gold, long and thin and drawing to a sharp point like a spearhead. He could feel the presence, the familiar power in the object. "This was the rabbit's foot, wasn't it?" he said.

"And now it is the spike that can destroy the Machine," Li'l Bill said. "It's a terrible burden to have to give you, son. You have learned to take animal form. You can cross. So it is up to you to bring Conker into the Gloaming. You will have to hold the spike when Conker drives it into the Machine."

"I'm not afraid, Father," Ray said, although this was not entirely true. There were too many things to worry him to even hope that he could actually help destroy the Machine. "But Conker and the others are in Chicago. That's halfway across the country. We don't have horses anymore. How will we ever get to them?"

"We will have to cross onto the Great Tree," Li'l Bill said.

"The branches that make the path back to the trunk are too brittle," Quorl said. "It is impossible."

"No. Not impossible," Li'l Bill said. "I found a path that

led me here. We cannot reach Chicago on the Tree. Those branches would break. But we are in a region of the Gloaming far from the dying portions. I think I could get us as far as the trunk, with your help, Quorl."

"And from the trunk we could climb down to where your pack guards the Wolf Tree's base," Jolie said.

"That's still far to Chicago," Ray said.

"I think it's the best I can do," Li'l Bill said. He looked at Quorl. "Can we do it?"

The rougarou lowered his scarred snout and gave a low growl. "We will have to be careful. It will be a dangerous journey."

Li'l Bill led them back up to the tunnel, and after walking for some time in the dark, he said, "We should cross."

Quorl said, "Hold on to my back."

"Ray," his father said. "You should practice carrying someone across. Can you do it again? Are you too weak still?"

"No, I can try," Ray answered. He took out B'hoy's feathers from the toby and found he could much more easily reach the state of mind to take crow form. As Quorl walked forward with Sally and Li'l Bill holding the fur at his shoulder, he disappeared in a bright burst. Ray circled and grasped Jolie's shoulder with his talons.

They were on the enormous limb once more. Ray released Jolie and returned to his form, weak and a little dizzy but able to walk with Sally holding his hand. The limb was as wide as the roof of a house. Despite its size, the bough swayed, and at times they slowed as they heard deep, disquieting cracking through the howling wind.

Quorl and Li'l Bill stopped on occasion to anxiously discuss the route at precarious points, but each time, the limbs held true. Walking behind Jolie in the dark, Ray felt Sally squeeze his hand.

"Are you feeling okay?" she whispered.

He still felt weakened and a little nauseous, but he said, "I'm all right."

"Are you angry with me?" Sally asked in a barely audible voice.

"Why would I be?" he answered.

"You told me to keep the rabbit's foot safe at Shuckstack."

"If you had done what I asked," he said, "I'm not sure we ever would have found Father, and we wouldn't have the spike. You found him, Sally. You've done a great thing."

She put her hands around his waist and hugged him tightly as they walked.

"Is there something else troubling you?" he whispered.

"It's just I'm so worried about Hethy," she said.

"I'm sure she's fine, Sally. Conker had healing water. He must have helped her."

Sally sniffled, "I shouldn't have left her behind. I should have trusted her. I wish I had brought her with me. I could have used her help when Quorl started changing. And, Ray. I, well . . . it's just . . . I've done things I wish I hadn't."

"Like what?" Ray asked.

"I forced this poor old tinker to bring me all the way from Iowa to Nebraska."

Ray chuckled. "How'd you manage that?"

"With one of those foot powder charms you told me about."

"Not bad," Ray said, still chuckling.

After a moment, Sally said, "I think I might have done something bad to Mister Nel."

Ray felt a chill rise up his neck. "What do you mean?"

"Do you remember that charm I was reading about in the *Incunabula*?"

"You mean when I left?"

"The Elemental Rose," Sally whispered. "It was a poem, and I thought I had figured it all out so I could give Mister Nel back his leg. It worked, and he has his powers back. And I was so glad, because I knew that meant I could save Father too. But there was a line in the poem I ignored. I didn't understand."

Ray frowned, waiting for Sally to finish.

"Mother Salagi said Nel's leg would bring some danger to him. I didn't understand at the time, but I've been thinking about it. And I think I know. Oh, I wish I had thought about it more before I did it, Ray. It was a warning, and I didn't listen!"

Ray smoothed Sally's curls. "It's okay," he whispered. "It'll all be okay."

But Ray felt Sally was right to be afraid for Nel. He remembered back to the night he found Jolie and Hethy during the battle at the Wolf Tree. That agent, just before he died, had laughed, saying the Gog knew about Shuckstack. How Shuckstack had been discovered, Ray couldn't imagine. He had half hoped the agent had been bluffing. But now he felt a cold fear, that this must be the danger Mother Salagi had seen.

The Gog was coming for Nel. And if Nel was in danger, then so were the children of Shuckstack.

Hours seemed to pass, but to Ray it just as easily could have been days for all the endless walking in the howling dark. Soon the faint light of dawn began to illuminate their surroundings. Li'l Bill stopped. "We have reached the trunk of the Great Tree."

Quorl was sniffing. "Yes, we can descend from here to my pack. I will lead us down."

Ray looked over the edge of the branch. Below, wispy clouds drifted around the trunk, and far beyond, the prairie spread out in every direction.

With the golden light of dawn spilling over the land, Quorl led them in a circling path down the trunk. Descending, descending, down the strange stairway fashioned from the bark of the Wolf Tree. When they seemed a mile from the ground, Ray spied wolves—the rougarou—trotting around the roots and a girl he knew must be Hethy.

Jolie turned to Ray. "We still have a long way to go to Chicago, and even when we arrive, how will we ever find Conker?"

Ray considered this as they continued. Soon he stopped and took out the toby.

Jolie watched him as Quorl lead the others across a narrow chasm of bark. Ray took the dandelion in his fingers. He clapped his hands three times, blew three breaths on the yellow flower, and called out, "Peter Hobnob—Peter Hobnob—Peter Hobnob."

Jolie gave a curious smile as the yellow eroded from the petals into gray wisps. The little seedpods drifted out into the prairie's wind and disappeared to the east.

Ray and Jolie descended until they were nearly to the base of the Wolf Tree. Quorl was already at the bottom, speaking urgently to a large black rougarou. But Li'l Bill and Sally waited for Ray and Jolie at the last step. Ray noticed how ghostly his father looked in the sunlight. His hair and beard, his face and clothes were all nearly colorless.

With Sally tucked against his side, Li'l Bill looked sadly at Ray and Jolie. "I wish this danger was not asked of you children. I wish that I alone could do what is needed to stop the Gog. But my powers are gone, and I can't leave the Great Tree. I am changed. I'm no longer a part of your world. Here I must remain."

"I'll stay with you, Father," Sally said.

Li'l Bill smiled down at her. "Thank you, child. But go on down with the rougarou. Let them tend to you. I can't. I'll be here, though, if you want to visit on occasion." His smile turned grim as he looked at Ray and Jolie. "Good luck to you two in all that lies ahead."

"Thank you," Ray said. "Goodbye, Father. For now. We'll come back for you."

Ray followed Sally and Jolie down to the roots of the Wolf Tree. Sally ran to Hethy, but before Ray and Jolie joined her, Jolie caught Ray's arm. "You do realize we will not see him again. Or Sally either."

Ray looked back up the Wolf Tree, where the faint form of his father watched high above. He wanted to contradict her, to tell her she was letting go of hope, but as Jolie slid her hand into his, he realized what needed to happen. A siren spring had to be formed to save the Wolf Tree. He had to lead Conker into the Gloaming and hold the golden spike over the Machine's heart.

Ray watched his father disappear around the trunk. He took Jolie's hand and walked down the final steps.

Hope was not in surviving.

Hope lay in making things right.

THE NOISE IN THE GALLEY OF THE *SNAPDRAGON* WAS unbelievable. Sitting between Si and Big Jimmie, Conker leaned back against the wall, his stomach distended to an uncomfortable size from the cook Etienne Beauvais's feast. He poked an elbow into Big Jimmie's ribs. "You taken on some new crew?"

The pirate pushed his emptied bowl to the center of the table and gave a gumbo belch. Half-finished platters of lake mussels and pungent cheeses lay precariously close to the edge as dancers and musicians bumped and knocked into one another. While Marisol watched the pirates with astonishment, Redfeather was entertaining a few of them by lighting their pipes and cigars with the flame dancing from the palm of his hand.

Jimmie looked around at his shipmates. "Who? I don't think we've picked up anybody since you were last on board."

Rubbing her thumb over her darkened hand, massaging the missing knuckle and finger, Si gave a nod. "That tall girl with the black hair."

Big Jimmie laughed. "That's Piglet!"

"What?" Conker said, looking closer at the girl dancing with Hobnob on the far side of the galley. "She sure shot up. Last I saw, she was just a runt of a thing. Greasy braids and a pug nose, from what I recollect."

Piglet was still skinny but was now taller, having caught up in height with many of the other pirates. She wore a fine blouse of black silk to match her hair, and men's woolen britches. A pistol protruded from the back of her belt, and as Hobnob said something to her, she drew it and aimed it at the little thief's golden head. He waved his hands dismissively, and after some apologizing on his part, Piglet holstered the weapon and continued their dance, leading him around the floor like a rag doll.

"She's grown up some," Big Jimmie said. "The Pirate Queen has taken her under her wing. I suspect she'll make captain one day, when our lady's ready to retire to Panama or Bermuda or some such a place."

"Where is the Pirate Queen?" Si asked, peering into the thick of the dancers.

"Haven't seen her," Jimmie said. "Come on, Si. You up for another dance?"

Big Jimmie was on his feet, extending a meaty hand down to Si. She cocked an eyebrow dubiously at his offer but then smirked and followed him. Conker watched a few minutes, listening to the odd tune Mister Lamprey was belting out from behind his button accordion: "Brigand's Joy." Several drunken pirates were vying for a dance with Marisol despite the copperhead coiled about her shoulders. To escape the offers, she finally pulled Redfeather awkwardly to the floor. Conker laughed and maneuvered his way out the door.

As he came up the gangway, the breeze from Lake Michigan was refreshing after the stench of tobacco smoke and armpits that filled the galley below. He peered up at the pilothouse, but the moonlight showed no silhouette in the window.

The pirates had tried to disguise the *Snapdragon* by painting it a sunny shade of yellow. From a distance, Conker guessed, it looked like any of the other pleasure boats bobbing in the lake. But standing on deck, he saw that the paint did little to mask the bullet holes and repairs from cannon blasts that the marauding paddle-wheel steamer had acquired over the years.

Conker continued around the cabin until he reached the foredeck, where he saw the Pirate Queen up at the steamer's battered bow. Her elbows rested on the railing, one hand holding a glass of claret, the other bringing her cigar languidly to her mouth.

"My lady," Conker called.

She cocked an eye. "Get up here, Conker."

Conker gave a wary glance at Rosie, the gnarled alligator shifting at her mistress's feet. He rounded the Pirate Queen, putting her between the alligator and himself. Conker rested his elbows on the rail and peered out at the shoreline, where the White City shone, casting pearly sparkles across water.

"I ain't bothering you, am I?" Conker asked.

"No," the Pirate Queen grunted absently.

"You thinking on Buck?"

She bit hard on her cigar and said through gritted teeth,

"I'm thinking on whether Rosie will choke on Stacker Lee's clockwork heart when I feed him to her."

"How are we going to find him?" Conker asked.

She blew a silver stream of smoke, dragon-like, from her nose. "If my guess is right, there's an old acquaintance here at the fair. Going to call in an overdue favor."

"Who is he?"

"Jefferson Jasper. A train robber, a horse thief, the former mayor of several mining towns before they got wise and run him off, as well as the self-proclaimed adopted son to Chief Iron Tail of the Sioux." The Pirate Queen waved her hand dubiously. "Last I'd heard he's taken up with Buffalo Bill Cody. His Wild West show is set up just enough outside the Expo grounds so that old cheat Cody doesn't have to pay the fair owners' rent."

Conker tilted his head to the Pirate Queen. "How can this Jasper help us?"

"He keeps up with things," she answered, her mane of red hair fluttering against the bandoleer crossing her shoulders. "He'll know a thing or two about where the Gog's head-quartered if anyone does. Tomorrow." She pointed her cigar at Conker. "Go get some rest if you can find a dry bit of deck."

Conker returned to the galley to help Redfeather, Marisol, and Si escape the pirate crew's enthusiastic attention.

The following afternoon, a rowboat was lowered from the stern for the Pirate Queen, Mister Lamprey, Marisol, Redfeather, Si, and Conker to go ashore. The Pirate Queen wore a green silk dress with a high collar, a tight bodice, puffy shoulders, and a billowing skirt. Si gave Conker a wink, but neither had the nerve to joke with the captain about her fancy attire. Mister Lamprey had adopted a similarly conceived disguise, but his choice, a plaid sack suit, seemed more fitting for a dandy boy than a grown man. He carried a lacquered walking stick.

As Mister Lamprey took the oars with Conker, the Pirate Queen put a finger to her collar with annoyance. "Put ashore just south of the Expo so we can go on foot around to the Wild West grounds. How you four managed to not be spotted by the Gog's agents is a miracle. Stick out like geese in a cockfight. Row faster, Lamprey!"

When they reached the docks Lamprey tied up the boat, and the six set off until they were several blocks into a bustling lakeshore neighborhood. The sidewalks were crowded with tourists making their way to the Expo. As they passed under an elevated train platform, a great coliseum came into view.

"There it is, my lady," Mister Lamprey said, pointing with his walking stick.

"Obviously, Lamprey," she said, leading the way in long strides ill-suited to a woman in such a dress.

Murals outside the coliseum depicted side-by-side portraits of Christopher Columbus and Buffalo Bill. The caption below Columbus read, PILOT OF THE OCEAN, 15TH CENTURY—THE FIRST PIONEER, and the one below Cody read, GUIDE OF THE PRAIRIE, 19TH CENTURY—THE LAST PIONEER. A large banner announced in red letters, WELCOME TO BUFFALO BILL'S WILD WEST AND CONGRESS OF ROUGH RIDERS OF THE WORLD.

The thunder of horses and roar of the crowd within resounded in the street. Tipping his head back to look up at the stadium's height, Redfeather nearly collided with a couple rounding the corner.

The Pirate Queen snapped her fingers at him and said, "Quit staring, Sparky, and hurry up."

Redfeather frowned, and Marisol whispered "Sparky" with a smirk as she passed him. They entered the back of the coliseum, following an alleyway until they came to a dirt clearing surrounded by a fence. On the other side, an enormous set of elevated tracks ushered in trains filled with tourists to the Expo. Tents and hastily fashioned cabins had been set up around the encampment. Decorated horses were staked together in threes and fours. A dozen or more bison stood soberly in a corral, along with elk and mules and more horses.

The encampment was also filled with men sitting together in odd assortments, laughing and eating and playing cards. They were Buffalo Bill's Rough Riders, and their outfits reflected their wide-ranging backgrounds: fringe-shirted cowboys and feather-headdressed Indians; Mexican vaqueros in wide sombreros and simple vests alongside Russian Cossacks and hussars in blue and red military uniforms and tall ornamented busbies; Arab horsemen in long robes and scimitars at their belts as well as South American gauchos in wide-brimmed hats and loose pants tucked into their tall boots.

The Pirate Queen marched through them all, her head turning as she scanned the hundreds of men. Her gaze fell on a short man with a thin ribbon of gray hair who was prodding his teeth with a toothpick. As the Pirate Queen came toward him, the man dropped his boot heel from the doorway of a cabin and fled to its interior.

Conker picked up his pace to catch up with her and Lamprey, while Redfeather, Si, and Marisol jogged behind. A commotion was rising from inside the cabin, and as Conker came close to the door, he saw half a dozen men braced against the walls or leaning back in chairs from where they had been eating. They scrambled to draw guns and level them on the Pirate Queen and Lamprey coming through the doorway.

The Pirate Queen threw up the bustle of her dress and withdrew a pair of fat-barreled guns—too big to be pistols and too small to be cannons. Mister Lamprey held the walking stick up to his shoulder, and as it clicked, Conker realized it was an ingeniously disguised rifle. Si, Marisol, and Redfeather hastily ducked back behind the doorframe.

The Pirate Queen roared with a manic smile, "I'll wager our three guns to your six that Mister Lamprey and I come out the better."

Five of the men—three cowboys and two Comanche—blanched, eyes wide and guns shaking in their hands. The sixth was a cowboy, a finely dressed man with a wide handlebar mustache and a velvet waistcoat that was cut for a slimmer man. He grinned but didn't lower his Colt.

"If Buffalo Bill sees you here, Lorene," the man said in a slow drawl, "he'll string us both up."

The Pirate Queen said, "Hindsight and soberness will make Cody rethink that threat he left me with. Besides, I'm not here for Cody. I'm calling in a favor, Jasper. You remember that hand of poker?"

"You're speaking of Deadwood," Jasper said with a sneer. "Back in seventy-six. Remember it like it was yesterday."

"Then you'll remember you'd have been shot in the back by that tinhorn if I hadn't come through for you."

Jasper lowered his gun. "I remember."

The other men looked less eager to let down their guard, but Jasper waved a hand to them, and the terrified bunch slowly let their pistols fall. The Pirate Queen hiked up her skirt and stuck the guns back in their holsters. Mister Lamprey lowered his walking stick back to the ground, leaning one hand on it with a jaunty pose.

As Conker stepped into the room, he saw a stately elder Sioux sitting in the corner, seemingly unperturbed by the proceedings. Si came to Conker's side, reluctantly followed by Redfeather and Marisol. Jasper called from his chair to Redfeather, "Shut that door behind you before half the world knows we consort with questionable characters."

"Aren't you the pot . . . ," the Pirate Queen said, pushing a cowboy from his chair and taking a seat before Jasper. She glanced over at the Sioux. He had long silvery hair streaking over his shoulders and a kindly pinch to his face.

"A pleasure to see you again, Iron Tail," the Pirate Queen said. "Keeping a good eye on Jefferson?"

"Always," Iron Tail said.

"What's this favor, Lorene?" Jasper asked. "I'm not getting mixed up with any heist you're cooking up at the—"

"You know I wouldn't trust a half-wit like you with one of my jobs," she said. "I'm here for information only." She looked around at the wide-eyed cowboys and Comanche in the room. "Get clear of here!" she snarled with a cock of her thumb.

Iron Tail remained seated, but the other men pushed to get out the door. When it closed, Jasper glanced up at Conker and then back to the Pirate Queen. "Information, huh? About what?"

"The Gog," the Pirate Queen said.

"I don't know anything about the Gog. He's just a Rambler legend."

The Pirate Queen shook her head. "His name is G. Octavius Grevol."

Jasper blinked sharply. "Mister Grevol?"

"You've heard of him?" she said.

"Course I have." Jasper shifted in his seat. "He's got Burnham and the rest of the fair's directors under his thumb. I've heard strange things about Mister Grevol, but . . . the Gog? That's ludicrous. The Gog fell, along with most of the Ramblers, back when John Henry destroyed his Machine."

"No, he didn't," Conker said. "He survived. And he's built a new Machine."

Jasper smirked and shook his head skeptically. "How would you know?"

The Pirate Queen leaned closer. "He's John Henry's son."

Jasper's eyes widened with momentary surprise. He quickly composed himself, running his fingers along his mustache. "So what is it you—"

"Where's Grevol's headquarters?" the Pirate Queen asked.

"That's not too hard, I guess," Jasper said. "I suspect finding him is the least of the hazards you're going to bring down on yourselves. Grevol has an exhibit hall that's called the Hall of Progress."

"The Shadow in the White City," Iron Tail added.

Jasper grunted in agreement. "That's what some call it. You've seen the White City. Half the buildings look like ancient temples and palaces. The rest are a hodgepodge of replicas of Spanish missions and Swedish castles and whatnot. But

Grevol's hall is different. It's got none of the beauty of the rest of the White City. His Hall of Progress is functional and daunting and painted completely black."

The Pirate Queen was listening intently, her fingers absently going to her mouth as if she had forgotten she had no cigar there.

Jasper continued, "It's said that no light can fall on the Hall of Progress's facade. That the designers built it to play on the shadows, like a mountain among white clouds. I haven't gone in it. Bill's kept us plenty busy here. But I've heard that when you enter, you go from the dark clinging to the exterior to an inside of enormous light, electric and clear. Brighter than Edison's Tower of Light over in the Electricity Building."

Conker looked down at Si, and she said, "We never went in that building, but I remember seeing it. Where's it located?"

"It's just to the west of Big Mary," Jasper said.

"The golden liberty statue," Conker said. "We know where that is."

"Then you'll find his hall easy enough." Jasper drummed his fingers on the table, working out his thoughts. "So you really believe Mister Grevol is the Gog?"

"We know he is," Conker said.

"And his Machine?"

Marisol answered, "We've seen what it does. In Kansas, where the Gog has been secretly building his Machine, good people have become his servants. Those that try to escape sicken and die. If Grevol brings his Darkness down on Chicago, not only will the city fall, we'll lose our friends . . . we'll lose ourselves. We will all become the mindless gears turning the Gog's engine!"

Jasper frowned and looked over at Iron Tail.

The old man said, "I'm no medicine man. I'm just an old warrior who's fought too many losing battles. But Samuel Lone Elk speaks to spirits. He says he's seen ghosts wandering the fair's grounds. Ghosts disguised as men and women, even children. They know not that they are ghosts, but some devil has stolen their spirits."

"What's happened to them?" Si asked. "Grevol hasn't brought down the Darkness yet. Are they people from Omphalosa?"

"Why would they be walking around?" Conker said through a clenched jaw.

"Surely Gigi and the rest from Omphalosa are putting together Grevol's Machine in the Gloaming," Marisol said. "And when they finish—"

"Look! This is suicidal," Jasper said. "Even if Grevol isn't the Gog, do you realize how powerful he is? He has an army of Pinkerton agents, not to mention he controls the mayor, the police, state militia. They all answer to Grevol. Give this up before you wind up like the rest of the Ramblers."

Conker spoke in his deep rumbling voice. "My father died trying to stop the Gog. I aim to finish his work. I'll die if I have to, but not before I see that Machine destroyed and Grevol with it."

The room was quiet. Jasper smoothed his mustache before nodding to the Pirate Queen. "And you, Lorene?"

The Pirate Queen stood. "I've gotten myself mixed up with lost causes before, haven't I? See you, Jefferson."

Jasper rose slowly from his chair.

The Pirate Queen headed out the door, followed by Mister

Lamprey and the others. Conker looked back once more at Jasper and Iron Tail. The cowboy touched a hand to his hat and gave him a grim nod.

When they left the encampment behind Buffalo Bill's coliseum and returned to the busy sidewalk underneath the elevated train tracks, Lamprey said, "I've seen the Hall of Progress on our rounds, my lady. I don't know how the sanitation crew enters, but we could—"

"Conker!" Redfeather said.

Conker was walking away from the others, headed toward the docks.

"Where are you going?" the Pirate Queen called.

Conker rounded. "You know where I'm going."

"Don't be a fool," she snapped. "If you're anywhere near that hall, agents for the Gog will spy you in a moment."

Si faced the Pirate Queen at Conker's side. "Buck's in trouble! And now we know where he and the hammer are."

Mister Lamprey was casting an anxious eye at the passersby, many of them unable to avoid noticing the strange group arguing in the thoroughfare. The Pirate Queen moved closer to Conker and Si, her voice lowered. "We'll do nothing hastily. Do you hear? I haven't gotten to where I am without following carefully laid plans. We rush into that hall without a plan, it'll be as good as turning a gun on Buck's head. Back to the *Snapdragon*."

The moment lingered with heavy tension as a clattering train passed overhead on the tracks. Marisol and Redfeather looked from Conker to the Pirate Queen. Finally, Conker growled and strode past the others, heading toward the docks.

* * *

Conker ate his meal silently, the noise of the galley all around. Si leaned across the table and snapped her fingers. "Conk," she called through the din.

He looked up slowly, his brow furrowed.

"You okay?"

Conker nodded and continued absently eating from the plate of chitterlings and apple-cheddar pie. He thought about Iron Tail's words. *They know not that they are ghosts, but some devil has stolen their spirits.* Who were these people? What was happening to them?

The possibilities chilled him. They had to hurry. They had to get back the Nine Pound Hammer so he could . . . so he could what? He couldn't reach the Machine in the Gloaming.

"Eat your meal in peace," the Pirate Queen said from down the table. Conker looked over at her, and her frown softened slightly. "I've got an idea, and we'll discuss it after we've had our fill of Etienne's slop."

Etienne looked up, his fork perched before his mouth and a look of hurt in his eyes.

"Toughen up, Frenchie," Mister Lamprey said, and the table bellowed with laughter. Big Jimmie clapped Etienne on the back, and the cook forced a grin.

The door behind Etienne burst open. The yellow shock of Hobnob's hair came through. "Sirens, my lady! Sirens at the stern! And they've brought Buck."

THE PIRATE QUEEN PUSHED AND BATTED HER WAY THROUGH her crew as she headed up the gangway.

As Conker reached the moonlit deck, he wedged through the crowd. Piglet was kneeling on the wet planks. Behind her, the pair of sirens—one blond, the other auburn-haired— huddled together, ghostly pale in strange woven gowns like the one that Jolie wore.

The pirates surrounded Piglet and murmured and gasped to one another. A man lay before her, drenched and shadowy and seemingly drowned.

"Buck!" Marisol cried.

The Pirate Queen dropped to Buck's side, pushing back the wet tangle of hair from his face.

"He's alive, my lady," Piglet said.

Hobnob leaned over the Pirate Queen's shoulder. "The sirens, they found him in the lake."

"He's bleeding," the Pirate Queen said, pulling the tattered front of Buck's shirt open. Black slashes crisscrossed his chest.

Buck opened his eyes, the pair of orbs seeming to glow in the moonlight. His lips drew back, and he groaned through clenched teeth. "Lorene?"

"What happened?" the Pirate Queen asked.

"Stacker . . ." Buck's face knotted, and he groaned again.

The Pirate Queen barked, "Get him to my quarters, Lamprey!"

"Aye," Lamprey called. "I'll get the medical kit and the whiskey." He dashed off.

Big Jimmie lifted Buck, and the pirates parted. Si and Redfeather followed the Pirate Queen belowdecks. The rest of the pirates drifted toward the galley, mumbling to one another and looking back at the sirens.

When Conker turned, he saw Marisol already speaking to them. "Thank you for bringing him to us."

The blond siren spoke in a sharp voice. "He was nearly drowned. We asked the waters, our grandmother, to spare his life."

"We did not know what to do with him," the other siren said gently, a hint of apprehension in her voice. "He was barely conscious. Mumbling names we did not know. Then your boat rowed over us. He heard your voices. He seemed to know you. You are a friend to this man?"

"An old friend," Conker affirmed. "You're sirens. Why are you here? Do you come from the Terre—?"

The blond siren grabbed her sister's arm and pulled her to the rail. "Go!" she said.

"Wait!" Conker called.

The auburn-haired siren leaped from the rail. The blond one looked back. "Our debt is paid to that outlaw." Then she followed her sister, disappearing into the black waters with only the faintest splash.

Conker furrowed his brow at the siren's strange parting words. "I didn't mean to scare them."

"It's okay," Marisol said. "We're strangers to them."

Conker put his hands to the railing, peering out at the waters. "Jolie said her sisters had returned to the Terrebonne."

Marisol shook her head. "Then they're a long way from home."

The following morning, Conker and Si waited at the top of the gangway as Mister Lamprey came up the stairs with a tray of empty bowls and plates.

"How is he?" Si asked.

"Stacker's slashes were shallow," Lamprey said. "Needed a little stitching, but Eustace has seen worse. Mostly just worn out from the ordeal. Go see him for yourself. He's awake."

Conker followed Si down to knock on the door. The Pirate Queen grumbled, "Come in," in a tired voice.

They entered to find Buck with his head propped on thick silk pillows and the brocade covers turned back at his waist. The ragged cowboy looked alien among the finery.

"How are you doing?" Conker asked.

Buck shifted a bit until he was sitting up. "All right, I suppose. I'm ready to get up from this confounded pouf, though!"

The Pirate Queen clapped a hand over him. "Stay put until supper. We'll let you join us if you're a good boy."

Buck scowled but dropped his head back to the pillow. He sighed heavily and held out a hand. "Let me feel it," he said.

Conker and Si exchanged curious glances.

"Your hand," Buck said. "I need to know how bad it is."

She let him take her by the palm. Buck traced his fingertips across her knuckles until he found the missing finger. "The tattoo?" he whispered in his gravelly voice.

"It's gone," she replied. "The powers have gone."

He dropped his hands from hers and contorted his face. "I should have stopped Stacker. I . . . should have done something, but I . . . I just—"

"I was there too," Conker said. "We just weren't quick enough."

"But you acted," Buck said. "I did nothing. Si, I can't tell you how sorry . . ."

Si slipped her hands back to his. "It's okay. You've given up your guns. You're walking a new path now, Buck. You can't blame yourself for something Stacker did."

"Believe me," Conker growled, "when I see that murdering ally of the Gog, I'm going to tear his—"

"I don't think he is," Buck said.

"Is what?" Conker asked.

"An ally to the Gog."

"But he serves Grevol," the Pirate Queen said skeptically. "He brought you to him, along with the hammer."

"Grevol has lost Stacker's loyalty," Buck said.

"He told you that?" Si gasped.

"No, but I can tell. Stacker wants the clockwork removed from his heart. He wants to be a man again, and he knows Grevol's never going to allow it." Buck shifted uncomfortably in the bed. "Don't get me wrong. Stacker's wicked. He's a killer through and through. But he's no ally to the Gog."

The Pirate Queen slumped down onto a cot against the opposite wall and fumbled through her coat until she found a cigar. "He's certainly not helping us."

"Isn't he?" Buck asked.

The Queen brought the cigar almost to her lips before freezing and staring dubiously at Buck. Si said, "What do you mean?"

"He could have killed me," Buck said. "By any measure he should have. But he didn't."

"He had a few bad swings with the razor," the Pirate Queen sneered. "He was busy shoving you in the lake."

"Murder is his art," Buck said. "If he'd wanted, he'd have killed me. It's not just that. He said something. Before he threw me in the lake. He said . . ." Buck paused and furrowed his brow. " 'Hope rises at liberty's feet.' No, that wasn't it. What did he say?"

"What does it matter?" Conker said. "You think he was spouting words of wisdom?"

Buck's lips were drawn tight, and a cough brought his hand up to his chest as he winced in pain. "No," he murmured. "It was like it was a hint or something."

"A hint about what?" Si asked.

The Pirate Queen rose and pulled Buck's covers up. "It doesn't matter," she said after Buck settled back on the pillows with a grumpy look on his face. "I wouldn't trust Stacker to tie my noose. You're supposed to be recovering. Doctor Lamprey's orders." She waved a hand at Conker and Si. "You two clear out and let Eustace rest."

"See you, Buck," Si said, giving his hand a squeeze. Conker followed her up the gangway and on deck.

By the following day, Buck was joining them for meals and had moved quarters down with the crew on the lower deck. "I wish I could tell you more about the Hall of Progress," he said as they gathered in the galley late that night to discuss their next move. Buck had told them about the upper level where he'd been held and about the displays on the main floor between the elevator and the main entrance.

"You've given us a good start," Lamprey said. "But we still don't know where the Nine Pound Hammer is."

"They said it was on display," Buck said. "I couldn't find it. Something seemed—" He began coughing, holding his hand to his chest.

"You're going to bust those stitches," Lamprey growled as he poured Buck a mug of water and slid it across the table to him. Marisol narrowed her eyes at him and then looked over at Redfeather.

"We'll need to be certain where the hammer is before we go after it," the Pirate Queen said, giving Conker a frown before he could argue again that they should sneak in that night. "Mister Lamprey, you're trying to get your trash crew transferred to his hall?"

"We're doing our best, my lady. Asked the boss for a switch, but . . ." He shrugged. "No luck yet."

"What about the crew that works Grevol's hall?" Conker asked. "Can't you ask them if you can switch?"

"Never seen them," Big Jimmie said. "They've got the three of us running ragged just to get through our route each night."

Mister Lamprey added, "There's hundreds of men on sanitation, lad. And these Expo grounds are enormous. No time to figure out who's assigned where."

Buck put a fist to his mouth as he began coughing again.

Big Jimmie gave a wide yawn before saying, "To be sure, if I find out which workers got the Gog's hall, I'll break their legs so they'll need replacing."

"Then there's no other choice," the Pirate Queen said, casting an irritable glance at Buck as he continued coughing. "We need to send someone through the front door, like the rest of the tourists. Only way we'll be able to get a proper look at the . . . Tarnation! Eustace, you sound like a barking dog with all that coughing. It's late. Why don't you get yourself to bed."

"I . . . I'm not feeling well," Buck said, pushing back his chair.

"I'd guess not," Lamprey said. "Floating in the lake and all. Lucky you en't come down with pneumonia."

Buck stood and then stumbled to one side.

"Whoa," Conker said, catching Buck and propping him back up.

Big Jimmie came around the table. "Come on. I'm due for bed myself. Let me help you down to the bunks."

As the two headed out the door, Marisol leaned forward and said in a quiet voice, "What do you think, Si?"

Si's eyes were still on the door as Buck's coughs reverberated down the stairs. She shook her head. "I don't know."

"What are you two jabbering on about?" the Pirate Queen barked.

"Remember that man we told you about?" Marisol said. "The one who showed up at Nel's. From Omphalosa."

"You mean the one who escaped from the Darkness?" Conker asked.

"The one who *died* from the Darkness," Si said, her voice barely above a whisper. "He coughed like that."

The Pirate Queen snarled. "Come now . . . Eustace never even went to Omphalosa."

"No," Redfeather said. "But he's been in Grevol's hall."

Conker frowned. "You said yourself, Grevol had to bring the Machine from Kansas to Chicago. He's still assembling it somewhere in the Gloaming."

"We don't know," Marisol said.

"He'd have unleashed his Darkness over Chicago if he was finished," the Pirate Queen said.

Marisol threw her hands out in exasperation. Javidos popped his head up and hissed from where he'd been resting her lap. "All I'm saying is that it's strange that Buck seems to be sick after he's been imprisoned in Grevol's hall. I hope I'm wrong."

"Me too," Conker said. "But if we're going to send someone into the Hall of Progress, we'll have to assume the worst."

Redfeather looked around at the others. "So who should it be? Who's going in?"

* * *

"I look ridiculous!" Marisol said the following morning. "This dress is about two decades out of fashion." She stood before a mirror in the Pirate Queen's chambers, brushing a hand across the green silk bustle skirt.

"How do you think I looked wearing it?" the Pirate Queen snarled.

Marisol's face became blotched. "You looked . . . lovely, my lady."

Si covered her smile with her hand.

The Pirate Queen called to the screen where Redfeather was dressing. "You suited up yet, Sparky?"

Redfeather came out in Mister Lamprey's plaid sack suit. "A little short," he said, looking down at the cuff riding several inches above his brown shoes.

"It'll do," Conker said.

"Tell me again why *we* need to be the ones who go in," Marisol said.

"You two went to Omphalosa," Si said. "You've seen the Darkness. If there's something going on in Grevol's hall, you've at least got Nel's charms to protect you."

"But you and Conker could use them just as easy," Redfeather said.

"I ain't going to fit in that monkey suit," Conker said. "Besides, you two won't stand out near as much as we would. You look like . . ." Conker paused to find the word.

Si offered, "Dandies?"

The Pirate Queen laughed. "Tourists. You'll pass easily enough. Now, Mister Lamprey's ready to take you ashore. He'll wait at the docks for you. Leave the snake here."

Marisol had Javidos halfway up her sleeve. "But what if we're caught by the Gog's agents?"

"That copperhead won't get you out of that fix," the Pirate Queen said. "And neither will we, so try to be careful. Now, get going."

Redfeather and Marisol glumly climbed the gangplank, where the pirates above howled with laughter as they emerged. Mister Lamprey helped them aboard a dinghy and rowed them to the White City's docks.

As the afternoon got late, Conker waited up on deck for Marisol and Redfeather to return. Other paddle-wheel boats and cruising yachts drifted up and down the lakeshore. Music and laughter seeped up from the *Snapdragon*'s galley. Conker looked up at the pilothouse and saw the Pirate Queen smoking a cigar in the darkness, watching the docks with a spyglass. A bandy-legged pirate named Malley kept watch down at the stern. Si and Piglet played a game with knucklebone dice on the foredeck.

Conker's thoughts returned to Buck, who was already asleep belowdecks. His coughing had continued, but according to Si, the Omphalosa man had survived for weeks after leaving the Darkness. Besides, maybe Mister Lamprey was right and Buck had taken ill from being in the lake or from the razor wounds. Conker felt that was almost too much to hope for, especially as Buck's face had an ashen look to it.

"My lady," Piglet said behind him.

The Pirate Queen was coming down the pilothouse's steps. When she reached the deck, she snapped the spyglass closed and said, "Lamprey's returning."

Conker followed her to the stern, and a few minutes later

the rowboat appeared. When it reached the steamer, Mister Lamprey tossed a line to Conker. He held it while Marisol and Redfeather climbed back onto the *Snapdragon*'s deck.

"Up to the wheel," the Pirate Queen ordered. "Lamprey, bring us coffee! Piglet, I want you and Malley and two others on watch. Make sure they weren't followed."

Conker hurried after the others up the steps to the pilothouse. Settling on a bench against the wall, Marisol and Redfeather loosened their collars to breathe. The Pirate Queen knelt to scratch the underside of Rosie's chin, and Si leaned against the console beside Conker.

"Well?" Si snapped.

Marisol took the pouch that Ray had sewn from around her neck and gazed down at it in her palms. "We went in."

Conker realized that Marisol's fingers were trembling. Redfeather looked shaken as well.

"And?" the Pirate Queen said.

Redfeather looked up. "It's as Jasper said. The Hall of Progress is like a black fortress. It's not beautiful at all, not like the other buildings. I suppose to the fairgoers it looks like something practical. Something functional. Like an engine or a mill. And I heard many saying such. That the hall represented the future, not a harkening to the past."

"I don't care about the aesthetics," the Pirate Queen said. "What's inside?"

Marisol shook her head slowly. "The strangest things I've ever seen. Engines that seem to run on little more than air. Armored locomotives, like the steamcoach we followed across the plains, but bigger and mounted with cannons. There was an enormous machine—"

"An analytical engine," Redfeather said.

"What's that?" Conker asked.

"I'm not certain," Marisol said. "But it could do all these calculations. Some of the visitors seemed awed by it, but we didn't really stop to find out."

"At each display," Redfeather said, "there were these clockwork men. What were they called? Automata, I think. Their skin was made from brass. They could speak through little horns placed in their mouths, and they explained each exhibit, just like a regular person would."

"Could they think?" Si asked.

"I don't know," Redfeather said. "They didn't answer if you spoke to them. They just talked, and they could walk and pick things up and move around just like they were alive."

Marisol's face tightened. "I'd have been delighted if I hadn't known these were the Gog's devices. There's a whole army of clockwork men in that hall! Other beasts too. Horses and dogs. Nothing like the Hoarhound. That would be too terrifying to display. What the Gog is showing to visitors excites them. It fills people with possibility at the future. If they only knew . . ."

"Did you see the hammer?" Conker asked, uncrossing his arms from his chest.

Marisol and Redfeather looked at each other before answering. Then Redfeather said, "The Nine Pound Hammer's there, Conker. It's on display at the center of everything."

"Like some trophy." Marisol scowled.

"Big crowds around it too," Redfeather said. "We had to push our way to the barrier just to read the display. It tells a story, the one most people have heard, about your father taking on a steam drill in a competition. About how he beat it and then died." He blinked hard before continuing, "But then it goes on to say, 'No more will slaves and laborers have to die to build our industry. The dawn of great progress, the end to suffering, the birth of wondrous machines has arrived.' It's like a rallying cry."

"But it's a lie!" Marisol's face grew red. "We saw those workers in Omphalosa. The Gog does not mean to end slavery. It's a secret enslavement he's starting. Those workers—poor Gigi's family and the others—they're nothing more than machines themselves now."

"What's happened to them?" Si asked. "If the Gog brought them all from Kansas, then where are they?"

Marisol's nostrils flared as she took deep breaths to calm herself. "I don't know."

"But we saw those people," Redfeather reminded her.

"What people?" Si asked.

"I saw this husband and wife," Marisol said. "Their skin, it was ashen like the way the workers in Omphalosa looked. But this couple, they weren't workers. They were dressed in nice clothes, not fancy but nice. I pointed them out to Redfeather and we watched them walk around the exhibit floor for a while. They never stopped to look at anything. They never spoke to each other."

"They just kept walking," Redfeather said, "like they were drawn to something."

"We followed them to a corridor at the far end of the hall." Marisol's eyes were wide. "There weren't any displays there.

None of the visitors wandered back there. It seemed like a service area or some such. And down the hall, a pair of agents were waiting before a stairwell. They stepped aside with not so much as a word, and the couple disappeared down the steps."

"The agents spotted us," Redfeather said.

The Pirate Queen grimaced. "You were supposed to be tourists. Unnoticed! If they realize you—"

"They didn't know who we were," Redfeather quickly explained. "They asked if they could help us, and Marisol said she needed air and that we were looking for the exit. We got away without raising suspicion."

"Doubtful," the Pirate Queen murmured.

"But don't you see?" Marisol said. "Those people. They were infected by the Darkness. Somehow the Gog has activated the Darkness within the walls of his hall—"

"Or," Redfeather interrupted, "they're getting sick just by being close to where the Machine is being assembled."

"Either way," Marisol said, "the ones who are growing sick are being taken somewhere. Someplace down those stairs."

"It must be where the workers from Omphalosa are completing the Machine," Redfeather said.

"Poor Gigi." Marisol twisted the hem of her dress. "We should never have left him in that awful place."

The Pirate Queen stood and from her front pocket took out a cigar, which she waved at Redfeather and Marisol. "We'll get you to describe the hall in detail for Mister Lamprey so he can work up a map."

"When are we going to get the Nine Pound Hammer back?" Conker asked.

The Pirate Queen put a hand on his arm. "Patience. We'll get it back. But not without a solid plan first."

Conker scowled.

Si slumped back in her chair, shaking her head. "You realize what this means. There's no doubting it any longer. Buck . . . he's been infected by the Darkness."

OVER THE NEXT FEW DAYS, THE GROUP GRUMBLED OVER
Lamprey's incomplete map of the hall, went back and forth
on possible plans, and generally argued over next steps.
Conker hardly slept for worrying over the plans and about
Buck, who continued coughing but so far seemed to grow no
worse.

It was late one night, as Conker was watching the moon set
over the lake, that a bit of luck came their way. "We were re-
assigned," Mister Lamprey announced before the rowboat
had even touched the *Snapdragon*'s stern. "Malley, Jimmie,
and me."

"To the Gog's hall?" Conker bellowed, as he caught the
mooring line. He pulled hard, and the boat smacked heavily
against the steamer's hull, nearly toppling the crew into
the lake.

"Easy there," Mister Lamprey said as he scuttled up on the deck. "Let's go first to the Pirate Queen's chambers."

As the others stumbled off to bed, Conker followed Lamprey to the Pirate Queen's door, where he gave a small rap. "Are you awake, my lady?"

"I am now, you idiot," she grumbled. "Come in."

Conker followed Lamprey inside. The Pirate Queen sat up in her plush bed and placed the pistol she slept with at her side. Rosie, sleeping beside her mistress on the floor, opened her beady eyes and then closed them again with a whine.

"What is it?" the Pirate Queen asked.

"The crew assigned to the Hall of Progress," Mister Lamprey said, "apparently they've disappeared. At least, the boss said they didn't show up for work last night or tonight. So he put us on their route. We got in."

"What about the danger of the Darkness!" she barked.

"Marisol and Redfeather, they already gave us those charms to wear," Mister Lamprey said, patting the front of his shirt. "Just in case we got in."

"But there's three of you," the Pirate Queen said. "Wouldn't one of you get—"

"Big Jimmie never goes in," he explained. "It's the routine. Two collect the trash in the halls while the third unloads it in the wagons."

Conker waved his hand impatiently. "Could you get the hammer?"

Mister Lamprey shook his head. "We don't go on the main floor. There's a service entrance around the back, down a ramp and below street level. All the trash for the hall is picked up there."

Before Conker could say anything, the Pirate Queen raised a hand. "We learn more before striking. Lamprey, memorize the routine of the guards at the service entrance. Do they use the same men every night? See if there's a chance to explore further in the hall. But be careful! No unnecessary risks."

"Aye, my lady." Mister Lamprey smiled and then nodded toward the door at Conker. Conker followed him down the hall and out onto the deck. Although he was trembling with impatience, he knew the Pirate Queen was right. And more important, they at last had a way into the Hall of Progress. The Nine Pound Hammer was nearly in his grasp.

One afternoon, just before Mister Lamprey and the others left for their evening work, Hobnob ran over to where Conker and Si were talking in the shade on the foredeck. "Ray!" he chirped. "Going to see Ray."

"What do you mean?" Si said, laying the book she had been reading to Conker across her lap.

"Reckon he's needing me, en't he?" Hobnob opened his hand to show them the small collection of gray dandelion seedpods. "En't but one that carries one of my dandelions around and that's Ray. I'm setting out straightaway once I get permission from the Pirate Queen."

He dashed off for the pilothouse, nearly colliding with Big Jimmie.

"Ray . . . ," Si said, looking at Conker.

"Think he's all right?" Conker asked.

"I hope so."

After a moment, Hobnob leaped down from the pilothouse. He waved his dandelion hat at Conker and Si before plopping it on his head. He disappeared in a scattering of white pods being blown away by the lake's steady breeze.

As Conker turned back to Si, Marisol came up from belowdecks and hurried toward them. "It's Buck," she said. "He's getting worse."

Throughout the evening, Buck's coughing spells racked him for minutes at a time. The Pirate Queen ordered him to stay in bed. She also wanted him to return to her chambers so she could keep a closer eye on him, but he refused.

"I'll cough just the same wherever I lie," he grumbled at the small mob surrounding his bunk in the pirates' sleeping quarters.

Si brought a damp cloth to his forehead, and although he frowned, he also relaxed. Buck was burning up with a fever and occasionally moaning insensibly about hope lying at liberty's feet. Conker frowned as he saw the cowboy's complexion. His skin was the ashen gray of the workers in Omphalosa that Marisol had described. How were they going to help him? If Nel had not been able to save the man Si had spoken of, the man from Kansas who had died at Shuckstack, how could they save Buck?

Conker thought with longing of Nel. He missed the old pitchman terribly. It was somewhat of a consolation that Marisol and Redfeather had sent the telegram to Nel so he knew that Conker was alive. But could he be sure that Nel had received it? Had he gotten the warning that Shuckstack was in danger . . . that the Gog knew of their whereabouts?

Overcome with anxiety for Nel and for Buck, Conker

went out on the deck. It was late. The lights of other bobbing boats were dimmed. A trail of cloud drifted across the setting moon. Conker strode to the bow and hooked his elbows on the railing, dropping his forehead to his arms.

He was there only a moment before a hand touched his back. "You okay, Conk?"

Conker lifted his head enough to see Si. "I'm tired of all this waiting around," he said. "When are we going to get my father's hammer back? It's so close and yet . . ."

She nodded sympathetically and then rested her head against his arm. Conker felt his worries subside. They could not disappear. Even Si could not do that for him. But with her at his side, he always felt reassured.

After a week of learning the guards' routines in the Hall of Progress, Mister Lamprey felt they were ready. Gathering the others around the table in the galley, the fish-eyed pirate explained the routine of the agents who guarded the service entrance, the procedures he and Malley had to follow in collecting the hall's waste, and their best guesses as to how the service entrance led to the main floor above, where the Nine Pound Hammer was displayed. With a crude map rolled out before them, Conker listened to every detail.

"In the other buildings on our route," Mister Lamprey said, "we have to pick up these big bins of trash on different floors. But not in the Gog's hall. They don't let us go more than a few feet inside. He's got all the trash sent to the one location in the basement."

"Who dumps it there?" the Pirate Queen asked, chewing on her cigar.

"In the other buildings, it's normally cleaning crews that work during the day," Lamprey said. "But not at the Hall of Progress. Mister Grevol has a kind of plumbing system built in. Air sucks the trash through a series of pipes."

"Vacuum tubes," Big Jimmie said.

Mister Lamprey paused and crooked an eyebrow, mystified.

Jimmie shrugged. "That's what the guard called them."

The Pirate Queen rolled her eyes. "So there *is* a brain in there! Go on, Lamprey. How do these tubes work?"

"Ain't sure," Mister Lamprey continued. "But after we shovel all the trash out, we're supposed to pull this lever one last time. To suck out any remaining trash around the hall. I guess they have stations on different floors where people dump the trash, and by the offices on the upper level. When we pull that lever, it makes a huge noise like a cyclone, and there's a howl of sucking wind. Terrible loud it is."

"Who cares about those tubes?" Si scowled. "How are we going to get the hammer?"

"Ah, there lies the problem," Mister Lamprey said. "None of the three of us collecting the trash can go."

"Unless we knock out the Gog's men," Big Jimmie said, his smirk clearly showing his eagerness for this course of action.

The Pirate Queen narrowed her eyes. "If one of them fires a shot, the whole plan fails."

"Right, my lady," Mister Lamprey said. "Best we not tip off the guards."

"What if I go with you?" Conker suggested. "I could stay hidden and sneak past the guards if you're able to distract them."

"I'd be better at that," Si said.

"You're forgetting," Mister Lamprey said. "Malley and I need those charms so we can enter the hall without being harmed by the Darkness. Whoever sneaks in to get the hammer will be exposed to the Darkness."

A hush settled over the galley. Marisol and Redfeather exchanged worried glances. The Pirate Queen held her cigar an inch from her lips, neither drawing on it nor lowering it, as she thought.

"Buck's already been exposed—" Big Jimmie began.

"He's too weak from the fever," Si said. "I'll go. Someone's going to have to do it, and it might as well be me."

"No," Conker growled.

"Yes!" Si snapped. "You can't get sick. We have to destroy the Machine somehow. It all depends on you, Conker."

"If I go in, I don't reckon the Darkness will get me sick," Conker said.

The Pirate Queen swished her cigar back and forth. "Wishful thinking and fool's hoping isn't going to—"

"I'm saying the Darkness won't affect me," Conker said.

He was met with a series of frowns and confused mumbles. "Why would you think that?" the Pirate Queen asked.

"When Stacker took my father's hammer from me at the roots of the Wolf Tree, I was shot twice. Once in the side and once in the leg."

"I didn't know you were shot," Si said. "You never told me you were injured!"

"Because I wasn't injured." Conker stood and pulled the tail of his shirt from his pants. "Not really. I didn't want to say nothing." He looked anxiously at Si. "Because of your hand

and all. Didn't seem right, you losing your tattoo and me healing so easily. But see . . ." He pulled up the shirt. The Pirate Queen and the others leaned forward over the table to look at Conker's waist. His skin was smooth and unblemished, except for what could have been a pockmark.

"It healed almost immediately," Conker said. "The leg too."

"What?" Redfeather stammered. "What . . . how could that be?"

Conker dropped his shirttail and sat again. "I slept almost a year in the waters of that siren well—"

"But gunshots aren't the Darkness," Si argued.

Conker gave a firm gaze. "One of Jolie's sisters came to the well, just before I woke. She took water from the well to heal her sisters in the Terrebonne who had been sickened from the Darkness. The sirens believe their waters can protect against the Darkness. I reckon it to have done the same for me."

"But you don't know!" Si snapped.

"I know," Conker said in a low voice. "I feel it in me, just as certain as I feel the power of the Nine Pound Hammer when I hold it. I'm going with you, Mister Lamprey. I'm getting back my father's hammer. So enough arguing. Tell me more about the service entrance."

The wagon rattled over the paving stone thoroughfares of the silent fairgrounds. Big Jimmie drove the team of horses, with Mister Lamprey and Malley on the bench at his side. The wagon had tall sides, big enough to carry half a ton of garbage at a time. Conker huddled at the far corner of the wagon, steeling his senses against the stench as the pirates dumped great bins of half-eaten food, discarded brochures and leaflets, and other soggy, fly-ridden trash around Conker. Unfortunately, the Hall of Progress was at the end of their route.

Jostling in the back in the dark, Conker heard Mister Lamprey's voice whisper through the plank siding, "We're almost there. Go ahead and get in the bin."

Conker stretched his cramped muscles before climbing over the garbage to the back of the wagon. Conker lifted the canvas flap and peered around. The fairgrounds were nearly empty. Another sanitation crew was driving their wagon in the opposite direction. Big Jimmie was leading them past the long fountain, the pearly white buildings all around, the golden statue of Big Mary perched at the far end of the fountain, gleaming in the moonlight.

Conker climbed into the bin. It was little more than a large iron box on wheels hitched to the back of the wagon. He settled down, his weight silencing some of its noisy clanking as it rolled.

After a few moments, the wagon slowed. Conker felt a descent as Big Jimmie led the horses down a ramp. "Little ugly, little ugly, and big ugly," a voice called out, followed by the chuckles of two other men. Three agents at the exit, Conker noted.

"Evening, fine sirs," Mister Lamprey said. His boots clapped to the stones along with Malley's. Conker heard the pitchforks scrape as they took them from the wagon's side. "And a fine evening it is. The ever-present perfume of refuse wafting in the night breeze."

One of the agents gave a weak laugh. As the bin was unhitched and began rolling, Conker lay flat against the grimy metal floor. The Hall of Progress loomed above him, and then he passed through a doorway to a hallway illuminated with a dim electric bulb.

"Good evening, *sir*," Mister Lamprey called, as a way of telling Conker that only one guard was posted inside tonight.

Lamprey had said there was usually a second one, but occasionally just the one. Before they left the *Snapdragon*, the pirates had offered Conker a ridiculous assortment of weapons, but Conker had passed on firearms. He had no experience shooting. Instead he settled on a blackjack and Jolie's shell blade that he still carried.

Conker checked the knife wedged into his belt with one hand and brought the heavy, leather-covered club up to his chest with the other as he prepared for his exit.

The bin jostled abruptly, and Mister Lamprey gave a howl. "That's it, you stupid mick. Third time you've run this bin into my heel."

"Then pull faster!" Malley snarled.

"Boys!" the agent called.

"Pull faster? Pull faster?" Mister Lamprey growled, his voice moving to the side of the bin. "I'll pull your ears off faster than you can say John Brown!"

"Let's see you try."

"Cut it out, you two," the agent barked, coming closer now. "Hey . . . hold on now."

There was a scuffle of feet and the slaps of fists on flesh. Bodies knocked into the side of the bin, and it tipped onto two wheels.

"Enough!" the agent said, attempting to break up the fray. "Hey! Ow. Stop it."

The bin rocked again, and before it could settle, Conker threw his shoulder into the side to topple it over. The bin landed with a loud clank. Conker saw the agent's back as he tried to pull the two fighting pirates apart. Then he spied the doorway, the one Lamprey had said led to a stairwell to the upper floors. Dashing for it, Conker pushed open the door and pulled it nearly closed.

Putting an eye to the crack, he watched the agent pull Lamprey and Malley apart. "Quit acting like a pair of mongrels and get to work."

One of the guards from outside came to the exit. "What's going on?"

"Nothing," the agent said, putting his bowler hat back to his head and brushing the sleeves of his black suit. "Right, boys?"

Lamprey and Malley exchanged venomous glances and then lifted the bin upright before picking up their pitchforks and going to the trash chute. Conker closed the door and started up the steps. As he reached the first landing, he heard footsteps above. Quietly scuttling back down, Conker looked for a hiding place. He spied the recess beneath the stairs and squeezed into the space.

The footsteps descended. Conker saw the back of an agent. The black-suited man paused as he reached for the handle. Don't look back, Conker willed. The leather handle of the blackjack creaked as he squeezed it. The agent opened the door and went out to join the others. "Look, it's little ugly and little ugly. . . ."

Exhaling sharply, Conker came out from the shadows and ran up the steps, stopping at the door on the next floor. He cast a quick glance down the stairs and then up to where the stairwell continued for many more flights. All was quiet and dark.

He eased the door open and peered out. The main floor loomed in shadows, an enormous cavern filled with darkened displays and exhibits. From what Lamprey had said, the stairs should put him at the northeast corner of the Hall of Progress. The Nine Pound Hammer was at the center. Conker headed down the first aisle, crouching and then stopping every few yards to listen.

Across the hall, faint voices sounded, their muffled words echoing softly in the expansive space. Other guards. As he continued, Conker hoped that they would never expect an actual intruder and would simply carry out their rounds with little attentiveness.

Conker peered around at the tall exterior walls to get his bearings. He was nearing the center. He came around a huge contraption and spied a tower at the hall's center. It was framed with metal girders and had wires, tubes, and cables running through it. A support structure for the ceiling, Conker thought. Buck had said there was a sort of mechanical lift called an elevator in the tower that led to the rooms above where he had been captive to Stacker Lee.

The windows above were darkened. Conker wondered if the clockwork killer was up there now, watching the floor.

Conker lowered his gaze to the base of the tower, where a tall, stage-like display was covered in velvet curtains. He moved into the aisle and slipped closer. A figure stood in his periphery. Conker whipped around with the blackjack.

A brass man stared at him. Conker brought up the club but paused. The clockwork figure did not move. Blackened slits were cut through the metal where his eyes should be. A circular cone formed a mouth that appeared to be making a surprised O. Conker poked the clockwork man's chest. The brass figure tipped back a fraction and then settled on its feet. Watching a moment longer, Conker decided the figure must have been shut off for the night.

He passed several more of the coppery figures, each perched motionless with strange mannequin-like tilts of their metal arms and awkward cocks of their heads. Conker crouched low when he came to an intersection in the aisles.

From his vantage, he spied it: the Nine Pound Hammer. It hung horizontally, fastened with clasps to a velvet-covered wall. Pasteboards of text spread below it, the words that Redfeather had repeated for them. Several feet in front, a low iron fence had been placed to cage out visitors.

Conker looked around, listening to distant footsteps slowly tapping against the marble floor and the low voices of the agents talking as they made their rounds. He took a deep breath and then dashed for the iron fence.

He was about to put one leg over when a voice said, "It's not what it seems."

Conker swung around.

Stacker Lee held his long pistol at hip level, trained on Conker. He said, "Didn't that idiot Buckthorn tell you—"

Conker lunged, his shoulder plowing into Stacker. The gun fired. A bullet lodged, hot and stinging, in Conker's stomach. The two toppled, Conker coming down heavily on Stacker. The clockwork killer's crisp Stetson fell from his head and slid on the smooth marble. Stacker grunted and struggled beneath Conker's weight. Conker reared up with the blackjack, as Stacker jabbed the barrel against Conker's temple.

Conker rolled aside before the shot erupted. He grabbed the iron fence and hurled it around at Stacker. The railing knocked him backward into several of the clockwork men. Stacker disappeared under the falling figures.

Conker dropped the blackjack. Voices shouted and feet echoed through the hall. Warm blood spilled down Conker's leg. He turned to the display. The hammer—that was all that mattered.

Bullets rang out around him. Gunfire filled the hall like cannon blasts. Conker rushed to the display, one hand grabbing the Nine Pound Hammer's handle, the other bracing against the display's wall. The velvet tattered in several places as bullets ripped into the curtains. Conker broke the Nine Pound Hammer free from its bracings with a heave.

Something felt odd about the hammer, but he had no time to wonder as he wheeled around and saw a dozen agents coming at him. Stacker was climbing out from under the brass men and looking about for his pistol. The wound in Conker's stomach seared, and he realized that although it might heal, he would never survive a shot to his chest or his head. The siren water could not protect him from that.

"Stop!" agents cried. "Stay where you are. You're surrounded."

Conker shoved the Nine Pound Hammer into his belt and leaped at the velvet display. The wooden structure fell backward, toppling against the steel girders of the tower. Conker grasped at the fabric, pulling as he climbed over the fallen display. A bullet grazed his ankle, and another caught him in the shoulder. But he kept climbing until he reached the tower's spiderweb of girders.

Reaching back, he snatched the velvet curtain and tore it from the display. He threw it over his head and shoulders and climbed, pulling and leaping as he grasped the girders. The curtain hung like a cape, and as the gunfire erupted, bullets swished through the curtain and sparked off the girders. Stacker began ascending after him, followed by several of the agents.

At an opening in the framework, Conker crossed into the interior of the tower and grasped the dangling cable of the elevator. With a leap, he swung to the other side of the tower's interior to put more of the structure between him and the agents' gunfire.

"Nowhere to go!" Stacker called.

A groan emerged from above. The cables hanging through the middle of the tower began moving, one up, the other down. Below, a small structure began to rise through the tower's center. The elevator.

Conker climbed quickly, but the clockwork killer ascended even faster. Stacker Lee reached an arm through the girders, his long pistol aimed at Conker. Conker leaped before the gun fired, the velvet curtain falling from his shoulders. His fingers grasped at the cables, and he grunted as the friction burned his palms. He fell, only a few feet, before his boots thudded heavily on the top of the rising elevator. Conker steadied his stance and looked up. The shaft where the elevator reached the upper-level rooms was approaching fast. He'd be crushed by it.

Splinters broke from the elevator's roof as the agents within fired. Conker dove, missing the girder framework but catching a large tin pipe running up the interior of the tower. The pipe held firmly, but its sides crinkled as Conker squeezed tightly to it. He could hear a droning from inside.

"You're at the end, Conker!" Stacker called, climbing closer up the far side of the tower. "Can't get into those rooms above. So it's either climb down and hand over the hammer . . . or fall. That marble's plenty hard down there."

Conker swung from the pipe to the girders. He looked up to where the elevator had disappeared into the uppermost level. Could he break through the floor above with the Nine Pound Hammer? Probably not before Stacker shot him dead. He looked down. It was a long drop. In the dimness, he could not gauge the distance, but he was certain it was too far. And even if he did manage it without breaking his legs or cracking his skull, he'd never get past the waiting agents.

On the other side of the tower, Stacker watched him with sparkling eyes. "What's it going to be?"

Two other agents had nearly climbed up to Stacker's position. Conker panted as his eyes darted around for some option.

"Shoot him!" an agent roared from the floor.

The two agents stopped their ascent and drew Colts from their belts. Conker climbed the last remaining feet, putting the wide tin pipe between him and the agents. Gunfire pinged and reverberated off the girders at his feet. Then one plunged into the pipe. An angry hiss formed at the hole.

Conker's eyes grew wide as he looked at the pipe. The vacuum tubes.

"You're cornered, Conker," Stacker lilted.

Conker pulled Jolie's knife from his belt and plunged it into the side of the pipe. A howl of air erupted. Not blowing out, but sucking in. Conker dove at the hole. His shoulder broke through. The head of the hammer caught on the opening, and he kicked helplessly at the empty air. The darkness inside the tube howled with a great rush of wind, whipping his shirt and stinging his eyes. Bits of debris and garbage knocked against him.

Conker roared and pulled until the hammer's head at his belt broke through the tattered tin. There was a whoosh and he was sucked down the tunnel, garbage all around him. Battered and bashed about, Conker flew through the network which was twisting this way and that so he could hardly tell up from down.

With a thud, he landed in a thin heap of refuse. The garbage sucked down with him buried him. Conker stayed still a moment to regain his bearings. He heard Lamprey's voice muffled through the trash, "That's the last of it. Pitch it up, mick."

Before their pitchforks could spear him, Conker leaped up from the trash. Lamprey and Malley jumped back, and the agent's eyes went wide. Conker drew the hammer from his belt. As the agent fumbled to grab his pistol, Lamprey stabbed his pitchfork down, pinning the agent's foot to the floor. He howled, and Malley swung the handle of his pitchfork into the agent's temple, knocking him out.

"Let's go!" Lamprey shouted.

Another agent came through the doorway, firing his gun at Conker.

Conker ducked behind the bin and shoved it toward the agent, plowing the man against the wall before he could take another shot. The third agent fumbled to draw his pistol as he came in. Before he had it leveled, Big Jimmie reared up behind him and brought a bludgeon against the back of the agent's head. His bowler hat tipped forward over his eyes, and the agent flopped unconscious to the ground.

Mister Lamprey wedged the handle of his pitchfork behind the wheels of the bin to trap the other agent and said, "On the horses."

Big Jimmie had already stealthily unhitched the horses from the wagon. Conker climbed on the back of the biggest of the beasts. Lamprey and Malley each leaped on a horse, and Big Jimmie cried "Hiya!" from his mount. The hooves of the animals clattered up the ramp and out into the moonlit thoroughfare of the Expo.

Gunshots popped behind them as agents poured out from the Hall of Progress. But they were too far away, and without horses at the ready, the agents would never catch up. Lamprey led their horses on a winding path through the white buildings of the Expo grounds to throw the agents off their route.

As they reached the waterfront, they slid from the horses and into the boat. Rowing out into the lapping waters, Lamprey looked at the empty shore and leaned back against the side of the boat. "Well, far from perfect, gentlemen. But we made it out in one piece, now, didn't we?"

Conker stared down at the hammer resting across his knees. He had lost blood from the gunshots, but the wounds were already closed.

"You okay, Conker?" Big Jimmie asked from behind the oars.

Conker felt cold and empty, and not from the loss of blood.

He had carefully carved the handle of the Nine Pound Hammer at the roots of the Wolf Tree. He knew every nick and scar in its iron head. . . .

"This ain't it," he said, lifting the hammer.

"What's not?" Lamprey asked.

Conker looked up, seething with anger. "This ain't the Nine Pound Hammer!"

THE SUN HAD JUST SET. RAY RESTED ON THE WOODED SHORE-
line of Lake Michigan, peering to the north at the distant city's
gas lamps coming on one by one. "How far away is the Expo?"
he asked.

Hobnob scratched at his yellow mane. "In steps to walk or
minutes to fly?"

Ray regarded him with a cocked eyebrow. "Neither. How
about in miles?"

"En't good with those kinds of fancy figures, you know."
Hobnob shrugged. "It's a fair distance."

"You couldn't have brought us closer?" Ray had been
eager to see the city and the Columbian Expo, but Hobnob had
led them to a sparsely populated section of the shore south of
the city where he had arranged with the Pirate Queen for them
to be picked up.

"And rouse suspicion?" Hobnob chirped. "That Jolie wouldn't have passed for even some foreign tourist in that dress of hers." Before Ray could point out that Hobnob didn't exactly blend in either, the little thief jabbed a finger. "Lookit! There's the *Snapdragon* coming."

Ray scanned the twilight waters. The lake was a busy waterway with all manner of barges, schooners, fishing johnboats, and pleasure steamers. "Where? I don't see it."

"Right there." Hobnob pointed gleefully.

"That yellow boat . . ." As Ray looked closer at the paddlewheel steamer approaching, he realized this was unmistakably the *Snapdragon,* despite the odd paint disguising it. He went down to the water's edge. "Jolie!"

She broke from the surface several yards out, her dark hair streaming in rivulets down her face. She looked at the steamer and then swam to shore to join Ray and Hobnob. Soon a little dinghy rowed out from the *Snapdragon*'s stern. Ray swelled with excitement as he spied his friend at the oars beside Mister Lamprey.

"Conker!" he shouted.

Conker waved, and as the boat slid to the sandy bank, he leaped ashore. He threw his huge arms around Ray and lifted him from his feet. "Ain't it something to see you again!"

Ray gasped, "C-Conk-er." As the giant put him down, they held each other's arms and stared with crooked smiles. "You've changed, Conker."

"I have?" Conker said. "Not so much as you. Look at you." He lifted a hand to level it at the top of Ray's head. "You nearly come up to my armpits."

Ray tried to shove him, but Conker didn't budge. "I'll be taller than you one day. Just wait."

Conker laughed. "Reckon you will. When I'm a hunchback old man." He embraced Jolie less aggressively than he had Ray, but with no less warmth. "You faring okay, Jolie?"

"Yes." She smiled.

He took the shell knife from his belt and handed it back to her. "Thank you."

"Back to the boat," Mister Lamprey said, beckoning. "There's a happy crew who's just dying to see you again, Ray." He held out a hand for Jolie to help her into the boat. "I'm Lamprey," he said with a little bow. "You must be Jolie. Heard so much about you, dearie."

"You too," Jolie said, climbing into the boat.

Lamprey gave a wink and said, "Don't believe anything they told you."

As the little dinghy reached the *Snapdragon*'s stern, the pirates crowded together on deck, and Ray had to push his way through clasping hands and jostling bodies to reach Si, Red feather, and Marisol. Jolie stared around at the reception with wide eyes, and Ray held tight to her hand as he introduced her to the Pirate Queen and her crew. Ray didn't recognize Piglet, and Big Jimmie found this terribly funny. The smells of Etienne's cooking came up from the galley, and they rushed down the gangway.

There were so many things to tell one another; so much had happened since they had all last been together. But as Mister Lamprey brought down his button accordion and musical mayhem overtook the galley, Ray and Conker, Jolie and

Marisol, Si and Redfeather found their way up on deck where the stars were out and the breeze coming off the lake was cool.

They talked about old times, the days aboard the *Ballyhoo* and the medicine show and gathering herbs in the woods for Nel's tonics. But they weren't able to escape for long. Soon Hobnob and Big Jimmie found them, and they were dragged back to the galley, back to the music and dancing, and the evening turned into a dizzying romp.

Ray woke in the morning with the alligator Rosie nestled against him. "Good to see you too, old girl," he said before yawning and crawling out from the overturned pirogue on deck. Most of the crew was already at work around the steamer, waxing the deck, refitting lines, touching up the paddle wheel's blades. Bleary-eyed, Ray followed the smell of breakfast down the gangway to the galley, where Conker, Si, Marisol, and Redfeather were eating at the long table with the Pirate Queen and Mister Lamprey.

"Where's Jolie?" Ray asked, sitting down to pour tea over a mound of sugar cubes in a chipped cup.

"Said she was going to sleep in the lake," Conker said.

Etienne placed a plate of fried ham, steaming crescent rolls, and poached eggs before Ray. He thanked the cook profusely before attacking the plate.

"Tell us what happened to you, Ray," Redfeather said.

Ray collected his thoughts as he finished off the breakfast. Pushing the plate away, he began the tale of his journey with Jolie deep into the Rocky Mountains.

"Your father . . ." Conker smiled when he told him about Li'l Bill. "At last you found him. I'm glad for you and Sally, Ray."

Ray winced. "It's not what I'd expected. Not what I'd hoped. He can't even come back with us. When all of this is over . . ." His voice trailed uneasily.

"*When?*" Conker murmured. "I ain't sure it's even *if*. With the hammer lost—"

"What!" Ray gasped. "Where's the hammer?"

Conker growled. He told Ray about what had happened, the attempted recovery in the Gog's hall. "But the hammer," Conker concluded, anger peppering his words, "it was a fake."

"So where is it, then?" Ray asked.

"Probably hidden somewhere by the Gog," the Pirate Queen said. "It could be anywhere! We were fools to think he would have the actual weapon of John Henry in plain view."

"We'll find it," Ray assured them. "We have to. And when we do, we'll be able to destroy the Gog's Machine at last." He opened his shirt to take out the toby, and from it he laid the golden spike on the table. "This is what my father forged."

Si sat up from her chair. "It's as Mother Salagi described!"

"What do you mean?" Marisol asked.

"The seers," Ray said. "Mother Salagi and the others. They had a vision. A weapon that must be used to destroy the Machine."

"They called it the 'light to pierce the Dark,' " Si said.

Conker picked up the spike. "How does it work?"

"It must be driven into the heart of the Machine, the very core," Ray said. "But only with the Nine Pound Hammer."

Conker balled his hands into fists in frustration.

"Then what good is this spike?" the Pirate Queen muttered.

"We'll never have another chance to get into the Hall of Progress."

Conker said, "Even if we get the hammer back, how are we going to reach the Machine? We need Li'l Bill to help us cross—"

"I can do it," Ray said. All eyes were on him now, but Ray stared at Conker. "I can cross into the Gloaming. If we can just find the Nine Pound Hammer, I can lead you to the Machine, Conker."

Conker rose, nodding his head. He walked around the galley until he stopped at one of the small windows and narrowed his eyes out at the lake. "Then we've no choice," he said in a low voice. "One way or another, we got to get the hammer back."

By afternoon, Jolie had still not returned. Ray tried not to worry. It seemed only natural that after their long journey, she would need time beneath the waves. The Pirate Queen said Buck was awake, so Ray hurried down to visit with him. He and Jolie had been eager to visit Buck the night before, but the Pirate Queen had insisted they let him rest. His condition was unfortunately worsening.

Buck lay on a bunk in the far corner of the crew's quarters. Although Marisol had assured the pirates that his illness was not contagious, most of the crew had been sleeping on the open deck—some skeptical of her words, some because the racking cough kept them up all night.

"Ray," Buck said weakly as Ray reached his bunk. The old cowboy's skin was an unnatural gray, nearly the color of the streaks in his ragged beard and hair.

Ray sat on the bunk across from Buck's. "How are you?"

His pale eyes stared up at the ceiling. "Not good. I won't lie to you." He began coughing, doubling up on the sweat-stained sheets. Ray watched closely and felt some relief that no blood came up.

"We're going to find a way to stop the Machine," Ray said. "Then you'll be better."

Buck settled back onto his pillow, and Ray handed him a tin cup of water. After swallowing, Buck wheezed, "I don't know if even that will cure me. Only the waters from a siren's well would do it. That's what I'm figuring."

Ray leaned forward eagerly. "Conker had the water Jolie carried back from that spring!"

Buck shook his head. "He used it all. Helping heal Si."

"Si?"

"Stacker shot her," Buck said. "In the hand. Didn't you notice? She's lost her little finger. The tattoo, its powers . . . they're gone."

Ray had not noticed. Why hadn't Si told him? But there had been so much to tell, and Si was not one to indulge in self-pity.

"Buck," Ray began slowly. "I found my father. I found Li'l Bill." Ray told him about his journey to the Bitterroots, and as he finished, he added, "The Wolf Tree is dying. Its survival depends on a siren's well." Ray paused before whispering, "There is a way for a well to be made."

Buck sat up. "No! You must not. Where is she? Where is Jolie?"

"She's in the lake."

Buck's voice cracked. "You must not let her sacrifice herself, Ray."

"Jolie knows there is no other way. She knows that if a well is not made, then . . ." Ray had hardly been able to think it. The knowledge lurked in the back of his every thought when he was with her.

Buck's voice came from his cracked lips, low and raspy. "I must tell you something, Ray. Something I had not intended for anyone to know. Come closer."

Ray got up from the bunk and knelt at Buck's side. The old cowboy reached out with a hand to take Ray's. "It pains me to tell it. My life has been filled with so many regrets and missteps. I am not the man I wanted to be. I was never a Rambler like your father and Nel. I wanted to be good—"

"You are good," Ray said. "You're one of the best men I've ever known."

Buck laughed grimly and broke into a shallow cough. "Thank you, Ray. But I don't deserve your admiration. I'm nothing but a worthless outlaw. I've wanted to redeem myself, for my sins. I've wanted to make amends. To deserve what you so freely express."

"You do deserve it, Buck."

"I don't," Buck said. "Listen. I need you to know for what I'm atoning. It's not just my brother Baldree. Not just Seth. Not just the other men who have died by my guns. I brought death to the one I loved the most, more than my brother. . . . Her name was Élodie."

Buck began coughing again and took his hands from Ray's to cover his mouth.

Ray sat frozen, the weight of that single name bearing down on him with a locomotive force. When Buck settled again, his wheezing returned to a shallow pattern. Ray put his hand on Buck's shoulder.

"You're Jolie's father, aren't you?"

Buck blinked, his lips parted with wonder. Before Buck could ask, Ray said in a whisper, "Jolie told me how her mother died."

"Does she know who I am?" Buck asked.

"No," Ray said. "How could she?"

"Does she hate me?" Buck whispered. "Does she hate her father? For what he . . . for what I did?"

"She could never hate you, Buck. You need to tell her—"

"No!" Buck growled in his gravelly voice. "I don't want her to know. Ray, I'm telling you because I'm not sure how much longer I will live. I intended for Jolie to learn. After I redeemed myself. I thought by giving up my guns, I thought by following a righteous path, that I might mold myself into a man worthy of being Jolie's father. But I have only stumbled further. I did nothing when Si was shot. I didn't prevent Stacker from taking the Nine Pound Hammer to the Gog. I have done nothing to right the ills of my own making or of the wickedness of Grevol. I fear I have lost my last chance at redemption."

He took Ray by the wrists firmly, pulling him closer. "Promise me, Ray. You will say nothing to Jolie or any other . . . at least not until I am gone."

"But why, Buck?"

"Promise me!"

Ray closed his eyes, struggling with what to say to convince Buck otherwise.

"Ray, you are dear to me. And I know you do not agree or understand, but if you hold any affection for me . . . swear that you will say nothing of what I told you."

"I promise," Ray said softly.

Buck's fingers relaxed. "Thank you. I won't allow her to sacrifice herself to save me. There is another way I might be healed."

"What?"

Buck was silent a moment, wheezing through gritted teeth. "The Hall of Progress," he murmured. "I feel it beckoning to me. My body longs for the Darkness. It draws me back."

"You can't—"

"Go," Buck said with a wave of his hand. "I can't even go up on deck in my state. Let an old man find some measure of peace, if only in sleep."

Ray watched Buck a moment longer and walked out into the bright sunlight of the deck. Gulls laughed from the air above the lake. A dark line of clouds was rising in the west. Ray looked out at the choppy waters, drawn to little peaks of foam by the rising wind.

By nightfall, there would be a storm.

"I can probably get into the Hall of Progress unnoticed," Ray said. The galley's table was covered with Mister Lamprey's map and scattered half-finished plates of fruit and cheese.

"As a crow?" Conker asked.

"I wouldn't need to cross," Ray said. "Crossing drains my strength. But just taking crow form, I could fly in an open door at night. It weakens me, but not as much as crossing."

"Even so, you could search the Gog's hall for weeks and never find the Nine Pound Hammer," the Pirate Queen said, running a finger along the edge of her wineglass. "What we need to look into is—"

The door to the galley swung open. Old Joshua stepped in, his sunken mouth writhing wordlessly.

"What is it?" Mister Lamprey asked.

Jolie came around the old pirate, dripping puddles on the floor.

"Where have you been?" Ray asked, standing.

"*Meu sirmoeurs!*" Jolie's eyes flashed. "My sisters, Ray! I found two of my sisters. But first, my lady, I think you should come out onto the deck. There are strange boats about."

The Pirate Queen followed Jolie and Old Joshua into the darkening air. Ray smelled the tang of the storm looming over the lake. No rain had fallen, but the wind was heavy with moisture. Lightning crackled over the land beyond. The Pirate Queen surveyed the lake. "The rest of you stay below. We don't want to arouse suspicion."

Ray held back with Jolie in the gangway's door. He watched as the Pirate Queen met Piglet on the stern. They spoke in low, urgent voices, and Ray saw the Pirate Queen tilt her head as she looked around surreptitiously.

"My sisters and I noticed the boats following the *Snapdragon*," Jolie said. "See, there and on the other side."

Ray looked from starboard to port. They were paddle wheelers, four of them, not unlike the *Snapdragon* but painted gray, and with their paddles mounted at the front like most of the pleasure cruisers. Ray would not have thought them to be any different than the myriad other boats going up and down the shore, except that these boats were only a hundred or so yards behind and traveling in a line toward them.

The Pirate Queen headed up the stairs to the pilothouse. Ray and Jolie backed from the doorway as Piglet approached. "Belowdecks!" she ordered, and the crowd clustering in the gangway scattered. Piglet grabbed Malley by the collar as he passed by her. "Ready the cannons. We might see some action tonight. I'm sending the lubbers with you so we can have fighting hands on deck."

"Aye!" he grunted, and before Ray could wonder who the "lubbers" were, Malley pointed at him. "Come on, you bunch! I'll show you how to load the smashers."

Ray looked around at the others, but Conker and Si were already charging past him. Redfeather shrugged. "After you," he said to Marisol.

"I don't think Javidos is going to like this," she said, guiding the copperhead up her sleeve to hide.

Pirates raced around the lower decks, loading rifles and donning blades and holsters. Grim glee crackled on every pirate's face except Old Joshua's. He sank into a chair in the galley and began gumming the cheese left on the plates like it might be his last meal. Big Jimmie came past, carrying Buck to the Pirate Queen's chambers.

Ray grabbed Jolie's hand. "Come on." They headed into the crew's quarters, where pirates had already pushed aside the bunks to clear room around the cannons. The smashers were short-barreled, squat guns mounted on sliding carriages on either side of the room. The gun ports were half latched to keep the cannons hidden.

"Gather up," Malley said as he slapped a hand to the pommel of a cannon. "Technically speaking, these smashers are carronades. No good at shooting long-range, but great at tearing things up in closer quarters. Start rolling shot over here," he said to Ray, Conker, and Redfeather. "Si, get those rammers down from the walls. Marisol and Jolie, see those trunks. They've got gunpowder cartridges. Start stacking them by the cannons."

As everyone set to work, a voice cried out thinly from above, carried by the wind, "Hail! Prepare to be boarded."

Rolling a cannonball across the floor, Ray caught a peek out the gunport to see a man standing on the bow of the nearest steamer. He held a megaphone and wore no hat, as the whipping wind would surely have carried it away. But he was dressed in a black plain-cut suit.

The Pirate Queen's voice carried without such a device. "Under whose jurisdiction?"

The man raised the megaphone again to his mouth. "The Pinkerton Detective Agency, under the ordinances of the state of Illinois and the mayor of Chicago."

"We're not on land, Pinkerton!" the Pirate Queen roared. "You've no authority out here."

"You're suspected of harboring criminals," the man continued. "Prepare to be boarded."

"Harboring criminals," said one of the pirates adjusting the turnscrew on the back of a smasher. "Ha! We've got nothing but criminals on board."

But Ray didn't laugh. These were not ordinary Pinkertons. These were agents of the Gog.

Malley and the other pirates loaded the cannons, showing

the lubbers how to ram home the shot with rope-padded rammers.

As Ray handed Malley a parchment cartridge, he looked out the port. Two of the steamers were veering together to cut off the Pirate Queen's escape. A third remained at a distance. The last, the one with the agent who had hailed them on its bow, moved closer to the *Snapdragon*'s starboard side. Men with rifles began to line up against their railing.

"Full steam!" the Pirate Queen bellowed.

The *Snapdragon* lurched, accelerating through the choppy waves toward the merging steamers. Gunfire opened from the agents, pinging off the metal plates of the hull. Pirates whooped and screeched from the other rooms as they rushed up on deck to return fire.

A squeal of twisting metal sounded. Ray and the others held on to the cannons to keep from getting thrown. The *Snapdragon* trembled as it broke its way through the steamers.

"Open the hatches!" Malley called. As Ray dropped the latch on the nearest gun-port hatch, he saw the vessels pushed aside, their paddle wheels mangled by the reinforced bow of the *Snapdragon*.

"Run out!" Malley shouted.

Ray wasn't sure what he meant, but as the pirates gathered around the cannons, grabbing onto the rope tackles attached on their sides, he and the others caught on that they were pushing the heavy cannons out through the ports.

Gunfire from the agents began to pepper the gun ports.

"You lubbers take cover," Malley ordered.

"Javidos is really going to hate this," Marisol said, as she got behind an overturned bed and nestled the snake against her stomach.

Jolie grabbed Ray's hand and pulled him to the safety of the floor. "I need to tell you something."

"Now's not the best—" Ray began.

But Jolie had already continued, "My sisters are held captive by the Gog."

"Ready, boys!" Mally shouted.

With all the gunfire and chaos ensuing, Ray struggled to train his attention on what she was saying. "What . . . how do you know?"

"Two of my sisters found me in the lake," Jolie said. "They said Cleoma never made it to the Terrebonne. She never brought the healing waters."

"Fire!" Malley shouted. The cannons blasted, filling the room with deafening noise and the smell of burnt gunpowder.

As the smoke cleared, Malley peered out a hatch. "What!" he growled. "The smashers ain't smashed nothing on them boats."

"Some sort of heavy reinforcement," another pirate said.

Malley scowled. "Reload. This time with canister shot."

As Ray helped pull the cannon back from the gun port, he called across the barrel to Jolie. "Do your sisters know what happened to Cleoma?" he asked.

"No," she said as Malley reloaded the cannon. "The others grew sick, all the ones who had ventured into the Darkness. They have been drawn up the Mississippi, up here to Chicago. The two who found me—Ediet and Yvonnie—they were not sick. They followed the sisters to where they disappeared in the Gog's hall. But Ediet and Yvonnie could not stop them, and they were afraid to enter—"

The *Snapdragon*'s hull resounded with a boom, and Ray fell backward into Redfeather. Piglet screamed down the gangway, "What just hit us?"

"Wasn't it a cannon?" Malley called.

The door to the engine room below opened, and a pirate stuck his head out. "Something's on the hull."

"On?" Malley said quizzically.

Conker was the first to his feet, racing through the door and down the stairs to the noisy engine room below. As Ray came down behind Redfeather, he saw a group of pirates—the four firemen and the lone engineer who operated the *Snapdragon*'s steam engine—staring at one of the sloped walls.

"What is it?" Conker asked.

"Shh," a coal-blackened pirate said. "Listen."

Small clanks and scraping sounded through the wall.

"That's below the waterline, isn't it?" Ray asked, trying to understand what was scratching at the side of the steamer.

"Aye," the engineer said. "Iron reinforcement over a wooden hull. Good for protecting against hundred-ten pounders, but whatever that is ain't from a gun."

"Can't be a person neither," another pirate said. "Hit the ship too hard—"

A shrill grinding noise began. Ray covered his ears and backed away a step along with Redfeather.

"Something's drilling through!" Conker shouted, looking around at the pirates. "Have you got weapons?"

The pirates gathered their wits and drew revolvers and cudgels from their belts. The whining got higher and higher in pitch.

"It's coming!" someone shouted just as a section of the hull, a circle of metal-plated wood, shot across the room, clanging against the engine and nearly hitting several of the pirates.

Water gushed in. It struck their legs, and had the engineer not grabbed Ray by the arm, he would have fallen. Steam hissed as the water hit the blazing firebox. The room was rapidly filling up with lake water.

Conker had ahold of Redfeather, tugging him up from the gush of water. "Get up above!" he shouted.

"What's that?" a pirate squeaked.

In the water blasting through the hole, a circle of spinning saw blades emerged. But then the saw was drawn back as a hinged case covered the blades. In its place, nearly as big as the hole, was now a metal face made of brass, which looked to Ray like some catfish or grotesque bottom-dwelling amphibian. A series of metal whiskers sprang from its face, catching on the floor and engine and flexing to propel the clockwork beast forward into the center of the deck. It thrashed with a long tapered tail, smashing a pair of the pirates up against the ceiling. They fell into the water and disappeared.

The remaining trio of pirates opened fire with their pistols. Bullets scattered and sparked off the brass scales, and had the others not taken cover, someone might have been shot. Realizing their mistake, the pirates changed course, throwing aside their pistols and attacking with cudgels. Conker grabbed the coal shovel and swung it sideways like an ax, chopping through the tentacle-like whiskers that were pulling the creature closer and closer to the far wall.

"It's going to drill through the other side!" Si shouted.

With half its whiskers gone, the creature thrashed, trying to hit Conker and the pirates with the crescent fins on its tail. Conker caught the tail, encircling his arms around it to stop it from swinging. With a grunt, he slipped the tip through the opening and pushed. Ray sloshed through the water to join Redfeather and the pirates as they helped. The clockwork beast fought but could not keep Conker and the others from forcing it into the hole, stifling the spray of water gushing in.

"You've got it!" Redfeather cried. "Keep pushing."

As Conker leaned his weight into the creature's face, a clanking of hinges sounded. The mouth began to open. Conker fought to keep ahold of the monster while shifting his hands away from the rapidly widening mouth.

As the hinges parted wider, a circular set of jagged teeth extended. Once fully exposed, they were as wide across as the fish's body.

"Conker—!" Ray began to warn.

But Conker was already jumping aside, grabbing as many of the others as he could to pull them away. Ray leaped just as the circular teeth started spinning.

Released from their hold, the Gog's clockwork fish shot across the deck, propelled by the water pressure behind it. It hit the far wall, and the drilling teeth began immediately grinding their way through the hull. Water once more poured into the engine room.

"It's too late!" the engineer shouted from the stairs. "There's no stopping it. The ship's already sinking."

As Ray swam with the others toward the stairs and made his way up to the gangway, he could feel the *Snapdragon* already tipping to one side. Piglet was coming down from the upper deck. "What hit us?"

"Would you believe me if I said it was a fish?" Redfeather quipped.

Piglet gave a quick frown of confusion and then barked, "We're sinking. Time to get out of here. Follow me!"

Jolie and the others were abandoning the cannons. As Ray reached her, he grabbed her hand and crouched to take cover from the gunfire as they came out on the deck. The skies were an ominous green-black. Heavy, whipping rain lashed across the deck. Pirates were ducking behind the bulwarks, firing rifles at the two steamers bearing down on either side. The other pair of steamers that the *Snapdragon* had rammed were far behind now, their broken paddle wheels no longer able to propel them. Gunmen returned fire from the vessels, outnumbering the Pirate Queen's crew five to one.

The deck lurched to one side, taking on waves. Piglet lowered a dinghy from the davit. "Get in! The Pirate Queen ordered you six off first."

"But if you're boarded, you'll need us to fight!" Conker roared.

"You can't be captured!" Piglet shouted over the groaning of the sinking steamer. "Captain's orders. You don't have the Nine Pound Hammer, and this is a gunfight. We'll hold them off as best we can. Now get!"

Marisol climbed into the dinghy first, followed by Redfeather. "She's right!" Si said, pulling Conker by his hand. "Get in."

The *Snapdragon*'s cannons fired again, but with the sharp angle the sinking steamer was tilting, the shot fired high over the pilothouse of the nearest of the pursuing ships. Then a cannon blast tore into the *Snapdragon*'s aft hull, throwing splinters of metal and broken boards into howling pirates.

Conker snarled as he followed Si into the dinghy.

Mister Lamprey was roaring orders from behind overturned boats on the deck. Big Jimmie, Malley, and the others were firing with their rifles, blunderbusses, and scatterguns. The glass had been blown out in the pilothouse, and the Pirate Queen struggled to steer her sinking ship.

The black-suited agent called through the megaphone, "Turn over the Nine Pound Hammer and your ship might still be salvaged!"

"What did he say?" Conker barked.

Ray looked back toward the steamer in confusion.

"Hurry!" Piglet shouted at him. Jolie was already in the dinghy. He was the last still on deck, and as he started down, he saw a small boat ahead, bobbing among the rocking waves off the bow.

"Now!" Piglet said, grabbing Ray's arm.

A man was rowing the small boat toward the *Snapdragon*.

"What's that?" Ray said.

Piglet looked up. "Some fisherman too stupid to get out of this storm." She shoved Ray, and he toppled into Conker's arms in the dinghy. Redfeather rowed them out from the *Snapdragon,* trying the keep the pirate's sinking vessel between them and the line of sight of the Gog's men.

"They're done for!" Si shouted.

Ray looked for the little rowboat, but the wind—which was already heavy—rose up, throwing water in his eyes. The others in the dinghy staggered as it struck them too. The strange wind blew harder and harder until Ray braced himself in the bottom of the leaping dinghy. He looked back to see the pirates cease their firing to grab onto railings and brace themselves against the force of the cyclonic wind.

"What is happening?" Jolie shouted into Ray's ear.

The *Snapdragon* pitched up behind them on a huge wave, rising so high that Ray had to look up to see the steamer suspended atop an enormous swell of black water. With the steamer half filled with water and sinking, the *Snapdragon* slid back down as the wave rushed forward. The wave rose higher until it collided with the two steamers pursuing her.

The boats rocked over on their sides from the force of the wave and continued rolling until their bilges were exposed like vulnerable bellies. The steamers began to sink, their paddle wheels turning helplessly to catch water. Agents called out to one another from the waters as the boats went down around them.

"What just happened?" Ray murmured.

Redfeather fought with the oars to turn their dinghy. With the *Snapdragon* slowly sinking, the pirates began abandoning their steamer in the assorted dinghies and pirogues.

"Where did that wave come from?" Si asked.

"From him!" Conker pointed out into the storm.

Ray twisted in his seat. The raindrops poured into his eyes and he had to wipe back his sopping bangs from his face.

The little boat was rowing closer now. Through the dark, Ray saw a figure raise a hand in greeting. "Hoy!" he shouted.

"Who—?" Si began.

"Tempestuous night!" the figure bellowed with a laugh. "I've been ferreting you out for days. Had not the faintest expectations to locate you in this foul weather, but here I am."

Conker roared with laughter.

"Who is it?" Ray asked.

"It's Nel," Conker said. "Nel's here!"

As THE BOW OF THE *SNAPDRAGON* SANK BENEATH THE STORMY waves, the crew caught up with Ray's dinghy. The Pirate Queen stood at the back of her pirogue and watched with a cold ferocity as her beloved ship disappeared. Rosie rose up from the bottom of the boat between Mister Lamprey and Buck and snapped her jaws glumly at her mistress.

The Gog's men had made their way from the water to the remaining two steamboats, but with the paddles broken, the vessels drifted harmlessly away on the tide. "I'd murder every last one of them if I could," the Pirate Queen growled, her voice choking momentarily on the last word.

The worst of the storm had blown off to the east, but a cool, steady rain fell, masking the sunrise with steely, swift-moving clouds. Nel led the small battery of boats up the lake.

They came ashore on a wooded beach about a mile south of the Expo's grounds.

Ray stared in wonder at the old pitchman. His silver mane of hair was as wild as ever, and his cheerful eyes sparkled from his dark face as he opened his arms wide. Ray's gaze fell to Nel's leg, now returned, and even though Sally had already told him, he could not help but gasp.

"How did you find us?" Si said as she hugged Nel.

"Your telegram, of course," Nel said, wringing out his fez and gesturing with the wet hat to Redfeather and Marisol. "I received your message that you were traversing to Chicago. And the news that you were alive, Conker."

The old pitchman's eyes softened as he looked up at Conker. The two embraced for a long moment before Nel pulled back to whisper, "But I could not bring myself to believe it until this very moment. My dear boy."

Redfeather pulled his boat up in the sand. "Those agents will get word back to the Gog. They'll be after us."

Nel turned to the Pirate Queen. "Yes. Is there anywhere that we can take refuge?"

"Nearly two dozen pirates and some Ramblers," the Pirate Queen said, sneering. "Sure, we'll take lodging at a hotel. Won't even cause a second glance."

"There's someone who might harbor us, my lady," Mister Lamprey said.

The Pirate Queen scowled. "Who?" Then she rolled her eyes and sighed. "Jasper?"

Mister Lamprey shrugged. "Well, not Jasper, exactly . . ."

"All right," she said, casting a pained glance back at the lake. "Piglet, you come with me. Lamprey, tend to the wounded. The rest of you, hide the boats in the trees and stay out of sight until I return. Hammers cocked at all times, boys. The daylight will be upon you soon, and if anyone comes this way, shoot first and make introductions afterward."

A small whoop answered her as the pirates set to work. The Pirate Queen headed out on foot with Piglet. Conker knelt by Buck, offering to carry him, but the old cowboy brushed him away and rose weakly to follow Nel and Ray. With the pirates hauling boats and camouflaging them with brush, the group moved away from the beach and into the thick of the forest.

"What about Shuckstack?" Ray asked. "We heard the Gog sent men."

"Sent men, he did . . . and a Hoarhound." Nel gave a meaningful frown. He braced Buck's elbow as they stepped over a log. "But they did not find Shuckstack. They found me."

"What do you mean?" Conker asked.

"I had ventured out to Mother Salagi's cabin," Nel said as they reached a clearing dripping with rain and settled to the damp earth.

"I was returning home with young Gabe and Tom. We realized we were being followed. We attempted to hide, we endeavored to escape, but no matter where we turned or what charm I devised to throw off its pursuit, the Hound knew where I was. Something drew the Gog's beast to me.

"I sent Tom and Gabe back to Shuckstack, hoping the Hound would follow me. As I ventured farther from home, and the Gog's agents continued to hunt me, my suspicions were confirmed. I could not return, lest the children were put in danger. The charms that protect Shuckstack would keep them safe, but only if I was no longer there."

"How was the Hound able to track you?" Ray asked.

Nel clapped a hand to his knee. "My leg. Mother Salagi warned that it was bringing some danger. I realized what it was almost too late. It was a Hoarhound that severed my leg. And once my leg was returned, a connection of sorts remained. Connecting me to the Gog's Machine. His Hound has infected me in a way. The Gog's clockwork servants are drawn to me. But I can also feel the Machine, ever so faintly, and it is growing stronger."

He smiled gently at the worried faces around him. "Take heart. That is actually good news, because it means Grevol has not yet completed his Machine. And we must hope he still has much more to do before he can unleash his Darkness."

"So what happened to the Hound?" Redfeather asked.

"I destroyed it, but mind you it was not easy." Nel plucked his briar-wood pipe from his soaking-wet jacket. "And I escaped from the agents, as they were no longer able to track me. I surmised another Hound would be sent for me and, well, there was only one place to go." He held out his hands and smiled. "Chicago. And here I am."

"And it's true," Conker asked, "you made that wave out there that saved us? Your Rambler powers are returned?"

"I walk as a Rambler once more." Nel chuckled and stomped his foot. "In more than one way. But it is clear that I cannot stay with you. My presence will attract danger to you all. So quickly tell me before I go everything that has transpired. Leave out not a detail."

As the morning continued with a steady chill rain and the group waited for the Pirate Queen's return, Ray and Buck and Si, Conker and Jolie, Redfeather and Marisol all took turns telling their parts in the long journey. As the story brought Nel to the battle in the lake, Conker sat upright as if remembering something. "I thought I heard that agent tell the Pirate Queen to give over the Nine Pound Hammer."

"I heard him say that too," Si said, sitting up straighter. "Why would they think we'd have the real hammer?"

"Maybe they don't know the hammer I took from the Gog's hall was a fake," Conker said.

"But that would mean . . . ," Redfeather began, his eyes blinking rapidly. "What does it mean?"

Ray said, "It means the Gog might not have the real Nine Pound Hammer."

"Then who does?" Nel asked. All eyes shifted around to one another, hoping someone would have the answer.

Buck rose from where he had been resting on the ground and staggered to the log by Nel's side. "I was there when Stacker gave the Nine Pound Hammer to Grevol," he said in his gravelly voice. "I could feel its presence. It was the real hammer. But then later, when I was escaping Grevol's hall, I tried to go back for the hammer, to where the agents had said it was displayed, but I couldn't feel it."

"So somebody switched the real hammer for the fake one," Conker said.

"Who would do that?" Ray asked.

"The Gog can sense intent and truth in people," Buck said. "He knew things about me. With that stick he carries. But not from Stacker. When Stacker brought me to the Gog, I got the feeling that Grevol could not draw truth from Stacker Lee."

"He has strange powers," Jolie agreed.

Buck wheezed, "Only Stacker could hide something from the Gog. Stacker must have the Nine Pound Hammer. He must have hidden it somewhere."

"Why would he do that?" Ray asked.

A grim smile appeared on Buck's face, and then he broke into a ripping cough. Nel put his hand to Buck's back as the cowboy doubled over. When the cough had settled, Buck sat up weakly and wiped his knuckles across his lips. "There's only one reason why," Buck said. "To redeem himself."

Conker snarled, "That killer has no desire for goodness. After what he did to Si!"

"Buck, are you all right?" Jolie interrupted, leaning toward the cowboy.

Buck stared at his hand. Slowly he brought it down to rest in his lap. Black oily blood was speckled across his palm.

When night fell, the Pirate Queen returned. They gathered their scant belongings and set out under the cover of dark. Buck would not allow Conker to carry him but walked at Nel's side for support. Ray looked back to see the Pirate Queen kneeling to plant a kiss on Rosie's nose before the alligator waddled out into the lake. She would give some poor fisherman a fright, Ray thought.

When they reached the neighborhoods south of Jackson Park, the Pirate Queen stopped. "This avenue leads all the way to Buffalo Bill's coliseum. It's a wet night and not many on the street, but there will still be plenty turning out for Cody's show. We spread out. Going just a few at a time so we won't draw notice. Blend in with the crowds when you can. When you go in the main entrance, say to the ticket collector that you're Buffalo Bill's 'special guests.' He'll know what that means and show you where to go. Got it?"

The Pirate Queen checked her pistol, drew back her cloak, and holstered it. "I'll lead the first group. Buck, you and Conker and Old Joshua come with me."

After the first group had left, Ray waited with the others in a wet corner of the park. Streetcars and carriages clattered on the avenue nearby. The few people strolling home in the damp carried umbrellas or newspapers over their heads. Ray was eager to get somewhere dry, eager for a hot meal, but then what?

Every ten minutes or so, another group of three or four set out up the avenue. "Ray," Nel said, coming to his side and draping an arm over his shoulder. "You've done fantastically, my boy."

"Thank you," Ray said, watching Hobnob set out with Si and a couple of other pirates.

Nel lowered his voice. "I won't be coming with you."

Ray nodded bleakly. "Where will you go?"

"I've got something I need to locate. Something that will be critical for us to face the Gog. Redfeather and Marisol are coming with me. I need their assistance." Nel nodded to the pair. "They are proving to be quite capable, don't you think?"

Ray looked up to see the two talking to each other in the dark a short distance away. Redfeather was hiding his tomahawk beneath his coat as Marisol caressed Javidos at her throat. They had changed so much from the bickering pair he had endured crossing the prairie. Ray saw Redfeather lean forward and whisper something. Marisol laughed.

Ray smiled before turning his gaze back to Nel. "You don't want me to come with you?"

Nel lifted a crooked finger. "There is little time left, I fear. Locate Stacker Lee. If Buck is right, he must have the Nine Pound Hammer. I urge you to remember he cannot be trusted. He's dangerous. He's a killer. But he is our last hope."

"Then at last we'll be able to destroy the Machine," Ray said, his words filled with more confidence than his heart contained.

"It will take more than driving your spike into the Machine's heart to stop the Gog," Nel said.

"What do you mean?"

"Mother Salagi has helped me comprehend the Gog's full nature." Nel took his arm from Ray's shoulder and stepped before him. "You know what the Magog is?"

"The Machine. It's the Gog's soul."

"Yes, but more than that. The Magog is a being. A demonic force of eternal darkness. Many men over time have bartered their souls for the Magog. To be possessed by this being gives them great power and ultimately ushers forth great evil."

"Why didn't my father and John Henry kill the Magog when they destroyed Grevol's first Machine?" Ray asked.

"The Magog cannot be killed. It cannot die. But only its servant the Gog can carry out its evil. So even if you and Conker manage to destroy the Machine, Grevol can build a new Machine to house his possessor."

"So the Gog must be killed as well," Ray said. "That's what you're saying, isn't it?"

Nel nodded, his heavy lids covering his eyes in shadow. "Grevol senses my presence. I can use this to distract him. To draw attention from you and Conker while you go into the Gloaming. I will be checking in with Hobnob. Send word with him when you are ready."

Ray's eyes were wide. "Then what?"

"I alone must face the Gog," Nel said. "I must destroy him."

Redfeather and Marisol approached. "We should go, Nel," Redfeather said.

Nel put a hand to Ray's shoulder, and a careworn smile broke on his face. "Much depends on us, Ray. We face what no others can. We are Ramblers, after all."

He turned and pulled his collar up as he headed back into the trees. Redfeather and Marisol looked at Ray, and then they too were gone.

Ray and Jolie followed Mister Lamprey and Piglet up the avenue. They were the last to leave. "Nearly there," Mister Lamprey said. His cane clicked on the paving stones, and Ray saw the pirate's finger tapping the button that transformed the cane into a rifle. Piglet looked around cautiously as she walked hunched against the rain with a hand beneath her coat.

An enormous arena rose up on the next block. The four crossed the street, going under the elevated train tracks just as a train full of tourists rumbled overhead. They joined the back of the line waiting to get into Buffalo Bill's Wild West show. When at last they entered the warmth of the lobby and came to the ticket booth, Mister Lamprey said, "We're special guests of Buffalo Bill."

The plump, ivory-haired man adjusted his monocle and snapped a finger. "Gilley."

A freckle-faced young man in a white pearl-buttoned

cowboy shirt stepped from around the corner and said, "Right this way, folks." Piglet cast a glance over her shoulder and flashed Ray and Jolie a grin.

Gilley led them up a narrow stairwell winding up several flights until they came to a landing. They were at the uppermost level of the coliseum's interior. Ray looked down at the huge circular floor below, scattered with straw. The show had not yet started, and as the crowd filled the wooden bleachers, a regiment of hussar soldiers in full uniform paraded their horses for preshow entertainment. A small mock Indian village of several teepees was erected to one side, with Buffalo Bill's performers—men and women in Sioux attire—seeming to carry on their daily lives on the plains despite the din of the crowd filling the coliseum.

"Come on," Gilley said. He led Ray and Jolie along the balcony. Men operating mirrored gas-lamp spotlights watched as the four passed. A door was cracked at the far end of the narrow passage, and Ray heard the Pirate Queen's bellowing laugh.

Gilley stopped and motioned to the door, backing against the hewn timber of the railing. "Just in there," he said, tipping his cowboy hat to Piglet and Jolie as they squeezed past.

As he entered, Ray was struck by the stench of the soaking-wet pirates scattered around the room, sitting on crates and bundles of fabric. Lanterns hung from the rafters above what seemed a storage area for the show. The Pirate Queen stood in the center, talking to Mister Jasper and a tall man wearing an outlandish costume of bright silk and fringed doeskins. His long, neatly combed hair fell over his shoulders from beneath his chestnut-colored cowboy hat. A dark mustache curled across his lips, but the long goatee hanging to his chest was streaked with silver.

"A pair of jacks!" he bellowed. "That's all that stood between me and that steamer of yours. She wouldn't be lying at the bottom of Lake Michigan if you hadn't cheated, my dear."

"I don't need to cheat at poker, Bill," the Pirate Queen said, plucking a cigar from her pocket.

Buffalo Bill hastened to take a box of matches out of his coat, and striking one to his gleaming boot heel, he held it before the Pirate Queen. She grinned through clenched teeth as she leaned forward and drew several puffs to light the tobacco.

Bill brought the match down with a flourishing wave to extinguish it. "I must attend to my audience. A few at a time can watch the show from the balcony, but don't be obvious."

"I'm never obvious," the Pirate Queen said.

Jasper put a fist to his mouth as he gave a mock cough.

Buffalo Bill cocked an eyebrow around at the motley party. "How many did you say were coming?"

"This is all," Mister Lamprey answered.

Buffalo Bill gave a low humph and then said to the Pirate Queen, "After the show, meet me and Jasper down in my chambers. I think a few hands are in order. See if we can put bygones behind us."

She blew a stream of smoke sideways from her lips. "Looking forward to it, Cody."

Then he turned, casting a quick glance around the room at the pirates and drawing a handkerchief up below his nose before sweeping out. Jasper winked at the Pirate Queen before closing the door.

The Pirate Queen turned to Ray and Conker. Her smile had vanished. "He'll give us a few days at the most. Then our welcome will draw thin."

A few minutes later, a roar rose from the crowd below. The Pirate Queen let a few at a time go out onto the balcony to watch the show. But as Ray waited for his turn, he fell asleep on a folded curtain in the corner and did not wake until late in the night.

RAY WOKE AS A SQUARE OF MOONLIGHT FROM THE SOLITARY
window settled onto his face. The room was droning with
snores and snorts. Movement caught his eye—a pale arm and
an ankle passing out the doorway. Jolie.

He rose, careful not to rouse Hobnob and the other pirates
piled up around him as he inched across the sleeping bodies.
Conker grumbled and rolled over as Ray stepped over him. The
Pirate Queen slept atop a table, her arms crossed over her chest
and holding pistols. Buck had been given a cot, and his breathing came labored and wet. Si was curled beneath his cot.

Ray left the door open as he went out onto the balcony.
Jolie was not there. He listened until he caught the faint *tap-
tap* of footsteps going down the wooden staircase. As he descended to the lobby, Ray spied Piglet sleeping, her chair tilted
back against the main doors. A rifle lay across her lap. He

considered waking her, as she was clearly to be on guard duty, but decided Piglet needed rest as much as any of them. Nobody would come through the door without waking her.

As Ray entered the coliseum, the wide straw-littered floor was cast in moonlight. Looking up at the raised benches and balconies encircling the performance space, he again saw movement and the unmistakable sheen of Jolie's skin. Ray followed a short set of stairs leading up to the balcony seats, and as he maneuvered around from booth to booth, he saw Jolie watching him several rooms away.

He reached her booth. A dozen plush velvet seats filled the space, reserved for honored guests of Buffalo Bill's show. Jolie sat in the far back, her bare feet pulled up beneath her. "Did I wake you?" she whispered.

"No," Ray said, sitting down next to her and leaning back in the soft chair. "A lot more comfortable down here. Were you going to rest some more?"

Jolie shook her head. "I could not sleep even if I were in the ponds of the Terrebonne." She took his hand. "What are we to do, Ray?"

Ray felt her warm, slender fingers laced with his. He did not want to think of what lay ahead, he wanted only to hold on to her for as long as he could.

"We have to find Stacker Lee. He knows where the Nine Pound Hammer is—"

"But then?"

Jolie knew as well as he did what they had to do. This was not what she was asking. To defeat the Gog, Ray would have to hold the golden spike as Conker brought down the Nine Pound Hammer. They would not survive the Machine's destruction. And to save those afflicted by the Darkness, to restore the Wolf Tree, Jolie had to bring forth a siren spring.

The words lodged in his throat, and they came up as a choke. "We must sacrifice . . ."

Jolie leaned closer to him. "Conker does not fear death. He died already and returned again. But this time . . . this time . . ."

She could not finish. Ray brought his arms around her, drawing her against him. The armrest between their seats wedged uncomfortably against his ribs, but Ray leaned heavily against it, ignoring the pain. If only he could get closer to her. He needed her strength to comfort him.

"Leave, Jolie," he whispered. "Escape and go back to the Terrebonne. You don't have to do this—"

"Yes, I do."

Ray winced. "What about your sisters, the two who didn't enter the Darkness?"

"Ediet and Yvonnie abandoned me with my other *sirmoeurs*." Jolie's voice held no anger or resentment, not as Ray had heard before when she spoke of her sisters. She seemed to be merely speaking what was true, as if reporting the weather or stating the phase of the moon. "My sisters can be brave and fierce, but sirens care little for the troubles of mankind. I realize I am not like them."

"The Gog brings harm down on sirens as well. It's not just mankind who will suffer."

"I know this," Jolie said, leaning back to look at Ray. "But it is not how my sisters see what is happening. Ediet and Yvonnie intend to rescue our sisters held captive by the Gog and return to the Terrebonne."

Ray felt his temple throb. He fought to keep his voice at a whisper. "Didn't you hear what Buck learned from Stacker? Your sisters are lost. Their hearts are full of clockwork now! There is no saving them without the siren spring."

Jolie nodded. "Yvonnie said they had found a drain in one of the big fountains in the White City. They sense our *sirmoeurs* through the waters. They believe if they can remove the bars covering this drain, they can reach our captive sisters in the Gog's hall. They intend to bring them back to the Mississippi, to heal them in one of the hidden springs in the south."

"Your sisters will die before they get them there," Ray said, feeling a swell of guilt as he realized also that it was his father's fault that the sirens had been captured. If he had not called out to them through the waters of the Gloaming, they would never have entered the Darkness. But Li'l Bill had been trying to save the Wolf Tree. He had not realized what harm he was bringing. Nonetheless, Ray felt the responsibility was his to bear now.

"Yes, I know," Jolie answered. "They cannot escape the Darkness. I tried to tell them this, but they would not listen to me." She took a sharp breath. "I feel I am no longer one of them, Ray. I do not know where I belong, but I fear it is not with my *sirmoeurs*." Her voice grew quieter. "But what will this matter soon?"

Ray's thought of Buck's confession. If they were to defeat the Gog, and if all went as planned, wouldn't Jolie rather know who Buck was to her? But he had promised Buck. Ray bit his lip.

"Let us speak no more of this, Ray," she said, resting her head against his shoulder. "Please let us talk of better things."

"What's there to talk about?"

"Tell me again about your life in the city, before we met."

Ray laughed. "You've heard all my stories."

"Tell me again."

That boy from long ago seemed to bear no relation to who Ray was now. But as Ray began talking—remembering stories of better times in the midst of all those past hardships—Jolie stayed close to him.

Ray woke to the sound of voices echoing through the coliseum. Jolie lifted her head from where it had rested against his chest.

"Buck!" Si's voice rang out again.

Ray and Jolie approached the edge of the balcony. Morning sunlight glowed from the high windows above. Si was standing in the middle of the great floor below. Others were moving around adjacent booths. The Sioux family came out from their teepees at one side of the floor.

"What's going on?" Ray called down to Si.

She spun around. "Where have you two been? We thought you'd disappeared too."

Conker and Mister Lamprey came out onto the floor to Si's side, and Conker called to them, "Is Buck with you?"

"No," Ray said. "He was sleeping when I left—"

"How long ago was that?" Mister Lamprey asked.

"I don't know. Hours ago." Ray turned to Jolie, but she was leaving the booth, heading toward the stairs.

"He must be around," Si said. "He couldn't have gone far . . . not in his condition. He's been half out of his mind, mumbling about liberty's feet and such."

Ray raced after Jolie, taking several of the stairs at a time.

They met Conker and Si in the lobby. Piglet stood anxiously with her back against the front doors.

"Didn't you see him?" Mister Lamprey barked.

"Never came through here," Piglet said. Ray did not have the heart to reveal that she had been sleeping at her post.

"Where would Buck have gone?" Jolie asked.

Conker looked around anxiously. "Maybe he went for food or water and passed out somewhere in the coliseum?"

Hobnob came in, followed by the freckle-faced young cowboy, Gilley, who had escorted them up to the storage room the night before. "Gilley and I looked everywhere," Hobnob chirped with a nervous turn to his voice. "No sign of Buck anywhere."

Other pirates were filling the lobby, and the Pirate Queen bashed her way through. Gilley looked up at her. "Didn't see your man anywhere, ma'am. He must have left."

"Well, he didn't go out this door," Piglet said. While she must have been harboring guilt at her lapse in duties, Ray agreed: Piglet had been sleeping against the door. Nobody could have gone out that way.

"Are there other exits?" Ray asked.

"They're all locked and bolted," Gilley said. "From the inside. Guess that doesn't mean he couldn't have gone out."

"Still en't explaining why ol' Eustace would want to leave," Hobnob murmured, scratching at his yellow mane.

"The Gog's hall," Ray said.

"What?" the Pirate Queen barked.

"He told me," Ray said. "On the *Snapdragon*. He said he felt the draw of the Darkness. He's dying from the exposure.

It's the only thing that can save him. . . ." Ray's eyes darted to Jolie, but he said no more.

"Why didn't you tell us that?" the Pirate Queen said, rearing up in front of Ray.

"He said he couldn't get there," Ray explained. "He was too weak. I never thought he would actually try to return."

"He's probably not got control over it," Conker said. "Not anymore."

"We've got to stop him," Si said, pulling Piglet away from the door and turning the handle. As the door swung wide, Buffalo Bill stood before her, his big, costumed frame filling the doorway.

"Where were you?" the Pirate Queen snapped. "You said to meet you for some cards!"

Cody's eyes darkened, and he stepped hastily inside. He caught Si's arm in a firm grasp. "Nobody leaves."

Conker took a step forward, but Cody released Si's arm as he pulled the door shut and turned to bolt it.

"We've got to find Eustace," the Pirate Queen said.

Cody swung back to face them, his long blond hair scattering over his shoulders. His frowning gaze moved over the mob of pirates filling the lobby. "I said, no one leaves. Agents of the Gog are all over outside."

"How did they find us?" Ray gasped.

Cody's eyes moved from Ray to the Pirate Queen. "I've just met with Grevol. I've had to strike a bargain."

THE PIRATE QUEEN ROUNDED A PUNCH TO BUFFALO BILL, but he caught her fist before it met his chin. The leather of his gloves creaked as he pushed her fist away. "Hear me out!"

"You betrayed us," the Pirate Queen said, her face rising to a red brighter even than the flame of her long hair.

"He figured you were here," Cody said. "And after the show, Mister Grevol sent one of his agents to bring me to meet with him. I had no choice!"

"Don't you realize who he is?" Ray said.

"I do," Cody said. "Jasper and Iron Tail have spoken with me about what you are doing . . . and about Mister Grevol."

"So why are you helping the Gog?" Si snarled.

"I'm not helping him. I'm helping you!"

"By holding us prisoner?" Si said.

Cody gritted his teeth. "Look, if any of you leave, you'll be captured by those agents waiting out there."

"Why doesn't he just raid the place now and take us all?" Conker asked.

"Because he knows he already has you trapped," Cody said. "He ordered me to hold you in here until this other Rambler comes back. Someone he's been hunting but hasn't been able to capture. A man named Joe Nelson—"

"We've got to get out of here!" Si said. "We've got to find Nel!"

Jolie pulled Ray's arm, urging him back through the doorway to the lobby. He could see as well that things might turn worse at any moment. Conker was growing furious, and the Pirate Queen had her hand beneath her coat. She looked wild and dangerous, and Ray imagined that she would be the type of animal that would chew through her own leg rather than stay caught in a trap. But Cody, despite his flamboyant exterior, looked like the sort who had handled worse than her.

With his jaw set, Cody stood his ground before the door as Conker pointed over his shoulder and shouted, "We can fight our way through those agents out there!"

"And go where?" Cody said. "Grevol has an army at his disposal in that Hall of Progress. He showed me things . . . clockwork men and mechanized beasts . . . horrors you could never imagine."

"We don't have to imagine," Si said.

"Then you should know," Cody said. "You'd never get more than a few blocks before he would unleash them."

"In broad daylight?" Ray shook his head. "With all the crowds of fairgoers around?"

Cody shrugged. "Believe me, I'm sure that's something Mister Grevol would like to avoid. That's probably why he's waiting until tonight to come for you. There's some important guests arriving for the Expo today. Some king or prime minister or somebody, and Grevol can't have gunfights in the streets scaring off his dignitaries. But I'm sure if you all decide to run for it, he won't think twice . . . he'll send whatever horrors he's got after you."

Cody's expression grew grim. "I'm not sure exactly who you all are or who this Rambler Nel is that Grevol's after, but I know that you pose an enormous threat to him." His eyes settled on Conker. "You're John Henry's son. You wield your father's weapon. He would risk anything to stop you. He knows he has you cornered."

"So what do we do?" Ray said, seeing Cody relax somewhat as he seemed to feel he had settled the mob before him.

"Before I was a showman," Cody said, "I was a scout. I was a soldier out in the western territories. I fought in the Indian Wars. I was with Custer in Wyoming and led the first battle against the Sioux after his massacre. So I know war. And I know a losing fight." He looked slowly around at the group. "This here's a losing fight."

"You're expecting us to give ourselves up?" Conker growled.

"Of course not," Cody said, throwing out his hands.

The Pirate Queen crossed her arms over her bandoleered chest. "Then what are you saying, Bill? Illuminate us."

"I'm saying some fights you have to fight even if they are

losing ones." Cody jabbed a finger at the Pirate Queen. "I'll despise what you've brought down on me this morning, Lorene, until the day I leave this fine green earth. But I've never steered from a worthy fight."

"You'll help us?" Si asked, disbelief on her face.

Cody swept his hat from his head, pulled off his calfskin coat, and handed them both to Gilley. "I can't speak for my men. Most of them are performers, nothing more. And the ones like Iron Tail and me who've seen war have a few too many years on us to be much good. But you can count on me, for what it's worth."

The anger had diffused, but as Ray looked at the others, he saw the expressions around him change as the reality of the situation sunk in. And as he began to speak, Ray realized he was voicing the worry in everyone else's hearts.

"Even if we had your entire troupe, Mister Cody, even if we had an army, it wouldn't matter," Ray said. "A fight is pointless. We have to find Stacker Lee and get the Nine Pound Hammer from him. Grevol's drawing us into a fight to keep us from doing what we need to do . . . to destroy his Machine."

"And now we are trapped in here," Jolie said. "We cannot even search for it."

"Maybe we're not," Ray said.

"Not what?" Conker asked.

"Trapped," Ray said. "I can cross. I can carry at least two at a time into the Gloaming. What if we crossed, here, into the Gloaming and traveled far enough to get away from the coliseum."

"Would that work?" Conker asked.

"It should," Ray said. "It's tricky because travel in the Gloaming doesn't exactly match with our world. It's not like you walk twenty yards in the Gloaming, cross back, and then wind up twenty yards away from where you started."

"But could it be enough to get us out of this coliseum?" Conker asked.

"There's only one way to find out," Ray said.

"Hold on," Si said. "You won't know where you're crossing back. What if you wind up in Grevol's parlor?"

Ray and Conker looked at each other. Conker said, "We'll just have to hope we ain't that unlucky."

"Let me just try it," Ray said. "Alone. If I make it, I'll be able to follow the same path back here."

"Okay," Conker said. "Try it."

Ray closed his eyes. The group filling Buffalo Bill's lobby grew quiet, but Ray heard their breathing, their shifting feet, the noise of others in the coliseum moving about. He listened to the sounds outside—the clop of carriages, the shouts of vendors setting up along the street, the clank of the train on the elevated tracks. Ray let his focus shift from his surroundings to his body. He felt it lighten, grow smaller. He leaned forward and extended his arms, and as he waved his hands, he felt feathers catch on air.

He opened his eyes to see the others gathered around him gasping and watching with wide eyes as he took flight. He made a circle around the lobby, heading through the entranceway to the stadium, and then he crossed.

A bright light flashed, and before he felt himself fully through, he heard the roar of grinding machinery. He felt crushed on all sides, gears and churning parts tearing at his feathers. Quickly Ray pulled back, back into the flashing lights, back through to the stadium.

He landed on the sawdust floor in human form.

Jolie was the first to reach him. "Ray!" she shouted.

He gasped for breath, feeling as if his lungs had been filled with fumes and smoke. He held his hands up, certain he'd find that his fingers had been torn apart. He was unhurt, but pain still shot through his body.

Conker put an arm around Ray's shoulders to support him. "You okay? What happened?"

"The Machine," Ray gasped. "I . . . almost crossed into the Machine. Too close . . . here."

"But we've got to get to the Machine," Conker said, "to destroy it! How are we going to get into the Gloaming?"

Ray took a few more breaths and then held on to Conker's arm as he sat up. Si and the Pirate Queen and the others were surrounding him, looking down with anxious faces.

"The hall," Ray said, standing slowly. "We've got to get into Grevol's hall if we're going to cross. Marisol and Redfeather saw the people infected by the Darkness going down some stairwell. That must be where we have to cross. Anywhere else and we risk winding up in the Gog's Machine."

Si frowned. "Which only does us any good if we can get out of here. We're still trapped."

Cody pushed his way through the mob of pirates surrounding Ray. His eyes seemed to glow as he stared at Ray. "I've met a few Ramblers in my time. I knew they had strange powers, but what you just did, I'd always took as exaggeration and legend. Until now." He gave a crooked smile. "So tell me, Rambler. How many?"

"What do you mean?" Ray asked.

"I can't work miracles here," Cody said. "I'm just trying to figure how I can help you. I can't tell you where Stacker Lee is or John Henry's hammer, but I'm a planner. Some would say a schemer. Comes with the business. Now, say for a moment you knew where to find Stacker Lee, how many would you send? What I'm getting at is who needs to go and who can stay to fight?"

Ray nodded. "Conker and me," he said. "We'd have to go." Then turning to Jolie, he added, "And her."

"I'm with you too," Si said.

Ray expected Conker to argue, but he said nothing, so Ray looked back up at Cody. "Four of us."

"Good," Cody said, clapping his gloved hands.

"Why's that good?" Conker asked.

"Because the four of you might be able to escape notice." Cody had an odd tilt to his mouth, one that Ray imagined the old showman often got as he devised a new act for his Wild West show.

Conker frowned. "How you reckon we're going to escape notice if we're supposed to be handed over to the Gog along with Nel?"

"Because the four the Gog thinks he's being handed will not be you," Cody said, splaying out his hands like a man showing a winning hand. "And by the time Mister Grevol realizes it, you'll be long gone."

"Decoys," Ray whispered.

Cody pointed at Ray with a smile.

A murmur bubbled around the mob in the lobby.

"It's a good plan," the Pirate Queen said, digging into her

pocket for a cigar. "But the only problem is, what are you four going to do? Knock on the door to Grevol's hall and ask if Stacker is home?"

"She's right," Si said. "What good is all this if we don't know how to find the hammer? This is hopeless."

Conker spun around to face Si. "What did you say?"

She waved a hand at him. "Spare me the speeches, Conk, about not giving up hope—"

"Hope," Conker gasped, his eyes wide.

Si looked over at Ray. Ray wasn't sure what had caused Conker to grow so still, but he'd seen that expression before, that look on Conker's face when he was figuring out something critical.

"He's lost it," the Pirate Queen murmured.

"No, what is it, Conker?" Ray asked.

A smile crept across Conker's face as he clapped his coal-shovel hands onto Ray's shoulders. "I know where it is," he said. "I just figured out where the Nine Pound Hammer's hidden."

The day seemed to alternate between alarming velocity and painful slowness. Ray was not sure which he preferred, as every moment seemed ripe with apprehension.

Cody's men had another show to put on and carried out preparations as they would on any other day. However, up on the uppermost level, in the storage room, the Pirate Queen led plans for the confrontation ahead. Hobnob had been sent to find Nel, and Ray went often to the window to peer out for signs of his return.

Around two sides of the Wild West's encampment ran the

elevated train tracks. On the other lay the Expo's Midway, marking the entrance to the fairgrounds, with its odd jumble of exotic buildings and, rising above them all, Mister Ferris's enormous mechanical wheel. Beyond, tucked into the other buildings of the White City, Ray could see the black mass of the Hall of Progress, unassuming yet chilling. Buck must be there by now, he thought grimly. Was he lost to them for good?

Then his eyes went to a gap among the Expo's buildings, where Ray remembered the long fountain called the Grand Basin rested. He thought he could just make out a glint of gold.

"Big Mary?" Ray said. "The statue of the Republic."

"She's liberty," Conker said. "Remember what Buck said when Stacker threw him in the lake? Something about hope being at liberty's feet."

" 'Hope lies at liberty's feet,' " Si said. "He's been mumbling for days."

"What does that mean?" the Pirate Queen asked.

"Liberty's feet. That statue's feet," Conker said. "It means Stacker hid the hammer beneath Big Mary somewhere."

"So Stacker wants us to find the hammer?" Ray asked. "Is that why he told Buck that?"

Conker tapped a hand to his chin as he thought. "When I went into the Hall of Progress to get the hammer, Stacker started to say something to me . . . something like 'It's not what it seems' and then 'Didn't Buck tell you . . .' "

"Tell you what?" Si asked.

Conker shrugged. "I punched him then, so I don't know what else he was aiming to say. But now I think I do. I think Stacker was trying to say the hammer in the hall was a fake and that he had expected Buck to tell me something."

"Probably to have figured out his message about liberty's feet," Jolie said.

Si scowled. "Why would Stacker want to help us? Why would he tell us where he's hid the hammer?"

"Buck thought Stacker wanted to redeem himself," Ray answered.

Si held up her hand. "The same Stacker who did this to me?" she snarled.

"I don't trust him either," Conker said. "And if I see him again, he'll be sorry for what he did to you. But if he did it, if he hid the hammer beneath that statue, then who cares why. Tonight, this is our last chance. We have to go there and hope Stacker hasn't changed his mind."

There was a cough, and everyone turned. "How do I look?" Big Jimmie asked.

Ray watched as Conker strode slowly over to stand before the enormous pirate. Jimmie's face had been darkened with a stick of greasepaint Gilley had brought from the show's makeup room. Ray had seen plenty of blackface performers on vaudeville stages, but never anyone as large and ugly as Big Jimmie.

Conker had his hand cocked under his chin as he inspected the disguise. Fortunately Jimmie had thick, curly hair, which after being cut passed for Conker's. Conker continued stroking his chin as everyone waited. Then he erupted into a bellowing laugh. "You look preposterous!"

Big Jimmie chuckled uncertainly as the others slapped their knees and pointed.

"You're still about a foot too short," Conker said. "But you're big enough. Besides, this is what the Gog's men will look for." He handed Jimmie the hammer he had taken from the Hall of Progress. "Your Nine Pound Hammer."

"Good enough, given it will be dark," the Pirate Queen said. "Get out here, Piglet."

Two pirates had been holding up a curtain for Piglet to put on her outfit. She stepped out slowly, her hands crossed over her chest. Mister Lamprey had fashioned a green gown from some of the fabric in the storage room. Piglet was barefoot and seemed clearly uncomfortable. Her arms and feet were as pale as an egg, but her hands, neck, and face were sun-browned with abrupt edges at her wrists and neckline.

"I feel half naked," Piglet said, rubbing her hands over her bare arms. "Where's there to hide a gun?"

Ray looked at Jolie, who was blushing at the strange vision of herself.

"At your back," the Pirate Queen said, coming forward to brush Piglet's dark hair forward across her face. "We'll need powder to cover your tan."

"I'll get some," Gilley said.

"We'll get to it later," the Pirate Queen said, waving a hand before the freckle-faced cowboy could leave. "She'll just manage to smear it."

"What about me?" Big Jimmie asked. "It's itchy."

"Wipe it off if you want," Mister Lamprey said. "We'll touch you up tonight."

"Leaves just Si and Ray," the Pirate Queen said.

Si sat on a trunk with her back to the wall, watching the proceedings with raised eyebrows. "There's only one I know small enough to pass for me."

Mister Lamprey nodded. "Aye, you're thinking of Peter Hobnob?"

Si smiled. "We can paint his hand, but what about that nest of hair?"

The Pirate Queen turned to Gilley. "Have you got wigs?"

The boy nodded, tipping back his cowboy hat. "Yeah, we'll have something that'll work."

"Which leaves us Ray . . . ," the Pirate Queen murmured. Her eyes scanned the room full of pirates.

Ray looked around as well. They were all a gnarled, ugly bunch, not one of them besides Piglet younger than thirty.

The Pirate Queen was frowning. "Even with makeup and in the dark, I don't see one among you fair enough to be young Ray."

Gilley cleared his throat before saying, "I could do it, ma'am."

All eyes turned to the young man, and the room grew quiet.

"It's too dangerous," Ray said. "There's no telling what will happen, Gilley."

Gilley clenched his jaw and his freckled cheeks grew red. "I've been in fights aplenty."

"This ain't fighting," Conker said. "This'll be killing."

Gilley looked around at the crowd. "I grew up reading dime novels about Mister Cody. How he killed Chief Yellow Hand and all. Why I joined up. Not to be an errand boy and not to be a performer. I can do this. And besides, you need me, right?"

The Pirate Queen asked, "You know how to shoot a gun?"

"Yes, ma'am."

She clapped a hand to Gilley's back. "You're in. We'll be watching over you."

As the attention returned to the planning, Ray could not shake the fear—fear upon fear. This boy might lose his life tonight.

Jolie's hand slipped into Ray's and she whispered, "We all have to make sacrifices."

After a moment, Ray went back to the window to look for Hobnob, an unsettling feeling in his chest.

Evening came, and noise rose as the coliseum filled with the evening's audience.

"You bunch had better just stay up in here for the show," Gilley said as he came through the door. "Special guests tonight. President Cleveland's here, along with some governors and diplomats and whatnot."

As they listened to Cody's voice filling the stadium and the cheers and mock gunfights and laughter, Ray tried to stomach a meal but could not force himself to have an appetite. He gave his hat and coat to Gilley, along with a Solomon's seal root from his toby, hoping the charm would offer a small measure of protection as well as a bit of hoodoo in case Grevol was looking for it. Si had laid out her tunic and loose pants for Hobnob and dressed in a simple set of dark clothes she had found in one of the trunks. No other clothes would have fit Conker, and Big Jimmie seemed convincing enough with the greasepaint and the hammer. Jolie wore a black silk frock belonging to one of the smaller performers to cover her luminous arms.

Conker began prying apart the boards of the ceiling to open a hole to the coliseum's roof for their escape later. Si and Ray and Jolie passed around a whetting stone to sharpen their knives. Mister Lamprey had urged them to take guns, but all refused. They did not know how to use them, and as Si said, they would hopefully have no need for one. Fighting was not part of their plan.

The door opened, ushering in the laughter and voices from the audience. Nel entered, followed by Hobnob and Marisol. Redfeather shut the door behind them.

As Hobnob slumped into a chair, Si tossed her tunic, pants, and the wig into his lap. "These are for you."

The little thief lifted the wig with a horrified look.

"Were you spotted?" Conker asked.

"How could we not be," Nel said, removing his fez and coat. "There must be a hundred agents surrounding this stadium."

"There's something going on," Marisol said. "The crowd is huge. Lots of talk about somebody at the show."

"It's President Cleveland," Ray said. "He's in the audience tonight."

Nel's eyebrows leaped. "I was afraid of something like this. By any sort of logic, Grevol should have captured you all this morning. He's waited until night for a reason, and I fear it has to do with our special guests out there." He sighed grimly. "Even though I can feel that Grevol has not yet finished his Machine, it might be ready enough."

"Enough for what?" Si asked.

"For what he's conspired for these luminaries visiting the

Expo." Nel nodded to Redfeather. "Unfortunately I doubt we'll be able to convince President Cleveland's party to take any of my handiwork."

"Your handiwork?" Conker asked.

"These," Redfeather said, opening his satchel. "We were fortunate to find the right plants."

"We need to pass them out to everyone," Marisol said.

Ray looked curiously at the hundreds of tiny pouches Redfeather was spilling onto the floor. "What are they?"

"Protection," Nel said. "Protection for when the Gog unleashes his Darkness."

As the performance roared below, Nel made his way around the room, speaking quietly to each of the children of the medicine show. The pirates were loading pistols, polishing and sharpening blades, sipping rum, and inspecting the tiny pouches Nel had instructed them to wear around their necks. Ray had seen them face battles before, and they did it with glee. But not tonight. He sensed in their overly loud voices and sidelong glances that tonight was different.

"Ray," Nel said, as he sat down beside him on a trunk in the corner. The old pitchman clapped his large hand over Ray's knee. "Are you ready?"

"Is that possible?" Ray asked.

Nel shook his head. "My choice in words has become trite in the face of all that's before us. Forgive me."

Ray peered up at Nel. "You never have to ask that, Nel."

"But I fear I must," Nel said. He sighed heavily. "You know that I have spent my later days trying to shelter you all from the dangers of the Gog. And now, what I'm allowing you to do . . ." Nel leaned forward, his face in his hands. "Were I able to go in your place, I would," he whispered.

"I know."

"But the Gog would know where I was, and our plan would be ruined," Nel continued. "Go to the statue and retrieve the Nine Pound Hammer. Get into the hall. Reach the Gloaming—"

"I know," Ray repeated gently.

Nel's expression softened. He clasped Ray's arm.

"Nel?" Ray struggled to ask the question that was gnawing at him. "How will you defeat the Gog?"

Nel stood as he forced a smile. "Don't worry about this clever old fox, Ray. I'll create the necessary diversion for you four to stealthily make your getaway. Then I'll attend to how to defeat Grevol. Focus on your own task. We each have our part to play."

Ray could hear from the long applause that the Wild West performance was ending. "That's our cue, lads and lasses," the Pirate Queen said. One by one the pirates stood, holstered weapons, and headed for the door. Many of them stopped to shake hands with Ray, as well as with Conker and Jolie and Si, offering well wishes and encouragement.

Nel opened the door, and the pirates filed out onto the balcony. As the group crowded the doorway, Redfeather and Marisol came to say their goodbyes. Redfeather took the copper from around his neck and slipped it over Ray's head. "You might need it," he said, and then embraced Ray. "We are Ramblers," he whispered into Ray's ear before releasing him.

Marisol approached Ray. She leaned forward and kissed his cheek. Then she turned back to Redfeather, taking his hand before leaving.

The door closed. Ray was alone with Jolie, Si, and Conker.

As the next hour passed, Conker pried away the final boards to open a hole in the coliseum's roof. The four climbed through and stood on the flat, circular rooftop with the stars hovering above them. Si carried a coil of rope and set off across the roof, away from the others. Ray followed Conker and Jolie to the edge, where the raw plank siding of the exterior continued another few feet higher to make a low wall.

Below, the fence had been knocked down, and surrounding the encampment was now a wall of agents in black suits and bowler hats, each holding rifles and pistols. More were filing in from the Midway.

"How many do you reckon that is?" Conker asked. "A hundred fifty?"

Ray exhaled slowly. "Maybe more."

"Too many," Jolie said.

Between the Gog's army and the coliseum, the scant band of pirates stood in a cluster. The *Snapdragon*'s crew looked hopelessly few compared to the looming army of agents. Ray spotted the Pirate Queen's flowing red hair at the front of the group. She drew back her coat to place her hands on the arsenal belted around her waist. Nel stood beside her, tall and jaunty. Redfeather had his tomahawk against his leg, and Marisol held his bow at her side, an arrow already notched. Toward the middle of the group, Big Jimmie, disguised as Conker, towered over the other pirates, and Ray spied Gilley and Hobnob and Piglet beside him. From where Ray watched, the costumes were convincing.

Buffalo Bill emerged from the coliseum, followed by a contingent of a dozen men—cowboys, including Jasper and some of the elder Sioux, although Ray noticed Iron Tail wasn't among them.

Across the yard, a few of the agents toward the center of the formation stepped aside. A tall figure strode forward. He wore a silk stovepipe hat and a suit of black and green. With each step of his gleaming black boots, he brought an ebony walking stick to the ground. The Gog stopped when he was a few yards in front of his men, nearly a hundred yards separating him from Nel and the pirates. Nel had his toby in his hands, untying its string.

"I thought you said no harm would come to my Wild West show!" Cody bellowed.

"And none will, Mister Cody, if you hand over the Ramblers as you agreed," Mister Grevol said, touching a hand politely to his coal-black hat.

Cody waved at the wall of agents. "You've brought a gun to a knife fight, as they say, Grevol."

"I mean to dissuade you and your men from interfering, Mister Cody," the Gog said.

"Can't speak for my men," Cody said. "But I've been known to stir up trouble in my time."

Ray felt that for all of Buffalo Bill's tough talk, he hadn't gathered nearly as many to join him as Ray had hoped. Conker whispered, "We ought to go."

"Almost," Ray said.

He watched as Mister Grevol waved a gloved hand. "I see,

old Joe Nelson, that you've decided to join us. You've eluded me for some time."

"I plan on eluding you a bit longer," Nel said. The old Rambler drew out a handful of powder. "My powers are returned, as you well know. Allow me to demonstrate."

Nel scattered the powder into the air. A faint blue light glowed and then dissipated as it rose.

The moonlight snuffed out. A heavy sheet of clouds moved over the Expo grounds. Many of the agents turned their gazes up to the sky. A fierce wind rose, tossing bowler hats into the air. A few scampered to grab them, but most lifted their rifles, readying themselves.

Grevol began laughing. "Oh, is it parlor tricks, then, old Joe? I'm not one of your bumpkins watching your medicine show."

Conker clasped a hand on Ray's shoulder. "Let's go." He turned and stayed low until he was far enough from the edge to stand without notice. Ray and Jolie followed him until they reached Si. She had just finished tying off the rope to a brace of stout wood at the roof's edge.

Rain began to fall. A few heavy drops, and then all at once a torrent unleashed, like the lake itself had been dropped onto Buffalo Bill's coliseum. Nel had urged them to not leave until they were certain the Gog's men would have their full attention turned to the confrontation. The storm was the first distraction. Nel was buying them time, toying with the Gog so they could escape.

"After you," Si said to Ray as she handed him the rope.

Ray felt the rain streaking through his hair and running in cold rivulets down his back. He could fly. He could take crow form. But it would exhaust him. Tonight he needed all his strength.

Grevol's voice, along with Nel's and Cody's, carried through the whipping wind.

Ray looked cautiously over the edge. The elevated tracks bordered the coliseum. Through the ironwork of the tracks, Ray could see three of the Gog's agents on the sidewalk below. Lightning erupted, and the men flipped up their collars as they continued their patrol.

Ray grabbed the rope, looped it once around his wrist, and leaned back over the edge. He eased down, feet against the wet wood of the coliseum's exterior, and fed the rope through his hands. He stopped when he was level with the elevated track. Casting a glance down, he found the three agents hunched forward and cursing the foul storm to one another.

From around the side of the coliseum, Grevol's voice carried. ". . . this is the last time I'll ask. Give over the Nine Pound Hammer! Give over the Rambler's charm! The pirates can rot, Mister Nelson. I only need you and your Rambler urchins."

Ray kicked off the wall and swung out on the rope. When he was over the elevated track, he let go. He landed on the wooden crossties and crouched motionless, watching the agents for any sign that he had been heard. The three continued walking.

Ray pointed up to Si, and she handed the rope next to Jolie.

Ray dashed down the elevated track until the encampment came into view. Nel stood before the small cluster of pirates and Ramblers. Buffalo Bill was poised with his contingent at the back gates to the coliseum. The winds lashed, and rain beat against the earth of the yard.

The Gog cupped a hand to catch the falling rain. He laughed. "Who are you trying to frighten with your hoodoo chicanery, Mister Nelson? The earthworms?"

Nel drew out a twisted root from his toby. With a swipe, he directed the root at the Gog, and lightning flashed. The bolt drew down on Grevol, encompassing him in blinding light. The wall of agents shrank back as the thunderclap roared over the encampment. Even the pirates and Buffalo Bill's men backed away at the explosion.

Grevol had fallen to one knee, his pristine suit smoking in the pouring rain. He stood. The glowing knob at the end of his walking stick crackled as it drew the last of the lightning within.

"Not bad." The Gog took a step forward. "I would love to watch more, but it seems it is time to demonstrate what I have been working so hard to bring to fruition."

Jolie reached Ray's side and clutched his arm. Conker was helping Si to the elevated tracks. The three agents below were peering at the encampment, oblivious to what was happening above them.

Nel backed away as Grevol held up his walking stick.

"For years now, I have been gathering workers," the Gog said. "Constructing the greatest achievement civilization has ever known. A creation that will shape mankind, will better it, will bring humanity beyond its primitive ways and into a modern era. Once my Machine fills the people of Chicago, and eventually all the citizens of this great nation, with their new purpose, we will see an end to poverty, an end to suffering and conflict. They will have collective purpose. They will fill this land with towering cities and technology that our forebearers could never have dreamed."

Grevol tipped his head to Nel. "I am pleased you are here to witness this, Mister Nelson. You and your kind. You are the last of a backward, superstitious breed. You would have mankind live as animals, wallowing in the forests and reeking of sweat and decay. But I am helping to elevate mankind beyond the savagery you Ramblers so desperately cling to. I'm fighting to bring mankind into a world of greatness and industry. The future citizens of this nation will celebrate my triumph.

"Oh, I'm so pleased, old Joe Nelson." Grevol smiled. "Pleased you have lived long enough to see this historic day. Pleased you will witness the esteemed guests who sleep in our city tonight coming to fully embrace my vision for the future. Pleased you will join me as my Machine brings a new dawn for mankind."

The Gog grasped both hands to the walking stick before him. A pulse of green light bloomed from the knob. The light filled the encampment, and with it the terrifying roar of engines rose. Ray covered his ears against the deafening screams of grinding gears and the howls of spinning turbines. He staggered as he realized that what he was hearing was coming from beyond the barriers of this world. Deep within the portion of the Gloaming corrupted by the Gog, the Machine had come to life.

The Gog's walking stick dimmed.

The thunderous noises vanished.

The world became dark.

THE DARKNESS WAS SILENT AND COLD. RAY COULD SEE nothing, hear nothing. He reached to touch the track at his feet, fearing for a moment that even it might have vanished.

But then Jolie touched his arm. He grabbed her and pulled her tight so he wouldn't lose her in the silent ocean of black.

Conker brushed against Ray and, fumbling a moment, found a grip on his shoulder before gasping, "I thought we lost you."

Si whispered, "How will we ever—"

A solitary point of green light formed in the encampment. The knob on the Gog's walking stick gleamed thinly. At first all Ray could see were the knob and the green light illuminating the Gog's smiling face. But as Grevol began speaking, the knob grew brighter and brighter, casting its sickly green light across the agents massing behind him.

"Now it is over, Mister Nelson," he said. "The people of Chicago, our visiting president, and other fine leaders are falling under the Darkness's sway, as you all are by now. My clockwork sirens will be ready soon for any who resist this revolution. So embrace the future, Ramblers. Come with me."

From the lashing rain, a flame rose. Fire, true and orange and lapping high in the air. Redfeather held up his flaming hand, and the bright light spilt over pirates around him. Nel said, "Your Darkness holds no sway over us, Gog!"

The pirates howled, clattering cudgels and blades against the barrels of their rifles. Nel drew a tin from his toby.

The Gog snarled and waved a hand. "Men!"

The wall of black-suited agents rushed forward. The Gog marched toward Nel. When he was only paces away, Nel cast out the tin, and a powder flew from it. A wall of blue flame erupted on the ground where it landed. Grevol's suit was quickly encased in the odd fire.

The Gog waved his walking stick, and the flames whipped apart.

Nel held out his hands and the flames drew back to him, disappearing for a moment in his palms. He thrust his hands out, releasing the flames once more at the Gog.

The Pirate Queen's men spread out as the agents drew closer. But before the agents reached them, figures suddenly emerged from the cabins and tents scattered over the encampment grounds. Among the agents were now cowboys firing pistols and Sioux and Comanche shooting rifles at close range and swinging clubs and hatchets.

The pirates shrieked a terrifying battle cry and rushed forward into the fray. The confusion seemed to linger only a moment before the Gog's agents reorganized, positioning themselves to face the charging pirates while fighting Buffalo Bill's men in their midst.

Nel fought to drive Grevol back with the flames and other charms from his toby, but with his stick, the Gog batted away each assault.

"Mister Cody!" Nel shouted.

With the rain pooling in the brim of his hat, Buffalo Bill drew a saber from his belt and lifted it as a cavalryman leading a charge. Several from his contingent pulled open the massive gates at the back of the coliseum. Lantern light spilled out from the interior across the encampment. A line of horsemen galloped out—hussars and Cossacks beside vaqueros and Arabs. Horse hooves thundered against the muddy earth. Behind them raced Buffalo Bill's army. Indian and Mexican fighters, cowboys and soldiers. Iron Tail fired a rifle as he led his men. The Rough Rider congress rushed into the battle beside the pirates.

Grevol smiled. "Mister Cody, I thought a showman like you might resort to theatrics." Then Grevol called over his shoulder in a booming voice, "Mister McDevitt, you may release them now!"

Half a dozen steamcoaches entered the encampment from the Midway. Agents hurried to unbolt the back compartments. As the doors dropped, ghostly white Hoarhounds rushed out onto the battlefield, roaring and snapping their steel jaws.

"Let's go!" Conker shouted, hoisting Si to her feet. "There's nothing we can do."

Ray and Jolie ran behind them, the rain whipping against

their faces, down the elevated track and past the battle raging on the encampment. Soon they reached the huge train depot for the Expo.

Jolie pulled his hand, and Ray followed her into the empty cavity of the Expo's enormous train station. Tomorrow thousands of new arrivals would reach the White City. But what would they find? What future would be awaiting them?

Si led them to the far side of the depot, where wide steps spilled down to the empty streets of the Expo grounds. The electric streetlamps flickered with only a thin light to guide their way. It was as if the Darkness had filled the air with an oppressive phantom haze. The grand buildings loomed all around, the echoes of gunfire and cries reverberating off their facades.

"This way," Si said as they came around the corner of a building. She pointed to a long fountain filling an enormous empty courtyard. At the far end, illuminated faintly by the ghostly light, was the golden statue Big Mary.

"Ediet and Yvonnie," Jolie gasped. "My siren sisters. They found a grate in the fountain. A drain. They said that is where my captive sisters went."

"The Nine Pound Hammer must be down in that drain," Conker said. "Let's go!"

They raced down the length of the fountain. The dark clouds that Nel had drawn hung low over the White City, phantom tendrils whipping at the rooftops and being sucked toward the battle. The ominous winds wailed around them. Rain filled the streets.

A wagon with sanitation workers had stopped midway along the thoroughfare. The men were transfixed by the noise of gunfire and shouts beyond the Expo. They turned their heads to watch the four pass them and brought their dumbfounded gazes back to the flashes and chaotic noises rising from Buffalo Bill's encampment.

Jolie reached the far end of the fountain first and leaped over the low wall to dive into the water. Ray stood on the fountain's wall and looked up at Big Mary. She stood on a massive pillar, rising well over sixty feet in the air. Plated in gold, she held a globe in one hand and a staff in the other.

Jolie surfaced. "I found the drain. The grate is off it. My sisters must already have gone down."

"Can we get through?" Conker asked.

"I do not know what is down there," Jolie said, climbing out onto the stone edge. "The current pulls hard, and I could not get too close without getting sucked in."

"If Stacker got down there and back, then we can too," Ray said.

"Unless it's some sort of trick," Si muttered.

"Like he wants to drown us?" Ray said. "He'd have found a more inventive way to murder us."

"We have to act quickly," Jolie said. "I will go retrieve the hammer and swim back up. Wait here."

"Hold on, Jolie," Conker said. "I should go."

"You do not know what is down there. I can breathe under the water and swim back out."

Conker hesitated before saying, "Well . . . be careful."

Jolie nodded. She exchanged a glance with Ray before diving into the water and disappearing.

The minutes passed as Ray anxiously watched the water.

After a time, Conker murmured, "She's been gone longer than I figured. How could Stacker swim down that drain and back and still hold his breath? That's what I want to know."

"Maybe he didn't," Si said. "Buck said Stacker wandered at night. He'd located the captive sirens, and Jolie said that drain is where the sirens entered Grevol's hall."

"So what's that mean?" Ray asked.

"Stacker might not have gone down this way," Si said. "There might be a way to get beneath Big Mary without going through the fountain. Some passage that Stacker discovered."

Conker knelt to the sidewalk, putting an ear against the ground. He rose quickly. "It's hollow beneath. I hear the echoes. There's some big chamber down there."

He leaped over the wall and splashed into the fountain.

"What are you doing?" Si asked, reaching for him.

"I've got a bad feeling," Conker said. "Something's not adding up here. I'm going down after her."

"What?" Ray said, leaping into the fountain, followed by Si.

"Conker, wait!" Si shouted. But he plunged beneath the dark surface.

Ray looked at Si. "What do we do?"

Si furled her brow. "Come on."

She and Ray took deep gulps of air and went under. It was not hard to find the drain. The water drew Ray to it with a powerful force. Fear rose. Fear of drowning. Fear of losing their lives in the fountain while Nel and the others fought to keep the Gog's attention away from the Hall of Progress. All for nothing.

Ray touched the rim of the great drain and felt Si's legs disappearing into it. He fought a moment against the pressure. He needed more air. He wanted to rise again for another breath, but the force of the water pinned him. His legs pulled into the opening, and he clutched at the sides with his fingers. But they were not strong enough.

He let go and was sucked down.

Ray found himself falling. There was a brief moment of open air, enough to trick his lungs into gasping, before he landed in a pool. His feet struck the bottom, slimy and thick with loose debris. He choked and fought to find the surface.

As he broke out, Ray coughed up water that stung his nose and made him retch. He realized he could stand. He could see nothing in the dark, but the echoing told him it was an enormous chamber.

"Conker?" Ray choked.

A hand clasped his back. "Quiet," Conker whispered.

Ray felt Si on his other side. The three huddled together and moved away from the roaring waterfall behind them.

"Ray." Jolie's voice came from the dark ahead.

When they reached her, Ray hissed, "What is this—?" But his words were cut off by the unmistakable click of a hammer being drawn back on a pistol.

Conker called out, "That you, Stacker?"

Light bloomed above the water several yards away as Stacker Lee pulled a hood from a lantern. It cast a thin light over the water, illuminating the clockwork killer in part as if only half a man, the rest consumed in darkness.

Stacker lifted the lantern, and a beam of light reflected from his hand. A pistol. He turned the long-barreled Buntline back and forth, making it flash in their eyes. He smiled as if this amused him. Stacker was standing on a stairway coming up from the water and leading to a small shadowy hallway. Next to the hallway, a series of wide pipes, smaller than the one they had come through, protruded from the brick walls, dumping more water into the basin.

And standing behind Stacker in the shadows was Buck.

Jolie started forward. "Buck! You are alive!"

As Ray peered up at him, he saw that Buck was struggling to speak, his long hair drenched with perspiration and his ashen face ragged. "It's . . . it's . . ." A wet cough brought up black drops that speckled his lips. "Trap," he gasped.

Stacker Lee gave Buck an amused look. "Yes, brave Buckthorn. I found him wandering last evening in the dark. I was certain he was being drawn by the Darkness back to Grevol's hall. But you will be pleased to hear that he was fighting those urges, trying to make his way to the liberty statue above us. Yes, despite your dimwittedness, Buckthorn, you did figure it out and come at last."

"So you never had the Nine Pound Hammer?" Conker growled. "This was all a trick."

Stacker gave a look of mock hurt. "No, of course not. I have the hammer right here." He motioned with his pistol to the top of the stairway behind him, and Buck and held his lantern higher.

Lying on the muddy bricks was the long-handled hammer. Its iron head gave a dull gleam, showing the octagonal faces covered in nicks and scars.

"Buck was right, then," Ray said. "You're helping us!"

Stacker broke into laughter. "Oh, Buckthorn and his grand notions. No, I'm not that generous. Let me explain what's going on here."

"I've had enough of your toying." Conker lurched forward, dragging his legs heavily through the water. "After what you did to Si, you know I ain't going to let you out of here in one piece—"

A girl sprang up from the water behind Conker. Long blond hair fell wet over her face and down across her green woven gown.

Conker's eyes widened. Then he growled and rushed forward past her toward Stacker.

The girl drew a shell knife from a braided belt at her waist and opened her mouth to release a piercing note.

Conker fell to his knees with a splash. The muscles across his back trembled as he struggled to rise. But the siren's note held him.

"Yvonnie!" Jolie cried.

Ray and Si slogged forward to help Conker. Another siren rose from the water before them. Her mouth widened, and her teeth shone against dark lips as a shell knife flashed up in her hand. The song struck Ray, terrible and stabbing. He tried to clamp his hands over his ears, tried to shut off the siren's voice, but he could not move. Si continued toward the one who had Conker, but as the siren pointed the tip of her knife at Conker's back, Si stopped, her teeth gritted with rage.

"*Sirmoeurs!*" Jolie shouted. "Release them!"

The sirens ignored her, glaring at their captives and issuing high, shrieking songs.

Jolie drew her own shell knife. But Yvonnie gave her a fierce look and pushed her blade against Conker's back, drawing a spot of blood on the back of his shirt. As Jolie looked over to the other siren, she held her knife against Ray's neck.

She turned angrily to Stacker. "What have you done to them?"

"I assure you," Stacker said, "I have no power over your sisters. They act of their own accord, for they understand our common aim."

"What do you mean?" Jolie asked.

Stacker reached back to pull Buck down the steps until he stood before him. Then he looked at Jolie pointedly and raised his pistol to Buck's head.

"Yes, I'm pleased you've joined your sisters," Stacker said to Jolie. "For I was counting on Buckthorn luring you to me."

"Me?" Jolie asked. "Why do you need me?"

"The Darkness has arrived. Grevol has forsaken me."

"What is it you want?"

"You are a siren." Stacker smiled at Jolie. "You will save your sisters held captive by Mister Grevol. And by doing so, you will also save me."

"No!" Ray cried. But Ediet's gaze was on him again, and her song stabbed into his skull.

"A siren spring," Stacker said. "I was so close once. Had I realized how such springs arose, I would not have left so quickly after killing your sister. What was her name? Cl—Clema—"

Jolie gasped. "Cleoma!"

Stacker's eyebrows rose in mock sympathy. "Yes, that was

it. Cleoma. I wonder if she created those healing waters. That's neither here nor there at this juncture. And your sisters have forgiven me my trespasses. For they want their sisters freed. Brave though they may be, Ediet and Yvonnie cannot bring themselves to do what is required to save the others. You, however, dearest . . ."

"What do you want of me?" Jolie asked again.

"I simply want to know if you love Buckthorn."

"Let him go," Jolie pleaded.

"And I hope to," Stacker said. "I've grown quite fond of Buckthorn after all. Please don't make me do anything wretched to him . . . to convince you."

Jolie hurried toward the staircase rising from the water, saying, "Convince me of what?"

As she reached the first step, Stacker responded by pressing the barrel of his pistol harder into Buck's cheek. "At-at. Stay right there."

Jolie stopped, her shell knife pointed down but her grip on the handle so tight her hand was trembling.

"Now, Buckthorn," Stacker said. "We need to convince our young siren. Jolie, is it? Convince Jolie that you are worthy of her love." Stacker flashed his teeth—half a snarl, half a smile. "I need a siren spring to rid my heart of this clockwork. Jolie can create one. But you, my blind friend, must convince her."

"I will convince her of nothing," Buck said. "I am no one to her."

Stacker smirked. "You forget, I have a way of understanding things, Buckthorn. Call it a gift. I have even figured out who you are to the girl."

Buck lurched back against Stacker's body. Stacker tightened

his arm around Buck's chest, pushing the Buntline pistol so hard into his face that Buck had to tilt his head to one side.

"Tell her who you are," Stacker said through gritted teeth.

"I will not kill myself to make the spring," Jolie said, and threw her knife with a splash into the water.

"Will you watch your friends die one by one?" Stacker asked, regaining the cold smile on his face. "I think not. Pick up the knife!"

Jolie did not move. Ray squirmed, testing Eviet's hold over him, but there was no escaping her song. He felt as if he could hear Jolie's thoughts, her struggle to escape Stacker's trap. If she did not kill herself, did not form the siren spring, they might all die by Stacker's pistol.

And if she did, then wasn't that her aim all along? She had come into the White City with the intent of sacrificing herself to form the spring that would heal the Wolf Tree, end the suffering of those afflicted by the Darkness, free her sisters. What choice did she really have? Except that to form the spring here might not get the healing water to her sisters. She had to create the spring beneath Grevol's hall. It was a risk.

Stacker nodded to Jolie. "Retrieve your knife." She glared at him. Stacker called out to Yvonnie and Ediet, "Bring the others closer. If I lose Buckthorn, I'll need other incentives. Who will die after Buckthorn, Jolie? Conker? Your old travel companion Si has already suffered my wrath. The boy I don't know, but I sense your affection for him. He will do just fine."

Against every urge to do otherwise, Ray walked forward, dragging his feet through the basin. Jolie knelt slowly and found the knife. Her knuckles were bone white as she clutched the shell's whorl handle.

"Now," Stacker said. "I've been distracted from my aim. Ah, yes. Buckthorn, you were telling Jolie who you are. It took me a bit to unravel it. Grevol discovered your connection to the sirens when we first arrived in Chicago. And I sensed something too. Pieces that did not come together until you tried to strangle me. Only then did I realize why you would be so upset over a siren's death. So go ahead, Buckthorn. I think it's best that you tell her."

Buck did not struggle this time, but he made no sound, his lips drawn tight.

Stacker sighed heavily. "If I must. Jolie, my dear friend Buckthorn here is your—"

Buck threw his head back, his skull striking Stacker's face with a crack. Buck grabbed Stacker's gun hand and pulled it down. Stacker howled and pitched forward onto Buck. The gun fired, echoing loudly around the chamber.

Buck was on one knee with his hands to his chest. Ray heard a terrible wet hissing coming from him as the cowboy gulped and gasped for breath.

Stacker stood, the pistol no longer in his hand, and sneered at Buck. He lifted his boot and kicked the cowboy with the heel. Buck splayed on the stairs, his hands falling out at his sides and smacking heavily on the wet stone. He did not move.

Jolie screamed. As she reached the top step, Stacker swung backhanded across her temple. Jolie fell from the steps, splashing into the water. She rose to her feet, a ribbon of blood running down her face. "No! No!"

"Let us try again," Stacker said calmly, motioning to Ray, "with another."

Ediet locked her eyes on Ray, the wail of the sirens' songs

filling the chamber. Ray ascended the steps. Si watched helplessly. Conker fought to stand but then fell back until his face was nearly submerged in the water.

"The knife, Jolie," Stacker said, taking Ray by the shirt collar. "Let no more die for you. You can make it quick. I find no pleasure in your suffering. You have this final task before you. Sacrifice your life and spare your friends."

Serenity came to Jolie's face. She took a step toward her sisters. Stacker snapped open his razor. Ray felt the blade draw up against the soft skin of his throat. Jolie's gaze met Ray's and a subtle flicker came to her eyes. An apology, maybe? A reassurance that she would not let Stacker harm him?

Jolie turned the shell knife around and with both hands placed the narrow point against her chest. Ediet and Yvonnie's eyes widened. Jolie faced Stacker. "Before I do this," she whispered, "I must know. What did you want Buck to tell me?"

Stacker licked his lips and gave a weary smile. "He was your father. You did not know this, did you? Even your sisters never told you."

Jolie squeezed her eyes shut and when she opened them, tears streamed. She whispered, "Then I am glad he will not see—"

The gunshot did not seem as loud as the last one. Maybe all the blood roaring in Ray's ears and the terrible siren song dampened the explosive noise. Ray's vision felt hazy, his mind thick and unable to understand at first what had happened.

Then he felt Stacker's falling hand brush against his chest and watched the razor clatter to the wet stones and disappear into the water. Ray looked back. Stacker was still standing, but his mouth parted wordlessly and his eyes stared upward.

The fabric of Stacker's shirt was torn and burnt. Pieces of metal protruded from his chest. The teeth of a small gear still turned rapidly.

Buck lay flat on his back, his head lifted only slightly. Stacker's long-barreled pistol smoked in his hand. Buck gasped, barely audible, "It's . . . never . . . too . . . late. . . ."

The next shot exploded, and Stacker fell into the basin. His crisp Stetson hat landed a few feet farther and was set adrift in the dark waters.

Buck's gun hand dropped against his stomach, and his head fell back against the wet brick as he wheezed and gasped for air.

The sirens stared at Stacker's body floating in the basin. Ray realized their song had stopped. Conker stood up slowly from the water. Si ran to his side, glaring at the sirens.

Yvonnie cowed a few steps back, her knife held out protectively before her. Ediet watched them fearfully and backed behind her sister. Then as Ediet's eyes found Jolie, tears streamed down her cheeks. *"Sirmoeur,"* she whispered. "Forgive us."

Jolie looked away without acknowledgment. She climbed the steps, hurrying to Buck.

Conker growled as he faced the sirens. "You'd force Jolie to sacrifice herself? You are no sisters to her!" As he reached for Ediet, Yvonnie had her by the arm. The two dove into the water, coming up at the wall where the pipes protruded. With a leap, one after the other the sirens entered the mouth of one of the pipes and disappeared.

As Ray turned back, Si was already rushing up the stairs to Buck. Ray and Conker quickly joined the girls.

"Buck," Jolie whispered, taking his face in her hands. The

cowboy lay motionless on the wet stone. Blood pooled around him. His eyes did not open. A thin hiss came from his lips. The gunshot had punctured his lungs, and Ray knew the cowboy would speak no more.

Slowly Buck took Jolie's hand. Tears ran down her nose and spilled onto his beard. She kissed his hand and said, "*Patriear.* Father. You—you should have told me.'"

Buck squeezed her hand. Si reached forward and stroked back the old cowboy's hair. Ray took Stacker's pistol from him and set it on the wet bricks. Buck had given up his guns to set himself on a new path. But now, at this final moment, he had taken them up again. His choice had saved Jolie.

Conker laid a hand on Buck's shoulder. "We're all here. We're all with you, Buck."

Buck's mouth relaxed, the cracked lips settling into a faint smile. The four knelt together at Buck's side. After a few moments, Jolie brushed a hand across her eyes and let go of Buck's hand. "He is gone."

You've done it, Ray thought. Whatever pain you've carried in your heart, Buck, you've let it go. You are redeemed. Be at peace.

Conker stood and walked to the top step. He knelt slowly and picked up the Nine Pound Hammer, the lantern light flickering off the iron head with a hint of iridescent sheen. As he came back down to Si's side, she put her arms around Conker's waist and the two looked down at the old cowboy. Ray held Jolie close. "He only wanted your love."

"He should have known," Jolie said, not taking her eyes from her father. "He had it all along."

JOLIE STARED AT THE PIPES PROTRUDING FROM THE WALLS. "They have gone to my captive sisters," she said. "I must follow them."

"They betrayed you!" Ray shouted.

Jolie looked at him sorrowfully. "Yes, but I still must go. It was not hatred for me that drove them to betrayal. It was love for our *sirmoeurs*. And the only way for them to be saved, for the Wolf Tree to be saved, is for me to form the well beneath Grevol's hall. I must go."

Conker walked solemnly to Jolie and embraced her. Si hugged Jolie next, speaking to her, but her words were lost to Ray.

His feet felt leaden and fixed to the floor. Once Jolie disappeared into the pipe, he would never see her again. Conker and Si backed away from Jolie, and she approached Ray. She stood before him, her arms hanging helplessly at her sides. Ray was trembling, a slight shaking that he could not master.

"At least we both will die," she whispered, so soft that Ray was certain Conker and Si could not hear. "I could not bear it if I were to live after you had given your life."

Ray could say nothing.

Jolie's hands came up to cup his face. A fragile smile emerged, and she lifted onto her toes until her lips met his. The kiss was short, too short for him, but all his time with Jolie had seemed fraught with fleeting moments.

She stifled a sob as she pulled away from him. She hurried to the opening of the pipe and crawled into the gushing water, crouching in its spout as the water broke against her body.

"Jolie!" Ray cried. She looked back. Her eyes were pleading, and there was so much more Ray wanted to say, so much more time he needed with her before they were parted for good. But his words seemed fixed in his throat

Jolie looked around once more at her friends, her gaze gentle and assuring. Then she disappeared into the dark.

Ray could not move. He felt frozen with pain and fear.

Conker stood at his side and held Ray's shoulders. "I need you, Ray. We must go."

Ray nodded. Conker did need him—to hold the spike, to help destroy the Gog's Machine. All counted on his bravery. They each had their part to play. They each had their sacrifice to make. He took a step, and then another, and reached down to pick up the lantern Stacker had left on the floor. Si was kneeling again at Buck's side, brushing a hand gently across his face.

Conker stood over her. "Si—"

"No," Si said. "I won't."

Conker sighed. "I said you could come with me part of the way. But now it's time. . . . Stay with Buck."

Si stood and snarled, "Tie me up, then, or break my legs! I won't leave you!"

Conker reached out to take her hand, but she pulled it away sharply. "Si," Conker said gently. "We go to our deaths. The burden is already too big. For you to die when you don't have to . . . I can't bear it."

"Mother Salagi said I'd come to a crossroads! Don't you remember? I'm not there yet."

"Please don't—"

"I'm not there *yet*!" she shouted.

Ray saw what Conker surely did. The ferocity on Si's face. They would have to restrain her if they were to keep her from coming with them.

Conker asked, "Will you go back before Ray and I reach the heart of the Machine?"

"Yes," Si agreed eagerly. "I'll find a way back. I promise I will."

"I don't know if there will be a way," Ray said. "Once we cross, I'm not sure I'll be able to lead you back."

"Just let me come farther," Si said. "Just a little farther. Please don't leave me yet, Conker."

Conker looked at Ray. There was nothing Ray could say. "Okay," Conker said, holding out his hand once more. This time Si took it. Ray held up the lantern, and they followed him into the tunnel.

The passage was narrow, and Conker had to crouch and walk sideways. Through the slimy brick walls, Ray could hear the gurgling pipes carrying water from other fountains or buildings or various places around the White City. Somewhere in there, Jolie was making her way to her sisters. Could she be just on the other side of the wall?

He knew if he let his thoughts linger, he would not be able to face what lay ahead. Ray brought his hand to the toby hanging around his neck. He felt the hard edge of the golden spike. He continued on.

Soon they were in a hallway, warmer and moist with the stormy air outside. Conker whispered, "This is the lower level of the Gog's hall. I was here before. The garbage chute is down there, and the service exit that goes outside."

"Probably the agents are all at the battle," Si said, holding her knife before her. "Probably . . ."

"How do we get to the main floor?" Ray asked. "We have to find that back stairwell where Redfeather and Marisol saw the victims of the Darkness go."

"Follow me," Conker said.

They reached a doorway to a series of stairs, and one flight up they came out on the Hall of Progress's main floor. The shadowy displays rose up around them, exhibits and booths showing visitors the wonders Mister Grevol promised would better their world.

Conker peered around at the high ceiling and cocked his head to listen. "I don't hear no one," he murmured.

"Marisol said the stairwell was in one of the back corners," Ray said.

They crept down the walkway between the exhibits, turning occasionally to maneuver the maze of displays. Ray lowered the lantern. "Did you hear something?"

"What?" Si asked. Then her eyes widened.

Footsteps. Low and rhythmic, echoing slightly in the massive space.

"Agents?" Si hissed.

"I got a bad feeling they ain't agents," Conker said. "Hurry!"

They ran, following the walkway toward the tower at the hall's center. As they reached the junction where rows of displays extended in different directions, Conker pointed. "Back that way!"

Ray raced down the aisle. Movement caught his eye. Spinning around, he saw them—scores and scores of clockwork men, their brass skin shining in the dim light of the hall, marching down the rows.

As they ran, Conker said, "They weren't working when I was here last. Must have left them active this time."

They reached the back wall, the walkway going right and left. "Which way?" Ray asked.

"Don't know," Conker said.

Ray looked back to see the clockwork men coming down the aisle, their expressionless faces fixed. Si held up her tattooed hand a quick moment before she seemed to remember that it could no longer guide her. With a curse, she sprinted to the left.

They passed a walkway, where three clockwork men stepped out. Conker rushed ahead of Ray and Si, swinging his hammer in swift blows, sending the broken automatons into a display of small engines.

"Go! Go!" Conker urged.

The aisle ended at the far corner, and a passage continued to the right, away from the displays. Ray ran to the first door.

He opened it and saw a set of desks stacked with papers, inkwells, and ledgers.

He went to the next door and the next, opening each one only to see more desks. When they came to the final door at the end of the hallway, he cried, "They're just offices!"

"Must have been the other direction," Si said.

The three peered back down the hallway. Dozens of clockwork men filled the passage, marching closer and blocking their exit. Conker's face knotted fiercely. He lifted the Nine Pound Hammer. "Stay behind me."

He rushed toward the automatons, swinging the hammer. The heavy iron head clattered on their armor. Metal twisted. Steam hissed. As several automatons took hold of Conker's arms, Ray feared the clockwork men would overwhelm Conker. But with a roar, Conker wrenched his arms free and quickly swung the hammer around. Brass heads and molded arms snapped from the nearest clockwork men. The ones coming behind were soon unable to reach Conker through the mass of broken automatons.

Conker leaned his huge body into the pile of smashed and severed parts. Pushing and grunting, he reached wide to contain the heap. Step by heavy step, he drove the tide of automatons back with all his strength. Ray and Si followed behind him as pieces fell to the ground around them, severed limbs, gears and forged parts, molded plates from shoulders, chests, and legs.

After several yards, Conker forced the wall of clockwork men back onto the exhibit floor. With one last heave, he released them. The broken bodies fell in a heap. Clockwork men beyond fought to climb over.

"Run!" he roared, bringing up the hammer.

Ray and Si squeezed past and raced down the aisle but saw more of the clockwork men coming toward them.

"We're trapped!" Si said.

Ray looked back to where Conker was pummeling with the hammer, swing after powerful swing. A solid blow to the head or chest was enough to destroy an automaton, but as Ray saw the sheer numbers coming at them, he feared that Conker could not keep up the fight. In the hallway, he had used the limited space to their advantage, but here, with more and more of the automatons surrounding them, they were cornered.

"Get behind me," Conker said. Ray and Si backed against the wall as Conker fought the semicircle of clockwork men closing around them. As fast as he brought one automaton down, another would clamber forward. Metal hands clutched at Conker's arms. Some fallen and half-working men grabbed his legs. Conker cried out as he fought, tearing the mechanical men away and trying to get back from the swell.

"We've got to get out of here," Si said. "Can't we cross now?"

"We've got to get to those stairs," Ray said. "Otherwise, we'll wind up crushed in the Machine."

"Well, Conker can't hold all of them off!" Si cried.

Ray handed her the lantern and stepped closer to Conker. He had stopped the Hoarhound. Were these clockwork men so different? He grasped the toby. It trembled and grew warm. Tingling spread out from his chest, sending the pulsations through his body and down his arms. He could feel them, these devices of the Gog.

He understood now. The toby drew the power of the

Gloaming. With its powerful and rare objects of the wild, each selected and made potent through Ray's hoodoo craft, the toby was every bit the opposite of the Gog's forged servants. His body, his hands, held a repellent force to those mechanical warriors.

Ray reached Conker's side. The giant was trying to swing the hammer, but too many hands clutched him now. Clockwork men clung to his back and neck, pulling him down.

A clockwork man leaped at Ray. The energy Ray had summoned erupted from his palms. The invisible force crushed in the shell of the clockwork man's body. Ray reached out with his hands, extending his palms to the automatons around Conker. A tension, like the resistance of like-charged magnets put too close together, pushed against his hands. Ray gritted his jaw and leaned forward.

Clockwork men swung their expressionless slotted eyes to him before their brass skulls crinkled and were crushed flat. Ray brought his hands around to Conker, and a cluster of the men flew from him, repelled or compressed until the mass was driven back.

Conker broke free and beat down with his hammer. "Let's go!" he shouted. Ray dropped his hands. They turned and ran with Si, leaping over the broken automatons. Only a handful of clockwork men remained, but others—dozens more—came down the rows.

Carrying the lantern, Si led them to the far corner of the hall. "It must be down here!" she said.

They turned the corner. The hallway had no doors except one at the far end. Ray panted as he ran, the exertion of calling up the power to drive back the clockwork men weighing down on him. The *click-click-click* of brass feet marched behind them. Ray was exhausted and worried he could not stop the Gog's guardsmen again.

Si opened the door, where a narrow set of stairs circled down into the dark. As Ray followed her, Conker slammed the door behind them. "There's no way to lock it!" he shouted.

Si called out, "It stops down here. No door. Nothing! We're trapped!"

Ray looked around the bend in the stairs to see the flat brick wall.

Conker grabbed the handle of the door. Behind it, Ray could hear the buzz and grinding of the clockwork men coming closer. Conker spread his feet wide, clutching the handle and leaning back.

Ray took the last few steps down to the bottom. Si held up the lantern and looked around with wide eyes. "Where do we go?"

A boom resounded from the door up the stairwell, and Ray heard the door groaning as the clockwork men tried the pry the door open from Conker's grasp.

"We've got to cross," Ray said, heading back up the stairs to Conker.

"Here!" Si said, following him.

"Conker," Ray said. "Get ready!"

"What about Si?" Conker gazed at her fearfully as he struggled to hold on to the breaking door. The wood cracked, and the hinges whined.

"There's no choice," Ray said. "She comes with us."

His fingers darkened as feathers formed. His body transformed, compressing into the form of a crow. As Ray flew down the stairs and circled to come back up, Si grabbed the lantern. Conker let go of the door and leaped to Si, holding her. Ray clutched their shoulders with his talons. Conker and Si disappeared. The door broke open, and clockwork men poured into the room.

Ray flew at the wall at the bottom of the stairs. Lights flashed and the noise of the clockwork men's machinery vanished.

Darkness swallowed him.

Ray knew they were somewhere on the Wolf Tree. But it was not in the branches. His wings felt weighed down by some terrible force. He toppled against bark, which was soft and rotten and came apart in his feathers.

Down they went. Ray saw flashes of light again.

Falling to a metal girder floor, Ray returned to his form. Conker and Si reappeared and toppled to the floor. The three lay panting. Ray felt dizzy and sick to his stomach. It took all his effort to open his eyes and lift his head from the floor.

The room was small with a ceiling and walls of metal. Except for a spare incandescent bulb mounted next to an open doorway, it was empty. The air was hot and reeked of oil smoke. A constant rumbling noise seemed to cause the floor to vibrate slightly beneath them.

Si took Ray by the shoulder. "You okay?"

The battle with the clockwork men and the effort of crossing had draining him. Ray had to fight to keep from slipping into unconsciousness.

With the Nine Pound Hammer in his hands, Conker stood to walk over to the doorway. He peered down and then looked back at them with wide eyes. As Si picked up the lantern and joined him, her gasp brought Ray to his senses. He rose stiffly and staggered over to his friends.

"Where are we?" Si whispered.

A spiral staircase wound down from the doorway to an enormous grid of conveyor belts and assembly tables that were lit by a network of spare electric bulbs mounted on poles. The room stretched out in every direction, fading into a haze of smoke and dimness. Filling the aisles of the factory floor were gray ghostlike workers, piecing together bits of machinery coming down the belts, oiling small parts, inserting dials and levers, and returning their work to the moving platform before taking another part to assemble. What purpose their individual tasks served, Ray could not tell. But he knew each piece was part of the larger Machine, something to be added to the ever-growing engine of the Gog's soul.

"We've reached the Gloaming," Ray said. "Or at least what the Gog has turned it into."

He looked up to see that their room was mounted into a ceiling of exposed rock and tangled roots. Conker said, "I guess we go down."

"I'm ready," Ray said, taking a deep breath. He was still winded and leaned on Si's shoulder as they followed Conker down the staircase.

The hot, fume-laden air was filled with the sound of whirling belts, churning gears, heaving valves of steam, and the incessant chug of some dark industry. Ray heard larger machines beating and pounding and could only imagine some foundry somewhere out there constructing the pieces of machinery for these workers to assemble.

As they reached the factory floor, workers turned to stare at them. Ashen-gray men, women, and children stood along a long aisle of machinery. They had no color, like people plucked from a blurry daguerreotype. Their hair was bleached and their skin drawn and sallow as if years had borne down on them, beyond whatever natural age they were.

The people paused only a moment to gaze blankly at Ray, Conker, and Si. Then they returned to their work.

"Who are you?" Conker asked a man working nearby.

The man cast a fearful glance at Conker over his shoulder. His cracked lips and toothless mouth worked to make words, but no sound came out except for a dry gasping. After wincing and hunching away from Conker, the man returned to clamping metal plates over small casings of gears no bigger than what would operate a pocket watch.

"The Darkness . . . has done this to them," Ray said. "They are servants to the Machine now."

"How can we help them?" Si asked, her eyes on a small boy sliding cogs onto tiny rods.

"We can't," Ray said.

"We can destroy the Machine," Conker said. "Wherever it is."

He furrowed his brow and looked around at the conveyor belts. "We got to find where these parts are being sent." He started down the aisle following the stream of machinery.

With Si's help, Ray followed him. They passed workers who cast anxious looks then busied themselves at their posts. After a hundred yards, they reached a place where the conveyor belts dumped the parts into a wide chute. It made an intersection, and looking to the right and left, Ray saw chutes at the ends of all the rows.

Conker leaned over to look down into the hole. "I think there's another floor below us."

"Let's hope there are stairs—" Si started to say, but Conker pulled her and Ray back.

A few aisles down, a clockwork man crossed an intersecting walkway and disappeared down a row of workers. "They're guarded here too," Conker said. "Let's head the other way."

They hurried down the aisle, wandering through the enormous buzzing grid. They passed more of the chutes and eventually saw mechanical lifts cut into the floor lowering large containers of the assembled parts.

Ray felt they were utterly lost. He could no longer see the spiral staircase rising up to the room where they had arrived. Just when he began to suspect they were passing the same workers again and again, Si said, "There it is."

The aisle ended at a circular stairwell in the floor. "Let's go," Conker said, leading the way down.

"More workers," Si said at the next floor. She began to continue down the stairs.

"Wait," Ray said. A worker had stepped back, showing his face in profile. Then he had moved close to the machinery, disappearing behind the other workers around him.

"What is it?" Conker asked.

Ray walked forward slowly until he stood behind the worker. He was a boy, about Sally's age. At his back, Ray could see that his hair had not turned completely gray. Faint hues of brown showed. Ray touched a hand to his shoulder. The boy flinched, spinning around.

"Gigi," Ray gasped.

The boy's mouth opened and closed. He struggled to speak, and his words came thin and distant. "Ra-a-ay. Is tha-a-at yo-o-ou?"

"Gigi," Ray said, taking the boy's arms. "Why are you here?"

"My fa-a-amily." Gigi's gaze drifted to his left, and Ray saw men working at his side, one older and several who seemed about his age. Gigi's father. His brothers. They had all been brought here along with the other workers from Omphalosa.

Gigi took something from his pocket and held it up for Ray. The black bat-shaped seedpod. The charm Hethy had given Gigi to protect him against the Darkness. In Omphalosa, it had worked. But here in the Gloaming, shackled to the Gog's machinery, Gigi was becoming like the others—a wispy phantom, soulless, little more than the shell of a person.

"Ray!" Conker said.

A clockwork man stood at the stairwell, the blank slots of its eyes locked on them. "Don't do anything," Si whispered, putting down the lantern.

The clockwork man walked forward, brass feet resounding on the metal floor. Ray tensed as it approached. Tiny gears buzzed as it cocked its head. A tinny sound came from the little cone in its mouth. "Back to work," it said.

Si nodded to Conker and Ray and then turned to squeeze between two workers at their posts. Conker pushed in beside Si, and Ray stepped between Gigi and his father. The clockwork man remained at Ray's back, hovering, and as Ray cast an eye back, the automaton just stood, watching him with its blank face.

Ray stole a glance over to see what Gigi was doing. The boy took a metal part from a box and attached some dials to its side while his father bolted on a lever. Ray reached into a bucket that had stopped on the assembly belt before him. He took out a small tin part, open on one side for the dials to be inserted. Ray reached over to the other box, where Gigi had taken out the dials. He stared at the pieces, not knowing what to do with them. Before he could work it out, hatred welled up in him.

This was for the Gog's Machine. He was doing a part, even a small part, in helping it operate. Helping it generate the Darkness. Helping it enslave more victims.

A squeal began, first faint and then growing. The part within his hand writhed, and then the metal began to compress, crushing in on itself as Ray had done to the clockwork men attacking Conker. The part grew hotter in his hand.

"Stop," the clockwork man said with its expressionless, tinny voice.

Ray dropped the broken part onto the work table and staggered back a step, dizziness returning. The clockwork man leaned forward and began trying to fix the broken piece.

As Ray started for the stairs, the clockwork man reached out to grab his arm. "Stay here—"

The Nine Pound Hammer hit the clockwork man's skull, punching it straight down. The brass skin of its chest burst open and pulsating rods and gears spilled out. The clockwork man crumpled to the floor. The small cone of its mouth, now somewhere buried within its chest, issued muffled words: "Back—work—stop—release—"

"Come on!" Si said, grabbing the lantern and running for the stairs.

Ray turned back to Gigi. The boy's pupils were covered in a misty haze. He could not bring Gigi with them. Only one thing would help Gigi and the other workers.

"Where does this machinery go?" he asked.

"Do-o-own," Gigi whispered.

The three ran to the stairs, spiraling past floor after floor until Ray felt he might collapse. Conker clutched him under the arm to help. The heat diminished as they descended. Each subsequent floor seemed taller, with larger and larger pieces of machinery being assembled. The floors filled with long assembly lines of workers gave way to floors with large, steampowered lifts and men working in clusters with white-hot torches and heavy drills.

At last the stairs ended in a cavernous room lit by more of the bare electric bulbs, now mounted to the ceiling. Large pieces of machinery attached to heavy hooks and cables came down through wide chutes. Waiting below was a line of workers with enormous rolling carts. Once the pieces were placed inside, the workers, oblivious to the three who had arrived in their midst, pushed the carts along iron tracks.

"Where do we go from here?" Si asked.

Ray watched the workers. The network of tracks led in one direction. "That way," Ray said.

They followed the tracks. After several hundred yards, Conker stopped and pointed. "Look."

Ahead was an enormous circular opening in the floor, several hundred feet across. The tracks joined together, workers stopping their carts as each fed onto a solitary line. That track reached a ramp at the edge of the opening, where empty carts were coming up a second track next to the other.

Ray followed Conker and Si closer to the rim. The side-by-side tracks were bolted to the walls of the pit and spiraled down into the black. The three fell in behind some workers and started down the ramp.

Ray shivered. These workers were bringing parts to add to the Machine. And it was somewhere down there in the darkness below. As he followed the others, he peered over the edge into the mouth of the vast opening. Like some gigantic well it descended, lit only by lanterns fixed on the carts. They made two side-by-side lines of lights, one going down, the other coming up. The steady movement of lights spiraled down the walls of the shaft until they disappeared into blackness.

"How far down you reckon it goes?" Conker asked, peering into the void and then looking wide-eyed at Ray.

The answer terrified him.

Far. Very far.

ROUND AND ROUND THEY DESCENDED. LOWER AND LOWER.
Ray realized that the walls of the shaft seemed to be of blasted
rock and shoveled earth, but all along pieces of roots stuck out.
Some were as thin as a man's finger. Others were as fat as an
oil drum. But what was obvious to Ray from the foul smell and
mushy black spots was that these roots were rotting. And with
them the Wolf Tree was dying.

The workers ahead and behind them pushed the carts of
machinery along the tracks, while just to their right other
workers passed them without a curious glance. None of them
spoke. Only the *clack-clack-clack* of iron wheels on iron tracks
resounded, but at such great numbers, the noise was overwhelming.

"Not all of these people could have come from Omphalosa
and the Expo," Si murmured.

"I was thinking that too," Ray said. "The Gog has been capturing workers for years, probably before he ever kidnapped Sally and the other Shuckstack kids."

"You'd think they'd be missed," Conker said, looking at the ashen-faced men trudging along before and behind them. "Ain't they got family somewhere who's wondering where they are?"

"Some, probably," Ray said. But most he knew were missed by no one. They were the lost. The anonymous. The ignored. Immigrants. Orphans. Poor and displaced people. These were the Gog's prey.

As they walked on, Ray watched Conker and Si ahead of him. The two of them had been trying to avoid looking at each other. Ray caught from time to time the tension in Conker's jaw, the painful sidelong glances at her when she was not looking. Si never should have come with them. Ray could not bring her back out from this dark portion of the Gloaming. Or he could, in fact, but he would have no strength to return to Conker. Besides, how could he ever find again this dark bottomland of the Gloaming that the Gog had usurped?

They would never return to their world. They would never again see the open air, the morning sun on Shuckstack, the mountains, the prairie, the windswept trees around Mother Salagi's cabin, the beautiful places they loved.

Ray was surprised to find this somehow reassuring. It honed his attention. It gave him strength. There was no saving himself or his friends. There was only this final task to complete—to find the heart of the Machine deep within this abyss and destroy the Gog's wicked source.

"We're nearly to the end," Conker said.

Ray looked down the huge shaft. Below, the lights from the carts seemed to stop a few turns below, with only blackness beyond.

As they got closer, they watched as the carts before them were unloaded by huge cranes fixed to the walls of the shaft. While the empty carts were transferred by the cranes to the track going up, other workers began bolting and fastening the parts and pieces directly into the rock and decaying roots that made the walls of the shaft.

Ray followed Conker and Si as they passed the last workers and continued down the empty tracks.

"You were wrong," Si said, turning up the flame on the lantern and holding it higher to illuminate the track ahead and the walls writhing like a black mass of insects. "We're not at the end."

"We've reached the Machine," Conker said.

Dull orange lantern light reflected off bolts and metal faces and spinning parts. The clatter of the carts dissipated above, leaving only the noise of the machinery all around them. The farther they descended, the louder the noise grew. Cogs whirled, pistons fired, valves sputtered and hissed, belts churned, and engines roared. It was as Ray remembered from the dream he had witnessed long ago, the dream Conker had been having of their fathers facing the Gog's previous Machine. But then he had seen only a small portion of the Gog's creation, and here—groaning and pulsating from the vast dark below—the Machine encased in the walls went on and on and on, deep into the abysmal well.

"Dim the lantern some," Ray said to Si.

She frowned. "Why?"

"We don't know how far down we'll have to travel. And we need the oil to last."

Si did not question him further. She turned the damper down until only the thinnest light illuminated the path before them.

They had been walking for what seemed hours when Conker whispered, "Something's following us."

Ray looked back. The lights of the workers had long since disappeared. Through the din of the Machine he heard it—the clunk of heavy footsteps.

"What do we do?" Si asked, tightening her fingers around her knife.

"Keep going," Conker said.

As they descended, the footsteps grew louder. Ray kept looking back, trying to find whatever moved in the dark. He could see nothing. He wanted to tell Si to turn off the lantern, but how would they find their way? Even if they didn't fall from the ramp's edge, they would have to walk slower, and that was not what they needed to do.

"What is it?" Si whispered.

"A Hoarhound," Ray guessed.

Conker turned to look at Ray. His eyes glowed orange from the lantern's flame. "We ought to be able to handle a Hoarhound."

Ray nodded. "We'll have to be careful. Not much room on this ramp for a fight."

They went farther. All the while, Ray tried to find a spot to lie in wait for the pursuing Hound. There had been short shafts, niches in the machinery every so often. That must have been where the Hoarhound had been hiding as they passed, a guardian placed by the Gog to protect his Machine. Why it had not attacked them already, Ray was not sure, but it was pursuing them now.

Ray heard a strange sound like the hissing of a boiler, and he looked up in time to see flames illuminate the dark hundreds of feet above. Then the fire and noise vanished.

"What was that?" Conker gasped.

Ray had not been able to see well, but it seemed the flames had shown a snout, some monstrous jaws.

"Whatever it is," Si said, "that's no Hoarhound!"

Then the pace of the footsteps increased, striking heavily on the ramp.

"Do we face it?" Conker growled, holding the hammer with both his hands.

"No," Ray said. "Just run!"

Si went first, the lantern before her. The slope was slight, but the iron gave little traction, and they ran hesitantly. There could be no misstep, no slipping or losing one's balance with that gaping void only feet away.

On the opposite side of the shaft, a dark form was moving. Si's lantern did not illuminate that far, but whatever was after them was getting closer. The ramp beneath their feet began shaking with the weight of the beast.

"It's coming!" Si shouted.

"Go!" Conker roared. "Go faster!"

Ray could hear the clockwork monster's claws ringing out on the metal rails, the scraping of iron, the pumping of pistons.

Conker stopped first to spin around. "Get behind me," he said, rearing up with the hammer. Ray ran past him and then turned to look back.

The beast skidded on the ramp a dozen or more yards away and opened its jaws wide. It gave a piercing hiss like leaking gas, and then flames jetted from its mouth. Ray flung up an arm, but fortunately the flames did not extend far enough yet to reach them.

"What is that?" Conker shouted. Ray stared openmouthed at the monster. Nearly twice the size of a Hoarhound, the machine bore little resemblance to any particular animal. It perched on four legs and had a long snout, but its body and head were nearer to a locomotive or some great engine than to a beast. It was a pulsating mass of moving parts encased in pipes and iron plates.

It growled, and as it did, glowing fumes filled its mouth. A monstrous assembly of grinding teeth spun on cylinders where its lips should have been. Whatever they touched would be sucked into ragged saw blades mounted in its gullet.

Its slot-like eyes glowed like a volcanic vent, and as Ray stared into them, he realized this creature existed only to protect the Machine. It had been forged and brought to life for this moment, to stop the next bearer of the Nine Pound Hammer who might fulfill John Henry's destiny.

"Conker," Ray said, hardly able to keep his voice from shaking. "You can't fight this."

"We got no choice," Conker said, not taking his eyes from the clockwork sentinel. He was bracing his stance, flexing his fingers on the stout handle of the hammer.

Si grabbed Ray's arm. "Give me the spike."

"What?"

"I can do it," Si said. "You've brought us here. I can help Conker. You've got to hold that thing off. Only you can do it, Ray."

Ray hesitated only a moment before unbuttoning his shirt. He pushed aside Redfeather's copper to open the toby. He snatched out the golden spike and put it in Si's hand.

The toby trembled against his chest. Ray felt the tingling rise in him. It was fainter. Although he was in the Gloaming—the source of the toby's collective power—he was in the most corrupted part of the shadow world.

"Good luck, Ray," Si said.

The clockwork sentinel took a step closer, bringing its heavy paws down to shake the ramp.

"You can't do this alone, Ray!" Conker said.

"I have to," Ray said, stepping past Conker and facing the hissing beast. "Si's right. She can hold the spike. You two must go. This is no Hoarhound."

"Which is why—"

"Conker!" Si shouted. "It's time to leave."

Ray took a step closer to the sentinel. His muscles tightened as he tried to draw up the power against this monster of the Gog. The iron tracks between him and the beast whined, the metal beginning to curl. "Go!"

Conker backed a step, then turned to run with Si.

The clockwork sentinel hissed as the metal track twisted before it. Ray felt his body trembling as he pushed out with his palms. The repellent force like opposing magnets grew, and the track began to tear from its bolts. Ray concentrated on the ramp, hoping to use it against the creature.

The sentinel threw its massive head from side to side and then leaped forward. The erupting rails pummeled its sides, but the monster fought through it, clutching for perch with its claws and driving itself forward. Smoke plumed from the glowing bores of its nose.

Still pushing out with his hands, Ray backed up, trying to find some other way to knock the creature into the void. He caught sight of Si's lantern from the corner of his eye. They were farther down, descending the immense spiral.

The momentary distraction was enough to weaken the repellent force coming from his outstretched palms. The beast lunged from the breaking track and landed a few feet before Ray, its claws squealing on metal.

Ray took a step back, nearly toppling, and thrust a hand forward. The clockwork sentinel snapped its massive head to one side but then brought its snout down as if pushing against some heavy object. Flames glowed at the seams of its skull as it took a step forward. The pressure from the beast's effort suddenly pressed back into Ray, lifting him from his feet and throwing him against the churning wall of machinery.

As Ray caught hold of a metal bracket, the string from the toby was sucked into the teeth of a gear. The cord drew tight against his throat. Hanging by one hand, Ray snatched at the string strangling him. It broke. Holding the toby tightly, he flipped to one side as the clockwork sentinel rammed into the spot where Ray had just been. The spinning cylinders of teeth ground into the wall, ripping apart machinery.

Ray found a toehold and kicked, reaching up with his free hand and clutching the edges of casing until he climbed higher. The beast reared up on its hind legs and snapped its grinding, saw-toothed jaws. Ray had time only to turn and catch a foothold before the beast lunged for him again.

Ray held out the toby. The repellent pressure returned, bearing down on the sentinel's skull. Crush it, Ray thought. He focused all his will on trying to drive back the sentinel like he had done with the clockwork men. But this monster was too powerful. The sentinel rose taller, grabbing at the machinery with its front claws and getting closer to Ray.

The grinding teeth whirled. The sentinel opened its jaws, exposing the iron inner works of its throat. Gas hissed from its gullet, and flame exploded. The white-hot jet blasted Ray. He shut his eyes. He was certain he was dead, but he felt no pain.

Ray realized the flames had gone out. He drew in a huge breath. He saw his hand was still extended before him holding the toby, nearly in the mouth of the clockwork sentinel. His skin and the fabric of the toby were not burned. Then he remembered Redfeather's copper.

Ray bore down hard with the toby, pressing out with invisible force against the sentinel. He pried the jaws wider and wider. But at the same time, the beast was leaning closer. Ray's hand was in the monster's jaws—those grinding, spinning teeth. Fire erupted once more. Ray forced open his eyes.

He could not falter for a moment. If the clockwork sentinel broke through Ray's spell, if it clamped those jaws shut, he'd lose his hand . . . if not more.

Ray felt all his energy directed into his palm, all his powers welling in that single outstretched hand. Had it been the same for his father when he had confronted the Hoarhound in the Terrebonne?

The iron frame of the sentinel's mouth shook as it struggled to bite down.

"No!" Ray cried, forcing every bit of strength into that hand. The broken string from the toby dangled near the whirling teeth.

The jaws drew closer.

In an instant, the string was caught in the teeth and the toby was torn from his hand before disappearing into the saw-blade depths of the sentinel's mouth.

Ray pulled his hand back just as the teeth closed with a terrible clank and grinding. Without the repellent force bearing down on the sentinel, it fell forward, driving its head into the machine-encased wall, tearing away metal in chunks. Ray leaped from his perch, falling out into the void.

His fingers disappeared. His arms and legs transformed. Feathers bloomed from his skin, and his body shrank.

The sentinel dropped to the ramp and reared out, snapping at the crow.

Ray circled around, gliding on outstretched wings. The sentinel spewed a stream of white flame. Ray banked, twirling over in a loop. He dropped down on top of the clockwork sentinel's back.

His talons clutched at a pipe running down its spine. As the claws closed over it, Ray crossed.

Lights flashed, and the enormous well of the Gog's Machine vanished.

In the dark, he felt his beak scrape against the soft, rotting wood of the Wolf Tree. The weight—of the dying Tree, of the Gog's terrible guardian in his talons—was tremendous, and Ray pumped his wings fiercely to rise.

Dropping back again and again, Ray fought to fly higher. He climbed slowly until he no longer could. He had traveled far in the Gloaming and knew he wouldn't come out in Grevol's hall, but where he would return he wasn't sure.

Ray crossed again, lights flashing as he left the pathway of the Wolf Tree and emerged in the open air.

He let go of the clockwork sentinel.

The breeze of the lake rose up under his wings. Rain pelted his back, beading off his oily feathers and trailing behind him. Lightning flashed, and Ray looked down as he flew to watch the sentinel—transformed now into a steel trap—fall into the waters of Lake Michigan. It splashed once far below and disappeared.

Ray pumped his wings, turning to the dim, ghostly lights of the Expo. Over the white buildings, he saw fires blazing and gunshots flashing off the heavy smoke and streaming storm clouds.

Dawn should have come hours ago. But the Darkness hovered over the city.

Lightning flashed again, striking in the thick of the battle.

Ray flew on. He could not go back for Conker and Si. They were alone now. He had to reach Nel and the others. He had to help defeat the Gog.

But how? The toby was lost.

CONKER LOOKED UP AT THE DARK. "WHAT JUST HAPPENED?"

Si stared and then cocked her head to listen. She brought up the lantern and opened the damper. Conker blinked in the brightness. The lantern light reached the far side of the shaft and a few levels higher on the circling ramp, but they saw and heard nothing.

"Ray!" Conker boomed. He cocked his head, but all he heard was the incessant roar of the Machine.

"He's gone," Si said.

Conker stared a moment longer. "That beast is gone too. I don't hear nothing."

Si lowered the lantern's flame and turned back to the path before them. She nodded at Conker. "Let's go."

"Whenever you're ready," Conker said.

* * *

Side by side, they walked past the clattering, chugging machinery. The darkness enveloped them but for the faint bubble of sooty light escaping from the lantern. Conker watched Si as she stared at the golden spike in her hand.

"Are you afraid," Conker asked, "of what we've got to do?"

Si closed her fingers over the spike and looked up at Conker. Fear filled her eyes. He had never seen Si look like that. Brave Si. Fierce Si. She was trembling. Conker brought his hand around her shoulder and pulled her close against his side.

"Can you do it?" Conker asked. "Can you hold the spike while I drive it?"

Si pressed her face against him. "And bring about our deaths?"

"And end the Gog's Machine," Conker said gently.

They walked on like this, Si shaking at Conker's side as they went deeper and deeper. Si murmured something, and Conker asked her, "What did you say?"

"Why us?" she repeated. "Why does it have to be us?"

"There's no one else. It's just you and me."

She wept for a time, her tears soaking his shirt. Conker said nothing, but he rubbed his rough palm across her arm and let her mourn.

"I should not have come with you," Si said after a time. She brought her sleeve up to her nose to wipe her face. She was still trembling, shivering almost as if with cold, but the Gog's pit was hot and thick with fume-laden air. "I should have stayed with Buck and never come."

"If you had, then I would be alone now. And who would help me?"

"Help you," Si scoffed halfheartedly. "By holding the spike—"

"That's not what I mean," Conker said.

Si looked up at him, her eyes red and her cheeks blotchy. "How am I helping you?"

"You give me courage."

Si scowled. "Don't make fun of me."

"I ain't."

She looked back up at him again. "Are you really afraid, Conk?"

"Yes," he said.

She stared at him while they walked and then lowered her gaze and slipped from his arm. She took his hand and drew in a deep breath. "You give me courage too," she whispered.

Deeper and deeper they spiraled down until Conker could no longer fathom the enormity of the Gog's Machine. The mass of writhing parts, turning and hissing and pumping, clouded his mind like poisonous black smoke.

They were walking slower now, each step a struggle and a terrible effort. But it was not his body that was weary. Each step brought Conker closer to a feeling of desperation, of hopelessness.

Si fell to one knee and did not try to rise. She lowered until she sat on the metal lip of the track. "We'll never reach it," she panted.

Conker sat beside her. He leaned back and looked at the shaft above. The black was as complete as anything he had ever witnessed. All other shadow was nothing more than haze compared to this void.

He sat up and planted one foot on the track's iron rail, forcing himself to rise. He held out a hand. "Come on."

Si shook her head, and he let his hand drop. He stared into the blackness below. "Give me that lantern."

Si looked up sharply and then after a moment's hesitation handed him the lantern. Conker took it and extended his arm over the side. He turned up the damper and bright light bloomed.

"The bottom!" he gasped.

Si leaped to her feet and clutched Conker's waist as she peered down. The light reflected off a damp floor several flights below.

"Let's go," she said, snatching back the lantern and hurrying down the ramp.

In a matter of minutes, they came to the end of the ramp. The track extended several yards, disappearing in a rotten, wet tangle of roots making up the floor. Conker and Si walked out. She held up the lantern so they could see their surroundings.

It was some sort of cavity with soft roots underfoot and walls encased with pulsating machinery.

"There." Si pointed.

Conker turned to face a gap in the machinery. They walked together toward the opening. Holding forth the lantern, they saw a tunnel extending into the Machine.

"The heart," Conker whispered. He pulled the Nine Pound Hammer closer to his chest. He looked down at Si. They nodded to each other, then entered the tunnel.

The walls were lined with machinery embedded in the roots. Although the passage was tall and for the most part wide,

Conker had to squeeze through sections where spinning rods extended out in their path.

After they had walked for a time, Si blew out her breath in frustration. "How far back is it?"

Conker shook his head, and as he did the lantern's flame flickered and dimmed. They looked at each other nervously, but the flame did not die.

"Reckon it won't last much longer," Conker said.

"I'll cut it down as low as it will go," Si said, and darkened it until only a faint light escaped. Their eyes adjusted. It was enough, and they continued forward.

They traveled farther and farther, and every so often the lantern's light sputtered. After a time they came to a junction. The path split three ways.

Conker peered down the passages and asked, "Which way do we go? Which way you reckon is the heart?"

"Straight?" Si suggested.

"What if it ain't? How long would we travel before realizing we'd gone the wrong way?"

"I don't know, Conk. What's there to do but pick one?"

"This is too important for guessing!" he growled.

Si narrowed her eyes. "Well, what else do you—"

The lantern's flame died.

Conker reached out quickly to grab Si, as if the empty blackness would devour her. Si was struggling with the lantern. "It won't light!"

"Stay calm," Conker said.

"Do you have any matches?"

"No."

"Conker!"

"Calm," he said slowly.

Si grew still and then bent to place the lantern on the floor. Conker reached out with a hand to find the wall. The tip of his finger caught in the teeth of a gear, and he pulled back. He felt again and leaned his palm against the cold metal.

"I'm touching the wall," he said. "We should be able to—"

"Conker," Si's voice called from the dark.

"Yes."

"This is my crossroads," she said.

"What?" he asked.

"The crossroads Mother Salagi and the seers spoke of. I've reached it."

Conker drew in several slow breaths through his nose. "What's it mean? This crossroads?"

Si moved closer to him, pressing against him for assurance. "Conker, I couldn't leave you. I made a choice. I stayed with you. Even though it meant following you to your death, I stayed with you."

"You did," he said, a pressure forming within his chest, painful yet full of joy.

"I feel it," she whispered and backed away from him.

"Feel what?"

She was quiet. A sparkle emerged, like a solitary star in the night. Then another rose at its side. The two lights, small and pure, hung for a moment together and then were joined by others, growing one after the other until the outline of Si's hand, her thumb, her three fingers formed.

Conker gasped and then bent down to Si with his cheek close to hers. The light from her hand glowed on their faces, and he saw Si smiling. They looked at each other, illuminated by the sparkling lights, and laughed.

"It's beautiful," Conker said.

Quickly Si kissed him, then again and again. "Yes, it is," she laughed as tears fell down her cheeks and wet Conker's face. "She was right. The seer was right. Mother Josara said you would return something lost to me, Conk, and you have. I had nearly forgotten, but look. My powers have returned."

"I didn't give you back your powers," Conker said.

"Yes, you did," she said. Then looking at the glowing constellations across her hand, she slowly turned.

"There," she said, her smile disappearing. Her lower lip trembled. She looked back up at Conker fearfully. "The passage to the right. The heart of the Machine is down there."

SHEETS OF RAIN LASHED THE EXPO. LIGHTNING CRACKED
like cannon fire. As Ray flew past Buffalo Bill's burning coliseum, the wind battered his weary crow body. He struggled to
stay aloft.

Other buildings were alight with flames. Although the low
storm clouds reflected the dull orange glow from the fires, the
Darkness dampened the light so that it was like moving through
mist. Ray could see that the battle had moved from the encampment. In its wake strewn along the grounds, among the cabins
and tents, were bodies. Dark-suited agents of the Gog lay
fallen alongside men from Buffalo Bill's troupe—horsemen
and warriors from all those far lands, as well as Comanche and
Sioux fighters and cowboys. Among them were the bodies of
several pirates from the *Snapdragon*.

Ray swept over the dead, searching fearfully for his friends.

There was Malley and a few others he recognized, even if he couldn't remember their names. How long had the battle raged? Many hours, possibly. The storm conjured up by Nel had surely slowed the fighting.

Ahead, a troop of Cossacks passed through the muted electric light of a streetlamp to take cover between two buildings on the Midway. They fired out into the street. Ray moved away from them, following the backs of the Midway's buildings. Down each passage, he glimpsed the chaos of battle—men firing at one another from the corners of buildings and trees, others engaged at close quarters, swinging cudgels and swords. A band of Arab horsemen were cornered by a Hoarhound against the steps of a music hall.

Ray flew between two of the buildings, keeping low, just inches above the puddles and rain-splattered ground. He saw Big Jimmie leap from behind a pushcart, the greasepaint streaked and the hammer abandoned. He roared as he fired a pair of pistols at a group of agents charging from the trees around a beer garden. One of the agents spun as he was struck, but the others fell back to the trees, returning fire. Jimmie dropped behind the pushcart to reload.

Ray flew farther, searching for his friends. Bullets whizzed and pinged all around. For the most part, he could not see the shooters or their targets, just misty forms racing this way and that, taking cover, charging from positions, falling to the paving stones of a nearby boulevard, never again to rise. He had not seen Nel or the Gog in the smoke and rain and confusion.

His arms grew heavy, the feathers fading. Ray spied a cove of boxwoods next to a building. His crow form left him, and he crashed through the bushes, striking the sopping earth and tumbling. His head hit the brick of the building's foundation.

Weakly he tried to sit up but found he didn't have the strength. He was not injured, although his head throbbed from the fall. Ray was drained—drained of all remaining strength and hope. The toby was lost. His friends were going to their deaths. Nel might already have fallen. What was there left for him to do? The Darkness filled his eyes.

Shouts echoed. Gunshots resounded. A Hoarhound roared, followed by another. Men and horses cried out in pain

Ray lay in the mud. The cold rain splattered against him. He realized this overwhelming weariness was not simply from crossing or taking crow form or the battle with the clockwork sentinel. This was something profoundly worse. Nel's charm had been lost along with his toby. There was nothing protecting him from the Darkness.

Feet sounded on the paving stones. A bullet sang as it struck the building behind Ray. A voice shouted, "Over there!" And more bullets thunked and pinged off the stone.

Ray felt the Darkness flood over him, as if he were sinking into a pool of thick black oil. He sank deeper and deeper. He wanted to struggle to stay conscious, but poison filled his heart. What was there left to struggle for?

He opened his eyes and saw Conker and Si. He almost called out to them. What were they doing here? But then he realized he was seeing them as they made their way down the circling pathway deep in the Gloaming. Suddenly the bolts broke free from the wall, and the ramp began to crumple. Conker dropped the Nine Pound Hammer as he grabbed the ramp. Si tumbled into the dark void. Conker reached for her, but not in time.

"No!" he roared. The ramp ripped away completely, carrying Conker down until he disappeared into the Gog's pit.

Ray opened his eyes again and saw the bushes around him. The leaves dripped with what at first seemed to be rain and then became an inky black fluid. Some part of his brain felt certain this was not real, but it was too hard to hold that thought.

Ray trembled with fear. He heard gunfire and shouting agents just around the corner. He knew he had to get away. He knew he had to help the others. But what did it matter? His friends were all going to die. They were never going to stop the Gog. They were never going to destroy the Machine. It was all too late. He closed his eyes and waited for the agents to discover him.

He saw Nel. The Gog had him trapped, surrounded in the Midway by scores of agents. The Pirate Queen lay dead at his feet, along with Hobnob and Buffalo Bill, and there were Marisol's and Redfeather's bloodied and motionless bodies. Nel desperately drew vials and powders from his toby, but it was no use. The agents opened fire, and he fell.

"It can't . . . be," Ray murmured. He tried to force the evil visions from his mind, but they kept rising.

He saw Jolie emerging from a pipe in a room deep beneath the Hall of Progress. Her sisters were locked in a cage, submerged in an enormous tank. Jolie dove into the water and broke open the lock. She opened the door, and slowly one by one her sisters swam out. Casings of machinery were bolted into the skin of their shorn heads and along their bare backs. Their faces were monstrous. Jolie tried to escape, but her sisters surrounded her, lashing with their claws and sinking their long teeth into her.

Ray shuddered violently. His vision swam in and out of focus.

He saw Stacker Lee standing before him. His once fine clothes were filthy. His hat was gone, and in the center of his tattered shirt, Ray saw exposed machinery, revolving gears and squeaking parts protruding from his chest. Stacker tried to speak, but only faint gasping escaped his blood-speckled lips. He reached for Ray.

"No," Ray said, squeezing his eyes shut tightly. He sank deeper into the Darkness until all sight, all sound vanished. Inky blackness filled every corner of his thoughts. The whole world seemed lost to him, and him to it.

He slipped deeper and deeper. . . .

A pleasant breeze seemed to be blowing across his face. Warm light filtered through his eyelids. Ray opened his eyes and blinked at the bright sunlight. Where was he?

He sat up from where he was lying in tall grass and saw the empty prairie rolling out to the horizon. For a moment, Ray thought he might be back with Sally and his father and the rougarou at the roots of the Wolf Tree. But as he turned around, he saw trees growing at the shore of a large lake.

This looks familiar, he thought. It wasn't so different from the wooded section of shore to the south of the Expo where he'd met the crew of the *Snapdragon*. But as Ray looked around, he saw no houses, no White City, no Chicago. There were no boats on the lake or signs of people anywhere. It was as if the world had emptied of all people and he was all that was left.

Something sat in the grass not far away. Ray squinted at it curiously. As he walked over through the windswept grass, he found it was a simple wooden table with a polished brass box resting on top. No decorations adorned it, except for a small button-like latch on the front. After a moment's hesitation, Ray pressed it and heard the latch click.

He backed away a step as the lid parted and tilted up slowly on its own with a *tick-tick-tick* of turning gears. When the lid had fully opened, Ray saw a metal cone rise from the center like a blossoming flower. Stacks of thin gears filled the box, their teeth meeting in swirling circles. Even after the cone had risen up from the box about a foot or so, the brass clockworks continued to turn with a chorus of clicks.

A voice, thin and tinny, came from the cone. "Hello, Ray."

He backed up another step. "Who are you?"

"You know who I am," the voice said.

Ray felt a chill wash over him despite the warm sunlight. "You're . . . are you the Magog?" he stammered. Then looking around at the lake and prairie and cloud-speckled sky, he said, "Where am I?"

"Chicago," the tinny voice replied, with a trace of laughter in the tone. "Or at least the place where Chicago is today."

"What am I doing here?" Ray said.

"I've brought you here to show you something."

Ray felt an uneasy knot forming in his stomach. "What?"

A panel opened on the side of the box. A lens, like a large

monocle, extended out on a metal frame. Once the frame finished telescoping out, the voice said, "Please. Have a look."

What was the Magog doing? Ray couldn't understand what it wanted from him.

"I promise it will bring you no harm," the voice said.

Ray frowned skeptically and stepped to the lens, looking through the glass. He simply saw the prairie beyond. It seemed no different than what he saw without the lens.

"I remember this age," the voice said. "Before man came. When it was nothing. It was a long time before the first people passed through."

Ray saw a party of hunters in furs, carrying spears, jogging through the trees. Startled, he pulled back. The men were not actually there, but as he leaned back to look into the circle of glass, he saw the hunters again, this time with women and children, butchering bison on the shore of the lake.

The tinny voice continued, "Even as time passed and new people came, little changed." The images in the lens came in and out of focus, each time showing a different scene—tribes people in hide tents, and then others building huts of branches and logs. Then Ray saw bearded white men in wool coats pulling boats up on the shore. "Others came. Trappers, soldiers, explorers, and eventually settlers."

Ray watched the images shift, each time revealing more and more huts on the shore, then a village with roads, then a town with a church and stockade. The number of people grew, each shift showing men, women, and children in slightly different styles of clothing but ultimately not that different in how they lived. They cooked over fires. They hunted. They gathered and grew their own food. They built houses from the trees and mud around the lake's shore.

The voice sighed. "A mundane history, and wearisome for me to watch. Savage people, all of them. Savage people living out savage lives. That is, until recently. Do you realize how rapidly the world has changed in the past several decades, Ray? A single generation has seen an explosion of innovation and growth that all the generations before could never have imagined."

Ray watched as the town rapidly expanded, wooden houses being replaced by brick and stone. Dirt streets being paved with cobblestones. Stores and churches and warehouses and factories being built as a city rose up where only prairie existed before. Finally Ray saw the Midway filled with the exotic buildings and mobs of smiling fairgoers. Overhead towered Mister Ferris's marvelous wheel and, beyond, the domes and spires of the White City.

"This Expo is a turning point," the voice said. "The world will never be the same. Electricity. Engines. Machinery big and small. If this much has changed in so quick a period, can you imagine, young Ray, what lies ahead?"

As Ray stared breathlessly through the lens, he watched as the buildings grew taller and taller, towers of lights and steel and glass that seemed to rise beyond the clouds. The scant trees and patches of earth that remained soon disappeared under cement. The streets were flooded with such a mob of people that none seemed to be able to even move. These were not the smiling faces of the fairgoers. These were lifeless, ashen-faced people. The lake was clogged with monstrous barges and the sky filled with winged airships. Stretching out to the horizon were endless crowded streets and colossal buildings. What had been earth and air and water was now blotted out like a gray mold covering a piece of fruit as the city of smoke and steel and darkness expanded.

Ray staggered back from the lens and saw that twilight had fallen over the prairie as he'd been watching the Magog's vision of the future.

A thin laugh came from the cone. "Impressive, isn't it? And shocking. What man is capable of. Consider this, Ray. My servant Mister Grevol, he did not make Chicago what it is today. He did not conceive of this Expo or its wonders. And neither did I. The Chicago that you just saw, the Chicago that is to come—that is to say, the very world that is to come—will arrive whether or not Mister Grevol or I are here to play our small part in it. What you saw is progress. What you have witnessed, Ray, is the inevitable."

Ray felt terror and anger welling up in him so fast that he grew dizzy. "No!" he said. "That's not true."

The grass around him was shriveling and dying, the waters of the lake receding into mudflats. The sky grew darker with no stars or specks of light overhead.

The gears continued to tick as they swirled around in the box. "You cannot stop it by stopping us," the voice from the cone said.

Ray stumbled, feeling as if the entire world was toppling around him. He shouted and reached for the box to slam the lid, to stop the Magog from saying any more, but he could not find it in the dark, and he fell.

The tinny voice said, "What place will there be for a Rambler in the world that is to come?"

Ray tried to sit up but the ground beneath him was no longer there. He seemed to be suspended in a black void.

The voice spoke one last time, but now it was not the thin, tinny voice from the cone but a low whisper that seemed to come from lips pressed to his ear. "So I have a question for you, Ray Cobb. What are you still fighting for?"

He couldn't move. He couldn't feel or hear anything. He saw only Darkness surrounding him. The Magog's words swirled in his head.

What was he fighting for? What hope was there in stopping what could not be stopped?

Something crept through the black of his mind. Sounds slowly emerged again. At first they were indistinct: A thud. Shuffling. Scraping. Then a sharp twang and another twang, like arrows being fired.

Ray recognized a voice, but it was barely audible through the Darkness filling his thoughts. "What's . . . happened . . . ?"

Ray couldn't tell who was speaking. He no longer cared. The world would embrace Grevol's aims no matter how this battle turned out. And even if Conker and Jolie and Nel succeeded and Grevol and his Machine were destroyed, the world would become a twisted, dark place that he could no longer live in.

Whirling muffled noises surrounded him. Through them, words emerged: "is . . . hurt . . . no . . . what's wrong . . ."

Ray felt a hand touching him, but it was as if it were through thick blankets. He tried to drive his concentration from whoever it was. He wanted nothing more than to slip back into the Darkness and disappear.

"Toby's gone . . . doesn't have . . . charms . . . protect . . . Dark." The voices came through clearer, closer. Despite his efforts, Ray cracked open his eyelids.

Marisol was kneeling over him. She was sliding her pouch from over her head.

Redfeather grabbed her hand. "No! You mustn't," he said. "It will take you too."

She hesitated but finally let go of the pouch. Ray's vision grew blurry and dim.

"Did you do it?" Redfeather asked, kneeling closer to Ray. Fire glowed from the cupped palm of Redfeather's right hand, casting an orange light into Ray's eyes. "Is it destroyed?"

Ray opened his mouth to answer, but couldn't muster the effort. His mind swirled with blackness, emptiness, despair.

"Ray." Redfeather spoke firmly and slowly, making sure Ray could understand him. "Nel is fighting the Gog. He needs you. He cannot defeat him."

Ray managed to murmur, "Doesn't . . . matter . . . anymore."

"Yes, it does!" Redfeather snapped, shaking Ray by the shoulder.

"Redfeather, don't . . . ," Marisol began.

Ray felt he couldn't hold his eyes open any longer. Redfeather wrapped his arm around Ray's shoulders, helping him sit upright. Ray's head slumped, his body as limp as a doll's.

"Listen, Ray!" Redfeather said. "Listen. You will not fall to the Dark. Don't you remember what Water Spider told us? You're a Rambler. Like your father. Greater even than your father! Don't you remember? Water Spider said you could resist the Darkness if you mastered the Darkness within you."

Ray struggled to think against the black gears growing in his mind. Hadn't his father told him this also, in the Gloaming? What were his words?

The only one who can stop the Gog and the Magog is the one who has mastery over his own Darkness. The one who can stand against his own black clockworks.

What was his Darkness? Ray thought it had been having to watch Jolie leave to sacrifice herself to heal the Wolf Tree and free her captive sisters. Or giving Si the spike so that she and Conker could destroy the Machine, even though it meant marching to their deaths.

But he had been willing to go with Conker. He too had been ready to die to stop the Gog. That had not been his Darkness. That had not been what had driven him to despair. Ray knew their sacrifices had purpose.

But then he'd seen the Magog's terrible visions of what was to come—of all that the Ramblers had fought for adding up to nothing in the dark world of machines and soulless cities that lay ahead. But hadn't the Magog also shown him his friends falling before they had done their parts in stopping the Gog? He'd seen Marisol and Redfeather dead. But here they were, Marisol leaning over him with tears on her cheeks and Redfeather with his arm around him. His dear friends. They had not fallen. They were alive.

The Magog . . . the vision it had shown him, it had not been true, or at least it had only been a possible fate, the darkest possible one. Nel was alive and still trying to stop Grevol. And Jolie might still make the siren spring that could save the Wolf Tree. Conker, he, and Si might still be able to reach the heart of the Machine.

And the world ahead, it would change. That was inevitable, just as the Magog had said. But it wasn't inevitable that it would be a world that would turn people into the ashen-faced slaves that Grevol desired. Mankind might still hold on to its humanity. There might still be a place for a Rambler.

It was as if an ember formed. A small and singular spark taking flight from a bed of dead coals. The flame grew and grew, becoming a blaze.

Ray reached out to grasp Redfeather's left hand.

Redfeather looked up sharply. Marisol leaned back in surprise. "Ray?" Redfeather said, pulling him to his feet. "What's happened?"

Ray staggered a step, but then felt strength flood into his body. A tingling feeling moved from his chest to his arms. "Where is Nel?" he asked.

Redfeather held up his hand as it burst with flames. "Let's find him."

Marisol said, "This way," notching an arrow before pushing back the bushes.

They ran around the back of the building. Buckshot-hard pellets of hail roared down from the storm. But Ray felt no cold, no weakness. He ran, with Redfeather and Marisol at his sides.

A terrified group of Javanese tribesmen stared out at them from their grass hut displays as the three passed. Continuing to circle the building, Ray came up behind the Pirate Queen taking cover from gunfire roaring across the Midway's boulevards. Marisol and Redfeather took positions against the wall, their weapons ready.

"Ray!" Mister Lamprey barked. Piglet was there, along

with Hobnob. They held guns, but the small yellow-haired thief kept switching the Colt from hand to hand, scratching at his palms.

"This is it," Hobnob simpered. "I'm quits after this. Never felt myself cut out for this sort of work—"

"Shut up and be ready with that peashooter!" the Pirate Queen shouted, loading the massive cartridges in her guns. "And, Ray, what are you doing here?"

"Have you seen Nel?" he asked, knowing there was no time to explain it all.

"The wheel," she said. "Last I saw, he and Grevol were at the base of that wheel."

Mister Ferris's wheel. The symbol of the Expo. The towering monument to the progress of the age. Ray would need no help finding it.

"Can you cover us?" Ray asked.

"With pleasure," the Pirate Queen said, chomping on her cigar.

Piglet peeked around the corner, and immediately a bullet resounded off the stone inches from her face. She looked back and smirked. "They're waiting for us."

"Wouldn't want to disappoint them," the Pirate Queen said before stepping out into the boulevard and roaring, "Looking for me, you dandies?" From under her coat, she brought out the pair of fat-barreled guns that were too big to be pistols and too small to be cannons. Each weapon boomed with great clouds of smoke.

The agents ducked behind a cart as it splintered with gunfire. Piglet and Mister Lamprey ran past her, firing their rifles and screaming as they charged and drove the agents from their hiding places. Hobnob followed, but as soon as a bullet rang off the cobblestones by his feet, he dropped his gun and smashed the dandelion hat to his head, dissolving in a cloud of seedpods.

Redfeather said, "Follow me." As he disappeared around the corner, Marisol and Ray sprinted after him. Marisol paused halfway across the thoroughfare to send a volley of arrows at the agents. The three kept running, keeping low until they reached a stack of beer kegs.

"There are more Bowlers ahead," Marisol said.

Ray peered around the leaking barrels to see the black-suited agents battling against the pirates and Buffalo Bill's men.

"We've got to find better cover," Redfeather said.

Ray looked hastily around and then pointed. "That booth!"

"Good enough," Redfeather said.

They ran as gun battles raged around them. Ray jumped across the counter of a tin-sided ticket booth, landing on the dusty wood floor. He fell against someone hiding. The person gasped and cocked a pistol, but Ray quickly pushed the barrel down.

"Gilley, it's me," Ray said.

"You scared the blazes out of me," the young cowboy said, his freckled face pale and his eyes wide.

"Glad you're okay," Ray said.

"Me too," Gilley said. "It's a miracle I'm in one piece."

Redfeather and Marisol burst through the door and crouched beside Ray and Gilley. Redfeather said, "What now?"

Ray peered over the counter. Staying low, Redfeather and Marisol came up beside him to survey the scene.

The towering wheel rose hundreds of feet above the Midway. Dozens of locomotive-sized cars were mounted to it, for visitors to ride and view the Expo. Although they were empty, the cars rose up and around and back down, following the huge circular path. Just beside the base of the wheel in an opening in the ground, the engine driving Mister Ferris's ride rumbled. Its pistons and gears clattered as they turned the great pulleys attached to the wheel's axle.

A line of agents encircled the base of the wheel. Ray saw bodies lying on the ground around them—some were Buffalo Bill's men, some were agents of the Gog. The shell of a Hoarhound smoldered to one side. From the black scorch marks radiating from it, Ray guessed the monster had been struck down by a bolt of lightning.

By the bottom of the wheel, the Gog stood with his back to Ray. He swung his walking stick like a conductor of some mechanical orchestration. Nel was pinned between the pit with the churning engine and the cars coming by every few moments. As each of the huge cars swung down, he had to duck to keep from being crushed.

As the next car rose over him, Nel held out a vial of glass that glowed suddenly. Lightning flashed down on the Gog. Ray's vision turned white. He pulled back from the counter, to squeeze his eyes shut as the light lingered in his sockets.

"He needs our help," Marisol said.

"You'll never get past those agents," Gilley said. "Iron Tail tried to attack them, but I think he was shot."

A whirlwind of seedpods filled the booth. As it began to coalesce into a form, Gilley backed nervously against the wall.

"It's okay," Ray said. "It's just Hobnob."

A moment later, the little thief pulled the dandelion hat from his head and fell back against the wall, panting.

"You okay?" Redfeather said.

"Do I look okay!" he squeaked.

"Is the Pirate Queen coming?" Ray asked.

"I don't know, I don't know," Hobnob said piteously. "None's the difference."

Marisol stole a glance over the counter. "I see her. She's coming this way with Lamprey and Piglet."

Redfeather said, "There's still too many agents between us and Nel. Even that one-woman army can't get us through all of them."

Ray looked over the counter with Redfeather to see how Nel was doing.

The old Rambler held up his hands and pushed his palms toward Grevol. A gale-force wind battered down, ripping at the Gog's coat. The Gog turned to one side to brace against the force, then flung out his walking stick.

The next car came down faster, and Nel was not ready this time. The enormous side of the car crashed into him. As it rose, Ray expected Nel to be lying on the ground, but he was not there at all.

"Ah, Joe Nelson," the Gog laughed, his voice carrying faintly on the wind. "You toy with me."

Nel clambered atop the rising car. The Gog walked slowly forward as the next car came down to the ground. When it reached the lowest point, he took hold of a bar running along one of the windows and stepped onto a metal lip on the side of the car. As his car rose behind Nel's, the Gog deftly climbed onto the roof, and the agents tightened their circle around the wheel.

Ray felt his hands tingle as warmth flowed from his chest down his arms. If he could only get up on the wheel, he might be able to help Nel. "We need a distraction," he said, his eyes settling on Hobnob.

Hobnob nodded in agreement, and then his eyes sprang wide as it seemed to dawn on him what Ray was suggesting. "No. No. Why's it always me that gets sent into this sort of madness? 'Just go lift the key from the sleeping sheriff, Hobnob.' 'Just go hobble the rangers' horses, Hobnob.' 'Just hold Rosie's jaws while I give her medicine, Hobnob.' Well, none of them worked, so why's this going to?"

"You're right," Ray said. "It might not work. But either you could agree now to help and get going, or we'll ask the Pirate Queen to convince you."

At that moment, several people bumped against the side of the booth. "Ray, you in there?" the Pirate Queen called from the other side of the wall.

"Yes," he said. "Along with Hobnob and—"

The Pirate Queen growled, "I was wondering where that little yellow-headed coward ran off to. Send him out here so I can speak with him."

Hobnob strangled the dandelion hat and cursed, "Tarnation! So what you want me to do?"

Redfeather replied, "Use your hat. Get on the other side of

that line of agents. Then get their attention so they turn around. Just long enough for us to make a good charge." He held up his hand, flames lapping through his closed fingers. "I'll take care of the rest."

"After this I'm quits," Hobnob mumbled. He slapped his dandelion hat over his nest of hair and faded.

As the last of the pods drifted away, Ray said, "You all ready?"

Gilley slid the last bullet in his revolver and shut the cylinder. "I'm ready.

Marisol notched an arrow, and Redfeather put his palms together, allowing the flames to encase both hands. He called out, "My lady, get ready to follow us."

"Aye," she growled.

Ray peered over the counter and saw Hobnob appear behind the line of agents.

"Any of you boys got change for a dollar?" he said.

The agents swung around, baffled for half a moment by the little thief. Hobnob quickly put his hat back on as gunfire opened up on the spot where he'd been.

Redfeather kicked open the door. "Here we go."

He dashed out from the ticket booth, running toward the agents who were still turned around and searching for Hobnob. Redfeather whipped out both his hands, sending streaks of flames at the backs of the agents' coats. There were shouts as clothes caught fire. Many dropped their weapons as they fell to the ground or ran in panic. Redfeather continued to lash out with the flames. As the other agents gathered their wits and lifted their rifles, Marisol volleyed arrows and Gilley opened fire from behind the counter. The roaring Pirate Queen charged along with Lamprey and Piglet, guns blasting. The agents scattered back toward benches and behind trees.

Ray ran, heading straight for the base of the wheel. He leaped over fallen agents and others rolling on the cobblestones to extinguish their flames. He was almost there when an agent came out from around the wheel's engine room and blocked his path. Ray froze as the agent's pistol leveled on him. He cocked the hammer back with his thumb. "Got you," the agent sneered.

Ray heard hooves thundering on the boulevard. The agent had only an instant to turn his head before a Comanche horseman struck him with the butt end of his rifle. Horses charged past Redfeather and the Pirate Queen and the others as the Comanches joined in the battle.

Ray reached the base of the wheel and watched the next car lower. He grabbed the door handle, shouldered the door open, and fell inside as the car rose back up. The storm beat against the car like war drums. Ray looked up through the rain-blurred window for Nel and Grevol.

The two were atop each of their rising cars, casting spells at each other. Nel drew on the powers of the world—storm and hail, lightning and wind. The Gog drew on the powers of his machinery—electric charges, magnetic forces, eruptions of light and heat that came from the glowing knob atop his walking stick. The two ducked and dodged, leaping around the roofs of the cars, bracing against the raging storm and each other's spells.

As Ray forced the door open into the howling wind, he saw the ground below. More agents and more of Buffalo Bill's men had joined the fight, converging below the towering wheel. The agents who had been driven back by the Comanche fighters came back with reinforcements. From down the boulevard, groups of Hessian cavalry and vaquero horsemen emerged, firing round after round. Then there was the Pirate Queen, barking and cursing and leading a band of her pirates. Marisol was now at Redfeather's side, firing arrows as he slung whips of flame. The battle was growing, and here the final stand would take place.

Ray reached for a handhold to get up onto the roof, his fingers half frozen. He tightened his grip and with a grunt hoisted himself up.

The car swung with the storm, and his foot slipped on the rain-slick metal. Ray slammed against the side of the car. He squeezed hard so as not to lose his grip on the bar. Rivulets of rain poured into his eyes, and he brushed his face against his soaked shoulder to try to see. He pushed with the toes of his boots but found no foothold. Looking up, he saw Nel's car reach the peak of the wheel.

Nel shot down a twin lightning flash that brought Grevol down on one knee. Grevol held up the walking stick with one hand as the lightning illuminated his body, a thin black phantom within a sun-bright crackling of electricity. But then the lightning coalesced, sucked into the knob of the walking stick. Grevol rose, laughing.

Nel's car began its descent, the Gog now above him. Grevol leaped for Nel, his coat flapping out bat-like in the storm. He knocked the Rambler backward and caught Nel by the throat.

"You are not whole, Joe Nelson," the Gog said. "You possess within your leg the link to my Machine."

Ray kicked and struggled to get atop the car, desperate to reach Nel in time.

Nel grabbed at the Gog's hand where it locked on his throat. His eyes were bulging and he gasped for breath.

The Gog lifted the walking stick, pointing the glowing knob at Nel like a sword ready to be plunged. A whirling noise rose from the knob, tiny gears churning and growling.

"Don't fear. I don't intend to kill you, Mister Nelson. I could have thrown you from this wheel already if that had been my aim." A wide smile slithered across the Gog's face. "No. You will join me. You will be one of my clockwork servants!"

Ray's feet pressed against the wet metal of the car. His arms shook as he drew himself up. When he was over the edge, he dropped to his stomach and rolled over. He rose and, with a leap, landed on the roof of the car above Nel and the Gog.

For a moment, Ray thought he saw a figure, a mere shadow, climbing onto a car at the bottom of the wheel. He narrowed his eyes to see who it was—Redfeather or Big Jimmie or someone else who might be of help. Or were the agents coming to help their master?

"Let us finish this, shall we?" the Gog said, bringing the knob to Nel's chest, pressing it over his heart. Nel's gaze flickered up to Ray, and the Gog glanced over his shoulder. Nel used the moment and kicked, catching Grevol in the stomach. Grevol shouted and bore down on Nel, thrusting forward with the walking stick. But Nel was not there.

A silver-furred fox twisted and broke from Grevol's hold. The knob of the walking stick struck the roof of the car with a flash of greenish light. The blast sent the fox sliding across the rain-slick metal until his hind legs fell over the edge.

His car was swinging again in the wild wind, and Ray clung tightly as he leaned over the edge and looked down.

The Gog spun around, reaching out with his free hand to grab the silver-furred fox. Nel scrambled, his claws scratching at the wet metal. The Gog's gloved fingers reached for the fox's neck but met empty air.

The fox fell. Nel fell.

The Gog peered down from the roof of his car.

Ray cried out as the fox flipped and tumbled. Then the fox hit the ground and was still.

"No!" Ray screamed. "No! No!"

Grevol looked back over his shoulder, locking his coal-black eyes on Ray. He smiled.

SI AND CONKER WALKED THE DARK PASSAGE HAND IN HAND. Si held her other hand aloft, for guidance and to light their way. She had begun trembling again, and Conker feared there was nothing left for him to say to alleviate the growing terror. They were deep within the Machine, and the Darkness was like a cloud—evil and encompassing and barring their ability to hope that somewhere the sun still shone.

They were cold, a deep, bitter cold down to their bones, although the air was sweltering. Despite the tall ceiling, the acrid smell of fumes and pulsating noises of the machinery drew thick around them. Si pressed close to Conker's side.

"Will we know if the Gog is killed?" she asked.

"I don't think so," Conker replied.

"And if Nel doesn't defeat him?"

"Hopefully Ray's gone to Nel. Hopefully together they're able."

Her voice came out as the faintest whisper, as if the Machine was listening, as if it would turn her fears against them. "But if the Gog kills them both . . ."

"Don't you think like that," Conker said, also whispering, but urgently.

"But if he does," Si said. "If the Gog isn't destroyed, even if we drive the spike into the Machine, Grevol will only build another one. Like after your father died. And who . . . who will be left to stop him?"

Conker was quiet for a time before answering. "Redfeather and Marisol," he said. "Maybe them."

"They're not like Ray. They're not like you."

"Hush on it."

"I can't," Si said. "I keep thinking we're going to die, and all for nothing. That we're making a mistake."

"We ain't," Conker said.

"We might be."

"We ain't. The Machine, it's doing this to us. Don't you see? It's putting these fears and doubts in our heads."

"Do you think so?" Si asked. "Really?"

"The Darkness," Conker said. "It eats at you, don't it? I feel it trying to stop us."

They struggled to continue forward.

"Si?"

Her voice trembled. "What?"

"Do you remember when we were kids? That first time you performed in the medicine show? You were all covered in chains, tied up and twisted all around and stuffed in that box."

"Yeah." She managed a weak chuckle.

"I asked you how you could stand to be in that box. I said, 'Don't it scare you to be locked up in there?' You remember what you told me?"

"No."

"You said the time in the box weren't nothing but a few moments. You just thought on what you'd do when you'd get out. What we'd do together after the show was over."

Si walked on in silence, her glowing speckled hand extended before her.

"Si."

"Yeah?" she whispered.

"This ain't nothing but a few moments. One way or the other, it'll all be over. And we'll be together." Conker's voice lowered. "Don't let this Darkness make you forget we're together. You and me."

Si squeezed his hand. "Always."

Then she gasped and stopped walking. "Look, Conker. Ahead."

A faint sickly green light formed down the passage. "What is it?" Conker asked.

They began walking, heading toward the eerie glow. As they did, they saw the light pulsate. Not rhythmic like a heartbeat, but erratic and jarring. Conker felt his stomach knot and his hold on the hammer weaken.

As they went farther down, Si slowed and Conker couldn't help but do so also. Each pulsation of the light shot waves of pain through him, electric and burning. Si uttered a groan and turned her head. "It hurts," she said, and drew back behind him to shelter her. "What's it doing?"

"Trying to stop us," he grunted. Conker had to force himself forward, each step bringing new and worsening shocks of pain. He held out the Nine Pound Hammer as a talisman before him. "Keep going."

"Conker," Si said weakly. "Please no."

He had to pull her by the hand to keep her behind him. "Almost there."

They were still a dozen yards from the end of the passage. How would they ever reach it? How could they keep enduring this?

The green light glowed from a circular metal plate mounted in the center of the wall of machinery. The metal skin grew transparent with each pulse, and beneath the surface a mass of gears and clockwork parts churned and writhed, insect-like.

"The heart," Conker said.

It was horrifying to see, as if, should they come any closer, the machinery might begin growing within them. His knees buckled and he dropped the hammer as he fell to all fours. He ground his teeth and turned his head away from the painful pulsating light.

He saw Si behind him, lying in pain on the metal floor. "I . . . can't," he gasped.

Ray realized now that Grevol had wanted Nel alive. He had wanted all along to corner the old Rambler and use the poisoned connection in Nel's leg to enslave him. But Ray knew Grevol did not intend the same for him.

The Gog swung the walking stick toward Ray. He had only an instant to leap from the roof of his car before the glass exploded and the metal body ripped open. He fell, half propelled by the blast, until he landed with a gasp on his stomach atop one of the heavy iron spokes radiating from the wheel's center. Quickly kicking a leg onto the flat girder, Ray climbed to his feet. The foot-wide spoke was horizontal—for the moment—and Ray ran swiftly down a few yards until he reached a supporting brace rising up from the massive spoke. After he got behind it, he looked back to see if Grevol was pursuing him and realized that when he had leaped, he'd landed on the spoke connected to the Gog's car.

Standing calmly atop his car, Grevol looked at Ray with the sort of playful malice of a hunter eyeing his trapped prey. "I have longed to see you again, young Ray." Grevol spun the walking stick around in a circle.

Ray turned to head farther down the spoke, but the angle of the walkway was growing too steep, and he had to hold on tightly to the support brace. The turning of the wheel would throw him from his spot, and Grevol—seeming to know this—watched eagerly as his car descended to the bottom.

"Pity you can't just fly away, little bird," the Gog called.

Ray put his heel on a metal bolt in the iron frame and climbed up toward the wheel's center, as far away from Grevol as he could manage. But gravity and the wet metal played against him, and he began to slide. He threw a leg around the framework and held on tightly as his spoke reached the bottom and began to rise. When he saw that soon he would be dangling from the spoke, Ray clawed his way around until he got to his belly on the other side.

He looked once more for the figure he had seen ascending the wheel but could not find him. Down on the Midway's boulevard, black swarms of agents fought the pirates and Buffalo Bill's men. The storm, Nel's storm, had vanished, gone along with the old Rambler. The Darkness remained like a poisonous mist over the city.

But Ray could not think of Nel or the Darkness, could not watch the battle raging below, could not consider what was happening with his friends. His spoke was rising up again, and as soon as it was horizontal, he had to be ready to run farther down it. As Ray got to his feet, his gaze fell to where a chasm opened in the ground below and a huge set of gears ground together. The engine that turned the wheel churned, sending clouds of steam and smoke into the air. Ray knew he would be crushed in an instant if he fell.

The Gog stood placidly atop his car. "Fly, little bird. Fly." He lifted his walking stick and pointed it at Ray.

Ray had no choice but to roll off the spoke as the blast erupted from the buzzing knob. The brace he'd been hiding behind twisted, and the entire wheel groaned and began to slow.

Ray caught the next spoke below, gasping as his arms jerked painfully. He swung back and forth, dangling over that pit of gears and teeth. As he looked back up for a better hold, he spied the figure above him now on the wheel, leaping from a car to the one below it.

"Most entertaining!" Grevol shouted. "Most entertaining indeed."

Ray struggled to hold on to the wet iron spoke, kicking a foot up onto the frame before he lost his grip, and knowing all the while that he was trapped.

The Gog rode higher on his car, rising a hundred, a hundred and fifty, and then two hundred feet over the Midway. As the Gog was almost three quarters of the way to the peak, he swung out with his stick and the wheel stopped, giving a groan that shuddered through the enormous metal frame.

As Ray climbed onto the top of the spoke, Grevol walked out along the one above him, watching Ray all the while. "I suppose it is time to conclude this, young Rambler," he called. The smile left Grevol's face. Then he stepped out and dropped. His boots clattered loudly as he landed on the girder before Ray.

"Give me the rabbit's foot!" he commanded.

Ray backed away, glancing behind him at the long spoke going to the center of the wheel. There was another support beam just a few yards away, but he could never get behind it in time. He looked over the edge, saw the gaping pit of grinding machinery far below, and knew that trying to drop to the next spoke was too risky to attempt again. "I don't have it."

"Don't play the fool!" The Gog brought up the walking stick. The knob glowed and whirled with intricate machinery. Then Grevol's eyes widened as a stricken look came over his face. "You don't have it," he gasped. "Where's that foot?"

"Gone," Ray said. "It's been made into something more powerful now." A tingling rose from his chest, moving slowly down his arms. "Soon it will be driven into your Machine and you'll—"

Grevol snarled and swung the walking stick. Ray closed his eyes and held out his hands.

The force of the blast hit his palms like a cannonball, propelling Ray backward. His shoulders slammed against the beam. Pain shot through his body, but it was quickly replaced by something else. Warmth flooded down his arms, filling him with strength. His toby was gone, but he knew he did not need it. He could draw on the powers of the Gloaming without it.

Grevol watched with openmouthed incredulity as Ray walked toward him. Extending his hands, Ray let the magnetic force erupt from his palms. Grevol growled as the force hit him. He stumbled back a step and pushed his walking stick at Ray.

Ray felt the magnetic force butt back against him, throwing his hands apart and knocking him on his back.

"Your newfound tricks are amusing," Grevol said. He began to lift the walking stick again when a figure landed on the roof of the car at the end of the spoke. Grevol looked back over his shoulder. "The prodigal son returns!" he said.

Stacker Lee rose slowly, one hand to his tattered shirt front where the exposed machinery churned within his chest. He opened his mouth as if to speak but no noise came out. His hat, the fine Stetson, was gone, along with his razor and pistol. Stacker walked to the edge of the car and held on to the outermost support brace as he stepped onto the spoke. Slowly, he came toward them.

"I feared you had abandoned me," Grevol said. "But you've seen what my Machine can do, haven't you? You've come home. All is forgiven, my general. I welcome you back. We will begin the grand work of leading mankind into a new, civilized world. Together, Stacker. But first let us finish with our little hoodoo conjurer here and then we will find where John Henry's son has hidden the rabbit's foot."

"It's too late," Ray said, struggling to stand. "Conker is in the Gloaming. He has the Nine Pound Hammer. He's reached your Machine. He's probably already destroyed it."

Grevol looked at the glowing knob on his stick and laughed. "He's destroyed nothing. He'll never be able to face the depths of my Machine. Even brave Conker will fall before its terrors." Then Grevol reared up with the walking stick.

Ray held out his hands to shield himself. As Grevol brought down the stick, the invisible force erupted from the knob. Ray's cupped hands caught the brunt of the blast. Even so he was slammed back against the hard metal of the support beam. Struggling to hold his hands up for the next assault, Ray felt his legs give out, and he dropped to one knee.

Grevol brought down the stick again. The blast was stronger this time, crushing Ray back against the metal brace. Grevol did not let up. He walked toward Ray pressing the knob at him. Ray gasped in pain, trying to hold his hand up, trying to drive the blast away. The iron girders at Ray's back groaned from the enormous pressure.

"You might be a Rambler," Grevol said, "but I have destroyed Ramblers much more powerful than you."

The knob capping the Gog's stick glowed brighter, and Ray felt his senses swimming. He could not withstand this any longer.

Then the blast stopped crushing him, and Ray collapsed on the spoke. A flash of light filled the sky. The illumination was quick, quicker even than lightning. Just a flicker that almost seemed to be daylight cutting through the Darkness. Ray would have thought he'd imagined it except that Grevol had a bewildered look on his face. The wheel began turning once again.

With an angry snap of his head, Grevol turned around to face Stacker. "What have you done?"

Gasping for breath and reeling from the pain, Ray leaned to one side so he could peer around Grevol. Stacker Lee stood on the spoke a few paces beyond Grevol. The fingers on his right hand were dug into his chest. He was clutching the edges of his clockwork heart, slowly prying it out.

Grevol held up a hand. "You forget yourself, Stacker!"

Stacker shook his head and growled, "No . . . I remember at last . . . what it is . . . to be human again." A snarl of pain gripped his face as he wrenched the clockwork heart from his chest. Caked in bits of blood and gore, the brass circle of gears and tiny parts in Stacker's hand gave one final click and stopped.

Sunlight broke momentarily through the Darkness, and Ray had to squint against the glare. Then the Dark descended once more. But little flickers of light, like lightning flashing in a thunderhead, crackled through the Darkness.

Stacker's clenched face relaxed, almost forming a smile, before he toppled from the spoke and fell.

Conker lay on the floor, no longer able to move as the pulsating green light of the Machine's heart sent waves of unbearable pain through his body. He wanted to reach Si, wanted to comfort her. They would not survive this much longer. He struggled to rise, desperate to reach her, but he could no longer move a single muscle.

The green light stopped pulsing. For a moment, the tunnel's end was dark except for Si's hand. An eerie silence surrounded them as the mass of machinery stopped. Conker felt the fear and pain that had stymied him vanish. He sat up and felt in the dark for the hammer. As he found the handle, Si whispered, "What's happened?"

Then the noise of the Machine arose once more. A glow grew behind the metal plate and the churning gears illuminated as the Machine heart began beating again with its sickening pulse. Whatever had stopped it had only been momentary. Conker knew if they didn't hurry, it would bring them down again.

He stood and turned back to help Si up. "Where is the spike?"

She stuck her trembling hand into her pocket and drew it out. She gasped with the next pulse as fresh pain was inflicted upon her. Conker felt it too but fought to push the pain aside.

"We must do it!" he said, dragging Si forward. "You and me."

Tears rolled across Si's cheeks, and she stared up at Conker with blind-eyed fear.

"You can do it, Si. We can do this."

"We'll be together?" she murmured.

He pulled her against his chest, stroking her hair. "Yes," he whispered. Si emerged from his arms and turned. She dragged each foot forward until she stood before the metallic heart. The next pulse brought her to her knees. She held the spike up with both hands so the point rested against the pulsating plate. The horrible green light spasmed, and the little parts within shrieked in a furious hive of movement.

Then another light grew, golden and pure. Conker watched

as the convulsions that wracked Si's body suddenly subsided. She looked back over her shoulder at him, her face fierce and lovely. He loved her for it and felt his own strength renew.

"End it," she said.

Conker braced his stance, one leg outstretched before the other. He brought the Nine Pound Hammer back in a slow arc, measuring it off from the base of the spike so he would not miss.

Before he could bring the hammer down, a roar grew from the depths of the tunnel behind them.

"What is it?" Si cried out.

With the hammer still ready to swing, Conker looked back into the shadow.

A hard wind battered into them, and Conker lost his footing, replanting it as he stared and searched the dark for what was coming. Vapor carried on the wind, speckling his face and hair with cool moisture. Each droplet tingled against him, seeping into his pores and filling him with vigor. The roaring grew and grew until Conker saw what was making it.

"Conker!" Si shouted.

A wall of water rushed down the tunnel toward them.

"Now!" Si shouted. "Strike it now."

Conker fixed his concentration on the spike, the golden glow within Si's hands, the piercing green light erupting from the circular plate at the Machine's heart.

The Nine Pound Hammer was above him, the iron head suspended.

He glanced down at Si. Her face was serene, smiling. "Wherever you go, Conker, I go."

He brought down the hammer. The head met the spike. It drove deeply into the screeching heart.

The Machine erupted as a wall of water met the fiery explosion.

Stacker's body lay just beside the gaping maw of machinery driving the wheel. Grevol looked from his fallen general back to Ray. Occasional light crackled through the Darkness overhead. The wheel was turning again, and the spoke that Ray and Grevol were on was tipping higher. Ray tightened his grip on the metal edge, knowing in a few moments he would no longer be able to stay on.

With a snarl, Grevol raised the walking stick over his head. "For you . . . it is over."

The knob glowed brighter. All the sinister mechanisms within churned and whirled. But rather than striking, Grevol looked up at the blinding knob with his mouth open.

The knob shattered with a surprisingly explosive force. Turning his head away, Ray clung to the girder as tiny bits of gears and debris rained down on him.

Grevol knelt, holding fast to the rising spoke and staring at the broken end of his walking stick. "No!" he roared. "No! It can't—" His black eyes went to Ray. The wheel turned, and the spoke rose higher so that the angle was such that they could no longer stay on. Half falling, the Gog sprang with his arms outstretched for Ray.

His fingers encircled Ray's throat, clawing and squeezing and slamming him back against the beam. The weight of the Gog's body tore Ray's grip away.

They fell together, Grevol clinging to Ray.

Ray brought his arms out wide, feeling the wind pressing against him and allowing his fingers to become feathers. Grevol's eyes darkened as Ray transformed into a crow. He tried to hold on to Ray's feathers, to tighten his grip on Ray's slick small body. But his gloves slid to one of Ray's wings, and with a twist Ray was free.

He whirled out in the air, opening his wings to catch the wind.

Below, the Gog kicked and screamed as he fell toward the mouth of the engine driving the wheel, where great teeth of gears ground together. The Gog fell upon them. As the gears turned, Grevol thrashed about until he disappeared, crushed and swallowed by the wheel's enormous engine.

Light blazed, white and intense and true.

As Ray banked in the currents of air, sunlight spilled over the city.

The Darkness was broken.

Ray flew higher, surveying the battlefield below. Bodies lay about, some dead, some dying. Most were the Gog's black-suited agents. Buffalo Bill and the Pirate Queen led their troops in driving back the last of the agents toward the far end of the Midway.

Ray circled until he returned to the wheel. To one side lay Stacker Lee. The little case of brass gears that he'd pulled from his chest lay broken on the cobblestones just inches from his fingers. Ray realized that Buck had been right about him after all.

A little farther from the wheel's base, Marisol and Redfeather knelt over Nel's body. When Ray landed, he transformed and staggered a step. He half expected to collapse in exhaustion, and though he was weary, the effects that had battered him before did not happen this time.

"Ray!" Marisol said, grabbing him around the shoulders and hugging him.

As she let go, Ray asked, "Is he dead?"

Marisol shook her head and knelt with him beside the old Rambler. Nel lay on his back, blood on his lips. His eyes were little more than slivers under the heavy folds of his lids. He was not dead, but Ray could see the old Rambler was near.

"Ray," he said weakly. "Why . . . are you not with Conker?"

Ray put his hand on Nel's forehead affectionately. "Si took the spike. She and Conker . . . they have done it. They destroyed the Machine."

Nel winced painfully, and his lips parted in an expression of terrible sorrow. "They have done it," he choked. "They have saved us all."

"The Gog is dead," Ray said softly.

He looked at Redfeather and Marisol. They said nothing. Ray knew what they were feeling. Grevol and his Machine were destroyed. But their friends had sacrificed themselves to bring about their destruction.

Footsteps resounded behind them, and Ray turned. Hobnob ran with Big Jimmie at his heels. "The hall," he called out and then panted the final steps until he reached them. "The Gog's hall . . . you en't going to believe it! It's collapsed."

"What?" Redfeather gasped.

"A flood. Water erupted up from the earth, and the hall fell."

"A flood," Ray said as understanding struck him. "The siren spring!"

Hobnob nodded. "Must be."

Jolie. She had found her captive sisters. She had given her life to heal the Wolf Tree. Ray felt his chest ache with the realization. She was gone. Conker and Si were gone. And no matter what he had done or had been willing to do to stop the Gog, his dearest friends had died.

Redfeather said, "Quickly! We've got to get Nel to that water if it's not already too late."

Big Jimmie's clothes were bloodied in spots and the greasepaint washed away, except for around his eyes and ears and the underside of his jaw. He scooped Nel up and the old Rambler groaned. Ray reached for Nel's arm. "Hold on, Nel."

Redfeather supported Marisol as she limped. Ray had not noticed before, but she had been wounded in the final fight. Blood covered her left leg. They hurried down the boulevard toward the White City awash in morning sunlight.

Along the way, they passed the fallen. Pirates and warriors from Buffalo Bill's troupe attended to the injured. Over by the Turkish Village, Gilley and Mister Jasper knelt over Iron Tail. The elder Sioux had been shot but was speaking to them, his eyes clear. Turks from the village had come out, stripping sheets for bandages and helping attend to the injured.

As they passed, Hobnob called out, "To the waters. Bring the injured to the waters." Ray looked at Nel. His eyes were swimming, and his body was limp in Big Jimmie's arms. He looked too far gone, and Ray's heart hurt, imagining he'd have to watch Nel die. When they reached the end of the

Midway, Redfeather gasped as he saw what remained of the Hall of Progress.

The west wall still stood, but the roof and the other three facades had collapsed, leaving an enormous pile of rubble. The siren spring bubbled up in a great fount from the ruins. As they ran down the steps from the Midway, clear water pooled and rushed through the streets.

"Get him into the water," Ray said to Big Jimmie.

The huge pirate sloshed through the flood a few steps and then knelt to lower Nel into the spring. Hobnob crouched by Nel, cupping water in his hands to help him drink. Marisol sank down and Redfeather pulled open the torn leather of her legging to bathe the wound. Others began to arrive behind them from the Midway.

Ray stood, staring at the ruins of the Gog's hall.

Voices rose up. He turned to see some of the *Snapdragon*'s crew and Buffalo Bill's men being driven back by a line of soldiers in dark blue uniforms. These were clearly not Pinkertons. Ray guessed they were militiamen called up to set order to the Expo or part of President Cleveland's retinue. The soldiers aimed their rifles, attempting to round up the motley band of warriors. The *Snapdragon*'s crew and Bill's men were weary and surely out of ammunition, for they gave no fight. But still they clustered together, unwilling to let the militiamen take them easily. A short distance away, other soldiers were leading a line of agents who had their hands up in surrender.

Then one of the soldiers dropped his rifle and shouted something to the others. One by one they turned their heads and pointed curiously. Ray looked around. Coming from the Hall of Progress, from the crevices in the great slabs of debris and bubbling waters, people emerged. Their clothes dripping and skin ashen, one by one they appeared, coming out into the street like dazed things, wandering and staring about at their sunlit surroundings. The militiamen left the others and approached these people with dumbfounded looks on their faces.

Ray returned to his friends. Nel lay back in the water with his eyes closed. Big Jimmie supported his head, and Marisol and Redfeather hovered over him. "Is he—?" Ray began.

Nel's eyes opened and he smiled. "It would seem," he said slowly, "the old fox has slipped peril's snare once more."

Marisol laughed, a sob breaking with it as she hugged him. Then Nel took Big Jimmie's hand and stood, although he was unable to put his weight on his returned leg. "I'm okay," Nel said as Ray gave him a concerned look. "Thank you, children."

"We best get out of here if we can," Hobnob said after casting a glance at the Pirate Queen and the last of the *Snapdragon*'s crew. "The agents are scattered. And these militiamen are distracted for the moment."

Ray stared at the people continuing to come out from the rubble.

Redfeather put an arm around Marisol to support her, but she walked from him, testing her leg, and said, "It's better already. But these people. Will they be able to survive?"

"The Gog's Darkness draws them no more," Nel said. "They will still suffer its effects, as will all the people of Omphalosa and Chicago, all who have endured the Gog's Darkness. They will need us to . . . Ray, where you going?"

Ray walked forward into the crowd.

Other militiamen had arrived, along with Buffalo Bill and

more of his men. Orders were shouted back and forth as the soldiers tried to sort out what to do with all the people coming from the collapsed hall. Buffalo Bill's booming voice carried: "That madman Grevol sent his goons to burn down my stadium, and now some invention of his has gone awry bringing down his hall. Lucky it didn't destroy the whole Expo. And who are all these people he had imprisoned inside? Got to help them . . ." The militia officers trailing behind him began following his orders as the master organizer took over.

But Ray did not answer. His eyes were fixed on a final group of people crawling up from the rubble. The morning sunlight shone brightly behind them, and Ray squinted to see young women in strange green gowns. He walked toward them.

"Ray, what is it?" Hobnob called. But Ray kept going.

A silver-haired siren stood atop the debris. She knelt and helped another up. Coming out one after the other, sirens emerged before fleeing toward the lake. Ray watched each one—each one of Jolie's rescued sisters—until they were all gone.

Marisol called Gigi's name. And Ray turned to see Gigi and his family scramble down and run to greet Marisol and Redfeather.

Ray felt frozen. Jolie hadn't come up with her sisters. Dizziness came over him. Hobnob grabbed him by the arms. Ray thought for a moment the little thief was comforting him or pulling him back to the others, but then Hobnob turned Ray until he faced the ruins of the hall once more. "Look, Ray. Lookit there! En't that her?"

A figure stood up from the debris, a mere shadow against

the blazing sunlight. Ray took a few steps and then ran toward her. She came down from the rubble and waited for him.

As Ray reached Jolie, he caught her up in his arms and did not let go. Her wet hair pressed against his face, and he turned to see her so he could be certain it was really her.

"You live?" she whispered incredulously. "You live."

"Jolie," he gasped. "How . . . ?"

She looked stunned, overwhelmed by whatever she had been forced to endure. But she stared at Ray and said, "They gave their lives. Ediet and Yvonnie. They brought forth the spring. My *sirmoeurs*, my sisters, are free."

Hobnob ran to them and stopped to stare at Jolie. Redfeather and Marisol and Nel surrounded them a moment later.

"Jolie," Nel gasped, coming forward to embrace her and Ray.

"We best go," Hobnob said. "Got to leave the city."

"Atsila is stabled not far away," Redfeather said. "There are other horses on the Midway. Their riders are fallen."

"Let's go, then," Nel said, turning.

Jolie was gazing across the fallen hall toward the lake

Ray came to her side. "Go with them," he whispered. "You belong with your sisters."

She looked at him. "Do you remember the night *The Pitch Dark Train* exploded?"

Ray nodded.

"I had to leave you then to save Conker," she said.

Ray listened.

"And at the foot of the mountains as we chased the steamcoach," Jolie continued, "you let those agents capture you. I had to leave you to search for Sally. Do you remember?"

"Of course," Ray said.

A smile grew on her face. "I have found that when I leave, you are not easy to find again." She slid her hand into his. "I will not take that chance this time."

Ray shivered, happiness filling him for the first time he could remember in a long while. "Okay," he said. "Let's go."

AUTUMN COMES TO THE PRAIRIE. THE GRASSES TURN A golden brown. Crisp blue skies, with not a cloud to fill the expanse, hover overhead. The breeze carries the hint of winter, coming and yet still some time away. An arrow of geese laugh as they pass what might have seemed to them like snow. It would be more likely in the late season. More likely than what they actually encounter on their flight.

Petals, white and voluminous, drift down in great clouds from the phantom Tree that rises up from the prairie.

At the roots of the Wolf Tree, a camp was made. Cookfire rings were constructed, and small three-sided huts of woven grasses to shelter them from the sun and break the cool winds that came at night. But even in the chilly starlight, the party was comfortable and warm, gathered around their fire beds and singing songs learned from Mister Everett and eating feasts gathered from the grasslands.

On that afternoon, Sally sprang over the rise with Hethy at her side. The girls ran with the grasses whipping at their legs and the fallen flowers underfoot. "They're here!" Sally called.

Ray stepped out from his shelter and put a hand to his brow to shield his eyes from the bright sun. When Sally and Hethy reached him, they jumped up and down, pulling on his hand. "Redfeather and Marisol are coming. And the others. The medicine man—"

"Water Spider," Ray said, spying the horses trotting up over the rise.

"Come on, Yote," Hethy said. "Let's go tell Quorl."

"All right," Sally laughed, and the girls dashed off.

Jolie came over to Ray and said, "Nel will be glad to see his old friend again."

Ray smirked. "He'll just be glad there's somebody else to entertain the girls for a change."

He looked back at Sally and Hethy surrounding Nel. Quorl sat by his side.

The rougarou had returned to their true forms. Their long hair was now the color that their fur had been, but otherwise, there was nothing about them to show they had been wolves. The rougarou were tall and regal and otherworldly with a shimmer to their skin. Quorl's silver-blue hair danced out in the wind as he stood to put an arm around Sally's shoulder, pointing over to the fire pit and giving the girls some task or another to keep them from underfoot.

Nel smiled from where he sat in the grass shelter. The fall

from the wheel had been great, and although the siren waters had spared him, his leg—the leg that Sally had helped return—no longer held his weight. The limb was lifeless, dead along with the Gog and his Machine.

"Will Water Spider go with Nel?" Jolie asked.

Ray nodded. "One last journey, Nel says, for the old Ramblers."

The sun set, and the sky grew orange. One by one the stars came out, pushed aside by an enormous yellow moon rising from the east.

Around the blazing fire, the group ate and talked and watched the night world from the warmth of their camp. The rougarou were there. The former children of the medicine show and Peter Hobnob. Iron Tail along with other elder Sioux and Comanche and old warriors who had lost their land and tribes before joining Buffalo Bill's Wild West troupe. Nel and Water Spider sat with others from the Indian Territory, men and women who followed the Cherokee medicine man.

"Then Marisol says, let's add some of these mushrooms I gathered," Redfeather laughed. "Just for flavor."

Marisol rolled her eyes and ran her hand along Javidos's back where he was coiled in her lap.

"Well, you do have to watch out for wild mushrooms," Ray said, taking a bite from the meal cake on his napkin. "They could be poisonous."

Redfeather laughed once more, bellowing and holding up a hand. "These weren't."

"How did you know that?" Hethy asked.

Before Redfeather could say anything, Marisol said, "They were buffalo chips. I thought they were mushrooms. It was dark. They looked like mushrooms."

Hethy squealed, and Sally gasped, "Yuck, you ate buffalo chips!"

"No," Redfeather said, wiping his eyes. "I didn't let her put it in the stew. But it was a close call, wasn't it?" He put his hand on Marisol's apologetically.

She scowled but could not help a smile from rising. "Just wait. Next time I come across something dried up on the prairie, it might wind up in your supper."

"I've been warned," Redfeather said. He turned to Ray. "We've decided we're going west."

Ray blinked with surprise. "Where?"

"Vancouver Island first," Marisol said.

"To my family," Redfeather added. "We want to tell them of the Wolf Tree. We want them to know that they can cross if they want to. It was Renamex's idea. To make sure others know."

Ray looked across the fire at the leader of the rougarou. The strange shimmering woman with the inky black hair was talking to Iron Tail as they ate.

Redfeather continued, "She says the path is open to those who want to leave this world. Your father can guide any who wish. They can go to the next world."

"We'll head south after Vancouver," Marisol said. "To my grandparents' people. But we'll meet others along the way. We'll carry the news to those that still believe in the old ways."

"And then?" Jolie asked.

Redfeather looked at Marisol and shrugged. "We'll find you. Sometime."

"Can I go?" Sally asked Ray. "Can Hethy and I go with them? I want her to see the mountains. And what's on the other side. We want to see the Pacific! There's just so much more to see."

"I don't think you two are invited," Ray said.

Sally and Hethy looked pleadingly at Redfeather and Marisol.

"You need to stay with your brother," Marisol said. "You need to help him. The victims of the Gog's Darkness need to be made whole. They depend on your understanding of the *Incunabula*. They need you, Sally."

Ray put his arm around Sally, and she leaned back against him. "Yeah," she said. "I want to help. Are you going to get a train again, Ray?"

"No train this time," Ray said.

"How we going to travel?" Hethy asked.

"Lorene's working on it," Ray said.

"Who's she, again?" Hethy asked.

Sally flashed her eyes at Hethy. "The Pirate Queen."

"Oh, her," Hethy said a little anxiously.

"We'll meet Mister Everett," Ray continued. "Once he's gathered the children from Shuckstack, we'll join them at—"

"Ray." Quorl came from the dark behind Ray and knelt beside him. "Come with me."

Ray looked up curiously at the rougarou. "What is it?" he asked.

Quorl cast his silver eyes around at the others, lingering on

Sally. Then he tapped Ray's shoulder. "Just come with me. Alone."

Ray rose and followed the rougarou. When they got outside the campfire's glow, Quorl stopped and looked down at Ray. "It's your father. He waits for you on the Great Tree. He asked to speak to you alone."

Ray ascended the crude passage that encircled the Wolf Tree's enormous trunk. After rising several hundred feet, he looked down at the little ring of light where the campfire shone on the dark prairie.

"Ray."

A shadow stood on the rise before him. Ray climbed to his father. Li'l Bill smiled as they met, and he put his hand on Ray's shoulder. Ray's eyes fell for a moment to the other hand, the missing one, the old scar that kept his father from joining the living gathered below at the fire. The rabbit's foot, his father's hand, was gone. It had cleaved the heart of the Machine and freed the enslaved from the Gog.

"I'm leaving soon," Li'l Bill said. "Nel and the others will ascend to the next world. But I ain't to join them. Not yet, anyway. I've got others to attend to. Lead them to that fair land beyond."

"Will I see you again?" Ray asked hesitantly.

Li'l Bill gave a lopsided grin, both playful and melancholy. That grin, so familiar from Ray's memories as a child. "That'll be for you to figure. One day."

Ray nodded.

Then Li'l Bill said, "I spied them."

Ray frowned. "Who?"

"In the heights of the Tree." Li'l Bill squinted. "I seen two ascending. Without a guide. Together."

Ray's voice barely came from his mouth. "Who were they?"

"A big fellow," Li'l Bill said. "And a smallish girl, I reckon. I couldn't make them out. They were far above. Climbing ever higher. Hand in hand they went."

Ray shuddered as warmth grew in his chest—bright and wondrous. His father then said, "Your sister and I already said our good-byes. She's a clever girl, Ray. And good. Full of goodness. Like you and your mother." He smiled, and Ray could see the memories sparkling in his father's eyes. "Go back to the others. Tell Nel I wait for him when he's ready."

Li'l Bill turned and climbed. After a dozen steps, he stopped and looked back over his shoulder. "I'll wait for you too. Might be years and years. You might be an old man. But I'll wait for you if you want to go." Then he left. His shadow rounded the curve in the trunk and disappeared.

They gathered at the mountainous roots of the Wolf Tree with the golden light of dawn spread out across the prairie. Nel said his good-byes. Water Spider helped support Nel as he embraced and spoke kind words to each of the children. When at last he reached Ray, the old Rambler turned pitchman, who had returned once more as Rambler, laughed.

"Never thought when I met you," Nel said, "that I'd be relinquishing my 'mystifying medicine show' over to you. Are you up for it?"

"I'm no performer, Nel," Ray said. "You know that. I've no gift for words either."

"And you think Peter Hobnob can handle the hawking," Nel said. "Does he have the proper disposition for leading the tabernacle?"

"He's so excited," Ray said. "I don't think he'd consider anything else."

Nel grumbled, "Your cast of performers hardly compares to my ensemble."

"Mister Lamprey is working up some new songs," Ray said. "And Piglet swears she has ideas for how that scruffy crew can be entertaining. Obviously the talent won't be tachycardial, but Lorene . . . the Pirate Queen, she's calling on old favors. Gathering funds to purchase a new steamer."

"She'll never be happy with this line of work." Nel shook his head fretfully. "Next thing you know she'll be robbing the tips at gunpoint."

Ray laughed. "We'll see. She's promised to help us. After that, who can say where her crew will wind up."

"In prison, if we're all lucky," Nel said, wringing his hands.

Ray said, "We have the tonics. The siren water. We just need to get them out to those who still suffer from the Gog's Darkness."

"It might take years."

Ray shrugged. "Then years it will be."

"And then?" Nel asked.

Jolie took Ray's hand, and he smiled at the old Rambler. "You worry too much, Nel. We'll be fine."

Nel's careworn smile creased his face. He nodded to Water Spider, and the Cherokee elder helped him hobble over to join Iron Tail and the others preparing to ascend the Wolf Tree.

The rougarou stood at the Tree's base, Sally and Hethy nestled between Quorl and Renamex. The pathway's stewards raised their hands in blessings as the group began slowly up the trunk. Ray looked up the Wolf Tree to where a faint figure stood high above. His father waited to guide them to the world beyond.

Ray and Jolie and Marisol and Redfeather and Hobnob and Sally and Hethy and the rougarou watched as the band of travelers rose higher and higher up the towering trunk to where the bark began to fade into luminous mist, higher still past the ghostly distant branches until the old Ramblers were gone from this world entirely.

ACKNOWLEDGMENTS

Bringing to life the world of the Clockwork Dark has been a labor of love and a dream that never would have been realized had it not been for the support and hard work of many people, only a fraction of whom are named here. I would like to thank my brilliant editor, Jim Thomas, along with Chelsea Eberly, Meg O'Brien, and all the rest of the wonderful team at Random House; my enormously talented agents, Josh and Tracey Adams, for their enthusiasm and guidance; my wonderful critique group of Jennifer Harrod, Stephen Messer, and Jen Wichman; John Gorely, my cowboy research assistant; Bill and Claudia Bemis, the Butcher family, Randy and Marge Bye, Pat Gorely, and the Bauldree family for all their love and support; Margaret Henderson, Carol McLaurin, Sharon Wheeler, and all the rest of the thoughtful people in my hometown of Hillsborough for their kindness and invaluable support;

Peter Kramer and Susan Gladin, for my inspiring writing cabin; Greg Hanson, my partner in all manner of things old-timey and creative; Rose, for making me laugh every day; and most especially Amy, for all your love, encouragement, and inspiration.

ABOUT THE AUTHOR

JOHN CLAUDE BEMIS grew up in rural eastern North Carolina running around the swamps and forests, reading fantasy and science fiction, playing violin, and having his head filled with his grandfather's stories of train hopping and rambling around the country. Writing the Clockwork Dark trilogy, John wanted to create a world that captures America's myths, draws on American legends and tall tales, and turns Southern folklore into epic fantasy.

A musician and former elementary school teacher, John lives with his wife and daughter in Hillsborough, North Carolina. Visit John's website at JohnClaudeBemis.com.